PENGUIN BOOKS

BRIDIE AND FINN

Harry Cauley has had two of his plays, *The Paisley Convertible* and *Let Me Hear You Smile*, produced on Broadway. He was producer-director of the Apple Hill Playhouse, near Pittsburgh, Pennsylvania, for thirteen years until he went to Hollywood and started writing for television on the ground-breaking series, *Mary Hartman, Mary Hartman*. He wrote and produced several other series and won the Writers' Guild of America Award for his film about a victim of Alzheimer's disease, *And There Were Times, Dear*. He lives in Cherry Valley, California, in the foothills of the San Bernardino Mountains. *Bridie and Finn* is his first novel.

HARRY CAULEY

Bridie and Finn

PENGUIN BOOKS

PENGUIN BOOKS

Published by the Penguin Group
Penguin Books Ltd, 27 Wrights Lane, London w8 5tz, England
Penguin Books USA Inc., 375 Hudson Street, New York, New York 10014, USA
Penguin Books Australia Ltd, Ringwood, Victoria, Australia
Penguin Books Canada Ltd, 10 Alcorn Avenue, Toronto, Ontario, Canada m4v 3b2
Penguin Books (NZ) Ltd, 182–190 Wairau Road, Auckland 10, New Zealand

Penguin Books Ltd, Registered Offices: Harmondsworth, Middlesex, England

First published by Penguin Books, 1994
1 3 5 7 9 10 8 6 4 2

Filmset in 10/13 pt Monotype Times
Typeset by Datix International Limited, Bungay, Suffolk
Printed in England by Clays Ltd, St Ives plc

For
Esther Sherman
and
George Towers

with affection and gratitude

PART ONE

I don't think a day goes by when Bridie doesn't come to mind. Lately, more often than usual. I suppose it's because I'm getting older and rather than face the future, with all the unpleasant inevitabilities, I escape into the security and comfort of the past. I'm so at ease with old friends, old clothes, old books and old times. Challenge doesn't interest me anymore and I find surprises surprisingly repetitious. Not that I've lost my sense of wonder, a gift for which I have always been grateful, but I seem to get the most satisfaction out of wondering about the familiar.

The last time I saw Bridie was fifteen years ago and we didn't even speak. There was so much to say yet there was nothing to say. It was an accidental meeting at Joe Allen's in New York. I was having a drink with Dorothy Monkhouse, a woman with whom I had had an affair so long ago that neither of us were quite sure it ever happened. As I recall, we discovered we were much better friends than lovers and the romance was over in a few weeks. It was back when we were both trying to take New York by storm, when everything seemed possible and we were too naive and inexperienced to be afraid. She was going to become the greatest actress since Duse and I was going to overwhelm the art world painting soulful, blank-eyed portraits like Modigliani. Fortunately, I've been successful as a wildlife painter and after years of working in regional theatre, Off-Broadway and doing bits on soap operas, Dorothy was finally making her Broadway debut. She was playing the grandmother in *The Shadow Garden*, an English play that had received very good notices and was a box-office success. And there I was, sitting with Dorothy in Joe Allen's, toasting her long-overdue recognition, when I saw Bridie. She was standing in the arch between the bar and the dining room, with a man and another couple, waiting for a table. After all those years, there was no mistaking her. She had the same open, defiant look on her face, the same easy, determined self-assurance. Someone said something and she threw her head back and roared with laughter. It was the raucous, uninhibited, explosive laugh I had heard so often, the laugh I had shared and the laugh that destroyed me when it was at my expense. Dorothy was talking about an actor in her show but I couldn't hear a word she said. I couldn't hear anything. Even the cacophony of show people, animatedly trying to outdo each other, stopped, as though I had suddenly been struck deaf. All movement in the room slowed to half time and the waiters glided from table to table as if they were in some surreal, special-effects ballet in a movie. I tried to look at the people she was waiting with but I couldn't take my eyes off her. There was Bridie, just twenty feet away, and I knew that any minute she'd start scanning the room and see me. What would we say to one another? I wanted to apologize and at the same time I wanted to say I forgave her and understood and still loved her, but it had been so long ago what difference would it make? Maybe, I thought, it would be best to avoid her, to slip out while she was being shown to her table. But it was too late. She saw me. Without a moment's shock or surprise she smiled, almost as though she was expecting to see me. She turned to her companions, said something, then started walking in my direction. By then, Dorothy had stopped talking, having realized something peculiar was happening. I touched her hand and got up and started toward Bridie. We met in the center of the room and stood for a moment reading each other's faces. There were tiny lines around the still-incredible green eyes and strands of gray were starting to invade the thick, shiny black hair. It was a shock because in my mind she had never aged. But we weren't young anymore. And I could see by the way she was looking at

4

me, white-haired and worn, that she was thinking the same thing. I wanted to apologize for allowing time to do this. It was never supposed to happen to us. I felt my eyes fill with tears and she looked at me with such tenderness I thought my heart would break. We held each other and I knew that this chance meeting, this unexpected moment, was the last time we'd ever see or touch one another. We were Bridie and Finn, together again. And suddenly the room was filled with the people who had made our world. Mom was there, holding Pop's arm and they were young and beautiful and smiling. And Fritz was standing next to them with Mina and the baby, Fritz's head tilted to one side as though he was trying to balance his crooked smile, the only imperfect thing about him. And Simon stood off to the side, wary and fearful of intruding. Mrs Ganis, with her flaming-red hair and bright lipstick, was shaking her finger in one of her happy accusations while Mr Ganis stared at the floor, sparing anyone from having to look at his crossed eyes. Laurie O'Connor had his arm around Kitty Neal, all starched and white in her nurse's uniform, and Honey stood right beside them, holding Mr Howe's enormous, gnarled hand. Big Tum and Little Tum, Mattie Horn and Sister Rosetta, as imperious as ever, were standing in the shadows with Turk and Sparrow and Tessie and Charles and all the girls. And Duke. There was Duke, wagging his tail, his eyes bright and shining like the eyes of a pup. And in the background I could see all the other faces, faces of the people who had molded our days. And I knew when I let go of Bridie, I knew I'd never see those faces again quite that way. Not as clearly as I saw them with her because we were seeing them as they were when we invented ourselves. Maybe we even invented them? The world created by Bridie and Finn. I wondered if she saw them, too? And if she did, were they as young and alive? Bridie gently pushed me away and everyone started to vanish. There was no way to hold on to them or her. Familiar faces were replaced by strangers sitting at tables, laughing and talking and ignoring us. The din of the room blasted as

though someone had turned up the volume. Bridie and I looked
at each other for the longest moment I can remember, then
she kissed me and turned and went back to the people in the
archway watching us and they left. When I got back to the
table, Dorothy had ordered me another drink.

'I hate nuns more than I hate the Japs.' That was the first thing Bridget Mary O'Connor ever said to me. It was Monday, January 6, 1942, just under a month after the Japanese attacked Pearl Harbor and there were no greater villains in the world with the exception, to Bridget Mary's way of thinking, of the nuns. She joined the fourth grade after the Christmas holiday. Sister Rosetta, the feared and tyrannical principal who moved through the halls with the silent, killer instinct of a shark, brought her into the class and we all jumped to our feet and said an automatic, singsong, 'Morning, Ster'. Ster being the Catholic grammar-school shorthand for Sister. She introduced this new girl, who stood in the front of the room, out of uniform and in a dress that was too small and needed to be ironed and who stared at the class with a fierce and arrogant animosity, as a welcome addition to the fourth grade. One look at this kid and I knew she was trouble. Sister Matthew, our fourth-grade teacher, who should have been retired ten years earlier, thanked Sister Rosetta as she glided out of the room sneering over her shoulder, letting us know she was boss. Sister Matthew was short, fat, deaf, near-sighted and bored with kids, school and life in general. She always smelled slightly of clean sweat. It was her habit every morning after roll call, the pledge of allegiance and the morning prayer, to give the class a reading assignment during which she took a nap. The addition of Bridget Mary O'Connor to the class in no way altered the routine and after she took her seat, right next to me, we opened our readers and Sister Matthew went to sleep. That's when Bridget Mary compared the nuns to the infamous Japanese. It was clear, from the first moment I saw her, she didn't fit in. There was something untamed about her, something so unlike any other kid I had ever met. Aside from her too-small, unironed dress, everything about her was a little messy and a little off. Her black hair was more chopped than cut, with one side longer than the other and too short bangs sticking straight out like a brush. She wasn't exactly dirty although she wasn't too clean either. But Bridget Mary's eyes were astonishing. Green as a cat's, piercing, questioning and demanding, there was something old and fearless about them, something that made them seem out of place in that pretty, heart-shaped face. When she sat next to me she was a little frightening but I was so fascinated I couldn't take my eyes off her.

'What are you staring at?' she said angrily.

'I don't know . . . your hair.'

'You like it? I cut it myself.' That explained it. I grunted noncommittally but she heard what she wanted to hear. 'Good. What's your name?'

'Timothy Finnegan. Everybody calls me Finn.'

'I'm Bridie. Don't ever call me Bridget or I'll vomit all over you.' She barely took a breath, 'So, who do you like better, the nuns or the Japs?' By now everyone, except Henry Watson who always took a nap when Sister Matthew did, was listening. Bridie was the most interesting thing that had happened to our class since we all met in fear and hostility the first day in kindergarten.

'That's a stupid question,' I said. 'Nuns are nuns and Japs are Japs.'

'And they're both enemies. There's nothing stupid about it.' She turned to the rest of the class. 'You all think it's stupid?' They were afraid to say anything. Even Anthony Bragiolli, who was several years older than the rest of us having been kept back in first, second and third grades, who already had pubic hair and was happy to display it at the drop of a trouser, whose hormones were creating such an itch that he sat in the last row

8

constantly playing with himself as he commented on everything said, was speechless in the face of this newcomer who had the nerve to liken the nuns to the Japs. Bridie had everyone exactly where she wanted them, in a state of mild shock. Before she made her next move she sized up her audience. I thought to myself, 'She's trying to take over the fourth grade and she's only been here five minutes.'

She stood up very slowly, then, staring at the sleeping, snoring Sister Matthew, she said, as though the idea had just occurred to her and she was making a practical and intelligent suggestion, 'We could kill that old nun and throw her body out the window and say it was an accident.' There was a rush of air, a sucking sound, a gurgling, an Oh my God, a couple Jesus, Mary and Josephs and Frances Peart went into a violent and uncontrollable fit of hiccups and started crying. Bridie beamed.

'Are you crazy?' I said, dumbfounded.

'Don't you think we could get away with it?' She said it as though the plan was really a possibility. Frances Peart cried louder and there was a mumble of incredulous protest. Not against the nunicide itself. The thought of knocking off Sister Matthew had probably occurred to every one of us. But the idea that the words had actually been formed on a tongue and spoken and that the big picture of Jesus exposing his flaming, bloody, sacred heart was hanging in the front of the room staring and listening and that any moment there'd be a clap of thunder and we'd all go up in smoke, horrified everyone in the room. Of the three categories of sin drummed into us daily, thought, word and deed, none of us seemed to take thought too seriously. But Bridie suggested, with the spoken word, that we kill a nun and she said it almost as easily as she might say, 'Let's play Double Dutch.' Whatever Bridie set out to achieve, consciously or unconsciously, she did it.

The general hubbub in the classroom roused poor old Sister Matthew who couldn't hear what the fuss was about so she assumed it was time to line everyone up and march them off to the lavatory even if no one had to go. We filed out of the room two at a time, holding hands with our neighbor. It was the first time Bridie and I ever touched and I was sure I was going to get warts.

'I don't want to go to the toilet. I don't even have to pee.' She looked at me. 'Do you?'

'None of your business.'

We walked a little further down the hall and she noticed my leg. 'What'd you do to your leg?'

'Nothing.'

'Then why are you limping?'

'None of your business.'

'Is that all you can say to people? I'm just trying to be friendly.'

'Well, I don't want to be your friend. I think you're crazy.' I tried to let go of her hand but she held so tight we both got sweaty palms. She kept looking down at my leg as we walked. I did pretty well in the halls but going down stairs slowed me quite a bit and I usually let the rest of the class go ahead. When I stopped to let them pass I tried again to shake loose of Bridie's hand but she wouldn't let go. I started hobbling down the stairs, holding on to the rail with my free hand, when it suddenly hit her.

'You're a cripple, aren't you?'

'So what if I am?'

'I think that's great.' Her face lit up and she was genuinely pleased. 'I never had a cripple friend before.'

'And you still don't.' I yanked my hand free. She didn't try to hold on anymore, it was as though she held tight until she got the information she wanted and then she didn't care. She jumped two steps at a time until she got to the bottom of the staircase then turned and watched me as I made my way down.

'Why are you a cripple?'

'You ask too many questions.'

'I know. Were you born that way?'

'Yes, I was born that way. Now, mind your own beeswax.'

'Is your leg all twisted and ugly? Is it shrunk?'

'You are crazy.'

'Maybe you'll show it to me someday.' The idea delighted her. She turned and skipped off to join the rest of the kids already lined up at the bathroom doors. There was no doubt about it, I hated Bridie O'Connor.

'Goddamn sons of bitches!' My father was pacing up and down the dining room while Mom, Fritz and I sat watching the food get cold on our plates. 'Too old! They're full of shit. I've never been in better shape in my life. Every day I'm lifting trunks and stuff a kid half my age couldn't get off the ground. I'm forty-two years old, for Christ's sake. Only forty-two. I am not too old, goddamn it!'

That day, my father had tried to join the army and discovered war was for younger men. The possibility of his being too old had simply never occurred to him. The night before, in the small hours, I heard him talking to Mom about enlisting and his voice was so full of enthusiasm that at first I thought he was talking about moving to a farm again. His dream was a place in the country. It was a boy's dream, idyllic and ridiculously romantic, but he could talk about it for hours lying in bed with my mother. He thought it was a shared dream but she would have gone to the moon sooner than move to the country. However, she put up with his talk and even encouraged the fantasy, knowing it would never happen. In fact, she liked hearing him talk about it. We all did. The livestock, the barn and the house became as familiar as the miniatures we put under the Christmas tree year after year. For Mom, it must have been like a very reassuring bedtime story. When he talked about it there was nothing new or threatening on his mind and everything was as it should be and she could lie there in his arms, half listening, comfortably saying her rosary and drifting off. Sometimes, when my leg bothered me enough to keep me awake, I'd listen to their conversations. If it wasn't too late when the pain came, I'd call

11

my mother and she'd give me a little whiskey in tea and eventually I'd fall asleep. Other times, if Fritz was still awake, I'd crawl in bed with him and he'd talk to me until I dozed off. But when the pain started very late, and I knew everyone was asleep, I'd lie quietly with the dog and listen to the sounds of the night.

'This war's going to be over in no time. Mark my words I'll be home before you know it.' The bedroom door was left open in case I needed them in the middle of the night so they always talked in whispers. When their door was closed, especially on Sunday morning after Mom came home from mass, I knew I wasn't supposed to bother them. Fritz had told me why.

'You were in the last war for God's sake, I should think that would be enough.'

'Jesus, Mae, will you use your head? What'll people say, everybody going into the service and Tom Finnegan sitting safe on his ass at home.' I never knew why my father worried so much about the approval of other people because it came to him so easily. Tall and handsome, with a body that was rock hard from years of lifting at the Railway Express, he was as vain as a beautiful woman. There wasn't the trace of a line in his face, which always had a shine as though he had just washed. If there was any sign of aging it was the slight graying of his temples, complementing brooding blue eyes. There was a sense of tension about my father, something withheld, something that could be confided any time he felt comfortable enough to trust someone and bestow upon them the distinct honor of intimacy. But I don't think he ever really trusted anyone except my mother. Back then, they were best friends and it was as best friends that they talked and argued in the middle of the night.

'I don't give a damn what other people think,' said my mother with the conviction of someone who really didn't. 'What about me?'

'When I joined the army in the last war I wasn't quite sixteen. I was younger than Fritz. But it made me feel like a man . . . a grown-up man. For Christ's sake . . .'

'Don't you feel like a man now? What do you want to do, go into service so you can feel like a man or so you can be sixteen again?'

'You don't know what the hell I'm talking about. How could you? You're a woman.'

'You start that with me and the conversation is over. You hear what I'm saying? My being a woman has nothing to do with this.'

'Shit!'

'Hush, you'll wake the kids.'

'They're dead to the world. Don't worry about them. Now listen to me and try to understand. You know I never liked working at the Express office . . .'

'If it wasn't for the railroad you'd of been out of work like everybody else in the country. You should thank God . . .'

'I know, I know. And I do. But that doesn't mean I like working there. Jesus Christ, you think when I was young my big dream was to spend my life lifting luggage for the railroad? I was going to have my own farm . . .'

'You're going to use the war as an excuse to quit your job? Is that what this is all about?' She was close to the truth and he couldn't stand it.

'There's no talking to you. Like it or not, tomorrow I'm enlisting.'

'Fine. You do that.' She knew she could really get to him by agreeing with him and minimizing what he was saying.

'I'm going to.'

'Good. Now turn out the light. I want to get some sleep.' The light went out and there was silence for a few minutes. I lay in the dark listening, knowing there had to be more.

'You make me so goddamn mad.' He said it softly, with an echo of apology.

'Tom, I don't want you to go.'

'I have to, Mae. You know it as well as me. That's all there is to it.' The argument was over. There was no doubt about it, he would enlist the next day. Her acquiescence was inevitable.

'Shut the door.'

When I heard the latch catch I called softly to Fritz. 'You awake?'

'Yeah, I heard them.' His voice was gravelly with sleep. 'Does your leg hurt?'

'Some.'

'Bad?'

'Enough.'

'Come on.' He moved over, making room for me as I slid under the covers into the warm spot in his bed. This was a comfort I had depended on as long as I could remember and it was part of the reason I loved my brother as much as I loved my mother and father. 'I've been thinking about joining up. I'm almost old enough.' It had never occurred to me that Fritz would ever go away, for any reason. We were all going to go on living in the house on Livery Street, with its ghosts and its smells and its same old furniture, until our world ran out of time. My father's going into the army was a possibility. He was forever telling stories about the wonderful times he and his buddies had had in Brownsville, Texas, in the First World War and it was a standing joke, one which I didn't understand for years, that somewhere in Texas or Mexico, Fritz and I had half brothers and sisters named Chico, Maria, Pedro and Carmen. Up in the attic, in a shoe box, there were pictures of my father in uniform looking young and skinny and foolish. Nothing about his going to war seemed dangerous and unnatural because fathers did things like fight wars. But Fritz couldn't go away, not to war, not to anyplace. He didn't fit into any context that didn't include me.

'You can't go, you're still in school.'

'Just till June. If the war goes on long enough, I'll have to go.'

'Pop said it would be over soon. Didn't you hear him?'

'It probably will. But if it isn't, I'll have to go.' He yawned. 'All the guys are talking about it.'

'I'm tired.' I didn't care about all the guys, only Fritz, and I couldn't think about it anymore.

'You want some whiskey? I'll get it for you.'

'No.'

'What do you want to talk about?'

'Nothing. Go to sleep.' We didn't say another word and a few minutes later I heard his slow, even breathing. He wasn't worried about going to war at all.

My father paced and ranted long enough to ruin dinner for all of us. Mom kept telling him to sit down and eat but he became more and more frustrated by the sheer impotence of his situation and he stormed out of the house, cursing 'the goddamn government' and slamming the door hard enough to rattle the windows in the dining room. We knew he was headed for the Alley, a bar whose clientele was a peculiar mixture of townies and college students. My father had taken me there once on a very hot day and I had the best ice-cold Birch Beer I have ever tasted even though the place scared me with its huge jars of pickled eggs and pigs' feet floating in brine like the dead unborn babies I had seen in the museum, looking naked and ashamed, trapped in their glass prisons like embarrassed seahorses. Pop wasn't really a drinking man. The potential was certainly there but my mother hated it so much, if he had drunk with any regularity there would have been hell to pay. There was always a bottle of rock and rye on the top shelf in the kitchen closet, which he took a shot of once in a while, and he did like his beer in the summer but he wasn't really a drinking man. However, if there was a legitimate excuse to tie one on he certainly used it, knowing my mother would have the good sense not to say a word the next morning. We picked at our cold food for a few minutes.

'Well, that's the last we'll see of him tonight.' She said it more to herself than us. Fritz offered to heat up supper but she didn't hear him.

'A new girl started school today.' I thought a different topic of conversation was timely.

'If he thinks we're going to sit around here while he's out getting pie-eyed, well, he has another think coming.'

'She's crazy. She wanted to kill Sister Matthew and throw her out the window.'

My mother didn't hear me at all but it certainly got Fritz's attention. 'What are you talking about? Who wanted to kill Sister Matthew?'

'Her name is Bridie and she's crazy. She thinks it's great that I'm a cripple.'

Mom stood up abruptly. 'Leave everything where it is. We're going to the movies. Fritz, get my purse out of the sideboard.'

'What's playing?' I asked, but I didn't really care.

'I don't give a damn.' Fritz got her purse. 'Let me powder my nose first. We'll eat at the diner on the way.' She started for the bathroom but stopped when she heard Fritz and I clearing the table. 'I told you to leave everything where it is. Let your father clean it up in the morning.' We sat down and waited while she went to the bathroom.

'What'd you say the crazy girl's name is?'

'Bridie. Bridie O'Connor,' I said, pushing my fork into the cold mashed potatoes.

Before coming to town and joining the fourth grade at Our Lady of Perpetual Help, Bridie and her father, Laurie, lived with his sister in Boston for a few months. Laurie O'Connor, a bartender by trade, had been working at a resort hotel on Cape Cod the previous summer. Bridie's mother was dead and, depending on Bridie's mood, the cause of her death was anything from childbirth to going over Niagara Falls in a barrel. She was, however, consistent about one feature of her mother's short but very dramatic life. The late Mrs O'Connor had been a beautiful Spanish dancer and, as Bridie put it, 'girlfriend to some king or something in some country in Europe or France or someplace'. It was years before I realized there was a remarkable resemblance between Bridie's exotic mother and the legendary and infamous Lola Montez. Like most people, Bridie created her own reality, but hers was haphazard and illusive, even lunatic, and she lived it with the dedication of a fanatic. And, blessed with the power to bewitch, she was capable of convincing other people that her reality was theirs. In all the years I knew Bridie, I was never quite certain of the truth of anything connected with her. I had my own escape, my own flights of fancy tucked away safely and privately, to be used when I needed protection from the possibility of the end of the world, the cruelty of the certainty of my parents' death and the agony of isolation. But Bridie's convoluted and frenetic sidestepping of the real world was public and seductive, especially to someone like me who was dazzled by the sheer audacity of the girl.

When Sister Matthew finally got round to putting Bridie in her proper place in the class, at least alphabetically, I was rescued from having to sit next to her. But even three rows away, I could hear her constant, compulsive talking, as though she had something vitally important to say. She didn't seem to be talking to anyone in particular, it was merely her opinion directed at the world. The class acknowledged her only when it had to but most of the time she was like a dead cat on a well-trodden path, everyone walked around her. The fact that she made no friends didn't seem to bother her in the least. She did, of course, have an imaginary friendship with me and as hard as I tried there was no way to discourage her. She was always cornering me, at lunch, in the schoolyard, even in church, and talking as though we had an ongoing dialogue. I remember them all as conversations started in the middle and I never knew what she was talking about: '. . . and that's what I told her so what do you think?', '. . . so, if God made us in his own image, does he look more like you or more like me?', '. . . and after that, there was no way I was going to eat a gizzard'. There was nothing I could say to answer her but I discovered she was satisfied if I just listened. Contact was all she needed and so long as she got it, someway . . . anyway, she was happy. Even if she drove people away, she was satisfied because she effected the retreat. And when a person actually responded and foolishly allowed himself to talk to her, her enthusiasm was so overwhelming she forgot where she was. Twice in those first weeks, when I was caught off guard and answered her, she followed me into the boys' lavatory. The only time I felt absolutely sure she wasn't lurking around a corner waiting to pin me against the wall was after school, at three o'clock, when the freedom bell rang and she went wherever she went and I went around the block to the safety of my own neighborhood. I didn't know how long it would be before she discovered where I lived but for the time being I felt relatively safe. There were days when, even with my bad leg, I ran home as though I was being chased by the Devil on horseback. Once I reached Livery Street, I imagined there was an impenetrable wall protecting me from Bridie. But in no time at all the wall came tumbling down. About a month after their arrival, the O'Connors moved into a house directly across the street from us.

We lived downtown where the middle to lower-middle class could afford to rent and sometimes buy their modest homes. There were a few shopkeepers and small-business owners but almost everyone worked for the university in one capacity or another. The men were gardeners, janitors, maintenance men or security guards and the few women who worked cooked or waited tables in the dining hall. My parents were the exceptions, Pop worked for the railroad and Mom taught at one of the two public schools in town. Some of the younger, unmarried women worked as secretaries or telephone operators but, for the most part, the university supported the townies and they, in turn, approached the university with a hat-in-hand, serf-like obeisance. It had, after all, seen most of them through the Depression and they were willing and expected to be grateful for the rest of their lives and their children's children's lives. This was the accepted social order and it would have gone on for ever if the Second World War hadn't happened. The university was also the dividing line between downtown, where the immigrant and first and second generation Irish and Italians lived comfortable if crowded lives, and uptown, where the old monied families lived in austere splendor. Except for a few downtowners who worked as servants in the big houses, they were staffed by blacks from Allen Street, which was in another neighborhood altogether.

Livery Street was two blocks of narrow houses of uninspired design, built in the mid 1800s. The sidewalks, cracked by the roots of handsome old maple and elm trees, met the front steps of every house, leaving no space for lawns or flower gardens. Everything about the street and its inhabitants was practical. It was named for a livery stable that had supplied the gentry with fashionable carriages for over a century prior to World War I. The two blocks were transected by Wilbridge Street, which ended three blocks away at the edge of the university campus. This small section of downtown was very nearly exclusively Catholic and Irish, with the exception of one German family, the Shultzes, one Greek, the Katsotases, two families of very mixed ancestry, the Wards and the Benlights who also happened to be the only Protestants in the neighborhood, and Mr and Mrs Ganis, elderly Hungarian Jews. The Katsotases were members of a Greek Orthodox church, St Sophia, in a town eleven miles away, the Wards went to the First Methodist and the Benlights were atheists and were therefore headed straight for hell. Some people were certain God was punishing them, the proof being their only daughter, Celeste, who was severely handicapped. The Benlights spent most of their time behind closed doors except in summer when they would occasionally prop up Celeste in a chair on the front porch so she might enjoy a cool breeze in the evening. When they did, most of the kids in the neighborhood would mysteriously disappear because they knew that Celeste Benlight was a witch and could put a curse on anyone who looked her straight in the eye. This was a secret carefully kept from adults. It wasn't enough that Celeste was a prisoner of cerebral palsy, trapped in a body wired wrong and unable to respond, we made matters worse by insisting she was a threat to us, capable of inflicting bodily harm or madness. I don't remember how the witch theory started, but the delicious fear of accidentally making eye contact with Celeste was so intense, most kids crossed the street rather than walk past the Benlight house.

Mr and Mrs Ganis, being the only Jews, would have been more exotic if it weren't for Mrs Ganis's need to socialize. There was a small circle of intellectual Jews at the university but Mrs Ganis, who had been in show business in the old country, thought they were snobs and bores and didn't want to have anything to do with them. A short, round woman in her sixties, she had carrot-red hair and wore so much make-up she always looked as though she was about to step on stage. She had been a ballerina in her native Hungary and she claimed she would have been a star if Mr Ganis hadn't been such a stage-door Sammy who came along and swept her off her feet. In his old age, Mr Ganis always wore a very proper dark suit and tie, even in the dog days of summer, and was content to spend most of his time at home reading, sheltered from people who couldn't help staring at his crossed eyes, made even more prominent by very thick glasses. But, having no children to occupy her, Mrs Ganis needed people. She especially wanted the company of other women to talk about husbands, food, clothes and the neighbors. Since she didn't have a temple to join, she did the next best thing and joined the Catholic Daughters of America. Although she didn't take part in the religious services, she was an active member, never missing a card party, a rummage sale or a meeting, and when the Daughters went to McConnell's Funeral Parlor or a home to say a rosary for a deceased member of the parish, Mrs Ganis sat quietly in the corner, crying.

While the nation was coming to grips with the fact that we were actually at war, that Hitler, Mussolini and Hirohito were threatening to enslave the world and put an end to freedom as we knew it, I had a real problem. Bridie O'Connor was living right across the street from me. I watched from the dining-room window, that Saturday, as she and her father pulled up in front of the house in his old Nash and unloaded their few belongings into the snow. There were two or three suitcases, some cardboard boxes and two folding army cots. They didn't have any furniture at all. I went into the kitchen where my mother was making a rice pudding and told her the crazy girl from school was moving in across the street and it didn't look like they had a pot to pee in.

'You don't know that. Maybe the movers will be bringing their things later. Anyway, it's none of your business.' She took an empty bottle of vanilla from the cabinet. 'Will you look at this! That makes me so mad. Who would put an empty bottle back?'

'You're the only one who uses it.'

'Well, it certainly wasn't me. You'll have to go to the store and get me some. This is ready to put in the oven.'

I had barely stepped off the front porch when Bridie saw me and came racing over, coatless, to tell me how great it was to be living across the street from her best friend. She insisted I meet her father and when I told her I was on my way to the store she ignored me, dragging me through the slush and up the stairs into the cold empty house that had been unoccupied since old Mrs Kenny died that September.

'Laurie, this is my friend, Finn. The kid I told you about with the bum leg.' I had never heard anyone call their father by his first name but it seemed quite natural coming from her.

'Well, Finn, it's a pleasure to meet you.' His voice was warm and energetic and musical, with the slight trace of a brogue. He smiled and shook my hand. 'We'd ask you to sit down if we had anything to sit on. Give us a couple of weeks and the place will be as grand as Mrs Astor's.' He had Bridie's smile but it was the only thing about him that was at all similar. While she was dark and ruddy, Laurie was fair and pale, like a photograph that had started to fade. His hair was almost red and his face almost freckled and his eyes were almost blue. The fine, classic features had the pallor of a night person and I had the feeling sunlight made him squint. He was about ten years younger than Pop, which somehow made him more accessible, and I liked him even though he was Bridie's father.

This would be the first house the O'Connors, father and daughter, would furnish together. Until she was five, Bridie had lived with her aunt in Boston but at her fifth birthday party Laurie decided he wanted his daughter with him and from then on they had lived in hotels and boarding houses up and down the East Coast, wherever he found bartending jobs. Over the next several years, I would hear endless stories about those places. Stories of such depravity and horror and obvious fabrication that I couldn't believe a word. But I listened to them completely mesmerized, waiting for the next fantastic embellishment. The job Laurie had taken in town, at the Prussian Inn, an exclusive hotel catering to the university and uptowners, was to be year round and permanent and the prospect of furnishing a whole house made him and Bridie as happy as a newly married couple.

'I have to go down and start the furnace before we all freeze to death. Finn, don't you be a stranger now.' He went down the hall telling Bridie to put on her coat until the place warmed up.

'My mother's waiting for some vanilla.'

She followed me as I went to the door. 'Laurie and me's going to buy a table and some chairs this afternoon. We figured the first thing we should get is something to eat on. I'm a good cook so you can come and eat with us sometime. Sunday or Monday cause Laurie don't get home till early in the morning when he works.'

'Maybe.' I had to get out of there before she included me in any more of her life. I was halfway down the stairs when she stopped me.

'I'll be over later this afternoon to meet your mom and dad. Careful on the ice, you don't want to fall and end up with two gimpy legs.'

Snow started to fall in big wet flakes as I walked to the store.

*

22

Mom, Fritz and I were at the table when there was one loud knock at the front door and, before anyone could answer, Bridie let herself in and found her way to the kitchen. Pop was at the Knights of Columbus planning the carnival that was held every spring in the back field, the unofficial center of activity downtown, as a fund raiser for the parish. As he told us before he left the house, 'I'll be goddamned if I'm going to let Hitler and that bunch stop the Knights of Columbus. Jesus Christ, life has to go on, doesn't it!'

'Hello, I'm Bridie O'Connor. I'm Finn's best friend.'

'She is not,' I protested.

Mom introduced herself and Fritz and offered Bridie some rice pudding and a glass of milk.

'I've been in five different schools and I'm only in the fourth grade. I've been in Catholic schools and publican schools and to tell you the truth I think I like the publican schools better. The nuns can work your arse off if you know what I mean. And they smell funny. Once you smell a nun you can never forget it. It's sort of like gasoline or skunk. You only have to smell them once and you never forget it.' She took a spoonful of pudding and a deep breath and continued. 'I used to live with my Aunt Theresa in Boston who was very nice except when she tied one on, which was every weekend, and started moaning about not having a husband. Well, Laurie and me think she's too set in her ways to ever get a man.'

'Laurie's her father,' I interjected.

'Oh yeah.' She ate another mouthful. 'Once, when Aunt Theresa was young and going to secretarial school, she fell for a guy named Joe Kerrigan, who she talked about every time she had a few too many. She was sure he would a married her if he didn't have to take care of his sick mother but it turned out Laurie knew him and said he was just another poor Irish bastard tied to his mother's apron strings. The truth, as Laurie and me see it, is Aunt Theresa's going to be an old maid and she better get used to the idea. She might try looking for a few

23

fellows who could take care of her when she gets itchy.' She stopped again to eat and we all took a deep breath. I couldn't believe Mom and Fritz. After all I told them about her, how crazy she was, they were hanging on her every word. 'I like your house, it's nice.'

'Thank you.' My mother was treating her like a sane person.

'Once, when Laurie and me was working on Cape Cod, I got a fish hook in my leg and they had to dig it out with a knife and you could look right inside and see the bone and all. Want to see the scar?'

'No.' I said it as quickly as I could. Mom and Fritz were ready to go along with anything she suggested. She had only been in the house for a few minutes and already she had won them over. Later, Fritz would tell me he thought she was the funniest thing since Laurel and Hardy and he couldn't understand why I didn't like her. I wasn't used to sharing Fritz with anyone but Mom, Pop and Mina Pascali, his girlfriend. I certainly didn't want to share him with the likes of Bridie. And when Pop finally met her it was love at first sight. He thought she was the toughest kid he had ever met and he admired toughness so he nicknamed her Joe Louis. He had never given me a nickname. Finn was inherited from him. I was Finn Junior or Little Finn to most grown ups. All my life I wanted a name of my own, a nickname no one else could claim, one that personified something special about me. My father only knew Bridie a few minutes and he gave her something I had always wanted. I felt betrayed by this intimacy and by his warmth and fondness for her. She sat on his lap and he hugged her and held her close and I never remembered him doing that with me. He tried a few times but it was unnatural for him and we were both embarrassed. Fritz was another matter. There was an easy, unselfconscious affection between them that went beyond parent and child. They were friends. They talked and argued and laughed like friends and they did things together. They hunted

and fished and went camping and, because of my leg, I was
excluded most of the time. On the rare occasion I did go with
them I felt as though I was intruding despite Fritz's efforts to
include me. Sometimes, Fritz and I would take Duke, my dog,
and go to the Pines for an overnight and I would astound him
with my knowledge of everything that walked, crawled or swam.
I knew every bird, tree and wild flower and I was fearless when
it came to handling animals, even snakes. I never went anyplace
without a sketch book and a pencil and on those camping trips,
while Fritz and I were discussing the problems of our world, I
drew pictures of everything that caught my eye. Fritz said God
gave me a special gift because He was embarrassed for what He
had done to my leg. I seriously doubted God cared one way or
the other about my leg. In fact, I seriously doubted there was a
God.

At first, my mother wasn't taken in quite so easily by Bridie.
She was concerned about her being in the house alone at night
when Laurie was working and she was amused by her, but she
kept her distance. My mother, like most people who think they
are strong, was a great admirer of independence and if there was
anything about Bridie she found attractive, that was it. Mom
was orphaned at eight when her mother died in childbirth and
her father, in such intractable grief, shot himself. His suicide was
a family secret and we were never, under any circumstances,
allowed to talk about it. Fritz said Mom pretended it never
happened and Pop went along with it. Having been shunted
from one relative to another until she was sixteen and went to
normal school, she learned at a very early age that she had no
one but herself to depend on. She worked her way through
college dipping chocolates in a candy factory while making
plans for a perfect life which included marriage to Tom
Finnegan, children, a teaching career and a house of her own.
And she managed to get it all. She considered herself a very
successful woman, blessed by a God she believed in deeply even

though He turned His back on her twice. Once, when I was born and again when, with very little warning, He took my baby sister, Deirdre. She was born two years after me and she was as perfect as Fritz. I heard stories when I was growing up about how frightened my mother was when she heard she was pregnant. Frightened she'd give birth to another deformed baby. But Deirdre was born with straight limbs and pink skin and hair as black as my mother's had been. There was a picture of her in a silver frame on the radio in the living room taken when she was nine months old, just two months before she died. She had on a white sun bonnet and she was smiling so hard her chin and eyes almost disappeared in wrinkles of baby fat, yet one could still see the best of both my parents in that happy little face. She died when she was convulsing from measles, in my mother's arms as she sat at the kitchen table trying to soothe away the sickness. No one knew the exact time she died but when my father came home from work he found my mother still sitting at the table holding the cold baby, talking to her just like she always did. The doctor said she had probably been there most of the day and that accounted for her nervous breakdown. She had to be hospitalized and couldn't go to the funeral. I was only three at the time but I can remember, with astonishing clarity, smells, images and colors, details that will stay with me as long as I live. Fritz and I were taken next door to stay with the Shultzes so out-of-own relatives could use our room. Mrs Shultz prayed a lot in German and I think it was then that the Shultz boys, Frank and Will, gave Fritz his name. For some reason, after the funeral, he was Fritz and never Tom Jr again. Fritz was nine and allowed to take his own bath but I was only three and Mrs Shultz gave me a bath and I was mortified to have anyone but my family see me naked. Someone bought us new suits which we only wore once, to the funeral. My mother burned them when she got out of the hospital, early one Saturday morning in her own secret ceremony in the backyard, and for the rest of that day she sat in her bedroom, detached and mumbling, almost as though she was having a conversation with someone. When we were finally taken back to our house, Deirdre was laid out in a tiny white coffin in the bay window in the living room and there were pink and white flowers and the air was so heavy with their sickish, sweet fragrance I could hardly breathe. My father took us to see her, looking neat and silly in a white dress, and I wanted to touch her to see if she was real. With her fancy curls and made-up lips and cheeks, she looked like a new doll, yet to be taken out of the box. There was a little blanket over her feet and I remember wondering if she was wearing shoes. People were all over the house, men drinking in the kitchen, women putting out food in the dining room and old women I didn't know, kneeling in the living room, moaning and crying and not making any sense. Kids, dressed in their Sunday best, were playing in the yard but Fritz and I weren't allowed to join them. At the church, the student body of Our Lady of Perpetual Help sat rigidly under the watchful eyes of the nuns, and six of Fritz's classmates, rigid and uncomfortable, carried the coffin. I couldn't understand why all those kids had to carry my sister when Fritz could have done it by himself. It was such a little box. At the cemetery, as they lowered it into the ground, my father cried out my mother's name and his knees buckled and he knocked me down. As people rushed to help him, Fritz pulled me out of the way of the crush. That afternoon we went home and after everyone left and it got dark Fritz and I slept in the big bed with my father who cried most of the night. Fritz cried too and I couldn't understand why because I was sure that when my mother came home she'd bring Deirdre with her, the way she did the last time she was in the hospital.

Pop always said Deirdre's death was the beginning of Mom's troubles. A few months after she got out of the hospital, she started to go through periods when her mind would wander and every once in a while we'd hear her talking to people who weren't there.

*

As Bridie and Laurie settled into the neighborhood, the nation settled into being a country at war. Like my father, as soon as war was declared, Laurie tried to enlist. The plan being for Bridie to go to Boston to live with Aunt Theresa until the war was over. He tried every branch of the service but he was 4-F, unfit for military duty because of a heart murmur. The classification of 4-F was a welcome relief for anyone who didn't want to go off and fight but to men like Laurie O'Connor it was a stigma that was almost unbearable to live with. But since he and Bridie were starting a new life in the house on Livery Street he did his best to disguise his disappointment. It was then that his drinking started to get out of hand.

The first man on the street to actually go into service was Mr Ward and, even though he was a Methodist, Father Boyle asked everyone in the parish to remember Mr Ward in their prayers. He joined the navy and Mrs Ward went to live with her sister in Wilmington and when they gave up the house my mother said it would be the last time we'd ever see the Wards in this lifetime, and she was right. The war changed everything, even something as timeless as Livery Street. Michael Foley, who lived at the end of the street and was a year ahead of Fritz in school, joined the army with his best friend, Jim Halley. They had intended to go into the seminary together when they finished high school but God and the Franciscans would have to wait. Frank and Will Shultz were the next to go. They enlisted in the navy and the day they left home my father told me to spend the afternoon with Mrs Shultz but not get in the way. Bridie, uninvited, went with me and never shut up from the time we walked in the door until we left for supper. Mrs Shultz sat in the kitchen with tears in her eyes, looking at her backyard, which was the most beautiful garden in the neighborhood, as Bridie rambled on about everything including Laurie's battle with hemorrhoids, which, Bridie informed us, was the curse of bartenders and anyone else who stood on their feet a lot. I had never heard the word hemorrhoid before and decided it must be something like a bunion or corn so I was surprised when Mrs Shultz started laughing at Bridie's father's foot problem.

If war and all its dire implications saddened adults, the effect on kids was positively exhilarating. Hollywood started pumping out movies with heroes who would forever replace cowboys in white hats, heroes happy to sacrifice their lives to keep the Japs and Germans from our shores. We all sang the National Anthem loudly and proudly with our hands over our hearts and chills up and down our spines. Sister Matthew taped a huge map of the world over part of the blackboard and stuck little flags on every far-flung place mentioned in the news. By the time school let out that June we'd all heard names like Corregidor, Rangoon, Manila, Java and Tobruk. The second week in April the spirit of the nation plunged when Bataan fell and news of the infamous Death March reached the home front. But on April 18, US planes, commanded by Col. Jimmy Doolittle, bombed Tokyo and raised hopes for a merciful and quick end to the war. In May, the aircraft carrier USS *Lexington* was sunk by the Japanese and Mario Pascali, the nineteen-year-old brother of Fritz's girlfriend, Mina, became the first man in town to be killed in action.

'Wouldn't you know,' said Mrs Cavanaugh, rocking furiously on her front porch, 'the first hero in town would be a damn wop.' She sat there in a dirty housedress, fat and unwashed, with her runny stockings rolled below her blubbery knees. 'The dagos have all the luck. Why couldn't it have been some nice Irish lad?' She spent every day on the porch, spring, summer and fall, watching, gossiping and disapproving. She stopped rocking and looked at me over the porch rail. 'Your brother's hanging around with that dago girl, isn't he, now? The sister of the one who got himself killed. I've seen them sitting on the porch kissing and carrying on enough to make a person sick to their stomach. Your poor mother, bless her soul, must be

29

brokenhearted. As if she didn't have enough trouble what with you being a cripple and her own little girl dying right in her arms. All I can say is that wop must be giving him something he can't get from a nice Irish girl. He'd better keep his pants buttoned. Your mother don't need no wop bastard running around the house.'

Mrs Cavanaugh never referred to my father. As far as she was concerned my mother was a widow. I never knew exactly what happened but some years before my father told Mrs Cavanaugh she was a bitch and should have been drowned with the rest of her litter. Mr Cavanaugh was in earshot and cheered Pop on and Mrs Cavanaugh knocked out his front tooth. It had all happened long ago and in the meantime Mr Cavanaugh died and when my father heard the news the first thing he said was, 'The lucky bastard.' There was a rumor, and everyone in the neighborhood seemed to think it was well founded, that Mrs Cavanaugh murdered Mr Cavanaugh when he was in the hospital for a gallstone operation. The story was that he was recovering nicely when they had another one of their legendary fights and she grabbed his pillow and pushed it down on his face until he suffocated. Of course, I believed every word of it and was scared senseless of the woman. I did everything I could to avoid talking to her but when I was trapped and unable to escape I agreed with everything she said as though it was Bible truth, just as I was now agreeing that Fritz should keep his pants buttoned.

'It's the goddamn foreigners taking over the country, that's what it is.' Her brogue was as thick as the day she left Ireland. 'And the Jews are the worst of the lot. This was a decent neighborhood until those two moved in. Her with the flaming, dyed hair and the crazy husband with the eyes that look every which way. And them Benlights, keeping that slobbering, idiot daughter at home! Wouldn't you think they'd put her away so nice people didn't have to look at her?'

I nodded yes to everything she said.

*

30

By spring of that year, Bridie was a fixture at our breakfast table. Laurie slept late and Mom didn't think she was eating a proper breakfast alone so she invited Bridie to join us and I was stuck with her every morning. Mom and Pop were hungry for the latest war news so the radio was always on but Bridie talked so much the war could have ended and we'd never have known. She blithered on about Laurie, what she fixed for dinner the night before, the latest furniture addition, Aunt Theresa, the kids in class and, her favorite target, the nuns. If there was anything she wanted to know, no matter how personal, she asked. Was Fritz going to marry Mina? Were Mom and Pop going to have any more kids? Was there any hope for me getting my leg straightened? These questions, which I insisted were none of her damn business, were all answered. Yes, someday Fritz and Mina would be married. Yes, Mom and Pop would have more kids, even though she was getting a bit old for that sort of thing, if it was the will of God. And yes, in a few months I was going to be fitted for a brace that might help straighten my leg. If, with the passage of time, Bridie endeared herself more and more to my family, her effect on me was exactly the opposite. She was the enemy and that would never change. It was bad enough that Mom, Pop and Fritz were charmed by her but when Duke, the trusted friend I slept with every night and to whom I confided secrets I couldn't even tell Fritz, allowed her to kiss him and pet him and even pull wood ticks off him, I felt my world was starting to crumble. Duke actually met her after school on the few days I stayed home sick that year. I was beginning to feel completely betrayed and alone. As fond as I had become of Laurie, I hoped with all my heart that he'd be fired and have to take a job a thousand miles away and I'd never have to see either one of them again. It was a few days short of a month later when everything changed.

Mom started spending evenings visiting the Pascalis. The little banner with the gold star went up in their living-room window and the reality of war settled on the town. Father Boyle said a memorial mass for Mario on a Saturday morning and the church was so full people spilled out on to the street. Laurie sat with Mom, Pop and me, and Fritz sat up front with the Pascali family, holding Mina's hand. Bridie was going to meet us there because she hadn't finished dressing when we left for the church. Since Mario had been lost at sea there was no body, just an empty box draped with the American flag. On top of the box was a framed high-school graduation picture of the darkly handsome Mario smiling happily at the congregation. Mina had the same smile. She was small and fragile, like Mrs Pascali, and everything about her was gentle. She always reminded me of a picture of the Blessed Virgin on a holy card I had won in a spelling bee. I could not remember a time when Fritz and Mina weren't together, she as dark as he was fair, complementing each other like shadow and sunlight, dawn and dusk. They had met in first grade and there had never been anyone else for either of them.

I kept turning around, looking for Bridie, and Mom kept yanking my arm, telling me to stop fidgeting. Father Boyle's sermon was about our brave boys, life everlasting, democracy and how much we should all pray for Franklin D. Roosevelt, the greatest man born into the twentieth century. Most of the congregation, being Democrats, nodded in agreement. He likened the President to Moses leading the Jews to the Promised Land and I looked around to see if Mr and Mrs Ganis were there. They were standing in the side aisle, halfway back, Mr Ganis staring shyly at the floor and Mrs Ganis, her red hair dramatically draped in a black shawl, wiping her eyes as she shook her head, saying no to the tragedy of it all. The priest started talking about the Pascali family and the sacrifice they were forced to make, the mystery of God calling such a young man to His heavenly home and the need for all of us to accept the wondrous ways in which the Lord worked. When he started his reminiscences of Mario as a child, remembering things only a pastor of a small parish who had the luxury of intimacy could recall, Mrs Pascali's head dropped to her husband's shoulder. There was muffled crying throughout the church. Mario the frightened child with the wondrous dark eyes on his first day of school, Mario the altar boy accidentally spilling the wine, Mario the basketball player racing down the court and winning the game in the last second, Mario with his white apron, stocking shelves in the Acme Market. I sat there wondering if Father Boyle would have as much to say about me if I died. As he went on the crying became more and more noticeable and even he dug his handkerchief out of his pocket, lifted his glasses and wiped his eyes. He seemed to lose his train of thought as he adjusted his glasses and in the silence that followed there was the distinct sound of suppressed laughter. Leaning over the edge of the pulpit he searched the congregation for the culprits as the tittering got stronger and louder. Mom, who wouldn't take her eyes off the altar if the vestibule was on fire, finally joined Pop, Laurie and me, bobbing up and down, trying to see over heads to discover the cause of the commotion.

Laurie was the first to see her. 'Mother of God, I don't believe me own eyes.' He sank down in the pew with his hand to his head.

I was too short to see anything. 'What is it?' I said, stretching my neck as I practically crawled up Pop's back.

'She'll be the death of me yet,' he said as he started to laugh.

'Jesus, Mary and Joseph.' Mom sat with a thud.

'Well, Joe Louis!' Pop just stood there, smiling.

Pushing past everyone I got to the end of the pew where I could look down the aisle. And there was Bridie, walking along, looking for us, dressed in her messy Sunday best and wearing the biggest, blackest picture hat with a veil so thick you could only see the tip of her chin. I looked up at Father Boyle, speechless with wonder, as he watched her make her way toward us. We made room for her as she slid into the pew and went to Laurie.

'Where in the name of the Saints did you get that hat?'

'Aunt Theresa. You like it?' She had no idea there was anything in the least peculiar about it.

'You might say it's a wee bit large.' Laurie patted her knee.

'All right now, everyone, just settle down,' said Father Boyle from the pulpit.

'What are they all laughing at?' she whispered to me.

'You and that stupid hat.' I was happy to be the one to tell her.

'What's wrong with it? It's a funeral hat.'

'Miss O'Connor.' It was Father Boyle. The church quieted and everyone's attention was on Bridie. It was the first time I ever saw her even slightly embarrassed. She lifted the heavy veil and sank back against Laurie.

'Well, answer the man.' Laurie nudged her.

'Yes, Father?' she said almost inaudibly.

'I like the hat.' Father Boyle smiled at her. 'And I'm sure Mario would have liked it, too.' He left the pulpit and went back to the altar.

She turned to me in triumph. 'See.' She pulled her veil down and sat up straight so everyone could get a good look at her. And after mass she was the last one to leave the front of the church, just in case there was a single person who didn't get to see her hat.

The Lord is my strength, my song, my deliverance.
Joyfully shall you drink from the fountains of deliverance;
The Lord will rescue; the Lord will bless His people.

Mrs Ganis, her hands dancing in the candlelight, said the Sabbath prayer as Mr Ganis, Bridie and I stood watching and listening to the hypnotic and musical Hebrew.

The Lord of hosts is with us,
The God of Jacob is our fortress.
O Lord of hosts, happy is the man who trusts in You.
O Lord and King, answer us when we call and rescue us.

Her head was covered with a white shawl and Mr Ganis wore his yarmulke. Bridie insisted our heads be covered too. She wore a doily and I wore one of Mr Ganis's fedoras, which was so big I could barely see. Even here, with Mr and Mrs Ganis, who were my friends, Bridie managed to insinuate herself. She convinced everyone, without even saying anything, that she and I were best friends. I had had Sabbath dinner with the Ganises often and sometimes Fritz and Mom and Pop were invited, too. The Ganises were like a part of our family and Bridie had no business butting in.

'You people say a lot more prayers than we do before dinner.' Bridie was stuffing her napkin into the neck of her dress as she sat at the table.

'That's why Jews eat so much. We get hungry waiting until all the prayers are over.' Mrs Ganis started passing the delicious-smelling food.

'I don't know what half this stuff is but I guess I can eat it,' said Bridie, piling the food on her plate. 'I can eat raw oysters.'

'Oy,' said Mrs Ganis. 'Just eat.' The table was always set beautifully with fine china, silver and delicate stemware, all brought over from the old country, and we ate by candlelight and everyone was washed in a sepia glow. To me, the way the Ganises ate their Sabbath dinner was the same way rich people ate in the movies. Mr Ganis poured a little wine in our glasses.

'Don't get drunk,' he said, not looking at us.

We raised our glasses and Mrs Ganis turned to me. 'So, Finn?'

'*L'chaim*,' I said proudly, knowing Bridie had no idea what I was saying.

We settled down to our meal and, as usual, Bridie did all the talking and said nothing. Mrs Ganis nodded her head, pretending to listen, and Mr Ganis stared at the side of his plate as he ate.

'It's almost time for the pigeon hunting?' he asked during an unexpected lull.

'Almost. I've got my eye on a couple of barns,' I told him. Mr Ganis enjoyed looking at my pigeons. One of his few excursions into the world, weather permitting, was when he walked uptown, sat on a bench at the bus stop on the Square and watched the people passing by. He always bought a newspaper on the way home and if I was in the yard he came in to visit with me and the pigeons. Most adults didn't really pay much attention to my flock but Mr Ganis knew which birds were mated, their off-spring, which were new and almost as many other details as I knew. And away from Mrs Ganis, he talked more and he relaxed so much when it was just me and him and the birds, he'd look me directly in the eye.

'Birds carry lice. They're dirty.' Mrs Ganis didn't approve of my pigeons. 'You should get maybe goldfish. What can be wrong with a goldfish?' She turned to Bridie. 'So, little miss, when are we going to find you a new mother?'

'A what?' Bridie didn't know what Mrs Ganis was talking about.

'Your daddy is a young man. He should get married. It's time he found some nice girl to take care of him . . . and you.'

'I take care of both of us. I don't need a new mother and Laurie don't either.'

'Sure, you take care of some things but some other things a woman has to take care of.'

'We don't need nobody,' Bridie insisted.

But Mrs Ganis wouldn't accept that. 'That's not for you to decide, is it?'

Bridie didn't answer but her mind was racing. She had never even mentioned the possibility of Laurie getting married and if it had occurred to her I'm sure she buried it in the darkest corner of her mind. As far as she was concerned, she was wife, mother and daughter and not only did Laurie not need anyone, there simply wasn't room for another woman in his life.

By the time we finished dessert, Bridie seemed to have forgotten the question of a new wife for Laurie. 'Can I ask you a question?' She leaned into Mrs Ganis.

'Could I stop you!'

'Are you circumcised?' I wanted to get up and go home. I couldn't believe she could be so stupid.

'This is some kid,' said Mrs Ganis to Mr Ganis.

'Aren't all Jewish people circumcised?'

Mrs Ganis looked at her a long moment while Mr Ganis and I sat with our heads down. 'That's for boys, not girls.'

'That's not fair.' Bridie was irate.

'Do you know what circumcision is?' Mrs Ganis asked.

'Something for Jewish people.'

'Listen, let's take some dishes and go into the kitchen and start cleaning up a little. We can have a talk. Just us girls.' They collected some of the dishes and started for the kitchen and Mr Ganis sat back, obviously relieved to have Bridie out of the room.

'I wouldn't get too comfortable if I was you, Sam,' said Mrs Ganis as she was leaving. 'With a kid like this, after I tell her, she may want to see.'

Toward the end of April, when the weather warmed, I went pigeon hunting with my friends Sparrow Foley and Turk Meegan. We called it hunting but our only weapons were our hands and a burlap bag. It was a yearly event made special that particular year when we went without our big brothers, a giant step toward manhood. Sparrow's brother, Michael, had recently gone into the army and Fritz was spending most of his free time with Mina and the Pascalis. Turk, Sparrow and I all had our own pigeon coops and we added to our flocks every year by taking squabs from nests in the local barns. The birds were a nuisance, fouling the hay, but the farmers didn't want to take responsibility for any kid getting hurt so we had to sneak into the barns. Climbing the dusty beams in the dark was dangerous

37

and over the years there had been several broken arms and legs in the quest for the best birds. My particular favorites were chocolate colored and I had decided to specialize and have a completely chocolate flock. Turk and Sparrow, not to be outdone, decided they would also specialize, with Turk opting for silver bars and Sparrow choosing pieds, birds with random splotches of white. Pigeon hunting was the one activity in which I excelled and although my leg could be a hindrance on the ground, once I started climbing the beams I was a marvel, as agile as a monkey swinging through the canopy of a rain forest.

About three miles west of town, Mr Howe's enormous, weathered old barn sat, as it had for a hundred years, at the edge of an untended apple orchard. In its day, the orchard had produced some of the finest apples in the State, but now, the tiny, spotty fruit only served as forage for deer in autumn. Left to be reclaimed by nature, the orchard was teeming with wildlife and once, when Fritz first got his driver's license, he took me for a ride past Howe's barn and we saw a pair of cranes, looking stately and fragile and out of place, poking through the debris with their great sharp beaks. Sometimes I would pack a lunch, get on my bike and Duke and I would go to the orchard and sit listening and watching as I drew the trees and flowers and songbirds, and Duke and I would talk and I remember those conversations as two-sided with Duke saying everything I wanted to hear. The one drawback, the fly in this Arcadian ointment, was the possibility of being seen by Old Man Howe. I had only caught a glimpse of him once but I knew he was the oldest man in the world. Pop said Mr Howe had been a waiter at the Last Supper. He rarely came out of the falling-down house but when he did he carried a shotgun loaded with rock salt. Fritz had told me that Old Man Howe actually shot at him once and a piece of rock salt lodged in his ass and he had to run to the lake and sit in the water, it stung so bad. He showed me where it was supposed to have hit him but there wasn't a mark so I didn't believe a word of it. But Fritz explained that rock salt left no telltale signs, that was the beauty of the damned stuff, it just burned the bejesus out of the person it hit. As luck would have it, the best chocolate pigeons in Christendom were nesting in Old Man Howe's barn.

'How'd you get away from your girlfriend?' Turk had a habit of sucking air through his crooked teeth after every sentence.

I pedalled along in silence, not wanting to encourage any conversation about Bridie but Sparrow, fat and glistening with sweat, wouldn't leave it alone. 'Yeah, Finn, we didn't think you went anywhere without her.'

I didn't say a word as I pulled ahead of them and turned into Riker's Lane, coasting down the hill. When we got to where the macadam stopped, where we had to slow down to avoid the ruts in the dirt road, I noticed the sky had darkened and thunderheads were almost over the barn.

'Hurry up, you guys. It's going to rain.'

'Let's turn around and go home,' Turk sucked in air. 'That old barn is scary enough when it's not raining.'

'Don't be such a big chicken,' I said, knowing he'd never turn back if I challenged him.

'Who are you calling a chicken?'

Duke saw something and rushed off into the field just as we arrived at the orchard. After hiding our bikes behind a tangle of blackberry bushes, we made our way from tree to tree, keeping a sharp eye out for Old Man Howe, until we got to the barn. A flock of more than a hundred pigeons, several of them chocolates, circled, cutting through the air haphazardly, ready to scatter if a hawk suddenly appeared. There was no trouble getting into the barn. After all the years of disrepair, all the doors had slipped their hinges. Inside, wings flashed in shafts of light as birds flew back and forth in the emptiness, disturbing dust motes hovering in the warm air.

'Let's hurry before that old fart shows up with his gun.' Sparrow liked owning the birds but the process of catching them made him uneasy.

39

I stuffed one of the burlap bags into my shirt and started spidering my way over the beams toward a nest I could see about thirty feet up. Turk climbed the other side of the barn and Sparrow and Duke stood in the middle of the floor watching us. As if someone had suddenly turned out a light, the barn went dark and there was a sharp clap of thunder.

'Oh shit,' said Sparrow, 'It's going to rain. Come on, hurry up.'

'Goddamn it! I got a splinter.' It was Turk, trying to hold on to the beam while he checked his wound.

'Will you keep it quiet! That old bastard will hear us.' Sparrow whispered loudly.

'Jesus, it's as big as a two-by-four. I'm coming down. Shit.' Turk started his descent. I could see the breast feathers of a bird on a beam several feet above me so I started to climb higher as big drops of rain splattered on the roof.

'Oh my God!' It was Sparrow and there was panic in his voice. 'Somebody's out there. I can see them moving around.'

Turk, who was almost down, jumped the last few feet. 'Shit, I think I twisted my ankle.'

'If you don't shut up, we'll get shot.'

Sparrow called to me, 'Finn, let's go. Now.'

'I've almost got this bird.' There were rumbles of thunder and flashes of lightning.

'You think my ankle could be broke?' asked Turk.

'Who gives a fuck, I want to get out of here.' Sparrow was heading for the door and Duke started running in circles, barking at the thunder. 'Shut up, Duke. I think Old Man Howe's out there. Finn, hurry up.' He was trying to look through the cracks in the walls to see who was outside.

I inched my way along the beam and, in a flash of light, saw the feathers again. I moved my hand in the darkness, very slowly and carefully, so as not to startle the bird. As soon as I touched the breast I knew I was in trouble. This wasn't a pigeon. This was a broad, feathered breast, almost as big as a chicken, and I knew I had my hand on an owl.

'Oh shit!' It was all I could say before I felt a sharp beak in the back of my hand. I pulled it away and the owl leapt off the beam and on to my chest, its talons digging into my flesh, and I felt myself falling back through the darkness. The huge roof timbers were lit by lightning and I thought I could see pigeons looking over the edge of the beams, watching with satisfaction as I fell to the floor, smiling with sweet revenge for all the babies I had kidnapped.

'Oh my God, he's falling!' I heard Sparrow shout just before I hit the ground. I wasn't sure if I was seeing stars or lightning when I cracked my head on the floor. I could hear Duke barking and I could see Turk and Sparrow looking down at me but there was no way I could respond. I wanted to tell them to help me up but I couldn't make my mouth move. Sparrow was crying and Turk kept walking away and coming back, looking at me as though he couldn't believe what he saw.

'He's dead. Oh shit! He's dead.'

'Oh shit, he's dead,' Sparrow repeated and started crying harder and louder. 'We have to get out of here,' he wailed.

I must have passed out because everything became very confusing with people, time and place all mixed together. Mom and Pop were in the backyard but I knew it was Christmas and it was cold and they didn't have any coats on and I was walking down the hall in school looking in the classrooms and there was no one there except Bridie. She was in every room, smiling at me as I looked in. Then Fritz and I were going down a swift river on a raft and we were headed for a huge waterfall and Fritz thought it was a joke. And somewhere in the background Duke kept barking and barking and the noise was hurting my head and I told God to stop him. God was looking right in my face and He looked old and tired with His long white whiskers and hair. He was putting a cold cloth on my forehead and I thought it was strange that God smelled of pipe tobacco and sweat. I knew I was dead.

'Are you really God?' I asked.

'Well now . . .' is all he said as he patted my arm.

'I'm dead, aren't I?'

'Damn near, but not quite. Close enough.'

'You're not God?' I tried to sit up.

'Some people think I'm the Devil. I'm Old Man Howe. And you're one of the Finnegan boys.'

'Mr Howe!'

Everything went black.

When I awoke, everything was stark white. Mom and Pop were whispering and Fritz was sitting on the edge of my bed holding my hand. I could barely make out Bridie and Mina standing by the door. My head was hurting and my chest felt like it was on fire. I looked around and realized I was in the hospital.

'Hey, look who's with us.' It was Fritz as he leaned over me smiling. 'Looks like he's going to live after all.'

'You're going to be fine,' said Mom as she kissed me on the cheek.

'You had quite a fall, sport.' Pop looked at me with more affection than he had ever shown.

'Can we go home?'

'Not right now.' It was Miss Neal, all freckles and red hair and starched white, standing by the window. She came over to the bed. 'We want to keep an eye on you for a while just to make sure you're all in one piece.' She held my eyelids up and looked deep into my eyes. I knew Miss Neal from school, she was the nurse for Our Lady of Perpetual Help when we had our TB tests and she was there every Wednesday afternoon in case anyone needed her.

'I don't have to stay overnight do I?'

'And I thought you liked me, Timothy Finnegan,' said Miss Neal as she took my pulse.

'Oh, I do but . . .' I suddenly remembered the most important part of the whole incident. I squeezed Fritz's hand. 'Guess who I saw?'

'Old Man Howe.'

'Yeah. How'd you know?'

'We all saw him. He just left.'

'I think the best thing for Finn is some rest so why don't you all say goodnight now,' said Miss Neal.

'Wait. How did I get here?' I asked.

'Well, if it wasn't for Joe Louis,' said Pop, and I looked at Bridie.

When I blacked out, just after Turk and Sparrow had decided I was dead and hightailed it for home so they wouldn't be implicated in the accident and therefore have to admit they were in Howe's barn, Bridie, who had followed us on her pathetic little girl's bike, and who indeed had secretly followed us many times before, came out of the shadows and to my rescue. She saw that I was unconscious and, not knowing how mean and dangerous Mr Howe was supposed to be, went to him for help. He carried me through the pouring rain into the house, put me on the sofa, dried me and covered me with a blanket. Since he didn't have a phone, Bridie had to ride to the nearest neighbor, a good mile away, and call for help. Mom and Pop were both working and Fritz wasn't at home so the woman called the police. In the meantime, Mr Howe did the best he could to dress the wounds on my chest. My shirt was shredded where the owl had scratched me from my collarbone to my waist. Bridie went back and waited with Mr Howe until the police came and took all of us to the hospital.

I had to stay in the hospital for two nights under observation because I had a slight concussion. Bridie visited me during the day and drove everybody crazy. She looked at the new babies and visited all the patients and came back and told me in gruesome detail what was wrong with them. There were flowers all over my room, flowers she collected from patients being released. She was underage and wasn't even supposed to be

43

there but the hospital made an exception because she was some kind of heroine. She also told me everything she could remember about Mr Howe. His house may have been old and dilapidated on the outside but inside it was immaculate. There were pictures of Mr and Mrs Howe when they were young and pictures of the Howe children. There had been eleven but only four lived. Mrs Howe had been dead for over forty years and Mr Howe still missed her as much as he did the day she died. The furniture was old but kept in perfect condition and looked like it came out of a store window yesterday. Mr Howe smoked a pipe and drank tea instead of coffee. When I was lying there unconscious, they both had two cups of tea in the nicest china Bridie had ever seen. There wasn't a chip in it. He also made her some toast and asked her if she wanted the crusts cut off, which, of course, she did because she thought it was more elegant. His name was Elias Howe, the same as the man who invented the sewing machine but they were no relation except for being forty-ninth cousins which Mr Howe said everyone in the world was. She liked the name Elias very much and hoped when she got to know him better she'd get his permission to use it. Mrs Howe's clothes were still in the bedroom dresser and closet, just as clean and nice as if someone had recently laundered them. She went on and on until even Mr Howe started to sound uninteresting. When she got to the color of the wallpaper in the bathroom, I dozed off.

When I was at home, feeling better and allowed to get up, Mom made a cake and Pop drove us out to Mr Howe's so I could meet him without thinking he was God. Bridie, of course, insisted on going along. Everything she had told me about Mr Howe's home was true. For once in her life she hadn't exaggerated. Mr Howe, still looking as old and tired as I remembered him, shook hands and invited us to sit down. He said I looked much better than I had lying in the hospital bed and asked how my scratches were healing. Bridie wanted me to take off the bandages and show him but he said he'd take my word that they were getting better. We had tea in his beautiful china along with the cake and when we were ready to leave he asked if I still wanted the pigeons from his barn.

'I won't go in there again, I promise.' I turned to Mom and Pop. 'This time, I mean it.'

'Well,' said Mr Howe, 'it's not such a terrible place if a fella does things the right way. For instance, if one person holds the ladder while the other one climbs up to the nests, pigeon hunting might be tolerably safe.'

'Could I?' I looked at Pop.

'We'll see,' he said as he went out to the car.

'And Finn,' Mr Howe's hand was on Bridie's shoulder, 'bring your best friend with you.'

I looked at Bridie as though I was seeing her for the first time. She was smiling at me and I thought, maybe everyone's been right and I've been wrong. She was crazy but maybe she wasn't so bad after all. 'I will,' I said, and we got in the car.

In the summer of 1942, America was singing 'I Left My Heart at the Stage Door Canteen', 'The White Cliffs of Dover', and 'Paper Doll'; while in Europe, the Nazis were beginning the systematic murder of millions of Jews. Field Marshal Rommel was dazzling the world with his Afrika Korps and German U-boats were sinking British and American ships faster than they could be replaced. The Japanese had their first defeat at Midway and the FBI captured eight German saboteurs in Florida and New York. American women, doing their damnedest to look like Greer Garson in *Mrs Miniver*, were leaving the home and working for the war effort. Mom quit teaching and went to work in the shipping office at the army depot in a town about twelve miles away and had to get up at five-thirty to be on the corner by six to get her ride. She also started making more money than Pop. At breakfast, Bridie took over as the woman of the house and waited on Pop, Fritz and me with the efficiency

45

of an assembly-line worker. School was out for the summer and since Mom was working Bridie took it upon herself to look after two households, even though we were doing quite well without her. Fritz and Pop were both good cooks and nobody dusted or scrubbed a floor better than me. Laurie started joining us for breakfast and lunch, and more often than not he was hung over. Bridie made excuses for him, saying it was the bartender's curse, and Laurie dismissed it all as just a few drinks with the customers.

In June, at Fritz and Mina's graduation party in the backyard, they announced they were getting married. Fritz had told me the night before, after all the lights were out in the house and we could hear soft snoring coming from Mom and Pop's room. He got out of bed and quietly closed our bedroom door.

'I've got something to tell you,' he said as he crawled back into bed.

'Yeah?'

'It's about Mina and me. We're going to get married.'

'I know.' Everybody knew.

'I mean soon. We're going to get married soon.'

I wasn't prepared for that. Someday, yes, but not soon. What would they do, live with us or with the Pascalis? Or would they get a place of their own? Fritz didn't even have a job, they couldn't get a place of their own. Fritz married. Mina Pascali would become Mina Finnegan.

'That's a terrible name,' I said.

'What name?'

I always assumed Fritz could hear what I was thinking. 'Mina Finnegan. It's terrible.'

Fritz chuckled. 'Mina thinks it is, too.'

'How can you get married? You're too young. And you don't even have a job.'

'Yeah, I do, kind of. I joined the army. Pop signed for me.'

'Jesus, Mary and Joseph!' I sat up so quickly I scared the hell out of Duke. 'Does Mom know?'

'Not yet. She's going to be mad at Pop.'

'She's going to kill him.'

'So, what do you think?'

I didn't know what I thought. Everyone else was going and I knew that one day Fritz would go, too. I had almost accepted that inevitability. A few months earlier, I couldn't imagine my world altering in any way, but the world was changing and there was nothing to do to stop it. Nothing would ever be the same. And it was all mixed up with movie images and propaganda, heroes and flag-draped boxes. Things were happening too fast. How could Fritz already have joined the army and not told me? Did he tell Mina? He didn't tell Mom.

'What do you think?' he said again.

'Where will you go?'

'Fort Dix, I guess. I don't know.'

'When?'

'Soon.'

Fritz told Mom just before people started arriving for the party. We were all in the kitchen. Pop, Fritz, Mina and I were sitting at the table when Mom, all smiles, came into the room with two little gift-wrapped packages.

'Mom, I have to tell you something –'

'Open your gifts,' she interrupted. 'I hope you like them.'

'They'll like them,' Pop said. He turned to Fritz. 'Go on, open them. She won't be satisfied until you do.'

'Okay. Open yours, too, Mina.' They started unwrapping.

'You shouldn't have done this, Mrs Finnegan.'

There was a gold Bulova watch for Fritz and a small gold locket for Mina, both inscribed with the date, June 5, 1942.

They thanked and kissed everyone, including me, and after Mom asked them a dozen times if they really liked their gifts, Fritz sat her down and finally blurted it out. 'I enlisted in the army.'

Mom stared at him for a moment.

'Now, before you say one word I want you to listen to me.' Pop was using his head-of-the-family tone of voice. 'He would have gone sooner or later so it might as well be sooner. I signed for him and that's all there is to that.' There was a long silence. Mom got up, went to the icebox and started taking platters of sandwiches and deviled eggs out.

'Well, aren't you going to say anything?' Pop's voice had lost some of its authority.

'What is there for me to say? It's already done, isn't it.' She was so angry she could barely speak. She started out of the kitchen.

'Mae . . .' Pop stood up and she turned to him.

'You'll get to play soldier again after all, won't you, Tom? Only this time it's through your son. I only hope you don't live to regret it.' She took the platters into the dining room and Pop followed her.

'It'll be all right, don't worry about it,' he said to Fritz as he went. 'Goddamn it, Mae, listen to me . . .' and he was gone.

'Don't talk to me because I'm not talking to you.' The three of us sat at the table waiting for more but they went upstairs.

'When are you going to tell them you're getting married?' I said it to break the silence.

'I don't know. Later, I guess.'

Mina took his hand. 'Maybe we should wait,' she said. Fritz shrugged.

'You like the watch?' I asked.

'Yeah, I do.'

'It cost forty-nine ninety-five.'

Aside from Fritz and Mina's school friends, the guests at the party included just about everyone in the neighborhood. Father Boyle was there and the Ganises, Turk and Sparrow, even though they weren't invited, Mr and Mrs McManus, known to everyone on Livery Street as Big Tum and Little Tum, Mrs Shultz, Mr and Mrs Pascali and even Mrs Cavanaugh. She wore the same dirty housedress and the same runny hose but in honor of the festivities she smeared very red lipstick across her sliver of a mouth and dabbed her cheeks with circles of rouge and looked exactly like the laughing, toothless, mechanical hag in front of the fun house on the boardwalk at Seaside Heights. Bridie, of course, dressed for the occasion. When Mom saw her she said she looked like a Russian refugee kid from the newsreels. Where she got the dress, nobody knew, but it almost came to her ankles, all dark flowers and leaves, like something an old woman would wear. Her hair, newly and oddly cut for the party, was tied up with a leftover Christmas ribbon and on her thin little wrists she wore junky, colored-glass bracelets which kept slipping off. I don't know if it was my new respect for Bridie or what but I thought she looked pretty.

People brought different dishes even though rationing had started and food was scarce. Big Tum and Little Tum brought beautiful cakes and cookies. Their sugar source remained a mystery for the duration of the war. Big Tum, who had worked for the water company all his life and retired a few years earlier, spent most of his time with Little Tum doing what they both enjoyed most, cooking. He weighed just under four hundred pounds and she was slightly larger. They had both emigrated from Ireland when they were in their teens and although they were born in villages not twenty miles apart they didn't meet until they arrived in America and were working at the Plaza Hotel in New York, she as a chambermaid and he as an elevator operator. When they married and moved to town they bought the big house on the corner of Livery and Wilbridge, anticipating a large family. But Little Tum only conceived once, in her early forties, and the child was stillborn. From then on every kid in the neighborhood was like one of their own and there was no better place to recuperate from an illness, be it too many green apples or the flu, than in the ample lap of Little Tum, resting your head on her pillow of a bosom and inhaling the healing scent of her ever-present talcum powder.

Bridie and I stuffed ourselves with sandwiches and cake and orange soda. She made a plate for Laurie and we took it across the street and put it in their icebox for him to have when he came home from work. By now the house had been furnished with the necessities and was very livable in in spite of Bridie's Gypsy taste in colors. Laurie either indulged her or had no taste at all because the decorating was all Bridie.

'I think I keep house real good,' she said, sitting at the kitchen table and straightening out the bright orange tablecloth. 'Don't you think?'

'Yeah. Why?'

'And I'm a damn good cook, too.'

'Sure,' I lied.

She was thinking hard about something, wrestling with one of her many demons.

'You like Mina?' She changed the subject.

'Course I do, what do you think?'

'Why does Fritz want to get married? Your Mom and me take care of him.'

'People get married ...' and I couldn't think of a good reason. Finally I said, 'To have children.'

'And cause they like to do sex.'

'Yeah.'

She shook her head. 'I don't understand it.'

'Are you thinking of Laurie?' I asked even though I knew she was.

'Do you think he has to do sex?'

'I don't know.' And I didn't.

'I don't think so.' She was quiet for a moment.

'We better get back. Fritz is going to tell everybody about him and Mina.'

'Sometimes I think nothing makes any sense. You ever feel like that?'

When Fritz finally made the announcement, just before it got dark and the party moved inside to get away from the mosquitoes, everyone had had enough to drink to make them very happy. The war was far away and real life was happening in our backyard. The world had receded to its proper size, the two blocks of Livery Street. Fritz and Mina stood hand in hand on the back porch, flushed with excitement.

'This is a great party and I want to thank everybody, especially Mom and Pop.' Fritz looked for them but they were on opposite sides of the yard, still not speaking. Pop smiled for the benefit of those gathered and looked in Mom's direction but she refused to acknowledge him. She stood rigid, facing Mina and Fritz, with a set jaw and blazing eyes.

'Mina and I have an announcement to make.' Fritz put his arm around her and pulled her close and some of their classmates started to hoot. 'We're going to be married – ' He didn't get to say any more. People were all over the porch hugging and kissing them and I wanted them to get away and give Fritz a chance to tell them about going in the army. As far as I was concerned, that was the big news. But he never got to say anything about it. Mom stood motionless by the lilac bushes and, after a moment's deliberation, Pop went to her. I couldn't hear what he was saying but she never looked at him once, she just walked up on the porch, past Mina and Fritz, and went into the house without saying a word. Pop stood with his hands in his pockets staring at the ground until he walked angrily through the gate and out of the yard. I knew he was headed for the Alley. Mrs Ganis was telling Fritz and Mina what beautiful children they were going to have while Bridie stood with me, watching the proceedings with such curiosity one would have thought she was watching a group of newly arrived Martians.

'I just don't get it,' she said, shaking her head with wonder.

Duke and I were lying in bed listening to the radio when Mom finally came upstairs after cleaning up the kitchen. Fritz was off somewhere with his friends and Pop hadn't come home yet.

'I thought you might need this, being on your feet so much today.' She handed me a cup of tea laced with the miraculous Irish whiskey. It was hot and harsh and sweet from the generous spoonful of honey. I sat up and sipped it.

'You'd better close your door tonight. His nibs will be coming in late and I'm sure drunk as a lord,' she said, meaning Pop. 'And who knows when your brother will be home.' She sat on the edge of the bed, petting Duke, her mind a million miles away.

'It was a swell party,' I said.

'Yes, it was.'

'Fritz liked his watch.'

'Did he? Well, I'm glad.'

'You still mad at Pop?'

'That's none of your concern.' She got up and turned off the radio. 'But if you must know, yes, I am. Now, drink your tea and go to sleep and not another word out of you.' She started for the door.

'Are you mad because Fritz is getting married or because he's going in the army?' I asked.

'I think you've been hanging around Bridie too much. There's no end to your questions, is there?'

'Why are you mad?'

'I'm mad,' and she stopped talking for a moment and looked at me as though she might find the answer in my face. 'I'm mad because Fritz is my son and he's too young to go off and fight and too young to get married and life is treacherous and men are fools. Does that answer your question?' She turned out the light and went back to her room and I could hear her talking to herself but I couldn't understand what she was saying. In the warm spill of the moon coming through the window I looked over at Fritz's empty bed. Once he left for the army, this was the way it would always be. There'd be no whispering into the night when the pain was in my leg, no warmth in the winter and no secrets confided. There'd be no Fritz to lie in the dark with, listening to Mom and Pop laughing and fighting in the night. It would be just Duke and me. I looked down at him, sound asleep, unaware things were changing, blissful in his dog ignorance of anything but the moment. His lip started to twitch and his legs jerked as he chased some night bird through his dreams.

It was a slightly muffled noise coming from somewhere downstairs that woke me. Fritz had come in while I was sleeping and was stretched out on his bed. I went to the door and opened it as quietly as I could.

'Ssh.' It was Fritz, up on one elbow, listening.

'Who is it?' I whispered.

'Pop and Laurie. They're drunk.'

I couldn't understand anything they were saying but the laughter was frequent and raucous.

'How long have they been there?' I asked.

'I don't know, I fell asleep as soon as I came home. Come on, maybe we can keep them quiet.' There was a particularly loud burst of laughter when we reached the foot of the stairs and Mom came storming out of her room, glaring at us from the top. I flattened myself against the wall, trying to disappear.

'Shut up, down there!' she yelled. 'You'll wake the whole neighborhood!'

'Go back to bed and leave us alone.' Pop saw us. 'You, too. Get upstairs.' We were caught between them.

'Laurie O'Connor, you should be ashamed of yourself. Drunk every night, leaving Bridie alone in the house. She'd be better off at St Stephen's.' St Stephen's was the local orphanage and the mere mention of the cold, gloomy, red-brick monstrosity chilled the heart of every kid in town. 'Go home where you belong.'

'You go back to bed and leave us alone.' Pop started back to the kitchen when Laurie appeared, barely able to stand.

'I'm going, Mrs Finnegan. I didn't mean to make trouble. Sure, you're the last person on the face of the green earth I'd want to upset. You know that, don't you?' He smiled at Fritz and me and whispered, 'You lads should be sleeping.'

53

'Don't go because of her,' said Pop. Laurie opened the front door. 'This is my house, too, you know.'

'You're only making things worse, Tom. Be a good fella and go to bed. I'll see you tomorrow.' He tiptoed out, quietly closing the door behind him, then fell with a loud crash down the three steps.

'I hope you broke your neck!' Mom shouted.

Pop looked at us, shaking his head in disapproval. 'Your mother is a terrible woman.' He faced her squarely. 'Well, Mae, I hope you're happy.' He started up the stairs. 'You've insulted a guest in our home.'

'You take one more step and I'll get the gun and shoot your foot off.' She really sounded as if she meant it. Fritz stifled a laugh. 'You're not sleeping up here tonight.'

'And where am I supposed to sleep?'

'I don't give a damn. Sleep in the gutter where you belong.'

'Well, the gutter would be a lot more pleasant than sleeping with you,' he said as the offended party. 'Jesus Christ!' He mumbled his way back to the kitchen.

'And I hope the two of you got an earful,' she said. 'Now get back to bed before you feel the palm of my hand. And I mean you, too, Mr grown-up Fritz.' And she went back to her room.

The following week was a period of intense activity and avoidance for everyone. Mom and Pop managed to keep busy every night so they wouldn't have to spend any time together. She with the Democratic Party, the Catholic Daughters and the war-bond committee, and he with the Knights of Columbus, the air-raid wardens and the Hunt and Fish Club. All meals were eaten in a silence that would have been the envy of cloistered monks. Laurie stayed away from the house, Fritz spent his time with Mina and their friends, and Bridie and I lunched almost every day with Mr Howe who was true to his word and helped me get the chocolates.

By the end of that week I felt I had known Mr Howe all my

life, thanks to Bridie and her incessant questioning, and he knew everything about the people on Livery Street, right down to Laurie's hemorrhoids. He was born on a flatboat on the Missouri River, four years after the Civil War. His father was a minister and the family was on the way to a new assignment in the Indian Territory when he decided, as he put it, 'to make an appearance'. He grew up on an outpost knowing more Indians than white men and Bridie wanted to hear the details of a scalping but Mr Howe was happy to say he had never seen one. He met his wife, Miriam, the daughter of an army captain, when they were both eighteen, and eventually they were married by his very own father. The young couple came East when Mr Howe's grandfather died, leaving him the land which they farmed successfully, raising corn and apples. He said they were as happy as Adam and Eve in Eden. Bridie asked if there was a snake and Mr Howe said sometimes life itself is the snake. Mrs Howe died and the children left and after years of trying to keep the place up he decided to let the land lie fallow. Of his four surviving children he saw one son, who lived in New York, heard from a daughter in Denver, and had no idea where the other two were. Bridie and I wanted him to come to Livery Street to visit and see the pigeons and have supper with us but he said he had overstayed his allotted time on earth and was sure the good Lord was going to call him any day and he wanted to be home to receive the call.

Some people measure a year by the calendar, some by the signs of the zodiac and some primitive peoples by sun, moon, tides, whatever. I measured the year by holidays. Memorial Day meant spring, the Fourth of July, mid-summer, Labor Day, the approaching autumn and, inevitably, school. Every other holiday had its own significance, along with my birthday and, if one went to a Catholic school, the wonderful Holy Days of Obligation, when we didn't have to go to school but the kids in the public schools did. That particular Fourth of July was special because Fritz left for the army the following day. Not long after the graduation party he was called for his physical and when he was classified 1-A he was given a short time to take care of things at home before he left. He and Mina decided to wait until he was home on leave to get married.

About a week before he was to go, Aunt Cassie, Pop's oldest sister, had a stroke and Mom and Pop had to go to Wilkes-Barre to see her. They still weren't speaking and Pop was still sleeping on the sofa and Fritz said it would be a hell of a long ride with the two of them sitting there, staring straight ahead, like a couple of corpses. Aunt Cassie was the matriarch of Pop's family and everyone was afraid of her, including me. When my grandparents died, long before I was born, she took over as head of the family and never relinquished control over her eight brothers and sisters. Mom wanted me to go with them, probably to have someone to talk to, but I didn't like Wilkes-Barre, it was in another State and so far away from New Jersey, I thought they got different news. Actually, it was only about a three-hour drive but I almost expected my Pennsylvanian relatives to speak another language. And I didn't like the way Aunt Cassie's house smelled. I begged not to go because I'd only be in the way and I hated hospitals but the truth was I wanted to stay home with Fritz. They finally agreed, after giving us a list of instructions, lock the door, feed the dog, turn off the gas, don't stay up all night and eat right. When they were putting the suitcase in the car, Bridie came over with a greasy paper bag full of sandwiches and fruit. The sandwiches were a specialty of Bridie's, peanut butter and anything else she found in the icebox. I'm sure Mom pitched them out the window as soon as they were a safe distance away.

With Mom and Pop gone, Bridie had Fritz and me all to herself for a few days and she took over the running of our lives with a vengeance. It was a Sunday night and Laurie was off work so she planned a supper for us, Mina included. We tried to get out of it, knowing what Bridie was capable of serving, but she wouldn't be dissuaded. Mina solved the problem by offering to help, an offer Bridie was delighted to accept because it made her feel more grown-up spending the afternoon with a high school graduate. We were informed that supper was to be served at six and asked to 'dress decent'.

It was the social event of the season for Bridie. There were enough flowers on the table for a derby winner and we could barely see the person sitting across from us. She borrowed candles and napkins from Mrs Ganis and, all in all, everything looked quite nice on the garish orange tablecloth. Four of the five plates were white, with the initials P. I. in gold and blue on the rim. Laurie was quietly filching a service for eight from the Prussian Inn. The menu was Italian and delicious, thanks to Mina, and the dessert was a Boston Cream Pie, thanks to Little Tum, who was happy to contribute when Bridie told her it was Fritz's going-away supper. The most astonishing thing about the evening was Bridie. Mina had given her one of her old dresses and Bridie wore it like a princess. Her hair, for a change, was combed like a normal person's and she even had a little lipstick on. Here was yet another Bridie. Since I decided to stop resenting her I kept discovering new things to like about her. She was still brash, irritating, aggressive and intrusive but she was also surprising and funny and fiercely loyal. And with a little help from Mina, she could also be civilized. At that strange little dinner party, she was in her element, self-assured and beautiful, and she knew it.

'I think this is the prettiest dress I ever saw.'

'Well, it never looked as pretty on me.' Mina smiled.

'You look just grand,' said Laurie. 'The picture of your mother.' There was a sad little smile on his face.

We hadn't seen Laurie since the night he and Pop got drunk and at first he was slightly nervous and apologetic but the attention was on Bridie and the conversation was easy and in no time at all he relaxed. Bridie and I told stories about Mr Howe, who had always been a mystery man, and we talked about Aunt

Cassie and Wilkes-Barre but the major topic of conversation was Fritz's imminent departure for the army. Laurie was reminded again of what he considered his uselessness and suggested a drink. He got out the bottle and poured a shot for himself and Fritz.

'You're one lucky lad,' said Laurie as they raised their glasses. 'If I didn't have a bum ticker . . .' and he threw the shot down. He started to pour another but Bridie stopped him.

'You said you wouldn't.'

'It's just a farewell drink to Fritz. I think we should have another for Godspeed. What do you say, Fritz?'

'No. No, that's enough for me, thanks.'

Laurie was disappointed. 'Well, just a quick one for me and that will be it.' He looked at Bridie. 'I promise.'

'All right,' she said grudgingly.

He drank the shot and put the top on the bottle and Bridie took it away from the table into another room. The effect of the whiskey was almost instantaneous. He was mellower and happier and, at the same time, sadder. He started to tell stories of his days working the resort hotels and those stories reminded Bridie of other stories and the two of them sat there like a vaudeville team, making us laugh until we cried. There was nothing Bridie liked better than sharing everything she had shared with Laurie. The two of them were like Mom and Pop talking about their childhoods in Pennsylvania. Fritz and I knew all the stories but we liked hearing them again and again because retelling the stories, Mom and Pop were always as happy and playful as children. They had known each other their entire lives and all their history and recollections were mutual and remembering the smallest detail never seemed to bore them. Bridie and Laurie had the same kind of connection and Bridie was only a kid. Her eyes glittered as she sat listening and talking, remembering the wonderful times they'd had together.

'Of course,' said Laurie unexpectedly, 'the best was when I had my Kath.' He sat back in the chair, his face changing to a look we hadn't seen before, as he thought about Bridie's mother. This was a part of Laurie's history from which Bridie was excluded. It was fine for her to fabricate stories about a dead woman she didn't know, stories that never included Laurie, but when this dead woman was mentioned in any real context, she resented it.

'I've been thinking about Kath a lot lately,' said Laurie, 'what with you two getting married and all. Those were the happiest days of my life. Oh, it's grand to be in love, now, isn't it?' Fritz reached over and took Mina's hand. 'The first time I ever saw her was on a trolley on Commonwealth Avenue in Boston, and the windows were open, it being summer and hotter than bejesus, and that black hair of hers, as thick as a horse's tail, was flying back in the wind and I thought she looked like the hood ornament on a Rolls Royce. I moved to the seat across the aisle from her but I was that shy I couldn't think of a word to say. I just sat like a great oaf staring at her until, finally, she turned to me with those yellow-green eyes of hers and said, "Kathleen Brennan. What's yours?" '

Kath sounded exactly like Bridie and his story reminded me of the first time I met her. I looked at her as she sat folding and refolding her napkin, glancing at Laurie occasionally. The glitter was gone and her eyes were clouded and secretive.

'Well, listen to me, going on and on,' he said.

'It's the drink,' Bridie said flatly, and she started clearing the dishes. Mina and I helped her.

'Anyway,' said Laurie, 'we lost her and that's the end of that story. If you'll excuse me, nature calls.' We all knew he went off to look for the bottle. Bridie slipped into one of her dark moods and try as hard as we could there was no getting her back. Laurie never came down to the party and after the dishes were washed and put away Mina, Fritz and I left. They were taking a walk uptown and asked me to go but I knew they wanted to be alone so I went home and Duke and I sat out by the pigeon coop in the dark and I thought about Laurie and Kath and

Bridie. I couldn't imagine living in so many different places and I wondered how it felt never knowing your own mother. Would Fritz and Mina remember like Laurie and Mom and Pop? And would I ever have stories to tell? Duke was no help at all finding the answers to my questions. Five minutes after we sat down the warm summer night lulled him to sleep. A few minutes later, I joined him.

I don't know how long I slept but when I woke up the sliver of a moon was high and the night was still except for the tree frogs and crickets. Duke was in such a deep sleep he didn't even move when I went inside. All I could think about was how angry Mom would be if she knew I had fallen asleep in the yard because she was convinced dampness did my leg nothing but harm. Since I knew my way around the house with my eyes closed, I didn't turn on any lights as I headed for the stairs.

'No, no, don't touch it. I'm so close.' It was Fritz, with a desperate kind of frenzy in his voice.

'Ssh, you'll wake Finn,' Mina whispered. They were in the living room, on the sofa.

'Oh God,' said Fritz as he exhaled loudly. 'I love you. So much.'

'I love you, too.'

I knew I shouldn't be listening, that I should go back out in the yard or up to my room, anyplace else, but I sat as quietly as I could on the bottom step, my heart beating so hard I was sure they could hear it. They didn't say anything for a minute or so but occasionally there were little sighs of pleasure and I could hear soft sucking sounds, like puppies nursing, and Mina was moaning.

'I don't want to wait anymore,' he said.

There was a slight pause and Mina whispered, 'I don't either.'

'Down here on the floor.' There was a rustle and thud as the sofa cushions hit the floor. 'No, no, let me take them off.' I could hear the hushed sound of clothes moving over skin. 'I wish I could turn on the light –'

'No, please,' said Mina.

'You feel so beautiful.'

'So do you.'

'Lie down.'

There was movement in the dark and I wanted to get up and run but I couldn't move, I couldn't do anything but imagine them lying next to each other.

'Are you sure?' Fritz sounded nervous.

'Yes.'

'You're not scared?'

'Yes, I am.'

'Me, too.'

I could hear them kissing, almost imperceptibly at first but it got more and more frantic and then I heard bodies moving, sliding over each other in the dark. Mina made a little sound deep in her throat and there was complete silence for a moment, then she choked back a painful sob so stifled and unexpected it frightened me.

'Are you all right?' asked Fritz.

'Yes.' She took a deep breath. There was no sound or movement for what seemed like a long time.

'Oh God, it feels so good.'

I couldn't see anything but I squeezed my eyes shut against the possibility and in my mind Mina was naked and dark and beautiful and Fritz was pale and perfect, as I had seen him a thousand times. And I could see him on top of her and Pop on top of Mom and Laurie on top of the dead Kath and it seemed fierce and scary and I knew why it was something that was whispered about. But what was this mixture of pleasure and pain and why was it so important to everyone? I could hear Mina and Fritz moaning through kisses, gasping and sucking for air, and it got louder and more frantic until Fritz cried out. They lay there quietly for a while after catching their breath until Mina started to soothe him like a mother soothes a child. I couldn't tell whether they were laughing or crying or both, but somehow I knew it was over. I crept back through the dining room and kitchen and out into the yard and when I sat next to Duke I was sweating and shaking and feeling very confused and strangely alone. All my life I had told Fritz everything that happened to me, but this, this momentous, extraordinary experience, was something I couldn't tell anyone, especially Fritz.

When Mom and Pop came home from Wilkes-Barre they were speaking again. Fritz said it was because they had to sleep in the same bed at Aunt Cassie's house, that sleeping together made not talking very hard. They were talking but there was something different between them, a kind of polite edginess, like two people who didn't really know each other. It was almost as if they were no longer friends. They had never been very affectionate, especially in public, but there were looks and little touches and intimate smiles Fritz and I would see once in a while. There was none of that now, only the necessary contact and only when it couldn't be avoided. Aunt Cassie was going to be fine, it was only a slight stroke and there would be no permanent damage. Mom said she worried more about us but from the looks of things we had done very well without them.

After the night on the stair, listening to Fritz and Mina making love in the dark, I expected them to look different. I didn't know how exactly but it seemed to me that if a person went through so much there'd be something different about them.

'What are you looking at?' asked Fritz when he caught me staring at him.

'Nothing.'

'The last couple of days, you've been looking at me funny.'

'No I haven't.'

'Yes you have. Like I'm some kind of freak or something. What the hell is it?'

'Do you feel any different lately?'

'What do you mean, different?' Fritz was completely puzzled.

'I don't know.'

'Honest to God, Finn, sometimes you're really strange.'

'Just forget it.'

'I know what it is!' My heart stopped. Was he aware of me there in the dark, listening to them do things they weren't supposed to do until they were married, and then only to have babies? I hadn't thought about it before but I had overheard two people commit mortal sin. I probably committed mortal sin just listening.

'What?' I asked.

'It's because I'm leaving in a few days.'

I was so relieved. 'Yeah, I guess so.'

'Hey, I'll be back before you know it. Nothing's going to happen to me. Quit worrying will you?'

'Yeah.'

'You're going to have it tougher than me. When I'm gone, you'll have to put up with all the shit from Mom and Pop.' It was then I realized Fritz was truly going away. Before that it had all been parties with his friends and idle talk but this was the first time just the two of us were discussing it. He was trying to minimize it, smiling, brows arched with wonder as if he was talking about a weekend at the shore. But deep in his eyes there was something else, some sense of a piece of our lives slipping away, a color fading, a candle being snuffed. He must have known I was feeling the same thing.

'Hey, I want you to do me a couple of favors,' he said. 'Mina's going to feel real bad when I go. Will you look after her? I think you're the only other person in the world she really trusts.' It seemed like an enormous responsibility but I was flattered so much I nodded yes. 'And take care of my graduation watch, okay? It might get broken or stolen and I don't want anything to happen to it. It cost forty-nine ninety-five, you know.' He smiled as he tried to fasten the watch on my wrist. 'It's too big. We'll get the ice pick and put another hole in the band.' I stood there looking at Fritz and the watch until they disappeared in a blur of tears. 'Hey, Finn, come on now, don't be such a dope.' His voice cracked as he put his arms around me and held me close for a few seconds until I ran out of the house to the security of the pigeon coop where Duke and I sat in the middle of the floor, showing off the beautiful watch to the uninterested birds.

Pop, Mom, Mina, Bridie, Duke and I rode to Trenton the day we took Fritz to get the bus to Fort Dix. The night before, we celebrated the Fourth of July quietly at home, just the family and Mina and Bridie. There were no fireworks, gunpowder was being saved for the war effort, and no farewell party. Mom roasted a chicken Pop got from Mrs Cleary, who was taking care of the farm alone until her husband came home from the navy. Father Boyle stopped by to have a drink and wish Fritz goodbye and at one point in the evening he looked at me and I was sure he could see mortal sin written all over my face so I went to the bathroom even though I didn't have to go. Bridie tied red, white and blue ribbons around Duke's neck and he spent the night rolling around on the floor trying to get them off. Mr and Mrs Ganis came over and gave Fritz a box of handkerchiefs and had a drink before Mrs Ganis started to cry and Mr Ganis thought it best they leave. Mom and Pop said very little to each other but they seemed to be in good spirits, with Pop telling stories about his days in the army and Mom and Mina talking about the wedding that would take place on Fritz's first leave. Bridie loved all the talk as she loved anything that made her feel more grown-up. I had never noticed before but she could be quite a good listener, even though she tried to listen to both conversations at once. About nine o'clock, Fritz borrowed the car from Pop and he and Mina went for a ride, Pop went to bed and Mom, Bridie, Duke and I sat on the front porch hoping for a little breeze and listening to the odd gunshot fired off in the distance to celebrate the nation's birthday. On the corner, in the yellow glow of the street light, we could see

Big Tum and Little Tum slowly rocking on the porch, and next door Mrs Shultz was gently riding through the night on the glider. Mrs Cavanaugh, halfway up the block, on the other side of the street, was sitting on the bottom step, fanning herself hard enough to work up a sweat, and when Mr Benlight put his trash cans out on the curb he nodded to her and she waved back with the fan. Someone was listening to swing music on the radio and Mom lazily kept time with her foot. At the end of the street, the occasional car moved along slowly, seemingly going nowhere in particular, just sailing, tail lights glowing like fireflies. Everything was exactly the way it should be and the idea that Fritz was leaving seemed absolutely absurd.

There was a large crowd gathered around the bus when we arrived at six o'clock the next morning. Mothers and fathers, sisters, brothers and sweethearts all gathered to say goodbye to boys who, for the most part, had probably never been away from home. Army personnel with clipboards and lists were passing through the hugging, laughing, crying people, trying to make some order. No one in our little group was saying very much except Bridie who had somehow heard about the theory of perpetual motion and had decided to change the name of our parish from Our Lady of Perpetual Help to Our Lady of Perpetual Motion. Mom thought it was sacrilegious but the rest of us thought it was pretty funny. There was a fellow about Fritz's age, leaning on a parked car and smoking a cigarette, who kept watching us. He was tall and thin with ordinary features and dull brown hair but his smile was warm and as broad as the smile of a jack-o'-lantern. Every once in a while, when he caught Duke's eye, he'd pat the side of his leg and Duke would start wagging his tail until, finally, Duke pulled at his leash trying to get to him.

'Can I let him go?' I asked Pop.

'No. Take him over there.' Duke was eager as I started off.

'Hey, what's his name?' the boy said, squatting down to pet Duke.

'Duke.'

'You're a good old boy aren't you, Duke? I had a Dalmatian dog once,' he said, rubbing Duke's ears. Bridie joined us.

'We got him free cause his nose is pink instead of black and the litter was sick,' I explained. 'Pop nursed him back to health and he's never been sick a day in his life.'

'How come you're standing here all by yourself?' Bridie asked.

'Well, I'm not now. You're here with me.'

'My name's Bridie, this is Finn and the dog is Duke.'

'Me and Duke already met. My name is Simon. I'm pleased to meet you.'

'How come you're here all alone? Where's your people?'

I started to say it was none of her business but Simon answered. 'Well, it was early and I didn't think anybody should come all the way down here . . .'

'Come on.' She took his hand and dragged him over to the family, even though he protested, and introduced him to everyone. Simon shook hands with Pop and Fritz, nodded to Mina and Mom and started to walk away but Bridie grabbed him. 'Hey, where you going? You and Fritz should get to know each other. You're both going to be soldiers.' Before either of them could say anything, a loud voice boomed out.

'Okay, you men, line up here when I call your names. And let's be quick about it. We got a war to win.' He called the names in alphabetical order and everyone started hugging and kissing, quickly grabbing at the last touch. He went through the As, Bs and and Cs, and then he called, 'Drubecki, Simon.'

'That's me. Good meeting you. So long.' And Simon got in the short line. Fritz shook hands with Pop, hugged Mom and Bridie and me and kissed Mina.

'Finnegan, Thomas, J.' Without saying a word he pushed his way through the crowd and stood in line behind Simon and, when all the names had been called, they filed slowly into the olive-green bus. Fritz smiled from the window as we watched it

66

drive off, everyone cheering and waving as if the home team was going to play a game in another town. Mom and Mina started crying and Pop reminded them that Fritz was 'only going to Fort Dix, for Christ's sake, not Germany', and he walked away to the car. Driving home, nobody said very much except Bridie who worried about the absence of Simon Drubecki's family.

That night, as I lay in bed waiting to fall asleep, I listened for the comforting sound of Mom and Pop discussing the day but they didn't say a word. They hadn't really talked into the night since Fritz and Mina's graduation party but I thought with Fritz's leaving they'd surely have something to say to one another. There was already an empty space, almost as palpable as death, in the house and it was something that demanded discussion. I was sure they were lying in bed as wide awake as me, their minds filled with so much they wanted to talk about, and I couldn't understand why they just didn't say what they were thinking. After a while I went over and crawled into Fritz's bed, hoping, perhaps, for some communion of spirit, some solace. But Mom had changed his sheets and even the scent of him was already gone from the room.

Toward the end of August, I was fitted for my first leg brace and the new pain in my leg slightly diminished the pain of Fritz's absence. Pop had to drive me all the way to Philadelphia to the specialist and even though gas was being rationed he got extra because it was a medical problem. Bridie rode along, assuring me there was nothing to worry about in spite of the fact that I wasn't the least bit fearful. The only problem I was having was figuring out why I was getting the brace at all. As far as I was concerned I got along just fine and didn't need a brace now or ever. Mom and Pop had explained a hundred times that the purpose of the brace was to straighten my leg, to slowly pull my right foot forward so that, eventually, I might have normal flexibility and mobility in my knee. I could ride a bike and I could climb a barn and that was enough flexibility for me. The doctor's name was Whiteshield, which made me think of castles and armor and knights, but there was nothing at all about him that King Arthur would have welcomed at his Round Table. Dr Whiteshield was the coldest, most unfeeling, person I had ever met and for the rest of my life my attitude toward doctors would be colored by that pinched-faced little man. I felt like a piece of machinery with a crooked component while he checked my leg, ignoring me as he explained to Pop that this would be the first of many braces. As I grew, the brace would have to be replaced to correspond with my growth. In the middle of this explanation he suddenly asked Pop where Mom was. Usually, mothers brought their children to doctors. Pop said it was easier for him to get off work at the baggage room than it was for Mom to get off at the army depot since luggage had no wartime priority. He seemed slightly apologetic and annoyed and it put him in a bad mood, which lasted the whole ride home. When I complained about Dr Whiteshield, Pop said he was a good doctor and that was all that mattered. What did I expect, a damn party? It would be over a week before the brace was ready and when the time came, war or no war, Mom took off work and, since she didn't drive, the two of us went to Philadelphia on the train.

Mina got a job as an operator with Bell Telephone and, what with work and Fritz being away, we didn't see her as much as we had. When she did come to the house she and Mom read parts of letters from Fritz to each other and once in a while even I had a letter to read. He and Simon were in the same infantry outfit and had become buddies and planned to come home on leave together because Simon really didn't have any family. Bridie, who had developed a crush on Simon from the one brief meeting, started writing to him and planning 'the best damn party Livery Street had ever seen'. Fritz complained about the food, his platoon sergeant, how tough it was, how tired he was and how much he missed everybody but, for the most part, he sounded as though he was getting along just fine. Pop would listen to them read the letters and comment on the army making a man of Fritz and Mom would get up and leave the room.

When I got the brace, a heavy chrome-and-leather contraption right out of the Spanish Inquisition, the new pressure on my leg was so painful I had to miss the first week of school. Fifth grade was important, I was finally on the downside of grammar school, closer to high school than to kindergarten, and I wasn't even able to go. Mom and Pop both had to work so I spent most of the week sitting on Little Tum's lap, rocking on the porch in the warm September sun, dozing in some phantasmagoric oblivion induced by the painkillers prescribed by the Devil Doctor, Whiteshield. Every afternoon, when school let out, Laurie would carry me across the street to our house before he went to work and Bridie would stay with me, fixing dinner for all of us and bringing me up to date on everything that was happening in school. Sleepy old Sister Matthew, who had snoozed through our fourth-grade mornings the year before, slept her life away that summer. Bridie said they found her propped up in bed, dressed in her nun nightgown, her rosary beads twisted around her bony hand, with nothing on her head and, rumor had it, she was as bald as an egg. Our new fifth-grade teacher, Sister Ellen Marie, had been at Our Lady of Perpetual Help for years and everyone loved her. Bridie thought she might be all right, as far as nuns go, but there was something fishy about her, something she just didn't trust. Maybe it was her one blue eye and one brown eye which 'a person didn't notice at first but kept you looking at her because you knew something was screwy'. The same kids were back, even Anthony Bragiolli, who had been kept back so many years, moved along to the fifth grade with the rest of us. Now, not only did he have pubic hair, he also shaved. Frances Peart had been to Canada with her mother to visit relatives and, according to Bridie, yapped about it so much a person would think she had been to Timbuktu. Sister Ellen Marie put a list of the kids' relatives who were in service on the board, a list twice as long as the year before, and Bridie added Fritz and Simon's names. She told everyone Simon was her cousin from New Orleans because she liked to say New Orleans and always wanted a relative there and maybe she did have a cousin Simon in New Orleans that nobody knew about so maybe it wasn't even a lie. Almost every day she brought get well cards crudely made out of construction paper, and read the messages out loud as if I was blind instead of crippled. The big news of the new school year was the SPCA poster contest with the first prize of a ten-dollar war bond, which Bridie thought was in the bag for me since I could draw better than anyone in the class. When I pointed out that the contest was open to every grade in all three schools in town she said I had nothing to worry about, even if I wasn't the best the judges would feel sorry for me because I was a gimp, especially since I got the brace. She had decided not to enter the contest, thinking it wasn't right to compete with her best friend but the truth was she couldn't draw a straight line if her life depended upon it.

One night, when I was still on the pain pills, I thought I was dreaming and the phone kept ringing and ringing and it wasn't until the light went on in Mom and Pop's room and I heard him going downstairs that I realized it wasn't a dream. It was early in the morning, maybe two or three, a time when a phone shouldn't ring. Mom stood at the top of the stairs trying to listen but I don't think she heard any more than I did.

'Who is it at this hour?' she yelled.

'It's Laurie,' said Pop as he hurried up the stairs. 'He's at Tessie's Place. He passed out.' Tessie's Place was a bar on Allen Street, the black section of town.

'Well, let him stay there. He might learn a lesson.' Mom had no patience with Laurie. 'And why the hell are they calling you?'

'What do I look like? A mind reader? Maybe he gave them the number.'

'Why didn't they call the police?'

'Use your head, woman. It's an after-hours place, for Christ's sake!'

'Well, don't holler at me. I'm not the drunk.'

'I'm not hollering at you. Just shut up about it.'

'I don't see why you have to go out in the middle of the night –'

'No, I'm sure you don't.' I heard the closet door slam.

'Stop making all that racket,' said Mom. 'You'll wake Finn.'

'Jesus Christ, if he's not awake by now he's as deaf as a post.' He went down the stairs and out the front door and I heard the car start and pull away from the house. Mom stood at the top of the stairs, staring down into the darkness long after the sound of the car faded into the night.

'Go to sleep,' she said, without looking in my room, and she went back to bed.

I crept as silently as I could down the hall and into the small front room we used for storage where I could look out at the street. The only movement was a cat making its way across, stopping every few feet, cautiously checking from side to side to see if it was safe to go on. The sky was sprinkled with the lazy light of late summer stars and I wondered if the Germans and Japanese looked at the same stars and, if they did, how could they do such bad things? I wondered if someplace over there where the war was being fought, there was a boy like me with a brace on his leg and a dog like Duke and maybe a father who was going out late at night to take a drunken friend home. I started thinking about Fritz going overseas and meeting a kid just like me and telling him all about me and how I had pigeons and could pick up snakes and was looking after his graduation watch until he came home. And maybe this foreign kid would have a brother like Fritz, and he'd tell Fritz all about him. It all seemed possible and the possibility was overwhelming. I had never thought about German and Japanese kids before, only grown-up men, soldiers with guns, sneering from posters. And if there were German and Japanese kids there were mothers, too. Did German mothers stop talking to their husbands because they signed for their sons to go in the army? Did young Germans and Japanese lie on sofa cushions on the floor and do what Mina and Fritz did? Suddenly, I was a million miles above the earth, looking down at everyone in the world living their lives and I felt insignificant, even infinitesimal, but at the same time I was the center of the universe and everything in the galaxy revolved around me. Sitting on the floor, looking at the night and waiting for Pop to bring Laurie home, I felt I understood something, something intangible that was already starting to slip through my fingers and something I'd never be able to explain, even to myself.

Headlights lit up the street as our car pulled around the corner and parked in front of the house. Pop got out and walked to the passenger side and dragged Laurie to his feet but he collapsed and Pop had to pick him up and carry him like a dead body across the street, up the steps and into the house. The light went on in the downstairs hall and after a few minutes in the upstairs bedroom. I could see Pop throw Laurie on the bed and I could see Bridie come into the room. Pop said something to her and she went to the windows and drew the blinds. The light stayed on and a few minutes later Pop came out the front door, crossed the street to the car, closed the door on the passenger side, came into our house and went to bed. He didn't say a word to Mom and she didn't ask anything. I waited there in the dark until I heard even, slow breathing, before quietly going back to my room. The next day, when I asked Bridie about the incident, she pretended not to hear me and rattled on about the nuns and school and how much she hated Frances Peart.

I hadn't seen Mr Howe for several weeks because I couldn't ride my bike with the brace on my leg but it didn't take me long to discover how easy it was to remove it and dangle it from the handlebars. In the meanwhile, Bridie developed a keen interest in my pigeons and we made plans for a flock of her own come the following spring. It appealed to her particularly because she'd be the only girl in town with her own coop. She decided to specialize in an all-white flock even though I told her white birds were rare in the wild because the lack of camouflage made them perfect targets for predators. The challenge made it all the more tempting to her. The incident in Howe's barn with Turk and Sparrow had been forgotten and somehow we were all friends again. For whatever reason, even Bridie was accepted. Perhaps it was because she had the guts to actually face Old Man Howe or maybe it was her ever presence, but Turk and Sparrow gave her the greatest compliment in the world when they decided 'she wasn't anything like a girl'.

When we finally did pedal out to see Mr Howe, on a cool Saturday in late September, Bridie was bursting with news. She told him all about Sister Ellen Marie and her peculiar eyes, the fifth grade, Fritz and Simon, who was her special new friend, the SPCA poster contest that I was destined to win and, most importantly, news of the upcoming wedding. The banns of matrimony had already been announced at Sunday mass and Mom and the Pascalis were busy making plans for the end of October, when Fritz would be home on leave. It would be a semiformal ceremony with Mina in a long white gown and Fritz in his uniform and the reception would be held at Fire Engine Company, No. 2. Nobody was supposed to know but Bridie told us the newlyweds planned to honeymoon in Atlantic City. Bridie knew all the details because she sat in on every discussion at our house and poked her nose in whenever possible.

'I'm going to be the dumb flower girl,' said Bridie as Mr Howe made the tea. 'What I would like to be is the maid of honor but Mina asked her sister Angie who is very fat and won't look good at all in a fancy dress.'

'Well, most folks will be looking at the bride, not the maid of honor,' allowed Mr Howe.

'I don't know,' Bridie shook her head, 'she's as big as your barn, for cripes' sake.'

The big question in my mind, the question that was yet to be addressed, was who would be best man? If Mina asked her sister did that automatically mean Fritz would ask his brother? Angie Pascali, aside from being very large, was also grown-up. She was two years older than Mina. I was only ten. Unlike Bridie, I would have been happy going through life completely unnoticed, even invisible, and when I pictured Angie and me walking down the aisle together, enormous her and skinny little crippled me, it made me feel kind of sick and I hoped Fritz wouldn't ask me. But at the same time, the very thought of Fritz asking someone else was out of the question.

'About this poster contest,' said Mr Howe, buttering our toast. 'Have you decided what you might draw?'

'I thought,' interjected Bridie, 'it should be something to catch their eye right off the bat. Like maybe a squashed animal on the road, like a dog or a cat, left by some driver who just didn't give a damn.'

'That seems a mite strong.'

'I don't draw squashed animals,' I said. 'I told you that a hundred times.' I turned to Mr Howe. 'I don't know what I'm going to do, yet. I've got a few ideas but I haven't made up my mind.'

'Well, it's a thing that takes some figuring, I suppose.' Mr Howe knew everything about everything.

'Yes, it is.' I looked at Bridie hoping she'd get the point and mind her own business.

'I have some old magazines, some of them must be fifty years old, that you should look at. Might give you some ideas. Seems to me there's some nice pictures of animals in them.' He got up and went into the other room.

'I wish you'd stop talking about squashed animals on the road,' I whispered. 'For God's sake, we're eating.'

'You do it your way then. Lose the damn contest. See if I care. You wouldn't know a good idea if it bit you on the arse. So there.'

Mr Howe came back with a stack of magazines and we started to look through them. The paper was so old the pages almost fell apart in our hands. Some dried leaves and flowers, so faded they were colorless, fell out of one of the magazines and Mr Howe picked them up as gently as one might handle a baby bird.

'Will you look at that! There's not a bit of color left in them. Like old skin.' He handed one to me and one to Bridie. 'You kids ever press leaves in autumn?' I had but Bridie hadn't. 'We used to do it with our kids every year. I'm sort of an authority on leaf pressing. You didn't know that, did you? If you want bright yellow, you get yourself an apple leaf, or a silver maple or a ginkgo, which is like a pretty little fan. Now, if you want red you look for a sugar maple or a sumac or maybe an oak if you want a real dark color. And once you start with flowers, well there's no end to that.' He took the leaves from us, looked at them long enough to drift off to a place we knew nothing about, then carefully replaced them in the magazine and I started looking for animal pictures.

We sat having our toast and tea, chatting about anything that came to mind and I thought Mr Howe was the easiest person I had ever talked to. He wasn't at all like an adult. He seemed to truly listen and to care about what we had to say and I never felt foolish or dumb and he never made judgments or gave orders or dismissed anything as unimportant.

'I want to ask you a private question,' said Bridie as she wiped some toast crumbs off her chin.

'Maybe I won't want to answer it but go ahead, shoot.'

'Did you ever take to drink?'

'Well,' Mr Howe thought for a second, 'depends on what you mean by that.' I knew she was talking about Laurie and the night Pop brought him home from Tessie's Place. She still hadn't mentioned it to me and I didn't tell her I saw the whole thing. I buried my face in the magazine and pretended I wasn't listening. 'Are you asking me if I ever drank too much liquor?'

'Yeah, I guess.'

'Then the answer is no. I don't think there's anything wrong with a drink now and then, you know what I mean, to warm you or maybe to celebrate something but there are some fellas who can't do that. The drink gets them and don't seem to let go.' Bridie listened intently, nodding her head in agreement. 'Now,' continued Mr Howe, 'I always thought a fella like that might think he needs the drink because he's got some kind of problem.'

'A problem?'

'Maybe. Maybe he don't even know he's got a problem. So maybe a person shouldn't be too hard on a fella like that.' He thought about it a bit and I tried to think of a problem Laurie might have but I couldn't come up with anything. 'Are we talking about anybody we know?'

'No.' Bridie casually poured herself some more tea. 'I was just wondering.' She put too much sugar in her cup and stirred until she made a whirlpool. 'Do all men want to do sex?' She fixed those green eyes on Mr Howe and he didn't even flinch. There was absolutely nothing she wouldn't say if it happened to creep into her mind. Suddenly, I wanted to tell Mr Howe about my experience on the stairs, my exhilarating, confusing, clandestine brush with real sex. If it had been Bridie sitting there, listening to Mina and Fritz in the night, she would have gotten up and announced it from the pulpit in church but, as much as I wanted to, I couldn't even tell Mr Howe.

'Well,' said Mr Howe, cautiously, 'I'm not sure I'm the right fella to answer that question. Mind you, it's a good question. There's not a thing wrong with it but I think you're better off asking someone like Finn's mother.'

As we rode home that afternoon, the precious old magazines in my bike basket, Bridie was oddly quiet until just before we got to Livery Street where we stopped long enough for me to put my brace back on. She held my bike as I sat on the curb adjusting the straps.

'Maybe the problem is not doing sex.' She seemed to be talking to herself so I didn't say anything. At the time I didn't know that Laurie might not be the only one with that problem.

Because of the war and food shortages Pop had been thinking about getting chickens to keep in the yard, and I'm sure it was also a way for him to realize a small part of his farm fantasy. He probably would have waited until the following spring when the new peeps hatched but things weren't getting any better between him and Mom and he seemed to be excluded from or uninterested in the wedding plans so, in the midst of all the other activities that early October, he went ahead and built a chicken coop. He was very handy with a hammer and saw and because Mom was making good money and there were few consumer products on which to spend it, he spared no expense and built a coop that was the envy of the neighborhood. Bridie and I helped. At least, I tried to help but every time he needed something he asked her to get it for him and only when she was busy did he ask me. I had thought, when Fritz first went away, that things might be different between Pop and me, that he might talk to me more just because he had nobody else. Especially since he and Mom weren't really talking. But our relationship got more strained and we hardly said a word to one another. My worst nightmare was being left alone with him for even a few minutes.

'How old are these chickens?' asked Bridie as we headed out to Cleary's farm to pick up the new occupants of the wondrous coop. Pop had arranged to get some young birds from Mrs Cleary.

'Oh, I guess about four or five months. They hatched last spring.'

'Do they lay eggs?'

'Not yet. Another couple months.'

It was a wet, misty day and the autumn leaves were sticking to the road as we drove out into the country through the woods surrounding the town. Pop seemed in a good mood, whistling softly to himself as Bridie and I discussed our Halloween costumes.

'I'm not going to be another damn ghost,' said Bridie. 'That's not a costume, it's just a dirty old sheet over your head.'

'I don't know what I'm going to be.'

'It doesn't matter what you dress up as, everybody knows it's you because of your limp.' She didn't have to remind me. 'Hey, I got an idea. You can go as a mummy, you know, wrap a lot of rags around your legs and walk real stiff. Nobody would know it was you.' I didn't want to admit it but it was a good idea.

Duke had his nose out the window, deciphering and classifying all the delicious new smells rushing into his face. We saw two pheasants picking their way through a harvested cornfield and just before we got to Cleary's farm a doe jumped the split rail fence on the side of the road and crossed in front of us without so much as a passing glance. As we turned up the dirt road to the house two scruffy dogs ran to meet us, barking and wagging their tails, and Duke went crazy trying to get out of the car. I had never been to the Cleary farm, in fact, I had never met Mrs Cleary. I did know Mr Cleary, who was in the navy, because he had been to our house a couple of times after Knights of Columbus meetings. Mrs Cleary came out of the house, dressed in overalls, with her dark brown hair pulled back in a kerchief. She was tall and thin and looked to be about Laurie's age.

'She looks like a movie star,' I said as she walked toward the car.

'I bet that's what my mother looked like.' Bridie opened the door.

'Hi, Josie, is it okay if we let the dog out?'

'Sure. These two old girls are harmless. They might lick him to death but that's about all.' She smiled at me and she looked even more like a movie star. Duke jumped out and the three dogs sniffed each other then ran tumbling across the fields as if they played together every day. Pop introduced Bridie and me and Mrs Cleary invited us into the house which was as neat and unfussy as the rest of the farm. She offered Pop coffee and Bridie and me cider and cookies. From the minute Pop got out of the car he seemed different. I couldn't tell what it was exactly but he wasn't at all like he was at home. He smiled a lot and even laughed out loud a few times. Mrs Cleary offered to show us the livestock but Pop told us to take our cider and look around on our own, he had some things to talk over with her. As we went out the door, Mrs Cleary said there was a litter of kittens under the corncrib.

'I think I'll look just like her when I grow up,' said Bridie as she played with a fluffy gray kitten.

'You can't decide what you're going to look like.'

'Yes, I can. If you could have one of these kittens which one would you take?'

'I don't know.' The one animal I could not have was a cat because Mom was scared to death of them. She said when she was little a cat scratched the boy next door and he got blood poison and died. Fritz really liked cats and always wanted a big marmalade Tom. 'I guess I'd take the orange.'

'That's mine. Pick another.' She put down the gray kitten and picked up the orange one.

'He's not yours. He's Mrs Cleary's.'

'I'm going to ask her if I can have him. She likes me. A lot.'

'She likes me, too.'

'You think Laurie would like her?' The wheels were turning as she shifted the kitten from hand to hand.

'Sure, why not.'

'If I have to have a new mother, I'd like her.'

'She's a married lady, for God's sake.'

'She can get a divorce.'

'No, she can't. She's Catholic.'

'So what!' She didn't want to talk about it anymore so she put the kitten down and ran through the drizzle into the barn and I followed her. It had the rich, timeless, evocative smell of earth and dung and animals and there was dry, satisfying comfort in the dust and cobwebs. Bridie had climbed a stall and was petting an old chestnut mare who nuzzled her, looking for a hand-out.

'I wish I could sit on top of this horse,' she said, rubbing the velvet nose.

'Go ahead.'

'No, she's too big. Let's see you do it.'

I climbed up next to Bridie, heavy brace and all, and tried to figure out how I could get the mare to stand still long enough for me to get on her back.

'Hold her mane until I get on,' I said.

'I don't want to pull her hair.'

'It doesn't hurt her, for God's sake.' Bridie grabbed two handfuls of the thick, coarse hair and held tight as I threw my right leg over her back and slid on. At first she shied a bit because of the brace but in a moment she settled down and I sat straddling the broad, muscular back, feeling powerful and enormous, as if the horse was part of me.

'I want to do it, too.'

'Okay, give me your hand and get on behind me.'

'If this horse moves and I fall down there in all that horse poo it's your fault.'

'Then stay there if you're scared.'

'Okay, give me your hand.' She took my hand and gritted her teeth as I pulled her on the horse.

'I am Sir Finn and you are my Lady Fair.'

'I don't want to be a Lady Fair. I want to be a knight, too.'

'There's no such thing as a girl knight. You have to be a Lady Fair.'

'Why can't I be the first girl knight if I want to?'

'Because you can't. Don't you know anything!'

'Okay, okay. I'll be a damn Lady Fair, for cripes' sake. So what do we do now?'

'Well, I guess maybe I should slay a dragon.' With my armor rattling we rode through the bleak, English countryside, Sir Finn and the reluctant Lady Bridie, banners unfurled, searching for dragons. I raised my visor, steely eyes searching the horizon for the scaly, smelly beasts, ready to defend m'lady with my very life if need be.

'I have to pee,' said m'lady. My armor clattered to the ground.

'Well, get off and go pee.'

'I can't get off.' The mare had moved to the center of the stall as I was cantering through the English countryside and we couldn't reach the wall to climb down.

'Give me your hand and just slide off.'

'Are you crazy! I'm not going to walk in all that horse poo. Make her move over.' I poked her sides with my heels and made all kinds of giddyup noises but the mare wouldn't budge. 'If I don't get off this horse, I'm going to pee my pants. It's all your fault.'

'You're the one who wanted to get on. It's not my fault.'

'Big Finn!' she screamed, frightening the horse who whinnied in protest. 'Help! somebody help us!'

'Don't call Pop! He's going to give us hell for getting on this horse.'

'Well then, get us off. Right now, I mean it.'

'I'm trying to. Come on, girl,' I said as I dug into the horse with my brace but she still wouldn't move.

'Big Finn, help!'

'Will you shut up! I'm going to slide down then I'll push her to the wall so you can get off.' Holding tight to her mane, I pulled one leg over and slowly let myself down. I felt like I was knee-deep in the muck. As I started to push the mare to the side, two figures suddenly appeared through the mist, running across the yard. Mrs Cleary wasn't wearing the kerchief and her long brown hair was falling around her shoulders.

'What the hell are you kids doing?' Pop was very mad.

'Get me off this horse, I got to pee.' Mrs Cleary opened the stall gate and Pop lifted Bridie down and she ran for the house. Pop grabbed me by the arm and yanked me out of the stall.

'Christ, look at your brace! It's full of horse shit!'

'Oh, Tom, it's not so bad.' She smiled her movie-star smile at me. 'We can have you cleaned up in a minute.'

Mrs Cleary put her hand on my shoulder and started walking me out of the barn. Pop closed the stall gate and followed, mumbling about 'damn dumb kids'. When we got to the house a very relieved Bridie met us on the porch.

'I made it,' she said, smiling. I sat on the step and took the filthy brace off.

'Let me ask you something,' Bridie said to Pop and Mrs Cleary. 'How come there were no girl knights?'

On the way home, with the ten Rhode Island red pullets in a crate in the trunk of the car, Pop was so angry he didn't say a word. He didn't even say anything about Duke getting the back seat all wet. It started to rain so hard the windshield wipers were practically useless. The whole time Bridie complained about smelling like a horse and said she had always wanted to meet a cowboy but now she wasn't so sure. I stared out the water-blurred window wondering what Pop would tell Mom and if he'd start yelling at me when we got home. But after we put the chickens in their new house in the back of the yard and Bridie went home and we went into the kitchen to dry off, Pop's mood completely changed. When Mom asked if I had a good time on the farm Pop insisted I go up and take a hot bath so I wouldn't catch cold. As I was going, Mom asked me what I thought of Mrs Cleary. I wanted to say she was the most beautiful lady I had ever seen and that she looked just like a movie star but something deep inside told me I had better not.

'She's okay,' I said as I started out of the room without looking at Pop.

*

As the wedding approached, the preparations seemed to get more and more complicated. There was all kinds of talk about dresses and food and who was going to play the organ and who was going to sing. Flowers were scarce in October but Mrs Shultz, whose garden was ablaze with chrysanthemums in spectacular autumn colors, was designated to decorate the altar. Mom took Pop's blue serge suit, his funeral suit as he called it, to the dry cleaners and I went to Ferris's Department Store and got my first pair of long pants and a maroon jacket with gold buttons. Mrs Ferris measured my inseam right in front of everyone in the store and I was so embarrassed I couldn't wait to get out of there. Bridie was planning on wearing her first communion dress, which was too small so Mom let it out and added to it until it looked presentable. Everyone in the neighborhood was making food for the reception and Laurie, who had been on his good behavior, was borrowing flatware and napkins from the Prussian Inn. Mrs Ganis, with the help of Mrs Shultz, was in charge of decorating the tables at Fire Engine Company, No. 2. She was the only one in the neighborhood with real silver candlesticks for the head table. Pop said if the troops in Europe and the Pacific had been as well organized as the wedding, the war would already be over. Mom spent quite a few evenings at the Pascalis', I didn't know where Pop was most of the time, and Bridie and I sat at the dining-room table doing our homework, planning for Halloween and fighting about the SPCA poster.

On October 13, 1917, the Blessed Virgin appeared to the three shepherd children at Fatima in Portugal, for the last time. In that October of 1942, according to Bridie, the Blessed Virgin appeared to her for the first and only time. Actually, it wasn't exactly an appearance, it was more like a wink and a shimmy. Sister Ellen Marie had been telling the mesmerized fifth grade the story of Our Lady of Fatima, about the letters with such dire predictions that they were kept hidden away in a vault in the Vatican and about the pilgrims crawling on their hands and knees and the miraculous cures attributed to the Virgin. The drama of those three little kids, dressed in their colorful peasant outfits, surrounded by all those sheep and talking to Mary in a tree, was a sure crowd pleaser. I never could figure out why she was up in a tree but I suppose that was quibbling. Bridie liked a good story, even if it was told by a nun, and the story of Fatima was one of her favorites.

When we left school that afternoon, she stopped in front of the church, fairly dripping with piety, and told me to go on home without her, she was going to make a visit and light a candle.

'Why?' I asked in total shock.

'Cause I want to. And I have some favors to ask.'

'What?'

'None of your damn business.'

'You shouldn't swear when you're going to light a candle.'

'Then leave me alone.' She started to go into the church.

'Wait a minute. I'll go with you.' We went through the door, made the sign of the cross with water from the holy-water font, walked up to the altar, genuflected and went to the statue of Mary. The sweetish smell of decades of incense mixed with floor wax was familiar and comforting. There were the usual older Italian and Irish women, black scarves on their heads, scattered around the back of the church saying their rosaries. Mrs Cavanaugh, in the same dirty housedress, mumbled her Hail Marys and I wondered if she was praying for 'some nice Irish lad' to be killed in the war so we could claim a martyr. Old Mrs Farrell, who spent so much time in church people suspected she never went to the bathroom, was sound asleep and brightly colored blue and red and amber by the sun coming through the stained-glass window depicting Jesus, looking a lot like Tyrone Power, as a shepherd surrounded by little children and lambs. Mrs del Fiore was there with Mrs Flynn, huddled together, whispering gossip, and tiny Mrs Donatelli, whose head barely appeared above the back of the pew, said her singsong prayers in Italian.

'Give me a nickel,' said Bridie. She wanted to pay for the candle.

'I don't have any money.'

'Okay.' She looked up at the statue. 'I owe you.' She lit a candle and we went to the front pew where she knelt, squeezed her eyes shut, and prayed with a vengeance.

'What are you praying for so hard?' I whispered.

'If you must know, miracles.'

'You're nuts.'

'Why? If the Blessed Mother would appear to those kids in Portugal, why not me? I bet nobody asks for a miracle anymore. When was the last time you asked?'

'Never.'

'See what I mean?' She looked up at the statue. 'Okay, do something.'

'What do you expect her to do?' I whispered.

'She's the Mother of God, she can do anything she wants.'

'I think you're nuts.'

'Yeah. Well, you won't think I'm nuts if suddenly your leg is okay.'

'Is that the miracle you're asking for?'

'One of them. Sister Ellen Marie said people got cured of stuff.'

'Well, you can save your breath. I gave up on praying for that miracle a long time ago.'

'Maybe people aren't supposed to pray for their own miracle. Did you ever think of that, smart ass?'

'Watch your language, you're in church, for cripes' sake.'

'Why don't you just shut up so I can pray.' It was clear that any conversation was over. She sat staring at the Blessed Virgin, shutting out the world, waiting for her miracles to happen. Mary, in her blue and white robes, which were badly in need of a touch up, smiled down on us with her painted-on cherry-red lips as she bravely stomped on the Devil, in the form of a serpent, with her bare foot, somehow managing to keep a rose between her toes. She had pencil-thin eyebrows and blank, empty, aqua eyes and round blots of rouge that made her look clown-like and grotesque. As I looked at her I thought the Mother of God was kind of scary. Surely, with all the responsibility she had, someone should have seen to it that she looked kindly and benevolent. Bridie knelt there, staring trance-like as I tried to figure out what, besides the miraculous straightening of my leg, she might be praying for.

'Oh my God, she moved!' Bridie slowly stood up, not taking her eyes off Mary. 'Did you see that? Did you see what she did? She moved and she winked at me.'

'Sit down, people will hear you.' I yanked on her arm, trying to get her to sit.

'I'm serious, she moved.' Her voice was getting louder and I looked around and the ladies in the back were watching her. Even the drone of Mrs Donatelli's Italian prayers stopped.

'The Blessed Mother doesn't wink at people,' I whispered. 'Sit down.'

'Oh yeah, well she winked at me.' She turned to the ladies. 'It's a miracle. The Blessed Mother moved.' Little Mrs Donatelli stood up, no taller than when she was kneeling, and looked to the other women trying to understand what was going on.

'*Che cosa fa Lei?*' she yelled at Bridie.

'She said the Virgin moved. *Miracolo.*' Mrs del Fiore tried to explain what was happening.

'She's a mad thing, that girl,' said Mrs Cavanaugh. 'Don't pay a bit of attention to her.'

It took a few moments for Mrs Donatelli to realize what was going on, to translate the alleged miracle, but when she did she screamed and blessed herself and disappeared behind the pew in a dead faint. She had probably prayed and waited for a miracle all her long life and the very possibility that it was actually happening was too much for her. The noise of the other women rushing to the aid of Mrs Donatelli awakened old Mrs Farrell who had no idea what was happening and started shouting about the Germans bombing the church. I wanted to disappear into the stained-glass window and sit through all eternity, with the lambs and children, staring rapturously at Tyrone Power. Bridie, unaware of the havoc she was causing, seemed transported to some heavenly somewhere not available to the rest of us. I'm sure she saw herself indelibly written into the Book of Saints.

'Somebody get Father Boyle,' said Mrs Flynn in a frenzied voice.

'No!' I shouted. 'Please don't get Father Boyle. This is all a mistake.'

'It is not.' Bridie was nose to nose with me. 'I saw her move, damn it!'

Mrs Flynn ran out of the church and Mrs Donatelli, who had come to, crawled out of the pew and started down the aisle toward the altar on her tiny hands and knees, praying her little heart out in Italian. Mrs Farrell, who still thought we were being attacked by the Germans, started singing 'San Francisco', just like Jeanette MacDonald as she stood in the rubble after the quake. Mrs Cavanaugh and Mrs del Fiore tried to get Mrs Donatelli up off the floor but she was dead set on supplication and all they got for their trouble was a few slaps, a couple of kicks and one solid punch in Mrs Cavanaugh's toothless mouth.

'The hell with you, you old blister! You can crawl until your skinny wop knees come off for all I care,' said Mrs Cavanaugh. She looked at Bridie and me with murderous eyes. 'Well, I hope the pair of you are satisfied. A cripple and the tramp brat of a bartender causing all this trouble. You should be whipped till you've got bloody behinds and I'd be that happy to do it.'

Father Boyle, followed by Mrs Flynn and Father Christopher, the curate, came hurrying into the church.

'What in the name of God is going on here?' he shouted. Mrs Farrell stopped singing, Mrs Donatelli kept right on crawling and Mrs Cavanaugh pointed at Bridie and me.

'It's all their fault,' she said.

*

It took the rest of that school year and most of the following summer for people to stop talking about Bridie's miracle. Father Boyle tried to tell her miracles were scarce and it was probably her imagination, that if you stare at anything long enough it seems to move, but Bridie was unwavering. The Virgin Mary winked at her and that was that. If Father Boyle and the rest of the civilized world didn't believe her it was just too damn bad. After days of trying to convince her otherwise, Father Boyle finally conceded that maybe she did have a sign from the Blessed Virgin but it would be best for all concerned if she kept the matter between the two of them. I still thought she made the whole thing up just to see what effect it would have on the ladies in the church. Mrs Donatelli wanted a miracle so much she never stopped believing and for the rest of her life, every time she saw Bridie, she blessed herself. Mrs Cavanaugh, on the other hand, thought Bridie was little more than a child of Satan, and mumbled curses under her breath, damning Bridie to ever-lasting hell. The kids in school were the most ruthless. Bridie was, and would always be, an outsider and this, mixed with their fear of her impudent independence, kept them on the offensive, ready to ridicule and deride as long as they could do it in a group and not risk actual one-on-one confrontation. I was guilty by association and accused of complicity. Their biggest taunt was my leg. If Mary had appeared to us, why was I still a cripple? Our only defenders were Turk and Sparrow who had become champions of Bridie and believed every word she said. They delivered many a fat lip and bloody nose that year in the name of me, Bridie and the Blessed Virgin.

The strangest reaction was Mom's. The night it all happened, I waited for Mom and Pop to come home from work, certain I'd be lucky to survive with my life. When I told them Pop raged, mostly about what people would think, but Mom was uninter-ested and vague, as though she wasn't really hearing what I was saying.

'What the hell's the matter with you?' asked Pop.

'I'm eating at the diner tonight. Anybody want to join me?'

'Have you gone deaf or what? Didn't you hear what he said? His nibs and Joe Louis are seeing visions now.'

'I didn't see a vision. It was just Bridie.'

'Just let me wash my hands and I'll be ready.' She started for the stairs and Pop grabbed her arm.

'I think you've gone completely round the bend, Mae. As crazy as a loon.'

'Let go of my arm.' Pop let her go. 'You want to know what's crazy? Crazy is sending a boy off to war because you're too old to go yourself. That's crazy.'

'Why don't you try singing a different tune. For Christ's sake it's been months. Give up on it, will you?'

'Never. I will never forgive you for that if I live to be a hundred.'

'Finn,' Pop turned to me, 'go across to the O'Connors'.' I hesitated. 'Now!'

'It's okay, go ahead,' said Mom.

'He would have gone soon, anyway,' I heard Pop say as I went out the door.

Whatever happened while I was across the street I don't know, but Pop started sleeping on the sofa again.

As it turned out, Simon was Fritz's best man. They came home on one week's leave the night before the wedding and it was all arranged for them to sleep in our room and, without even asking, Pop put up a cot in the little front room for me.

Everyone was at the house waiting for them to arrive. Mina and the Pascalis, the Ganises, Mrs Shultz, Laurie, who had taken a few days off because he was going to tend bar at the reception, some girlfriends of Mina's and, of course, Bridie, trying to look all grown-up for Simon. Duke, who usually liked company, stayed upstairs out of harm's way. I kept standing next to Angie Pascali, who seemed bigger than ever, trying to get some picture in my mind of what the two of us would look like as a couple. She obliterated me. I felt like a flea next to her and the very idea of us walking down the aisle made my face hot and I broke into a sweat. I asked Bridie how she thought we looked together.

'Really stupid.' Something had to be done.

Fritz seemed different when I saw him. I didn't know exactly what it was but the Fritz who left home in July was not the same Fritz who walked through the door with his friend Simon. He looked handsome in his uniform, taller and filled out and his boy's face was starting to be replaced by the man's. There was such a clutter of people it was a while before he saw me.

'Hey, kid, how you doing?' He put his army cap on my head and bent down and hugged me. I tried to say something but I was so happy to see him I couldn't get any words to come out.

'For Christ's sake, don't start blubbering.' Pop was pouring shots for Laurie and himself.

'Pay no mind to your father,' said Laurie. 'If it was me own brother I hadn't seen for months, I'd shed a tear or two, believe me.'

I wanted them all to go away and leave me alone with Fritz so I could talk to him.

'I have to tell you something. Private and alone.'

'Now?' He held me at arm's length. 'Can it wait a little? Okay?' Everyone was watching us because they all wanted Fritz as much as I did.

'Okay,' I said grudgingly. He kissed me on the cheek and went to Mina. I noticed Mom, standing at a distance watching him, with a strange, detached look on her face. Mrs Ganis couldn't get anyone up to dance so she was having a wonderful time doing a solo. Bridie, holding tight to Simon's hand, was introducing him to everyone as though he were her private property. I had never seen her act so downright silly and I thought she was making a fool of herself. The only thing I remembered about Simon was the broad smile that used up his face, otherwise, this was a stranger Bridie was escorting around the house and I wasn't sure I liked it.

'Why is Bridie acting so dumb?' I said to Mr Ganis as I sat next to him in the corner where he was watching Mrs Ganis dance.

'Women! Oy, Finn, they get crazy when they fall in love.'

'Love! She's a kid.'

'Oh, sure, a woman's a kid a little while but even when she's a kid she's starting to be a woman, if you know what I mean. And love is the first woman thing they learn.'

'Hey, Finn, where's my buddy, Duke?' Simon shook hands with me.

'Upstairs.'

'And this is Mr Ganis, our dear friend and Jewish neighbor.' Bridie was being very grand.

'Hello, Simon. Finally, it's good to know you.'

'Well, you too, sir. I got a little Jew in me. Someplace way back. I think on my father's side.' Simon smiled warmly.

'Sure you do,' said Mr Ganis. 'How else could you explain your good looks?'

'He is good-looking, isn't he? Come on, I want you to meet some other people.' Bridie dragged him away and as they passed Mrs Ganis she grabbed him and they started dancing.

'He's a nice boy.'

'I guess,' I said.

'The problem here is, he's an older man. What is he? Seventeen, eighteen? Women like older men. I'm almost ten years older than Mrs Ganis and when she first laid eyes on me she said, "This is some man! Who needs Clark Gable?" Of course, Mrs Ganis was older than Bridie when she met me so I don't think you have too much to worry about, Finn.'

'I don't care what she does,' I said unconvincingly.

Fritz and I finally had a few minutes alone on the back porch. It was cold so he took off his jacket and put it around my shoulders.

'How's your leg? Does the brace help?'

'I don't know. I hate it.'

'I guess you have to give it some time.'

'That's what everybody says.'

x

'Yeah.' He lit a cigarette, something I had never seen him do. 'So, Mom and Pop giving you a lot of shit?'

Once I started I couldn't stop. I told him everything that happened since he went away. About Dr Whiteshield and how Pop refused to go to Philadelphia after the first trip. How Pop had to get Laurie at Tessie's Place in the middle of the night and how all Bridie talked about was whether Laurie needed sex, even to the point of asking Mr Howe. All about the strange way Mom was acting and how she was still mad at Pop because he signed for him to go in the army. I told him about Mrs Cleary and the way Pop was different when he was around her, almost like a kid, and how mad he was when I slid off the mare and got my brace covered with horse shit. Fritz had already heard about Bridie's so-called sign from the Blessed Virgin and he said he would have given a month's pay to see Mrs Donatelli punch Mrs Cavanaugh in the gums. I knew he'd have to go back to the party soon and I still hadn't said anything about Angie Pascali but I couldn't think of a right way to say it.

'Mina's going to have a baby.' He said it just like that, without any introduction. 'Mina's going to have a baby.' I stood there, speechless and shivering. My first thought was that I had probably heard it happen. I may have actually heard Fritz and Mina make a baby. I wondered if that compounded the mortal sin, which I had been carrying around all those months.

'A baby?' Suddenly, Mom and Pop and all the other problems didn't seem important. Fritz was going to be a father. Little by little he was becoming less my brother and more something else. He was being redefined and there was nothing I could do to stop it.

'Nobody knows but Mina, me and you. Nobody. Course, it won't be long before the whole town knows but what the hell, we'll be married so it won't make any difference.'

'I'm going to be an uncle.' The only kid my age who I knew was an uncle was Charlie Collins, whose mother had twenty-one children. Charlie was one of the youngest. Sometimes she'd have a baby in the middle of the night, right in the bed, next to Mr Collins, and he'd never even wake up. The next morning when she was serving the other kids their breakfast she'd announce they had a new baby sister or brother. Pop always said Mr Collins should have been taken to a veterinarian and fixed when he was starting to itch, and when I was little I thought Mr Collins had the mange.

'Mom and Pop will be grandparents. God! When are you going to tell them?'

'I don't know. Later. I don't want any crap. But I wanted you to know.'

'There's one more thing.' I had to say it and get it over with. 'I can't be your best man.' He was so startled it took him a moment to respond. In that split second it occurred to me that quite possibly he never intended for me to be his best man.

'What are you talking about! I was counting on you.' Whether it was true or not, I'll never know, but hearing him say it made relinquishing the honor so much easier. I told him the truth, that I wouldn't be able to walk down the aisle with Angie Pascali, that I was certain everyone would laugh.

'Please, I just can't do it.'

'Okay. I'm disappointed but I know how you feel. Maybe I'll ask Pop?'

'No.' I said it without thinking. 'Not him. Somebody else. How about Mr Ganis.'

'I can't ask him, he's Jewish. It has to be a Catholic.'

'Ask Simon.' Bridie would really be upset that she wasn't maid of honor when she saw Simon walking down the aisle with Angie Pascali. 'Yeah, ask Simon.'

Mr Howe surprised everyone and came to the wedding. Bridie and I had been asking him for weeks but he begged off, using the same excuse as usual not to leave the farm. He was sure the Lord would be calling him soon. He must have decided church would be as good a place as any to receive the call because, without saying a word to either of us, he showed up. His hair and beard were trimmed and he wore his old-fashioned suit with the dignity of a diplomat. As I ushered him down the aisle, holding his huge gnarled hand, showing off my special friend to the assembled congregation, there was the strong and distinct aroma of Bay Rum. I sat him a few rows behind the immediate family, with Big Tum and Little Tum.

I suppose the wedding went as planned but I was so distracted by Mom I couldn't pay much attention to the proceedings. I remember the altar with all the flowers, and Mina, looking more beautiful than ever in her satin and lace, walking down the aisle with Mr Pascali, who was crying, and Fritz and Simon, both of them pressed and shiny like new toy soldiers standing at attention. And I remember Bridie, embarrassed to be what she thought was the oldest flower girl in the history of the world, angrily dropping petals in fistfuls rather than strewing them. But Mom was so peculiar I couldn't take my eyes off her. She never once looked toward the altar. Instead, she seemed to be focusing on a place the rest of us couldn't see. She sat with her purse clutched to her breast and every once in a while her brows would knit or her lips would twitch and then she'd smile as if she remembered something amusing. Pop didn't notice but Mrs Ganis, who was sitting behind us, did. I was very frightened and I think she knew it because when I looked at her she smiled and put a reassuring hand on my cheek. I could hear Father Boyle's voice but I wasn't paying attention to anything he said. Mom's eyes would open wide as if she was witnessing some shocking thing, then she'd smile and mouth soundless words to some unseen entity. When the service was over and Fritz and Mina kissed, Mom closed her eyes for a moment and when she opened them she seemed to come back to reality. In that short time, not much more than the blink of an eye, the unsettled, distant woman I didn't even know disappeared, and my real mother came back from whatever lonely journey she had been on. She looked down at me, took my face in her hands and kissed me lovingly on the forehead, then she slipped her arm in Pop's, startling him with the familiar touch he hadn't felt in such a long time. At first he didn't know how to respond. He searched her face for a moment, as though he wasn't sure of what was happening and when Mom stretched up and kissed him lightly, then put her head on his chest, he put his arms around her and held her close. I looked at Mina and Fritz as they left the altar and started down the aisle and I thought maybe everything was going to be all right. That perhaps Mom and Pop, like Fritz and Mina, would have a new beginning, that somehow the wedding had made whatever was wrong, all better. But there was an uneasiness deep inside and as much as I wanted to I didn't really believe it.

At the reception, Bridie tried to get me to dance whenever Simon was unavailable. Mr Delaney, who was a retired fire chief, sat at the piano and pounded out one tune after another with hardly a stop to get his breath. Whenever he did take a break, someone played records over the loudspeaker and the dancers jitterbugged and waltzed and rumbaed to the latest music. Every combination of parent and newlywed danced to oohs and ahs and when the crowd had gotten its fill, people relaxed into the partners they danced with most of the night. Mrs Ganis and Mr Howe were the strangest couple, he being almost twice as tall as she, but everyone said they were the best dancers on the floor. I wondered if the dead Miriam, whom he had been mourning for so many years, was as good a dancer as Mr Howe and I tried to imagine them as a young couple, back in the Indian Territory, dancing the night away. Even Big Tum and Little Tum waltzed together, their arms stretched as far as possible, just to touch each other. Simon, being one of the few young men there, was pursued by all the unattached girls and more than a few of the married ones. Bridie didn't like it one bit.

'You'd think they never saw a man, for cripes' sake.'

'Look who's talking.'

'What's that supposed to mean?'

'Why don't you leave the poor guy alone so he can dance with somebody his own age? You look stupid dancing with him all the time.'

'I do not look stupid. I'm a damn good dancer. Everybody says that.'

'Everybody says you look stupid.'

'Like who for instance? Who says I look stupid?'

'Everybody.' Actually, I hadn't heard a single comment. Bridie's jaw was set and her eyes were narrowed and I could see she wanted a fight but before we could get into it I noticed people had stopped dancing and were watching someone in the middle of the floor. Bridie followed me as I pushed through the crowd and when we got to the edge of the floor there was Mom dancing frantically all by herself. There was laughter and applause and had I not known better I would have thought she was drunk. But she was off in her own eerie world again, dancing with some mysterious, invisible person, laughing and talking and seemingly having the time of her life. I looked for Pop but I couldn't see him anywhere. Mrs Ganis, realizing something was wrong, went to her and tried to get her to stop dancing. Mr Ganis called for Pop and shouted for someone to turn off the music while Mr Howe and Mrs Shultz ushered people back to their tables.

'What's happening?' asked Bridie.

'Something's wrong with Mom.'

'What?' she said as she started to go toward the crowd gathering around Mom who was still dancing even though the music had stopped.

'You stay here.' Laurie grabbed her. 'There's enough confusion, they don't need your help.' He put his hand on my shoulder. 'It's going to be fine, Finn. Don't you doubt it for one minute.' His face was red and his words were slurred and I could smell the whiskey on him.

Pop suddenly appeared with Fritz and Mina and the Pascalis. As he made his way through the people surrounding Mom I got a glimpse of her, glistening with sweat, her hair stuck to her face, rigidly standing with her hands pressed to her ears. There was a half smile on her face and her eyes were squeezed shut.

'We're taking you home.' It was Mr Ganis and Mr Howe steering Bridie and me out of the hall.

'I'll be along as soon as I can,' said Laurie.

Mina and Fritz didn't get to Atlantic City for their honeymoon. Instead, Laurie arranged for them to have a room for a few nights at the Prussian Inn so they could be close to Mom in case anything happened. While Bridie and I were being taken to the Ganises', Pop took Mom home and Dr Lorman was called. Mrs Ganis stayed with Mom and Mr Ganis and Mr Howe made tea and toast for Bridie and me and did their best to assure us that nothing was seriously wrong. We eventually sat in the living room listening to the radio but I couldn't concentrate. I was thinking about Mom and wondering if someday she might slip away from us, through some unknown dimension, into that illusory and irrational private world and never come back. It was all too much to bear and leaning securely against Mr Ganis with his reassuring arm around my shoulder, I fell asleep.

When I awoke, it was dark and I was lying on the sofa, covered with a blanket. I didn't know where Mr Howe or Bridie were but I could hear Mr Ganis talking softly to Mrs Ganis in the kitchen.

'How's Mom?' I asked, standing in the doorway, squinting against the light.

'Oh, sweetheart, did we wake you up?' Mrs Ganis reached out for me to go to her. 'Your mother is sleeping. Dr Lorman gave her such a shot you could knock an elephant out.' She picked me up and held me on her lap.

'What did I tell you, Finn? Everything is going to be fine,' said Mr Ganis.

'This happens to women sometimes. Exhaustion. Your mother works hard at the depot and what with the wedding and worrying and the baby coming –'

'Fritz told them?' With all that went on the past two days I couldn't imagine when he found time.

'Fritz told them what?' asked Mrs Ganis.

'About the baby. He said he was going to wait.'

Mr and Mrs Ganis looked at each other for a moment. 'Oy vay.' She looked at me with disbelief. 'Fritz and Mina are having a baby? Oy vay.'

'Maybe we should have a glass of tea,' said Mr Ganis.

'What tea! Get the schnapps. Three glasses.' Mr Ganis went to the cupboard.

'Have I got a big mouth? I should have my tongue cut out with a dull knife.' Mrs Ganis started beating her breast.

'Stop it, already. You didn't know,' said Mr Ganis, trying to calm her.

'Neither did Finn.' Her eyes were closed and she was shaking her head.

'Know what?' I asked, thoroughly confused.

'That your mother is having a baby.'

'So, now he knows,' said Mr Ganis, filling the little glasses.

I chose to spend the night on the sofa even though Mrs Ganis insisted I go to bed in the guest room. After neatly folding my new long pants over the back of the chair along with my jacket and shirt, I put on one of Mr Ganis's pajama tops and just before slipping into the crisp white sheets, after the Ganises were finally convinced I had everything I needed and left the room, I took off my brace and laid it on the floor beside the sofa. I felt warmed by my shot of schnapps as I lay awake peering into the darkness, trying to make some sense out of everything that was happening. I was worried about Mom and I thought Duke must have been confused because I wasn't home for the night and I wondered if he was sleeping with Simon. And I thought about

Fritz finally being a married man after all the planning for the wedding. Mom and Mina were both going to have a baby and I was going to be an uncle and a brother. Maybe at exactly the same time since Mom and Pop had to sleep together when Aunt Cassie had the stroke and they went to Wilkes-Barre, which was the same night I sat on the steps listening to Mina and Fritz in the dark. I wondered how many other babies, all over the world, would be born because of that night. And how many puppies and kittens and whatever else? And that was only one night. It occurred to me that in every moment of every day something happened in each little faraway place on earth that changed the world for ever. And for this brief moment, I was aware of it all. I was less than a dust mote yet I was witness to the most subtle change in the universe. Disconnected images started to slide through my mind, tumbling over each other as I dozed off thinking of war and babies and pigeons and Duke and crippled, naked, dead bodies.

It was still dark when I heard Bridie whispering in my ear.

'Finn, wake up.' It took me a moment to remember where I was.

'What do you want?'

'Get up. Quick.'

'How'd you get in here?'

'The back door. Will you get up, damn it!'

'What's the matter?'

'Laurie's not home. He didn't come home all night. He's never done that. Ever. We got to find him.'

'What time is it?' I sat up, not quite understanding the desperation in Bridie's voice.

'Almost seven. Will you put your clothes on?'

'Turn your back.'

'For cripes' sake, you afraid I'm going to see that little worm of yours! Who gives a damn?'

'I said to turn your back.' She did and I sat on the edge of the sofa putting my brace on as we discussed the possibilities. 'Maybe he's at Tessie's Place.'

'Where?'

'The place Pop got Laurie the night he had to carry him up to his bedroom.' Bridie and I had never talked about that night and apparently Pop hadn't told her about Tessie's because she had never heard of it.

'Well, hurry up. We got to go there.'

'Are you crazy? That's way down the end of Allen Street. They don't like white people down there. Let's get Pop.'

'No. If Laurie's got a snootfull I don't want anybody to know he fell off the wagon. So, you going with me or are you too scared?'

'You're damn right I'm scared and I'm not going with you.'

'And I prayed to the Blessed Mother to straighten your crooked old leg! Thanks a lot.' She started out of the room.

'Well, the prayers didn't work. All you did was make people think we're nuts.'

'Whether they worked or not don't count. I still said the damn prayers, didn't I?'

'Wait till I get dressed.'

It was cold and damp as we walked along the nearly deserted Allen Street. The neighborhood was all black and the houses were neat and dull, not unlike the houses on Livery Street. The few people we did see, sweeping the porch or coming home with the Sunday paper, looked at us suspiciously, not, I'm sure, because we were white but because we hurried down the street on a cold October morning with no overcoats, me limping along in my maroon blazer and Bridie in the wrinkled first communion dress she had slept in. It never occurred to me that we were odd unless I stood back and looked at us through the eyes of other people. Certainly it wasn't unusual to see white people on Allen Street because it was the main thoroughfare to the hospital but two kids, all alone at seven-thirty in the morning, hurrying along as though they had someplace important to go, must have raised a few eyebrows. Bridie asked me all kinds of questions about Mom and I told her everything Mrs Ganis had said except the news about the baby. For some reason I wanted to keep it from her but I didn't know exactly why.

Just past the hospital the sidewalk ended and a ragged dirt path led through a section of marginal businesses. There was an auto-repair shop with rusty old junker cars scattered around, a meat locker with mean-looking metal hooks hanging in the window and an icehouse with a wooden flatbed truck dripping a steady stream of water. Next to the icehouse was a windowless, faded, clapboard building with a bright green door and a small hand-painted sign that read TESSIE'S PLACE. Hanging in the little window in the door was the flag with the blue star, informing everyone that a member of the family was in the armed forces. Bridie and I didn't know quite what to do.

'I guess we should knock,' she said tentatively.

'Yeah.'

'Go ahead.'

'I knew it would have to be me.' I knocked lightly and there was no response. 'They're all asleep.'

'Well, knock louder and wake them up.' I knocked harder and when there was still no answer Bridie started pounding on the door.

'What the hell is going on down there?' It was a deep man's voice that sounded as though it was coming from the second floor.

'I want to talk to somebody!' yelled Bridie.

'About what?'

'I'm looking for my father.' There was a long pause.

'Go around to the back.'

'That must mean he's here,' said Bridie as we walked down the alley, past the garbage cans, to the back door. We waited a few minutes and when no one came. I knocked.

'Wait a goddamn minute!' It was the same voice. When the

door finally opened, a huge black man, as big around as Big Tum and much taller, glowered at us, not saying a word.

'I'm looking for my father.'

'What's your name?'

'Bridie O'Connor.'

'And you?' he said, looking at me.

'Timothy Finnegan. Finn.'

'Get in here,' he said harshly.

We went into a small dark hallway, lit by a single bulb hanging from a cord at the foot of a long flight of stairs.

'Wait here.' The big man lumbered up the stairs, stopping halfway to catch his breath and turning to make sure we weren't doing anything wrong. When he was gone, Bridie and I looked at each other, too scared to say a word. The place smelled of pine soap and kerosene mixed with some strong, sweet perfume. There were two doors, one on either side of the hall and the one on the left was slightly ajar. It was too dark to see into the room but I had the feeling someone was in there, hiding in the shadows, watching us. Bridie and I stood there in the silence, no sound coming from anyplace in the building, and I knew she wanted to run as much as me. There was a soft rustling sound in the dark room and Bridie grabbed my hand.

'My name's Honey,' said a voice in the blackness. It startled us so much we jumped back, smashing into the opposite wall. The door opened a bit more and I could see a figure about my size but I wasn't sure if it was a boy or a girl.

'I'm Finn and this is Bridie.' My heart was pounding so loud I could hear it.

'Are you a kid?' asked Bridie.

'I live here.'

'Well, what are you doing hiding in the dark scaring the hell out of people?' Bridie was peering into the room trying to see who she was talking to.

'Is that your daddy upstairs?'

'Is he all right?'

'You go to school?' asked Honey, ignoring Bridie's question.

'Well, of course we do. Everybody does, for cripes' sake.'

'Don't you go to school?' I asked.

'No, but I can read and write.'

'Honey, get up here.' A beautiful woman, the color of milk chocolate, was coming down the stairs. She was dressed in a fancy nightgown and robe and wore very high-heeled slippers. 'You hear what I said? Get upstairs.' The door slowly opened and a boy about my age came out of the room. He was the most astonishing person I had ever seen, like some pristine visitor from an unknown world. When Bridie saw him she made a warm little indistinguishable sound, as if she couldn't find words to express her pleasure. He looked like something pure and unborn with skin and hair as white as paper. His barely pink lips were the same color as his eyes, which he seemed to shield even against the dim light of the hall. He smiled shyly as he pressed himself against the wall and started up the steps.

'He's not slow-witted, if that's what you're thinking,' said the woman on the stairs as she took a cigarette from a pack of Chesterfields and lit it.

'He's beautiful,' said Bridie, completely captivated by this strange and wonderful creature. 'Angels must look like you.'

The woman laughed. 'Well, you're no angel, are you, Honey?' She dragged hard on her cigarette and turned to us. 'Come on up, girl, if you want your daddy.' She took Honey by the hand and started up the stairs. Bridie and I followed them. 'I'm Tessie,' she said.

Walking through the door at the top of the stairs was like Alice going through the looking glass. The apartment was a jumble of rooms all decorated in pale blues, pinks and greens, with pictures of delicate, elongated, cat-eyed women dressed in leopard skins or peacock feathers, posing seductively before sumptuously draped curtains. The furniture in the living room was over-stuffed, plush, fan-shaped purple chairs and a sofa. Top-heavy lamps with beaded shades were supported by naked chrome women, breasts pushed forward and backs arched as though they were preparing for a dive. The perfume smell was almost over powering.

'How's your mama?' asked Tessie as she led us down a hall, past several closed doors, still holding Honey's hand.

'How'd you know she was sick?'

'Laurie wouldn't call your daddy cause your mama was sick, that's why he stayed here last night.'

'She's all right, I guess.'

'Seems like a nice woman. And real good-looking with all that pretty dark hair hanging down her back.'

'Mrs Finn has gray hair,' said Bridie. Mom's hair was short and streaked with white. She said premature gray hair was the price the Irish had to pay for having such fine skin.

'Gray!' She turned and looked at me a long moment before she said, 'I must have your mama and daddy mixed up with someone else.' She took a deep drag on the cigarette without taking her eyes off me. I realized she was talking about Josie Cleary and I wondered if Pop had actually told people she was his wife. But the town was too small for that. Everyone knew everyone else's business with the exception, perhaps, of someone like Tessie, who was isolated in her after-hours world of men who probably said little or nothing about their families. 'Come on, girl, let's get Laurie out of here so I can get my beauty sleep.' She yanked at Honey and continued on down the hall until she came to a door at the back of the apartment. Pushing it open, she stood aside so Bridie and I could go in.

Laurie was lying on a narrow bed, fully dressed except for his shoes, with his arms folded on his chest, looking more dead than alive. The room smelled foul and I could see a stain where he had wet his pants. There was a small lamp lit on the night stand with a red scarf draped over the shade, washing the room in a gaudy pink light.

'For cripes' sake, he peed himself! Laurie, wake up!' Bridie shook him hard but there was no response. 'Finn, get his shoes on him.' While Honey helped me with the shoes, Tessie stood in the doorway watching but saying nothing. 'Damn you, wake up!' Bridie was rocking him from side to side and after a few minutes he started to moan, slowly coming to.

'You kids ain't never going to get him out of here. Wait a minute.' Tessie went back down the hall. Honey, Bridie and I managed to get Laurie to a sitting position but he sat with his chin on his chest, unable to raise his head. Bridie started to cry.

'You promised, damn it! You promised! And I even got a sign from the Blessed Mother. Well, I'm never going to say another prayer. Never as long as I live. How could I be so dumb to think there's such a thing as a miracle.' The tears were more tears of rage and frustration than tears of hurt. Honey reached over and petted her arm.

'What's wrong with your leg?' he asked, without looking at me.

'It's crooked. I was born this way.'

'I was born this way, too,' he said. Our eyes connected, recognizing each other's isolation. 'I'm supposed to be a nigger.'

'Is she your mother?'

'My aunt. My daddy's sister. My mama run away after I got born. My daddy's in the army.' All the while he was touching Bridie, trying to soothe her.

Tessie returned with the big fat man.

'Maybe you should leave him here to sleep it off?' the man said.

'No. I want to take him home.' Bridie wiped away her tears. 'Get him up.'

'Take him downstairs, Charles,' said Tessie as she walked out of the room.

'All he needs is a little air.' Bridie shook Laurie and he tried to lift his head but couldn't. Charles pulled him to his feet and picked him up like a baby, carrying him down the hall and stairs to the back door. Tessie and Honey stood in the doorway watching as Charles propped Laurie against the wall near the garbage cans.

'We don't have a car,' she said, lighting another cigarette. 'I'll pay for a taxi.'

'No. We'll get him home. Where's our car?' asked Bridie.

'Well, you can't drive,' I said, knowing she'd be willing to try anything.

'I know that! I just wondered where the damn car was.'

'How the hell do we know?' said Charles. 'If he ever comes to, you tell your daddy to stay away from here.'

'Hush your mouth, Charles.' She took Honey by the hand and went inside, followed by Charles who slammed the door shut behind him.

'Come see me,' called Honey from the other side of the door.

The cold morning air seemed to revive Laurie and I think for the first time he realized we were there. It took a few minutes to put things in order, to understand he was sitting on a garbage can behind Tessie's Place, with Bridie and me doing our best to steady him, and to experience the utter shame and degradation of the situation. His eyes brimmed with tears and he covered his face with his hands.

'Don't start,' said Bridie. 'We gotta get you home.'

'Oh Christ,' he wailed, 'I wet meself.'

'And you stink. Come on, get up.' After a few stumbling attempts, we managed to get him walking. He leaned heavily on us and every once in a while his knees would buckle and he'd go down on all fours. We only got as far as the icehouse when he fell, and this time, no matter how hard we tried, we couldn't get him to his feet. He lay there, his face in the dusty path, and started retching.

'Oh God, please . . .' said Bridie, unconsciously breaking her vow never to pray again. 'Finn, what are we going to do?'

'I'll get help. I'll go to the hospital.'

'No!' said Laurie between gags. 'I'll lose the job. Call your father. There's a good lad.' He started shivering violently.

'Hurry up, Finn, before he dies!'

I ran past the meat locker and the auto shop until I got to the circular drive of the hospital. An ambulance was parked at the emergency room door but I didn't see anyone around so I went to the main entrance. Just as I started up the front steps, the door opened and Miss Neal, the school nurse, came out, buttoning her coat against the cold.

'Timothy Finnegan, what are you doing here? Somebody sick?'

'Please, you have to help us.' I grabbed her hand and started pulling her across the hospital lawn. 'It's Laurie.' I was too out of breath to explain any more. When we got back to Bridie and Laurie, Mattie Horn, a woman who lived nearby and worked as a maid in one of the big houses uptown, was helping Bridie tend Laurie. She was dressed in her Sunday best and right away I noticed she had vomit on her good coat.

'Miss Neal, this man is sick. Lord what the drink can do!' Mattie Horn shook her head. 'These children shouldn't have to see this.'

Miss Neal knelt beside Laurie. 'I think we can get him to the hospital. Help me get him up, Mrs Horn.'

'No. No hospital. Get me home. If I'm dying I'd like to die in me own bed if you don't mind.'

'Oh God,' wailed Bridie.

'Stop that fool talk in front of the children. You ain't dying though I think maybe you deserve to.' Mrs Horn took a handkerchief out of her purse and wiped Laurie's face.

'You could have alcohol poisoning,' said Miss Neal.

'He'll lose his job if they find out. I can take care of him at home. We'll say he has a bad cold. Please,' Bridie pleaded, 'he hasn't had a drink for a long time. But it was a party and you know how men get. Please, he can't go to the hospital. Please.'

Miss Neal looked at Mrs Horn and without saying a word, in that secret way adults always have of communicating, they decided to take him home. 'I'll get my brother's car,' said Mrs Horn. 'It's always the children that suffer.' She was shaking her head and mumbling to herself as she walked away. Laurie seemed to relax and drift off, his head resting in Bridie's lap, as we sat in the dirt waiting for Mrs Horn to come back with the car. Miss Neal's white stockings and shoes were streaked with brown dirt.

'My mother's sick, too,' I said.

The following week, I finished my poster for the SPCA contest. I wasn't allowed out of the house except to go to school so I had plenty of time. All hell broke loose when we came down Livery Street in Mrs Horn's brother's car. The Ganises had discovered I was gone and apparently, when I couldn't be found at home or at the O'Connors' and, to compound matters, Bridie and Laurie were missing, the police were called. I didn't know what happened after they got Laurie into the house and in bed because I was sent to my room and no one was allowed to have anything to do with me, not even Duke. I wanted to see Mom but Pop wouldn't let me. He did tell me she was still sleeping from the shot Dr Lorman had given her. Simon's toilet articles were on the dresser but I had no idea where he was. The house was completely quiet except for someone periodically coming upstairs, opening and closing Mom and Pop's bedroom door, then going downstairs and out the front door. For what seemed like hours, I sat on the side of the bed waiting for something to happen, knowing that any minute Pop would come storming into my room. The old magazines Mr Howe had given me were under the bed so I got them out and started planning my poster. As I was leafing through them, I wondered about Bridie and Laurie. Were Miss Neal and Mrs Horn still at their house? Were Pop and Simon there? And where was Fritz? The bells at Our Lady of Perpetual Help rang for the nine, ten and eleven o'clock masses and still no one came to say anything to me so I missed Sunday mass and besmirched my soul with yet another mortal sin. As quietly as I could, I unlatched the door and listened for any sign of life downstairs. There was nothing. Without making a sound I crept down the hall, past Mom and Pop's closed door, to the little front room where I sat on the floor and looked out the window at as much of the neighborhood as I could see. Mrs Horn's brother's car was still parked out front. Big Tum was sweeping the porch and Mrs Cavanaugh, wrapped in a fur coat that had long since shed most of its hair, was at her usual station in the beat-up rocker, making sure she wouldn't miss a trick. Fritz came out of the O'Connors' house and started across the street, stopping when Mrs Cavanaugh said something I couldn't hear. I raised the window about an inch and ducked down so I couldn't be seen.

'It's nothing, Mrs Cavanaugh,' Fritz was being very nonchalant. 'Laurie's feeling a little under the weather. A bad cold.'

'A bad cold my arse,' she answered. 'What's the nurse doing in there? And that uppity nigger woman?'

'Just stopping by for a visit, I guess.'

'You'd lie to the Pope hisself, just like that no-good father of yours.'

'And the top of the morning to you, too, Mrs Cavanaugh.' He crossed the street and came into the house. I met him on the stairs.

'How's Laurie?' I asked.

'He looks like he's got one foot in the grave. Pop and me had to give him a bath. Twice. We got him cleaned up and put him to bed and he threw up all over the place. Jesus, I don't know how much he had to drink but it must have been a shit load. Miss Neal says it could be serious but he won't let her call a doctor.'

'Where is everybody?'

'Wait a minute, I want to check on Mom.' He opened the door and we both went to the bedside. In a deep sleep and pale as marble, she was lying on her side, facing the window. The covers were perfectly smooth as though she hadn't moved once during the night. She looked much younger, like she did in my favorite picture of her, taken when Deirdre was only a few months old and the two of them were sitting on the side porch.

'She's going to have a baby,' I whispered.

'I know. Come on.' We left the room, quietly closing the door behind us.

'Is Pop real mad?' I asked when we were back in our room.

'Mad! You'll be lucky if he doesn't beat the shit out of you. What'd you expect, going to a whorehouse like that?'

'Whorehouse! What's a whorehouse?' I was very well versed in the matters of sex, what with having an older brother who was willing and anxious to discuss anything, but somehow the concept of a whorehouse had never come up. He explained it succinctly by telling me it was a place men went for sex and ladies did just about anything the men wanted depending on the amount of money they were paid. At first, I didn't believe it. I couldn't imagine people doing those things with strangers.

'That's why Laurie goes there!' The realization was shocking.

'Sure. A lot of guys go there.'

'I guess Bridie's been wasting her time worrying about him doing sex.' Fritz laughed. 'Pop goes there with Mrs Cleary.'

'What the hell are you talking about?'

'That Tessie told me. She thought Mrs Cleary was our mother.'

'Bullshit.'

'I swear to God. Ask Bridie.'

'Jesus Christ!' Fritz slapped his open palm against the wall hard enough to rattle the window. 'I didn't think he really fucked around.' He opened the door. 'I gotta get Mina. She's still at the Prussian Inn. I'll be back. Son of a bitch!' Even in the back of the house I could hear the car door slam as he drove away.

It was at least an hour before Pop came to my room. In the meantime, I had decided my poster would be a wreath of animal faces; dogs, cats, birds, horses, sheep, goats, pigs, all interwoven, with the words *Our Friends* boldly printed in the center.

'It's not enough your mother is sick, you have to pull something like this. What have you got to say for yourself?' I didn't have anything to say so I just shrugged my shoulders. 'Christ Almighty, it wouldn't hurt you to think once in a while before you do these stupid things. You and Bridie can cause more trouble than an army of kids. You don't think about anybody but yourselves.' There was some slight consolation knowing, for a change, he blamed Bridie as much as me. 'You're nothing but trouble. We had the goddamn police looking for you! You know what that means? Everybody in town will know our business.' He started down the hall for his room when the thought struck him, 'And there'll be no goddamn Halloween for you, either. You hear what I'm saying, mister?' I nodded my head and he went into his room and closed the door. Bridie must have told him everything because he obviously didn't want to hear any of the details from me. I heard the clicking of Duke's nails on the steps and in a moment he sheepishly poked his nose into the room, making sure the yelling was over and the coast was clear. He came to me, put his head in my lap and looked up, confused by what was going on but happy I was home where I belonged.

Both Mom and Laurie stayed home from work the rest of that week. Both claimed the flu and both were successful with their cover-up. The war went on without Mom at the depot and drinks were served at the bar in the Prussian Inn without the expertise of Laurie. Bridie and I weren't allowed to see each other after school so we did all our note comparing at lunch, recess and walking to and from. Pop was right about one thing; because of the police, everybody knew something happened but nobody knew any of the details and they didn't get a single word out of Bridie or me. Not even Sparrow and Turk, our good friends and staunch defenders. On Wednesday afternoon, when Miss Neal spent her two hours in the nurses' office to listen to any complaints the kids might have, I saw her in the hall and she touched me on the shoulder and smiled a little conspiratorial smile as she passed by. She was Bridie's new heroine. Bridie told me she and Mrs Horn stayed the whole day, right up to the time

Miss Neal had to go home and change to go back to the hospital on the night shift. She said the house was like Grand Central Station that day with Pop and Mina and Fritz, Simon and the Ganises all helping her look after Laurie. In contrast, our house was like a morgue. People would quietly check on Mom and leave while I sat with Duke in my room wondering if I'd ever eat again. Mom finally woke up at supper time but I wasn't allowed to see her. I heard Pop and Mrs Ganis talking to Dr Lorman and once I thought I heard Fritz yelling at Pop but the only people who came to see me were Simon and Mina when they brought me a tray with supper. They only stayed a few minutes because Pop said I was to be left alone in my room until it was time to go to school the next morning. Mina and Fritz had one more night at the Prussian Inn and, because I was being shunned, Simon was spending the night at the Ganises. Just before he left for the night, Fritz came up to tell me not to let Pop get the best of me.

'I won't.'

'He can be a son of a bitch. Mom's fine. A little dopey but she wanted to know how you were.'

'Does she know what I did?'

'No. She's still kind of out of it. She doesn't even know what happened to her last night.' He noticed the magazines spread on the bed and I told him my idea for the poster. 'That sounds great. When you finish it maybe somebody can take a picture and you can send it to me.' He put his arm around my shoulder and pulled me close. 'Is the watch keeping time?'

'Yeah. I only wear it for good. I don't want anything to happen to it.'

'You're my favorite brother, you know that?'

'I'm your only brother.'

'That's why you're my favorite.' He kissed me on the top of my head and went to the door. 'I gotta go before Pop has a shit fit cause I'm up here talking to you. I'll see you tomorrow.'

'Yeah.' After he left I went to the dresser and got the watch out of my sock drawer. I hadn't worn it for a long while and I had no idea of the time so I couldn't set it but I wound it anyway. I took off my brace, put on my pajamas and crawled into Fritz's bed. Duke jumped up and I fell asleep with the watch pressed to my ear, listening to the ticking.

Life on Livery Street had settled somewhat after the incident at Tessie's. I didn't win the poster contest but I did get an honorable mention. Bridie had been right, the judges were looking for drama and an eighth-grade girl from the public school won with a beautiful drawing of a sad-eyed, starved pup and a caption which read, *He needs you.* My rather fanciful animal wreath, which Mr Howe claimed was the most imaginative and well-executed poster in the contest, hung with the other winners in the First National Bank for almost a month. Bridie dragged me in to look at them at least twenty times, always ending up in front of the winner, where she would sigh deeply and say, 'What did I tell you?' Mom and Pop said they were very proud of me and bought me a war bond as a consolation prize, Mr and Mrs Ganis gave me the usual box of handkerchiefs and Sister Ellen Marie gave me a holy card with Saint Luke's picture on it because he was the patron saint of artists.

Not long after the wedding, Fritz and Simon were shipped overseas and all we knew was that they were someplace in North Africa. This should have been more momentous but Mom was having a baby and that surprising turn of events took center stage. I received a letter from Fritz saying he was collecting coins for me from different countries and, if he could, he'd send them home. Having been so intimately involved in everything that happened the week of the wedding, Simon had quickly become a member of our family. We knew nothing about his family except that he lived with a much older cousin in a tiny walk-up apartment and, from everything he said, there was very little communication between them. Simon liked me and I knew it and his close relationship with Fritz in no way seemed threatening. He was open and considerate and gentle and, although I knew he would never reach the degree of perfection Fritz had, I liked the idea of having another brother. Mom and Mina exchanged bits of information from their letters and this, coupled with the fact that they were both pregnant and expecting at the same time, brought them closer together than ever. Rarely, after her frenzied dance at the wedding reception and almost a week of sleep as a result of Dr Lorman's medicine, did Mom seem at all odd. Once in a while she'd have moments when she'd drift away or she'd get up and leave a room abruptly without saying anything but this was dismissed as the natural moodiness of a woman in her condition. If she worried about having a baby at her age I never heard her say a word. The only person it obviously bothered was Mrs Cavanaugh who told Bridie and me that Pop was a sex maniac. For the most part, after Mom went back to work at the depot and we all settled into our routines, she was very much her old, dependable self. She and Pop seemed to get along and he moved upstairs and into their bed but there was no talk in the night, just the hollow silence of two people lying awake in the dark, thinking lonely, separate thoughts.

Bridie and I wanted to see Honey again but the idea of going to Tessie's Place was out of the question. If we had, and anyone found out, we were certain we would have been shipped off to St Stephen's orphanage. I never told her what Fritz had said about it being a whorehouse and we never discussed Pop's being there with Josie Cleary. The wondrous Honey, with his translucent paleness, obliterated almost every other memory. We imagined him the child king of a race of privileged creatures reluctant to have their whereabouts known except to a few select, sensitive and trustworthy people like us. I secretly imagined his mission was to make life more tolerable for anyone who was different. The beautiful and elegant Tessie was one of his handmaidens and the monstrous Charles was his bodyguard and, when strangers weren't there, we were sure he wore red velvet robes and a golden crown. Bridie had no idea that the castle we were conjuring was really a whorehouse.

The greatest change, in those few months, was in Laurie. As far as anyone knew, he never took a drop of liquor. Bridie told me he cried for two days straight before going back to work. He wouldn't eat or talk, he just stayed in his room crying. Bridie didn't want anyone else helping her care for Laurie but she couldn't do it alone so Pop and Fritz did whatever was necessary. Miss Neal and Mrs Horn, feeling some kind of accountability for his welfare, visited regularly, bringing food and whatever solace they could offer. In fact, everyone in the neighborhood brought food and Bridie said she had enough to feed an army. When he did start talking, he spent hours with Miss Neal. Bridie didn't know what was said but she was sure Miss Neal was an angel, solely responsible for the miraculous change in Laurie. When he was feeling better, just before he went back to work, Laurie came over to visit Mom, who was still confined to her room. He was shaky and ashen as I took him up the stairs.

'Mrs Finnegan, you look the picture of health,' he said as he stood in the doorway. Mom sat in the corner of the room, her rosary in her hand, smiling the peculiar half smile of someone heavily sedated. 'Do you mind if I come in and talk to you?' he asked.

'Please,' she smiled. She couldn't forgive Laurie for his drinking and what she considered his neglect of Bridie but in her narcotic haze she apparently managed to push her feelings aside.

'Thank you, Finn,' he said as he started closing the door. 'Mrs Finn, I want to apologize . . .' and the door was shut and I couldn't hear any more but I knew they were making their peace.

On December 8, Mom and Mrs Ganis took Bridie and me to New York to have lunch at the automat and go to Radio City Music Hall. It was the Feast of the Immaculate Conception and we didn't have school. This was an annual trip for Mom and me and Fritz, when he was younger, but we hadn't been able to go the year before because the Japanese bombed Pearl Harbor on

December 7 and, although I didn't think it was reason enough not to go to Radio City, Mom was too upset. But a year had gone by and people were living with the war and that cold gray day, after seven o'clock mass and breakfast at the Ganises', we bundled up and walked through the university to the train station to get the shuttle to the Junction, where we stood freezing on the platform, waiting for the train to the city. Bridie had never been to New York before and she had driven everyone crazy, talking about nothing else. The train arrived about twenty minutes late and we pushed our way into the smoky car, crowded with servicemen standing in the aisle and as it pulled away two sailors gave their seats to Mom and Mrs Ganis. Bridie wedged herself in between Mrs Ganis and a soldier and I half sat on the arm of Mom's seat. A soldier sitting across the aisle noticed my brace and asked if I wanted his seat but I thanked him and said no.

'Wasn't that nice?' said Mom as she smiled at him. 'He looks like your brother.' He didn't look at all like Fritz. 'They all look like your brother,' she said softly. 'All of them.'

Mrs Ganis and Bridie were flirting with the soldier sitting next to them, telling him everything about themselves and doing their best to get as much information out of him as possible. Did he have a girl? Was he engaged? When was he getting married?

'I have to go to the bathroom,' said Mom as she slid out of her seat. 'It's the worst part of having a baby.' She made her way to the end of the car and I settled back, watching people talk and laugh or lose themselves in their thoughts. I loved riding on a train. The excitement of going someplace, anyplace, was always mixed with an elusive sense of melancholia, as innate as the wistfulness of an autumn day. Maybe it was seeing all those new faces and knowing they were attached to stories, wonderful stories, I'd never know. Maybe it was an unconscious awareness of using up one of however many train trips were allotted to me in my lifetime. I never knew why it made me feel both happy and sad. But I loved the sound of the wheels on the tracks and the swaying back and forth as I sat secure on the dusty, stale, tobacco-smelling plush, being thrust forward through day or night, summer or winter, all the times and seasons.

Pennsylvania Station was so crowded, Bridie and I had to hold tight to Mom and Mrs Ganis so we wouldn't be swept away. The war had everyone on the move. Uncle Sam was pointing at us from posters, saying he wanted us, and the marble floors and vaulted ceilings echoed the loudspeaker announcements and the din of people shouting to be heard. It was almost impossible to get through the crowd and as we were passing the Savarin Coffee Shop on our way to the street, Mrs Ganis was ready to give up.

'We need a cup of coffee. Bad,' she said, leaning against the wall.

'We just got here. We can have coffee at the automat. We're going to eat before the show,' said Mom.

'Two cups of coffee couldn't hurt. It's my treat.'

'Come on or we'll be late for the movie.' Mom headed for the taxi stand and we all followed. There was a huge crowd mobbing each cab as it pulled up to the curb. 'We'll never get one.'

'Sure we will,' said Mrs Ganis. 'Look pregnant.' Mom was in her fifth month and hardly showed at all.

'This is the best I can do.'

'Where are all these people going?' asked Bridie, completely in awe.

'Who knows. It's New York. I hate it.' Mrs Ganis was trying to get to the curb.

'I love it.' I knew Bridie would feel the same as me about New York.

'I told you it was neat.'

'Why don't we walk? It's not that far,' said Mom.

'Are you crazy? In your condition! And what about Finn's leg and my high heels.' Mrs Ganis shouted to the crowd, 'We've got a lady here who's going to have a baby!' No one paid any attention as she was pushed and jostled by people fighting to get ahead of one another.

'Come on,' said Mom, grabbing Mrs Ganis's hand and pulling her out of the crush. 'We'll be there before we know it.'

'What kind of a world is this?' yelled Mrs Ganis. 'War is war but pregnant is also pregnant. Someday, you'll all know what I'm talking about and all I can say is, colic.' Mom was laughing so hard as we started uptown she had to run into a bar to use the rest room because she was afraid she'd wet her pants.

To me, New York was Camelot, Oz and Babylon all rolled into one magnificent city. I knew, the first time I saw it, when I was about five and we passed through on our way to Coney Island, that someday I would live there. One day, when I was old enough to do whatever I wanted, I would go to New York where everything was possible and anything was probable. I would ride the subways or hail taxis as I rushed to go somewhere important to meet someone doing great things. First New York, and then the rest of the world, would know me as a famous painter. The people flowing through the streets like a river out of control would one day propel me to my destiny. There was no doubt about it.

Two Hasidic Jews, in their flat black hats and suits, with their long beards and side-curls, walked past talking loudly in what Mrs Ganis said was Yiddish.

'Did you see them?' said Bridie, wide-eyed.

'Hasidim,' said Mrs Ganis.

'What are they?'

'Old-fashioned Jews. If you ask me they look like they smell. *Meshuga.*'

As we hurried along the street, it seemed we passed enough servicemen to win ten wars. Bridie and Mrs Ganis talked about everybody and Mom kept looking at the young men passing by as though she was searching for someone she knew. Every so often she'd whisper something and smile at one of them and, if she happened to catch his eye, he'd smile back and nod as he moved away. I couldn't hear what she was saying and when I asked she didn't seem to hear me, she just kept walking and started to laugh. Mrs Ganis and Bridie were too busy to notice what was happening and I didn't know whether I should say anything but I was starting to get a sick feeling in the pit of my stomach. Mom was taking long strides and I was having trouble keeping up with her and my brace suddenly felt like it weighed a ton and my leg started to hurt. When I complained about it she didn't pay any attention to me and kept right on walking, dragging me along.

'Mom, please, my leg . . .' She dropped my hand and walked on without me. 'Mom!'

'What's the matter here?' said Mrs Ganis as she caught up to me.

'It's Mom. She's acting funny again.'

'Oh my God.' She hurried ahead and grabbed Mom by the arm, stopping her. 'Are you all right? What's the matter with you running away like that?'

Mom looked at her for a long moment as though she was trying to figure out who this intruder was. 'Was I running?' she said finally. 'I didn't mean to. It's the combination of the cold air and the city, I guess.' She looked at Bridie and me and smiled. It was a peculiar, detached smile. 'I'm sorry if I was going too fast.'

'We should have waited for a cab. What did I say?' said Mrs Ganis as she linked arms with Mom. She turned to Bridie and me. 'You two hold hands and stay close so you shouldn't get lost and give me a heart attack for God's sake,' and she started off down the street holding Mom very close.

Like the rest of the city, the automat was jammed and, once again, some soldiers got up and gave us their table.

'You two be the waiters and Mae and I will be the customers. If you're good, you maybe get a tip.' I could tell Mrs Ganis was worried and wanted to keep close watch on Mom. 'I'll have a tuna sandwich and a black coffee. Mae?' She turned to Mom as she handed us some money.

'The same but cream in the coffee, please.' She seemed to be normal and I felt better as Bridie and I hurried to get change. Standing in line, waiting to get our nickels, we watched a woman with no teeth unwrap a whole pack of gum, one stick at a time, and dunk each stick in coffee before she slipped it in her mouth. Bridie was fascinated.

'Look at her! She's got a whole pack of gum in her mouth.'

'Ssh. She'll hear you.'

'Damn, I love New York!'

When we got our change we had to stand in another line waiting to get to the little windows with the sandwiches. I tried to keep an eye on Mom and Mrs Ganis but Bridie kept distracting me.

'Look at that sailor, the one leaning against the wall. He looks a lot like Simon.'

'Yeah,' I agreed. I wondered where Simon and Fritz were and what they were doing way off in North Africa.

'My Simon's better-looking.' Bridie claimed Simon as her own personal property. Laurie was still the most important person in her life but over the past year he'd had to make room for several others. Aside from Simon there was Mom and Pop, Fritz and Mina, the Ganises, Mr Howe, the newly acquired Kitty Neal and, I was certain, me. At moments like that, when I stood back and looked at Bridie, I couldn't believe she was the same terrible kid who had walked into the fourth grade just under a year before.

We dropped our nickels into the slot and waited for the little windows to pop open and after taking out the food we stood transfixed, watching the shelf revolve and magically be refilled by some unseen sandwich machine. It was all too mysterious and wonderful for any logical explanation and even though I occasionally saw a hand replace an item of food, I really didn't want to know how it all was accomplished.

Mom seemed to enjoy her lunch even though she didn't join in the conversation. She smiled too much and several times Mrs Ganis asked if she was feeling all right but Mom always said she was fine. I knew Mrs Ganis was worried and that made me even more nervous.

Just before we were finished eating Mom reached over and took Bridie's hand. 'Are you having a good time, Deirdre?'

I felt a wave of nausea.

'Mrs Finn, I'm Bridie.' She said it timidly, almost as though she wasn't sure she should say anything.

'She knows you're Bridie,' said Mrs Ganis trying her best to minimize what was happening. 'Don't you, Mae? You know this is Bridie.'

'I'm sorry, Bridie.' Mom's eyes came back into focus. 'Did I call you Deirdre? Sometimes I think maybe she would have been like you. She would have been as pretty as you.' She took Bridie's face in her hand and held it. 'You are very pretty.'

'Maybe we shouldn't go to the movie. Maybe we should better go home.' Mrs Ganis was nodding her head, hoping someone would agree with her.

'Don't be silly,' said Mom. 'Can't a person make a little mistake once in a while? I'm fine. Really, I am.' And she seemed to be. 'Now, Mr Fred Astaire and Miss Rita Hayworth are waiting for us at Radio City and I think we should get going.'

Bridie was positively dazzled by Radio City Music Hall. The incredible vastness, the atmosphere of glittering grandeur, the wide staircases, the arcs of recessed lights in the ceiling and the paper-doll perfection of the ushers and usherettes was almost too much for her to bear. I was so overwhelmed by the size of the place I always had the feeling I'd slipped into another dimension and, by some cosmic jolt, was rendered lilliputian. While Bridie and I were agog with the wonder of it all, Mrs Ganis told us the toilet was clean.

Walking down the aisle to find our seats, Mom seemed to be having as good a time as the rest of us and I again felt slightly relieved. A few minutes after we settled down, the lights dimmed and the whole auditorium reverberated from the first thundering chord played on the giant organ rising from the floor. The nimbleness of the organist's hands and feet flying over the keys and pedals was all Bridie needed to decide then and there she'd like to play the organ. And when the corps de ballet danced on, demure and gossamer, skirts gracefully floating as they sailed through the air, she thought a ballet-dancing organ player was what she really wanted to be. However, both the organ and ballet were quickly forgotten when the glamorous and beautiful Rockettes, all perk and precision, kicked their way into her heart. There was no question about it, when she grew up she was going to be a Rockette.

'Enough already,' said Mrs Ganis as she pulled Bridie back in her seat. 'We'll talk about what you want to be going home on the train. Now be quiet, the picture's going to start and I want to listen to Fred Astaire. You I can listen to anytime.'

'I think I'll make a quick trip to the ladies' room.' Mom started to get up.

'I'll go with you,' said Mrs Ganis.

'No you won't, now, I'll be fine.'

'Bridie, you go with her.' Mrs Ganis was not about to trust Mom alone.

'Bridie, you sit. I said, I will be fine.'

'Either Bridie goes with you or we all go. And that's the last word.'

Mom knew she meant it. 'Oh, all right. Honestly. Come on, Bridie, so we don't miss anything.'

No matter how charmingly Rita and Fred sang and danced, neither Mrs Ganis nor I could pay much attention to what was happening on the screen. Mom's behavior had been so mercurial I had a pervasive sense of dread and I was sure Mrs Ganis felt the same because every few minutes she'd turn and look into the blackness to see if they were coming down the aisle.

'Shouldn't they be back by now?' she said after what seemed like a very long time.

'Maybe I should go look for them.'

'What, in the ladies' room? I should go. You don't move and don't let somebody take our seats. And don't talk to strangers.' But before she could get up we heard Bridie.

'Mrs Ganis, come quick!' She was yelling as she ran down the aisle. 'Something's terrible wrong with Mrs Finn.'

'Oh my God, I knew it. I knew it. It's all my fault. Come on, take the coats,' she said as she grabbed my hand and the three of us ran back up the aisle. 'What is it? What's wrong?'

'I don't know what she's doing.' Bridie tried to explain what was happening but she didn't make any sense. Several ushers were standing with a small crowd in the restroom doorway and a policeman was making his way through as we got there. Mrs Ganis pushed Bridie and me ahead of her into the ladies' room.

'It's going to be okay, lady, just try and relax,' the policeman was saying as he approached Mom. She was by the sinks, rocking back and forth, mumbling something. Wads of toilet paper were stuffed in her ears, and her face, hair and dress were soaked with water and there were puddles all around her on the floor. Her face was pale and her eyes were half closed and her lips were drawn tight across her teeth.

'Mae, my God!' said Mrs Ganis as she went to her.

'You know this lady?' asked the policeman.

'She's my friend. His mother,' she said pointing to me.

'What's the matter with her?'

'What do I look like, a doctor?' Mrs Ganis pushed him aside. 'Mae, darling, it's me, Sophie.' She tried to take the paper wads out of Mom's ears but she pulled away.

'Don't,' she said angrily. 'They won't stop talking.'

'Who? Who's talking? Nobody's here to talk. Darling, believe me. Who would say a bad word about you?' Mrs Ganis tried to soothe her. 'Oh my God.'

'Come on, lady. We'll take you to a doctor. He'll make you feel better.' The policeman, in spite of his tough New York accent, was being very gentle but when he stepped toward Mom

123

she started wailing. Bridie and I tried to go to her but strangers held us back.

'She's pregnant,' Mrs Ganis turned and said it to everyone.

'And he's a cripple.' Bridie offered the information as though it had something to do with what was happening to Mom. The policeman went to the ushers and said something and came back to Mrs Ganis.

'Try to calm her down. I sent for an ambulance.'

Mrs Ganis started to cry. 'An ambulance! We have to call her husband. Oh God, I'm going to have a heart attack or maybe a stroke.'

'Please lady, don't you start. I got enough on my hands here, you know what I mean? I never had to take care of anything like this before.' He said it as though it might excuse any wrongdoing on his part.

'Where's a phone?' Mrs Ganis turned to Bridie and me. 'You have to go to the bathroom? Do it now.'

I hadn't noticed that Bridie was holding my hand. 'Don't be scared,' she said in a small, unsteady voice.

It was hours before Pop and Laurie arrived at the hospital. Mrs Ganis would check on Mom every so often but Bridie and I weren't allowed to leave the emergency waiting room. We spent the afternoon huddled together, watching and listening to people bleeding and in pain, people coughing and spitting and vomiting, experiencing every degree of misery imaginable. Servicemen who had been in fights, mothers holding sick babies and old people fighting to get their breath, waited in fearful silence for someone to tell them they had nothing to worry about. I wanted to run away from it all but Bridie seemed to find the whole experience fascinating. The nurses were too busy to pay much attention to us but every so often one of them would ask if we wanted anything and try to assure us that Mom would be all right.

Pop didn't say anything when he finally arrived, he merely touched my shoulder before going to the desk with Mrs Ganis, then he disappeared down the hall with one of the nurses and

Laurie and Mrs Ganis sat with Bridie and me. Mrs Ganis told Laurie what happened and he shook his head in disbelief, muttering, 'Mother of God', or 'Jesus, Mary and Joseph', whenever her story got to be too much for him.

'Are you kids okay?' he asked.

'How could they be okay, seeing such a terrible thing?' said Mrs Ganis before we could answer. 'I shouldn't say this because I'll probably be dead in a minute but sometimes I don't think God knows what He's doing. God forbid He should hear what I just said but what did Mae ever do that this craziness should happen to her?'

'Poor Mrs Finn,' said Bridie.

'Poor Mrs Finn, indeed,' agreed Laurie. 'The baby?' he whispered and Mrs Ganis shrugged her shoulders. Later in the afternoon Pop came back to the waiting room and told us Mom was asleep and that the doctor said she would be all right. He pulled Laurie and Mrs Ganis aside and talked to them for a long time and Mrs Ganis started to cry. When I saw Laurie wipe tears from his eyes, too, I was certain Mom was stretched out on a bed with a sheet over her face and Pop was lying to me but Bridie said fathers didn't lie to their children. At least, as far as she knew, Laurie had never lied to her and that's why she would never lie to him.

That night Pop stayed in New York and Laurie drove us home and no one, not even Bridie, said anything until we pulled off Route 1 and were crossing the bridge heading for town.

'There isn't going to be a baby,' said Laurie as we watched the headlights follow the white line in the road.

Pop and Dr Lorman decided, ostensibly in the best interests of all concerned, that I should be out of the house when Mom came home to recuperate. They were afraid she'd have another spell and Dr Lorman couldn't predict the effect it might have on me. I thought Mom would want me there, especially after losing the baby and Fritz being in North Africa and me being her only available child, but Pop didn't care what I thought. At first a week at Aunt Cassie's in Wilkes-Barre was suggested but I raised holy hell at the very mention of her name and that option was quickly forgotten. I wanted to stay with Bridie and Laurie or with the Ganises but Pop said I wouldn't be able to keep away from Mom if I was that close to home. It was Mrs Ganis who came up with a solution acceptable to both Pop and me when she suggested I spend a week with Mr Howe. He was more than happy to have me as a guest, the first in more years than he could remember, and when Mom came home from that hospital in New York, Duke and I were already comfortably settled into one of the big musty old bedrooms in Mr Howe's house and I wasn't allowed to see her.

With everything that was happening I felt lonely for Fritz and the first night I was there Mr Howe and I sat at the kitchen table while I wrote him a letter. Pop had told me not to mention Mom's illness or the loss of the baby so I wrote about the trip to the city, the automat and the lady stuffing gum into her mouth and Bridie's decision to become a Rockette but I didn't tell him we never even saw the movie. The letter seemed short and Mr Howe suggested the weather as a safe topic to fill some space. He said just about every letter ever written had a lot of weather talk, which was proof enough for him that people's lives were fairly ordinary and there really wasn't much of interest happening to anybody, and if there was it was usually something that had to be kept secret like the bad things happening to Mom.

There was no snow so I was able to ride my bike to school and Mr Howe had to keep Duke in the house, feeling abandoned and confused, until I came back everyday, when he would do everything short of cartwheels at the sight of me. Some afternoons Bridie would come with me and we would have our tea and apprise Mr Howe of the doings of the day. Bridie hadn't seen Mom or Pop but Mrs Ganis, who was acting as nurse, told her to tell me that Mom was getting wonderful care.

'Is she getting better?' I asked.

'I don't know. Yeah, sure she's getting better. Why wouldn't she? Mina's there a lot and so is Miss Neal. She's a real nurse. For cripes' sake, you shouldn't worry so damn much.' Bridie was doing her best to be reassuring but her performance lacked conviction. 'But the baby . . .' her voice saddened and trailed off and we pedalled along in silence for a while. I think Bridie wanted the baby even more than I did. She planned on a beautiful little girl to play with and pamper and pretend was her very own. From the moment she was told Mom was pregnant Bridie started mapping out the future of the child-to-be, a child whose birth, she decided, would have no less impact on the world than the birth of the Baby Jesus. And then Mom had the miscarriage and there wasn't going to be a baby and Bridie was almost inconsolable.

Mr Howe did everything he could to make my stay with him a holiday. We played both checkers and Chinese checkers and most of the time he let me win. We sang Christmas carols, especially 'God Rest Ye Merry Gentlemen', which we were both partial to, as we made cards from pictures cut out of old magazines, and Mr Howe was very creative helping me decide what to give everyone on my very limited budget. As far as his gift was concerned, all he wanted was a drawing.

'Anything that comes into your mind. Anything at all. You're the artist and you know best.'

'How about a drawing of the barn?'

'That would be perfect. That's where we met for the first time. At least, that's where I met you. Of course, you don't remember cause you were out cold from your owl attack.' I could almost feel the scratches on my chest.

'Maybe I should draw some pigeons on the roof,' I said.

'I'd like that. I really would. It would make it more authentic-like. Now, that's the kind of picture a fella should have. Pigeons on a barn. I really like that.' His enthusiasm was contagious.

'Maybe I'll do a drawing for Mom and Pop, too. And maybe Fritz.' It seemed I had the answer to all my Christmas giving.

'Good idea,' said Mr Howe. 'And how about Sophie and Sam. And maybe you could do a picture of Duke for Simon?' I liked hearing Mr Howe talk about the Ganises and Simon as casually as he might talk about people who had been a part of his life for a long time. It made me happy knowing that my friends were his friends, too. 'You've got a lot of work to do between now and Christmas.' He decided we shouldn't listen to the war news on the radio because we had enough troubles of our own and he couldn't see how news of sinking ships and battles lost could help our situation one little bit. Every night after supper we took turns reading *Great Expectations*, his favorite book by his favorite author whom he reverentially referred to as Mr Dickens, never daring to presume to use his first name. Bundled against the December chill, Mr Howe and I shared our fire with Pip and gentle Joe Gargery, mad Miss Havisham and the cold and aloof Estella, Biddy, scary Abel Magwitch, Uncle Pumblechook and all the other characters who lingered in the shadowy corners of the room waiting to be brought to life, who, along with Mr Howe, helped me escape, even for a little while, from my frightening realities. When the week was up and Pop came to get me, as anxious as I was to see Mom, I didn't want to leave Mr Howe. In his way he gave me the same sense of security, the same love and respect, Fritz had always given me.

Driving home, Pop told me Mom looked well but I should prepare myself because she was different. She didn't talk very much and when she did she seemed to be talking to someone who wasn't there. My orders were to spend as little time with her as possible because Dr Lorman thought rest was the best medicine in cases like hers. I wasn't to mention the baby or Fritz or Mina's baby and I was to see to it that Duke didn't go into their bedroom. Dr Lorman said Mom should stay in her room until she started to feel better and even her meals should be served on a tray.

Miss Neal and Mrs Ganis met us at the door and Mrs Ganis

started crying the minute she saw me. I expected Bridie but she wasn't there.

'Did you have a nice time, Finn?' asked Miss Neal.

'I made some Christmas cards.' I couldn't think of anything else to say.

'Mr Howe is a nice man,' she said.

'I made a Christmas list, too, but I forgot you and Laurie.'

'Boy, we're going to have some Christmas,' said Mrs Ganis. 'Hotsie totsie. And such a Hanuka!'

'You better come and see your mother.' Pop started up the stairs with my suitcase and I followed, fearful of what I might find when I got to the top because the last time I had seen Mom she was strapped down in the ambulance, thrashing her head from side to side and screaming. But there wasn't a sound as I slowly walked up the steps with Mrs Ganis and Miss Neal standing at the foot of the staircase, watching.

The blinds were down and the room was dark and Mom was sitting on the side of the bed laughing at something one of her invisible friends was saying. Dressed in her bathrobe, with her hair brushed back and held in place by a ribbon, she looked fresh and clean. Her eyes were unnaturally bright and her cheeks were splotches of red as though she was wearing too much rouge.

'Here's Finn, Mae,' said Pop from the doorway. 'Give your mother a kiss.' I went to her and kissed her on the cheek and when she looked at me I thought I saw an instant of recognition but she started laughing and turned back to her secret conversation. Her rosary beads were on the floor next to the bed and I picked them up and offered them to her but she ignored me. 'That's enough,' said Pop. 'I think we'd better let her rest.'

That night, I made the drawing of the barn for Mr Howe's Christmas present. I tried to remember it as clearly as I could as I drew it from several different angles but I didn't like any of them. One, from the viewpoint of the orchard, wasn't too bad but it didn't capture the mood I wanted. It was like a drawing of a barn I didn't really know. Then, without even thinking about it, I started drawing the interior and I remembered every detail with startling clarity. I automatically drew the inside of the barn as it was the day I had fallen; dark and mysterious, stormy and violent and empty, with dusty, naked beams and cobwebs. It was a lonely, ghostly place, ominous and Godforsaken. Hidden away in a corner, sitting on the floor, was a figure so small it was barely discernible. There was no face but it was a figure in torment and isolation, arms clutching legs to breast, head hanging down hopelessly. I looked at it a long time thinking I had drawn a picture of myself before I realized it was a picture of Mom.

Mrs Ganis was true to her word and, in spite of everything, tried to make the best of Christmas and Hanuka. The brass menorah, which had belonged to Mr Ganis's father, who had been a rabbi in a small village in the old country, was polished to a gleaming gold and reflected the little flickering fires of the candles a hundred times. Bridie and I took turns lighting them and she was so taken with the custom she decided that when she became a Rockette she would also become a Jew and Mrs Ganis said if she did she wouldn't be the first Jewish lady to kick up her heels. We were each given fifty cents a day for the eight days and told we could spend the money any way we wanted but Mr Ganis suggested we save it until next summer so we'd have spending money when we went to the shore. I knew Bridie wasn't capable of keeping money that long so I offered to hold on to it for her and she told me to mind my own beeswax. One night, after we lit the candles, both Mr and Mrs Ganis cried when they started talking about friends and family in Europe. Bridie asked why they were crying and Mrs Ganis took her in her arms and rocked her.

'Oh, Bridala, you ask too many questions. Such terrible things aren't for such young ears.'

'What is this?' said Mr Ganis, taking off his thick glasses and drying his eyes. 'What kind of a party is this? We're supposed to have a happy time here. Now we got Hanuka and in a few days we got a Christmas tree to decorate at your house so we should be smiling instead of crying. No more tears, Sophie. Enough already. Maybe we should sing. Or maybe I should tell the Hanuka story?'

'Better we should eat,' said Mrs Ganis as she went to the kitchen.

Mom stayed in her room chatting and laughing with her phantoms and Bridie and I would visit and tell her what was happening and talk as though she understood what we were saying but we both knew better. If Pop wasn't home we took Duke into the room and she always reached out and petted him, trusting that his reality was no threat to hers. Dr Lorman said she was making definite progress and Mina and Kitty Neal made feeble attempts at reassuring me by saying they could see her improving every day and, although I wanted to believe them, in my heart I knew she was slipping deeper and deeper into a place we couldn't go, a place from which she might never return.

The day before Christmas, when Bridie and I were making last-minute preparations for our tree-trimming party, Dr Lorman came to the house with a younger man dressed in hospital whites and they both went upstairs to see Mom. Mina was there and the Ganises and Laurie and Miss Neal but they all seemed to be avoiding us as they sat quietly around the kitchen table, staring into their coffee cups. Pop had acted strangely all morning. If he wasn't going out to the back of the yard for no apparent reason but to lean against the fence in the cold, he was opening the front door as though he expected someone to be there. I tried to talk to him several times but he'd brush me aside and go on doing nothing. After Dr Lorman had been upstairs with the stranger for a while, Laurie came to me and said Pop wanted to see me in the yard. He told Bridie to stay with him, that I was to go alone. Pop was standing by the pigeon coop.

'Did I do something wrong?'

'No.' He started to walk toward the fence. 'It's your mother. She doesn't seem to be getting any better.' He took a deep breath. 'Oh Christ, they're taking her away.'

'What do you mean?'

'To a hospital. For treatments. It's not my fault, goddamn it.' He hung his head as though it was. 'I didn't want to tell you any sooner than I had to.'

'For how long?' I asked.

'I don't know. Not too long.' For the first time he really looked at me. 'It's just going to be the two of us for a while.' He pulled me close and held me. 'We're going to have to take care of each other. Oh Christ, Finn, I don't know what's happening to us.'

I didn't want him to touch me. 'I'm going to say goodbye to Mom,' I said as I pulled away from him and started for the house.

'We'll be all right. You'll see. Everything is going to be fine.'

I walked through the kitchen, past everyone who knew what was happening and didn't tell me and I wanted them all to die.

Bridie and I stood by the undecorated tree as Dr Lorman and the other man came down the stairs with Mom. She was smiling, almost as though she was happy to be going on a trip. I don't think she saw any of us but just before she went out the door she petted Duke. I noticed she had her rosary beads in her hand. They took her to Franklin Village, the State hospital.

PART TWO

Honey and I sat on the dune, huddled together against the November chill as we looked down on Bridie and Simon walking along the beach, occasionally stopping to pick up some treasure. Bridie, at thirteen, was almost as tall as Simon. Her body was still boyish, all skinny angles and flat chest, yet there was something about her, some intangible, womanly essence, which was starting to assert itself. Her hair was down to her waist, black and shiny as coal, and with her fierce green eyes and perfect skin she was beautiful. She and Simon were laughing at something they found as she stood in the surf, coatless and barefoot, not noticing the bone-chilling wind.

'She's going to catch her death,' said Honey as he tightened the scarf holding the big straw hat protecting his whiteness from even the possibility of sunburn.

'She could sit naked on an iceberg and it wouldn't bother her one bit.' I thought she was indestructible.

'Out there somewhere is Europe.' He took off his dark glasses and squinted at the horizon. 'All the places my daddy told me about. Places he been to in the war. Someday, I'm going to go over there on a airplane.' Honey thought about it for a minute. He still hadn't been to school because Tessie and his father thought people would make fun of him, being so different. But his curiosity was insatiable and his intelligence so obvious they supplied him with every possible tool of learning. 'I got lots of maps that shows where Europe is. And Asia and the rest of the world. All kinds of different people. I'm going to all those places someday.'

'Me, too. I want to go every place in the world. Especially Italy. And the Alps. I want to see where Hannibal rode the elephants.'

'We should go together. We start saving our money and one day we go over there. Just the two of us,' said Honey.

'And Bridie. Bridie will want to go.'

'Oh yeah. Bridie will want to go,' he echoed as though it was a given that had slipped his mind. The sky darkened and threatened rain as we planned our trip to Europe, watching a fishing boat appear and disappear in the heavy swells as it headed for the security of the inlet leading to the bay. 'Maybe, when we go over to Europe, we'll find your brother?'

'Maybe,' I said, although I didn't believe it.

'I think so. I think maybe we find him.'

'Maybe.' I didn't like to talk about Fritz and Honey knew it.

'I'm sorry.'

'That's okay. Forget it.' Bridie, arms outstretched and head thrown back, was running through the surf, kicking up foamy sprays, getting Simon wet. 'Don't go too far!' I yelled. 'It's going to rain.'

'So what!' shouted Bridie as she raced along the beach, 'I can't get any wetter.'

'She's crazy!' yelled Simon.

'She sure is,' agreed Honey. There was a flash of lightning way out at sea and the clouds turned orange and white and red as muffled thunder moved across the water. 'That's a discharge of electricity in the atmosphere,' said Honey. 'Lightning. It's beautiful. I read about it.'

'I like thunder and lightning.'

'Me, too. I like it a lot. It's like fireworks.' We sat there pondering lightning for a while.

'You be in high school next year. Maybe you can teach me what they teach you in the high school?'

'Yeah, sure. But I bet you already know all that stuff.'

'I can't talk no language but English. You got to learn how to talk other languages in high school. Like French. I like to talk French someday.'

'Someday.'

'Someday, maybe.'

'Damn it, you got salt water in my eye.' Simon started toward the dunes blinking his good eye.

'What a baby,' taunted Bridie, 'afraid of a little water.'

'Come on, Bridie, we have to go. Pop will be mad as hell.'

'I didn't even tell my daddy I was coming here. He going to kill me.'

'I'm blind as a bat, damn it.' The sky lit up and there was a crack of thunder and the rain started to come down as hard as icy bullets. Bridie ran to Simon and they started up the dune as Honey and I headed for the car.

The war ended for me the day Dr Lorman took Mom to Franklin Village. Patriotism was a luxury I could not afford. The survival of the nation was unimportant compared to my own survival and Fritz was off fighting for something I no longer cared about or understood when he should have been home helping Mom and me fight for our lives. All the absolutes and certainties were gone and I didn't know what to do about it. Pop and I had always lived more like strangers than family but now, being alone in the house, we were creatures from different planets, unable and unwilling to try to communicate on any level. The awkward silences were interrupted with the occasional clatter of dishes or Duke's nails clicking on the linoleum or the flush of a toilet but rarely with words. Fortunately, Mrs Ganis and Bridie, two of the greatest talkers in the history of mankind, were at the house a good deal of the time and when they were there the distance between Pop and me was less noticeable.

It was several weeks before I could forgive the Ganises and Laurie for not telling me Mom was going to be taken away. I could forgive Kitty Neal since she was new to my family through her connection with Laurie, but he was another matter. How could he keep such devastating information from Bridie and me? And Mr and Mrs Ganis, whom I trusted implicitly and who had been dependable allies as long as I could remember, betrayed me. I was determined never to speak to any of them again but as the days went by and the absence of Mom became more and more pervasive I needed them and my determination started to crumble and I forgot to be angry and it wasn't long before I forgave them. Not Pop. I could never forgive him.

'Maybe you're being too hard on your father,' said Mr Howe one freezing February afternoon when Duke and I visited him. 'It's not easy telling kids bad things, you know.'

'He should have told me, anyway.'

'I guess he should, but he was just trying to spare you. I expect there's not much worse than telling a fella his mother is going away to some hospital. You see how hard that would be?' I knew he was defending Pop because he was trying to make me feel better but it didn't make any difference.

'I hate him.'

'Lord, I don't like to hear you say a thing like that, Finn.' He made a face as though he was in pain. 'Hate is a big load for a little fella to carry around.' He put down a bowl with some meat scraps he had saved for Duke.

'I know it's a sin but I hate him.'

'Well,' he thought for a minute, 'I don't rightly know what a sin is. I leave that up to churchgoing folks. To tell you the truth, I always thought the good Lord had too much on His mind to worry a whole heck of a lot about who's sinning and who isn't. Seems that would be the least important part of the job of being God. But I do know one thing for sure. Hate is real bad for the digestion.'

'My digestion is just fine. Come on, Duke, let's go.'

'We haven't even had our tea yet.'

'I can't today, Mr Howe. Come on, Duke.' He was still licking the bowl.

'We've always been able to talk about things, you and me.'

'We still can.'

'Not if you leave like this. Friends should be able to disagree. That's what friends do. It pains to know you're mad at me.' I wanted to say he should have thought about that before he started taking Pop's side, but I just didn't feel like talking about it anymore.

'I'm not mad,' I lied. 'Come on, Duke, we got to go.' By the time Duke and I got to Livery Street I was feeling guilty about the way I treated Mr Howe and there was no one I could discuss it with. Not even Bridie. As far as she was concerned, there were two perfect people in the world, Laurie and Pop, and she wouldn't listen to a bad word about either one. Pop was a rock in her life, and since Laurie had stopped drinking he'd been elevated to sainthood.

It was almost spring before I was allowed to go to Franklin Village to visit Mom. After months of idle talk about her coming home any day, it was decided that perhaps it would be a good idea for me to see her. Dr Lorman and Pop, once again, had thought it was best for all concerned that I wait until Mom started feeling better, so week after week my visit was postponed until there were no more plausible excuses. Pop saw her every weekend, taking flowers and candy, almost like a young man trying to impress a new girlfriend. I wondered if secretly he was taking flowers and candy to Josie Cleary, too, because the Cleary farm was on the way to Franklin Village. Sometimes, when he went to see Mom, Mrs Ganis or Laurie went with him and when they came home they always said she was looking better. No one ever said she was getting better. I wrote to Fritz and, along with all my other problems, I told him they wouldn't let me visit Mom and I always thought the only reason Pop decided to take me to see her was because Fritz wrote and gave him hell.

Mina and Bridie went with us so the twenty-some-mile ride didn't seem nearly as long as it would have had Pop and I been alone. Mina was hugely pregnant and expected to have the baby any day. She and Fritz had decided to name the baby Mae, after Mom, or Mario, after Mina's brother who went down on the *Lexington*, which meant there would be a Little Mae or probably a Little Fritz in the family because I couldn't imagine anyone calling a Finnegan, Mario. Being Little Finn, I already felt sorry for the baby. For a change Pop was the talkative one on the trip. I think Bridie, Mina and I were too nervous at the prospect of what we'd find when we saw Mom to think of anything to say. He talked about the icy roads and the grip winter was keeping with spring just around the corner.

'I never remember it being this cold so long,' he said not really expecting anyone to react. 'Hell, it's damn near the first of spring. It'll be colder than bejesus on St Patrick's Day. If the birds come back they'll freeze their asses off.' We rode along in silence for a while. 'I hate a cold St Patrick's Day.'

'Will Mrs Finn know us?' asked Bridie.

'No, I don't suppose she will. Well, maybe. I like to think she knows more than she can let on.' He looked at Mina sitting next to him. 'Tell her Fritz sends his love.'

'He does. Always.'

'Maybe she'll understand that.'

'Won't she even know Little Finn?' asked Bridie as she took my hand.

'Maybe. There's just no goddamn way of telling what she knows. We'll have to wait and see.' We hit a patch of ice and the car skidded a few feet and that ended the talk about Mom. As we rode along in silence I looked at the naked trees silhouetted against the cold, clear sky and thought about the birds coming back too soon and finding there wasn't a hint of spring and I wondered if they'd turn around and go south or whatever warm place they spent the winter.

The guard in the little entrance booth, recognizing Pop, opened the gate and we drove up a long hill through rocky, barren fields before we saw the village. The first thing to break the horizon was a slim, slate-covered steeple, which quickly sucked the biggest, darkest building I had ever seen into view, stretching as far to the left and right as I could see. Dead ivy clung to bricks the color of dried blood and the building itself was a nightmare jumble of turrets and curved glass and gray stone staircases leading to huge, heavy, double doors. A few spindly trees dotted the common but for the most part the place looked like a bleak fortress surrounded by a brooding, lifeless landscape.

'This is creepy,' said Bridie. 'If a person wasn't nuts when they got here, this place would make them nuts.'

'Mom's not nuts,' I said defensively.

Pop parked the car in one of the spaces designated for visitors and we went up the center stairs to the reception area where two men were mopping the tile floor and the place smelled so strongly of disinfectant my eyes started to water. Several people, sitting quietly on straight wooden benches, looked at us when we came through the door, probably wondering, as I was wondering about them, which loved one we had come to visit. The huge, high-ceilinged room was freezing and everyone was wearing their overcoats and the place looked more like a bus station than a hospital. A tall nurse wearing a thick sweater over her uniform was standing behind the desk, picking her teeth with a piece of folded paper.

'They moved her,' she said when she saw Pop. 'She's in building H. Go out the front door and turn left. It's right behind us. It's a long walk so you might as well drive. There's parking.'

'How is she? Is something wrong?' asked Pop.

'I don't think so. H is for people they want to socialize. Talk to the nurse, okay.' She went back to picking her teeth and turned to two young men in white uniforms who were leaning against a filing cabinet, smoking.

Building H was one of several smaller buildings clustered behind the fortress, obviously the village part of Franklin Village. There was a sign over the door that read simply WOMEN. Next to the building was a fenced recreation area with tables and swings, almost like a schoolyard. The lawn was winter dead and brown except for the edges next to the fence where there was a path worn through to dirt. An old woman with short, white hair was riding a swing, talking to a stuffed animal so dilapidated it was difficult to distinguish what it was. Another woman, short and fat, was yelling at a cadaverously thin woman every time the woman stepped off the worn path. On the other side of the yard, two women stood with their arms around each other, foreheads together, both talking at the same time. Mina was so unnerved she wouldn't look but Bridie and I stopped for a moment and the short fat woman ran at us, ripping her coat open, exposing huge, pendulous breasts.

'My God,' said Bridie. 'Will you look at that.'

'Come on, you two.' Pop had us by the shoulders and was steering us into the building. The woman started pressing her chest hard against the fence, flattening her breasts and making a checkerboard pattern on them. 'Don't pay any attention to her and she won't do that. Christ!' We went into a small waiting room and a nurse took Pop away, leaving Mina and Bridie and me alone.

'Did you see that lady?' Bridie asked Mina.

'Out of the corner of my eye. It was awful.' Mina was looking a little pale.

'She had titties like watermelons for cripes' sake. Big ugly old things. Enough to make you sick.'

'Just forget about it,' said Mina, wanting to change the subject.

'Forget about it! Are you crazy! That must of hurt like hell, squashing her titties like that. I'll see those big old things in my dreams.'

A woman came in the front door, all bundled up against the cold, and when she pushed the scarf back from her face we could see she was about Mom's age and very pretty.

'It is so cold!'

'Terrible,' said Mina.

'My name is Mildred. I haven't seen you here before,' she said, smiling warmly.

'This is our first time. We're visiting my Mom.'

'What's her name?' asked Mildred.

'Mae Finnegan.'

'Oh, I know her. She has that nice thick gray hair. That's Mae, isn't it?' She didn't wait for an answer. 'Everyone is so nice here. Sweet and kind and understanding. They're very good to the patients. I am not a patient, by the way. I am in charge of new arrivals. I tell them what they can and cannot do. Also, who they can and cannot trust. It's very important to know who you can trust in a shitty place like this.' Mildred's voice became pointedly confidential. 'For instance, Miss Webster, the ugly nurse with the birthmark on her neck, cannot, I emphasize the "not", be trusted. On my birthday, that bitch stole my cake. My boyfriend, Teddy, he's in the men's building and I see him when they show movies, saw that bitch with half of my cake.' Mina started backing away, making strange little fearful sounds in her throat. 'I know she would like to get her hands on Teddy, too. He's very good-looking and will be downright handsome when he gets his teeth. If she ever kisses him I'll slap her face.'

'My father's going to be here any minute,' I said, in case Mildred was getting any violent ideas.

'You know, of course, you're in the wrong ward. Crippled children are in building B. That's B as in boy. Polio?'

'No. I'm only here to see my mother.'

'Do you know who the father is?' she asked, noticing Mina's swollen belly.

'Of course she does,' said Bridie indignantly. 'What the hell's the matter with you?'

'Mina's my sister-in-law.' I took Mina's hand and held tight.

'They won't let you keep it, you know. It's a rule. I make sure everybody follows the rules. After all, that's my job. Mina. What a pretty name.' She leaned close and whispered, 'I think they sell them to Germany because Germany needs babies.' Mina backed away. 'That's better than selling them to the Japs cause they eat them.'

'Why don't you keep quiet about babies,' I said. 'You're getting her all upset.'

'New patients are like that,' said Mildred. 'She'll get over it in no time. At first you'll miss the baby but you'll forget about it.'

'You're a crackpot,' said Bridie.

'Will you shut up. We don't want to make her mad.' I wanted Mildred to go away and leave us alone.

'She can't make me mad,' Mildred flopped down in a chair. 'Sticks and stones, you know. Maybe I am a crackpot. So what? I'll tell you a secret, a cracked pot lets in more light. So, I'm smarter than you.' She took a beat-up, old cigarette out of her pocket. 'You got a light?'

'She's as crazy as a bedbug.'

'Why don't you look for Pop?' I wanted to get Bridie out of the room before she and Mildred came to blows.

'And miss this? Not on your life!'

'I'll go,' said Mina, anxious to get away from Mildred. But just as she was about to leave Pop returned with Miss Webster, the nurse with the birthmark.

'Hello, Miss Webster.' Mildred was all smiles. 'You're my favorite nurse. I just love you.'

'You big liar,' said Bridie.

'That's enough out of you,' said Pop.

'Well, she is a liar.'

'I said, that's enough, damn it!' Pop took Bridie's hand and pulled her close to him.

'Mildred, why don't you go out in the yard with the other ladies?' Miss Webster ushered her toward a door.

'It's too cold out there. But if that's what you want me to do, Miss Webster, I'll be happy to go outside.'

'Just for a little while, please.'

'Next time we have crafts I'll make something for you, Miss Webster. Something nice.' She turned to us. 'It was lovely meeting all of you. Really, really lovely.' And she was gone.

'We have no idea how Mildred manages to get out. But she never goes very far.' We went through another door and started down a hall that smelled strongly of the same disinfectant I smelled in the fortress.

'I bet old Mildred tries to see her boyfriend, Teddy,' said Bridie as we walked past several closed doors.

'She told you about Teddy, did she?' Miss Webster chuckled. 'They're quite a pair. A regular Romeo and Juliet.' She stopped at a door with a small smoked-glass window. 'Mrs Finnegan is here on the sun porch. You can stay just as long as you like.' She opened the door. 'Now, don't you children be afraid.'

There were four people on the sun porch, Mom and three older women, all sitting as still as statues. Not one of them turned to look at us as we came through the door. Mom was sitting closest to the window, staring out at the cloudless, cold sky. Her hair was cut shorter, like all the other women we had seen, and she wore a shapeless gray dress and a heavy gray cardigan sweater. Someone had tried to dress her up for her visitors by putting a bow made out of Christmas ribbon over her ear. I thought she looked ridiculous and I was angry she let people do stupid things like put bows in her hair.

Pop went to her, kissed her on the cheek and knelt down in front of her. 'I brought you some visitors, Mae.' He waved us over. 'Give her a kiss.'

Mina leaned over and put her arms around Mom and held her for a moment. 'Fritz sends his love, Mom.' It was the first time I ever heard Mina call her Mom.

'Mina's going to have the baby any day now,' said Pop, smiling. 'If it's a girl they're going to name her Mae, after you.' Mom never took her eyes off the landscape.

'I miss you, Mrs Finn,' said Bridie as she snuggled up to Mom, putting her head on Mom's shoulder the way she had done a hundred times. The touch was too much for Bridie and her chin started to quiver as her eyes welled up.

'Now, we'll have none of that,' said Pop with a slight crack in his voice. 'Come on, Finn. You're next.' Bridie went to Mina. 'Go on, give your mother a kiss.' I didn't want to kiss her, I wanted her to see me and know I was there. And I wanted her to stop being so ridiculous. I went to her and stood in front of her.

'Mom?'

'She can't hear you,' said Pop.

'Stop looking out there and look at me.'

'I told you, she can't hear you.' He leaned against the window and looked down at me. 'I know how you feel. We all know how you feel. You want her to be all right. Believe me, I want that, too. But I'm telling you she can't hear you.'

'Why not? She's not deaf,' I said angrily.

'That'll be enough. You hear me? Now, give her a kiss.'

'No.'

'Don't you start making trouble, mister. I'm warning you.' His voice was loud and one of the other women looked at us and started laughing.

'Mom, look at me,' I said, ignoring him.

'I told you to give your mother a kiss. Now, you give her a kiss and that's final.'

'Go on, Finn,' said Mina. 'Please.'

'Give her a kiss for cripes' sake.' Bridie didn't want any trouble.

'She's my mother, not yours, so mind your own damn business!'

'That's enough, mister. You're walking on very thin ice and I'm not going to put up with any of your crap. Now kiss your mother.'

'No. I want her to look at me.'

'Goddamn it!' Pop's arm shot out and he grabbed me by the back of the neck. 'We got enough trouble without you starting. Go out and wait in the car. Maybe that'll cool you off.'

'Don't hurt him!' yelled Bridie, and as she came to me, for one hundredth of a second, Mom looked at me and there was a flash of recognition. There were no phantoms between her and me, and she wasn't hearing strange voices. For that moment my mother and I were looking at each other and she knew it was me.

Pop pushed me to the door. 'I don't care if you sit out there and freeze.'

'I'll go with him,' said Bridie.

'You will not. You came to visit and visit is just what you'll do,' and Pop closed the door, leaving me in the hall.

It was cold in the car but I didn't care if they never came back. I didn't care about anything. Mom looked at me and she knew me and that was all that mattered.

Mina had the baby when I was in Philadelphia with Mr and Mrs Ganis. Mrs Ganis had planned on taking me to my appointment with the dreaded Dr Whiteshield and, at the last minute, Mr Ganis decided he'd go with us, and since he never went anywhere he left even Mrs Ganis speechless.

'Maybe we can have lunch with the Steinmans?' Before Mr Ganis retired from the jewelry business he had worked with Mr Steinman.

'I don't like Sarah Steinman.' Mrs Ganis was washing the breakfast dishes.

'You don't like anybody,' said Mr Ganis without looking up from his morning paper.

'Finn, finish your egg so I can wash the dish while the water is still hot.' She was clearing the table.

'Finn, take your time. We got plenty of hot water. She's a crazy person. I'm going to trade her in for a new model.' He winked at me.

'I'm finished,' I said, taking the dish to the sink.

'Sarah Steinman thinks she's better than anybody else. Hoity toity.'

'The woman has had a lot of *tsoris*. You have no heart.'

'I have as much heart as anybody. We all got *tsoris*. Life isn't easy. So? She still thinks she's better than everybody.'

'So? That means we can't have lunch with them? Morris is my friend.' He folded the paper neatly. 'You don't like Morris, either?'

'Morris is a *mench*. So call and make a date for lunch.' She ran some more water into the sink. 'Who said I don't like him? What's not to like? Any man who could live with her is a saint.'

'Are there Jewish saints?' I asked.

'Two,' said Mrs Ganis. 'Morris Steinman is one and I'm the other.'

Bridie couldn't go with us to Philadelphia because it was a school day, and I was delighted to have Mr and Mrs Ganis to myself for a change. Mr Ganis told me about his first train ride when he was a boy in the old country and the thing he remembered most of all was everybody eating and the whole train smelling of garlic. He didn't have any idea how fast the train was traveling but he thought if they didn't slow down they were going to go off the end of the earth. Mrs Ganis told stories of touring with her ballet company and all the flirting that went on in the train, which she attributed to the fact that there was nothing else to do. Mr Ganis said she would flirt anyway and they argued back and forth, sometimes pretending to be angry and sometimes hurt but there was laughter under all of it and before I knew it we pulled into 30th Street Station.

Dr Whiteshield still treated me like something attached to the brace, barely speaking to me except to order me to turn or walk or sit. Instead of asking me questions he directed everything at Mrs Ganis.

'Does it hurt the child when he walks?'

'Maybe a little. Finn, does it hurt when you walk?'

'Does he keep the brace on all day?'

'Darling, do you keep the brace on all day?'

'Does the child try to do most of his normal activities?'

'What is he, invisible?' Mrs Ganis, unlike Mom and Pop who had a subservient, almost religious, reverence for doctors, was tired of translating for Dr Whiteshield. 'Ask him, he's sitting right here. And he's not the child. He's got a name. Finn.'

Dr Whiteshield stiffened. 'That will be all. My nurse will give you your next appointment.' He directed everything to me. 'Where's your mother?'

'Well . . .' I didn't know what to say. Of all people, I didn't want to tell Dr Whiteshield my mother was in the State hospital. Mrs Ganis came to my rescue.

'On vacation. His parents went to . . . Maine.'

'Who are you?'

'His grandmother.'

'His grandmother!'

'From Dublin.'

Mr Ganis had arranged for Mr Steinman to pick us up in front of Dr Whiteshield's building and, as we stood on the curb waiting for him, Mrs Ganis was fuming.

'Calm down, Sophie. You'll have a stroke.'

'Everything you said about that man was true, Finn. They should take away his license.'

'He's a good doctor.'

'He should be in the prison. Treating a child such a terrible way.' She leaned down to me. 'Do you have to go to the bathroom?'

'No.'

'How about you, Sam. Do you have to go?'

'None of your business.'

The Steinmans lived on the outskirts of town in a brick house in a row of brick houses as similar as the little houses on a Monopoly board. The only things distinguishing one from the other were the shrubs planted in the small front yards. Mr and Mrs Steinman were what I expected although I didn't feel Mrs Steinman thought she was better than other people, she just seemed plain and quiet. She was everything Mrs Ganis wasn't. Her hair was graying and pulled back in a soft bun and she wore round horn-rimmed glasses and no make-up or jewelry. Compared to her, Mrs Ganis was kaleidoscopic with her flaming-red hair, scarlet lipstick and rouge, huge earrings and necklace and brightly flowered dress. Mr Steinman was tall and handsome with unruly white hair and constantly smiling blue eyes and I was immediately comfortable with him because he had the graciousness to include me in the conversation, something most adults forget to do with children. But my biggest surprise was their granddaughter, Rebecca. For some reason the Ganises hadn't mentioned a granddaughter. She was about the same age as Bridie and me but she was much smaller. Everything about her was soft, her light-brown hair and her dark, sad eyes and her unnaturally pink lips imbued her with a fragile delicacy, a breakability that set her apart and made her almost unapproachable. We liked each other the moment we met in the car.

'Does the brace hurt?' Unlike Bridie, she was too polite to ask what was wrong with my leg and chose instead to inquire about my comfort.

'Not anymore. I was born with a crooked leg and the brace is supposed to straighten it out.' We were sitting on the back porch after lunch, just the two of us, while the adults sat around the dining-room table with their coffee, listening to old, scratchy Italian opera records on the Victrola. There was still a chill in the air but the sun felt warm and promising on my skin.

'Do you like the music?' she said after a moment.

'I guess. I never heard it before.'

'It's Puccini. I like him.'

'He sounds like a lady.'

'No, no. Puccini is the composer.'

'Oh,' I said, wondering if I should have known who Puccini was. We listened to the music for a while and, although I didn't understand anything the lady was singing about, I liked it.

'I want to show you something.' She led me to the back of the yard and, tucked away in a corner, under a forsythia bush just starting to show yellow buds, was a small patch of violets in bloom.

'They're early,' I said as I bent down to pick one.

'Don't.' She grabbed my arm and I was surprised at the strength in her hand. 'I like to look at them growing there. That's a cemetery. You don't pick flowers in a cemetery.' She held my arm for a moment and I was very aware of her touch and didn't want her to take her hand away.

'Finn, what are you doing?' It was Mrs Ganis on the porch.

'Nothing.'

'Well, come up here and do nothing in the sun where it's

warm. We're going soon.' She went back into the house, singing along with the lady on the record.

'What's buried there?'

'Some birds and a cat's head.'

'Just the head?'

'That's all I found. It was in the gutter out front. I don't know what happened to the rest of it.'

'Was it your cat?'

'No. I never saw him before. He was yellow and his eyes were open and they were yellow, too. I wrapped him in a lace handkerchief and buried him with the birds. My grandmother is still looking for the handkerchief. Sometimes I wonder if it was wrong to bury them together. Maybe he killed the birds. I don't know about things like that.' She had a slight accent. 'Would you have buried them together?'

'They're dead. I don't suppose it matters.'

'I wonder about that.'

'Where were you born?'

'South Africa. We lived in Munich, in Germany, but my parents were in South Africa and I came very much earlier than I was expected.'

'Are you a German?'

'American, just like you. My father was born right here in Philadelphia. In this house.' I felt so inadequate. I had only been in three of the United States, New Jersey, Pennsylvania and New York, and here was someone my own age who was born in Africa and lived in Germany.

'Did you ever see Hitler?'

'I don't think so.'

'My brother, Fritz, was in Africa. North Africa. Maybe he's still there. We haven't heard from him in a while.' I told her about Fritz and Mina expecting a baby and before I knew it I had told her all about everything in my life. About the people on Livery Street, and Duke, and the kids at school, and Simon and Mr Howe and even about Mom being in Franklin Village. I told her I wanted to be a famous artist and live in Manhattan someday and she asked if I wanted to be an Impressionist, her favorite painters, and I said yes even though I didn't know what an Impressionist was. I felt I could tell her anything but for some reason I didn't tell her about Bridie. I thought about it but it just didn't seem like the right thing to do.

'I don't know where my father and mother are.' She said this after politely listening to me go on and on. 'I haven't seen them in four years.' We started back to the house as she told me her father had brought her to Philadelphia from Germany but because her mother was a German citizen, and for some other reason Rebecca didn't understand, her mother wasn't allowed to leave the country. Her father left Rebecca with her grandparents and went back to get her mother and for a while they heard from him but the war happened and it had been a few years since they received the last letter. 'I have to look at their pictures to remember what they look like. Sometimes at night, lying in the dark, I try to remember their faces but I can't. I see their shapes but the faces are blank. I get up and turn on the light and look at the pictures. My favorite is one taken of the three of us by our car in the backyard in Munich. Mama is sitting on the running board, posing like a movie star, showing her knees, and Papa is holding me and pretending to be shocked. She's very pretty in the picture and when I look at it a long time I can remember her skin, pale and very soft, and I can smell it, sweet with powder and perfume. And I remember my father always smelled of tobacco and cologne. I remember what they smell like but I can't remember their faces.'

'Come on, Finn, we're going.' Mrs Ganis was standing in the doorway. 'You better go to the bathroom.'

It seemed the three of us had too much to think about on the train ride home so we didn't talk. We weren't out of the station long when Mr Ganis dozed off and Mrs Ganis sat staring out the window but she didn't seem to be paying attention to the countryside slipping by. She looked old and tired and there was

154

just the trace of a sad little smile and I noticed her lipstick was running into the little creases around her mouth. I almost asked what she was thinking about but I didn't want to start a conversation. There were so many things I wanted to remember about Rebecca as precisely as I could. I had just met a kid who knew the name of an Italian composer and knew that there were different kinds of painters. Someone who was born on another continent and spoke other languages and buried the head of a cat in her own secret cemetery. I was overwhelmed and decidedly jealous and I knew if I lived to be a hundred my life wouldn't be as exciting as hers had already been. Bumping along on that crowded train, I had no way of knowing Rebecca and the story of her mother and father would inspire me to do the most adventurous thing I would ever do in my life. Just as I started to seriously speculate about the fate of the headless body of the yellow cat I fell asleep and before I knew it the train was pulling into the Junction and Mrs Ganis was telling me to wake up.

'Well, for cripes' sake, I thought you'd never get home.' Bridie was on the Ganises' front porch with Duke when we came around the corner. 'Mina had the baby.'

'The baby's here!' Mrs Ganis shouted at Mr Ganis.

'I heard, I heard. So? What is it?'

'A girl.' Bridie came down the porch steps and Duke did his usual welcome-home dance. 'Mina didn't even get to the hospital. She had the baby in her own mother and father's bed. Her water broke in the dining room and it was a mess. Really disgusting.' She came over to me and stood nose to nose. 'I saw the baby before you,' she said triumphantly.

We all hurried to the Pascalis' with Bridie in the lead giving us a vivid moment-to-moment description of the day.

'She popped that baby out as easy as shelling peas. Her sister, Angie, fainted. Imagine trying to get big old Angie up off the floor! Cripes, she must weigh a thousand pounds.' Bridie had never forgiven Angie for being Mina's maid of honor.

'She's a very pretty girl,' said Mrs Ganis, 'and your father would give you a smack if he heard you talk like that.'

'The baby has black hair, just like me. She even looks like me.' Of all the people the baby could resemble, Mina or Fritz, the Pascalis, Mom or Pop or even me, Bridie, of course, decided the baby looked like her. 'She's got my nose.'

'She's not even related to you,' I said.

'So what?'

'How could she look like you?'

'Nature's real funny, isn't it?' She didn't want to talk about it anymore so she ran ahead of us.

'She's my niece!' I yelled.

'Who cares?' she said as she ran up the steps of the Pascali house. 'She still looks like me.'

Mrs Pascali hugged me so hard it hurt. She hugged Mr and Mrs Ganis and everybody started to cry and laugh at the same time. The Pascalis looked as though they had just been handed the moon.

'Such a beautiful baby,' said Mrs Pascali through her tears.

'She looks just like Mina when she was a baby.' Mr Pascali was leading us upstairs. 'Perfect.' He opened the bedroom door. 'You two got company.'

Mina, looking tired and flushed, was lying in bed holding a tiny bundle.

'Darling, are you all right?' said Mrs Ganis as she pushed past the rest of us and went to the bedside. 'You look so beautiful.' She leaned over and kissed Mina and looked at the baby. 'Oh my God, she's beautiful.'

'I've seen her already,' Bridie reminded me.

'We won't stay long,' said Mr Ganis as he went to Mina. 'You must be so tired.' He touched her shoulder and gently moved the blanket away from the baby's face. 'Now that's some baby! Her daddy will be one proud GI Joe.'

'Finn, aren't you going to look at your niece?' Mina smiled and held out her hand. I wasn't too anxious to see my brother's baby on the off chance she'd look at me and somehow know I was hiding in the dark listening to her conception. It had been on my mind quite a bit as the actual birth approached. Would I have some kind of special attachment or would the baby instinctively know and resent me? Hers was the only conception I was connected with except for my own and I remembered none of the details of that.

'This is your Uncle Finn.' Mina positioned the baby so I could get a good look at her. I didn't know what everyone was making such a fuss about, she wasn't pretty at all. She looked red and sore and her skin was like bread dough with indentations for features and a fringe of dark hair. She was like one of those dolls with a shrunken apple for a head.

'She's beautiful,' I lied, wondering if everyone else had lied, too.

'Now, I think mother and baby should get some sleep,' said Mr Pascali, and we all started downstairs.

'Don't you think she looks like me?' asked Bridie.

'Exactly.' I suddenly realized someone was missing. 'Where's Pop?'

'We don't know. We called the railroad but they said he took the day off. He still doesn't know he's a grandfather. Maybe he went to visit your mother?' Mrs Pascali was helping Angie put food on the dining-room table.

'Maybe,' I said, but I thought he was more likely visiting Josie Cleary.

That night, when he came home and was told about the baby, he was so happy he stood by the kitchen sink and cried uncontrollably, repeating Mom and Fritz's names over and over again, but he never offered an explanation as to where he had been all day.

'I baptize you in the name of the Father, the Son and the Holy Ghost.' Father Boyle poured the water on the baby's head and she didn't even wake up. 'Mary Theresa Finnegan.' Since there was no Saint Mae, the baby was named Mary, like Mom, and the plan was to call her Little Mae. But with Fritz overseas and Mina living with her parents, Mary, quite unintentionally, became Maria, and she was Maria Finnegan, a very suitable name as far as I was concerned, for the rest of her life. Angie Pascali and I were destined to stand side by side in Our Lady of Perpetual Help, the fat lady and the skinny cripple, and we finally did when Mina and Fritz asked us to be godparents. Mina told us she and Fritz had wanted us from the time they knew she was pregnant. I wasn't really old enough but Father Boyle made an exception because of the war. Bridie was certain, when she heard I was to be godfather, that she would be asked to be godmother but once again Angie Pascali had stolen her thunder and she was furious and sulked all through the service. Pop and the Ganises stood at the back of the church at the baptismal font with Laurie and Kitty Neal, the Pascalis and Mina, and scattered about the church were the regulars, Mrs Farrell, Mrs del Fiore and little Mrs Donatelli. We all witnessed as little Mary Theresa was absolved of the hideous stigma of original sin and was initiated as a soldier in the army of Christ. Now, if she died, she would be welcomed into heaven by God and the Blessed Virgin and all the saints, by cherubim and seraphim and all the other angels in the celestial hierarchy. But if she died and Father Boyle hadn't dribbled that water on her head she'd go straight to Limbo, for something she didn't do, and wait out eternity with all the other lost souls. It didn't make a bit of sense to me.

That summer, the war news was all about General Eisenhower in the European Theatre of Operations and General MacArthur in the Pacific, about B-17 Flying Fortresses and about the fall of the Fascist government in Italy. The Japanese offensive ended and the Red Army was on the counterattack. Once in a while we'd get a letter from Fritz but most of it was blocked out by the censors. They obviously thought the Finnegans were part of a spy ring and didn't want any information getting into enemy hands. We did know from the letters that he received news of the baby's birth and he loved and missed us all. Like the rest of the world, things were changing at home, too. Frank Shultz was the first boy from Livery Street to be killed. The gold star went up in the window right next-door but we were all tolerating death a little better and it didn't seem nearly as shocking as Mario Pascali's death had been. His body was shipped home and there was a high mass for his funeral and a proper military burial in Our Lady of Perpetual Help cemetery. Mrs Shultz, whom Bridie and I had kept company the day her sons, Frank and Will, went off to the service, visited the grave site every day and, before long, made a point of visiting every grave flying the small American flag. She spent whole mornings with the dead, talking to boys she had never even met when they were alive.

There were other changes at home, not quite as dramatic as death but equally as permanent. The Benlights moved away for ever. We would never again have poor Celeste, sitting on the front porch, jerking through her violent spasms, scaring the hell out of us. A couple in their mid-forties, Mr and Mrs Wilson, moved in and never had anything to do with anyone in the neighborhood. They were so similar in every way they even looked alike. They both wore glasses, had short light hair and dressed in clothes that were always freshly pressed and starched. Bridie swore they were brother and sister and for all anyone knew she may have been right. As unsociable as they were, they did have a profound effect on Livery Street. They were the beginning of a slow but steady stream of newcomers, people with whom the rest of us had no history and people who had no interest in assimilating. They minded their own business and didn't seem to be in the least interested in anyone else's. Although we weren't aware of it, it was the beginning of what, over the next few decades, would end the communal consciousness known as the neighborhood.

It was also the summer when more and more older and less fit men were finding ways to go into the service, when every day something new was rationed and when everyone was singing 'Coming in on a Wing and a Prayer' and 'Mairzy Doats'. In August, Simon was wounded and sent back to the States to a veterans' hospital in upstate New York, where, in spite of their best efforts and the latest medical technology, they couldn't save his left eye. Later that year he was released from military duty on a medical discharge and came home to live with us.

Every weekend Pop and I went to Franklin Village, almost always with a third party in tow. Bridie or Mrs Ganis or Laurie and, once, we even picked up Mr Howe and took him to visit Mom. Mr Ganis wouldn't go. Mrs Ganis said the thought of Mom being so lost and alone broke his heart. I was on friendly terms with Miss Webster, the nurse with the birthmark, and every time I saw crazy Mildred she'd try to assert her make-believe authority by insisting I go to building B, for boys. Occasionally, Pop would have a conference with the doctors and they always said Mom was making progress and they expected a breakthrough anytime. They never mentioned anything about her being released. She was like a prisoner with a life sentence that nobody wanted to talk about. Even though she didn't say anything, I was certain Mom knew who we were. Sometimes she'd look at me and there was something in her eyes, a look of collusion, as though we were sharing a secret. And sometimes I had the feeling she was asking why we weren't taking her home. No matter what anyone said, I was sure she was aware of something. The day Mr Howe visited she actually brightened when she saw him and any mention of Duke brought an almost imperceptible smile to her lips. But the biggest change was her appearance. She wasn't letting them do silly things like put bows in her hair, and for some reason she started to look more like a person in control.

That year, Bridie and I had the best beach summer ever. Both

Laurie and Kitty Neal worked nights and whenever they could get the gas we all went down the shore. If the sun wasn't too hot, Mina and Maria went with us and by the end of the summer Maria's fat little arms and legs were a soft, tawny brown. We walked the boardwalk at Seaside Heights and Bridie flirted with the soldiers and sailors, considering it her patriotic duty to talk to every single one of our men in service. Sometimes she'd embarrass us by assuming a ridiculous kind of piety and telling them she was praying for them. When I told her she was making a fool of herself she was quick to remind me of her special relationship with the Blessed Virgin and said her prayers almost certainly assured the safety of our men in uniform. She thought half of them looked like Fritz or Simon, and the rest like Clark Gable or Jimmy Stewart. I thought most of them looked like high-school kids playing soldier. By the end of June, Laurie and Kitty, our relationship was on a first-name basis by then, had been seeing each other for nine months, ever since Kitty and Mattie Horn had helped Bridie and me get Laurie up out of the dust in front of the icehouse on Allen Street. Laurie hadn't had a single drink since then and both he and Bridie credited Kitty with his salvation. If Bridie felt at all replaced, the peace of mind she enjoyed as a result of Laurie's sobriety more than compensated for any loss. And Bridie truly liked Kitty. She was gentle and dependable and willing to share herself, with no strings attached. Kitty wasn't as classically beautiful as Josie Cleary, who Bridie had thought would be a good wife for Laurie and mother for her, but she was pretty in her own freckled, frizzy red-haired way. She was big-boned and rangy and her eyes were almost as green as Bridie's. The neighbors were happy that Laurie and Kitty were 'keeping steady company', despite the fact that some were scandalized by her coming and going at all hours. Everyone knew a man simply wasn't capable of raising a child by himself and Laurie had been trying long enough. It was time there was a woman in his life. Even Mrs Cavanaugh admitted Laurie showed good sense 'fooling around with his own kind instead of some wop or Jew or other dirty foreigner. Never mind that a woman who'd come out of a man's house in the wee hours of the morning is a whore. At least, she's an Irish whore.'

By some miracle I managed to keep the existence of Rebecca a secret from Bridie until midsummer. Rebecca and I had started writing to one another and I had to hide her letters. But on a particularly hot and sticky July day, when we were taking turns with Mr Howe cranking the ice-cream maker, he accidentally mentioned Rebecca and she was no longer a secret. It wasn't a breach of a confidence. When I told him all about her, right after the trip to Philadelphia with the Ganises, it never occurred to me to swear him to secrecy.

'I was thinking about your little friend, Rebecca.' We were sitting on the porch in the shade of an old, broken trellis thick with morning-glory vines and Mr Howe was pouring us more iced tea.

'Who's Rebecca?' Bridie was glistening with sweat from the cranking. Mr Howe knew right away he had said the wrong thing and looked at me apologetically.

'Somebody I met in Philadelphia with Mr and Mrs Ganis.'

'How come you never told me about her?'

'I guess I forgot.'

'You told Mr Howe.'

'Yeah, I guess I mentioned it.'

'Well, who is she?' She stopped cranking and was looking me hard in the eye.

'I'm going to get some more ice.' Mr Howe slipped quickly into the kitchen.

'Her grandfather is Mr Steinman. He worked with Mr Ganis in the jewelry business. I told you we had lunch with the Steinmans.'

'You never said anything about this Rebecca. How come?'

'I told you, I forgot. Crank the ice cream or it will never get done.'

'You crank the damn ice cream.' She went to the steps and sat in the full sun with her back to me. 'I tell you everything.' That was true, Bridie did tell me everything whether I wanted to know it or not. If I had been able to explain why I wanted to keep Rebecca a mystery it would have been easier but I honestly didn't know why. And only a mystery as far as Bridie was concerned. I couldn't think of anything to say so we sat in silence for a few minutes while Duke, who was sprawled in the deepest part of the shade, mistook the silence for his turn to contribute and started banging his tail against the floor.

'She has an accent,' I said finally, as I took over cranking.

'An accent! What is she for cripes' sake?'

'She lived in Germany.'

'A Nazi!'

'No, she's not a Nazi. What's the matter with you?'

'Does she talk funny?'

'She has an accent. That's all.'

'How old is she?'

'Like us.'

'Is she pretty?'

'I guess.' I knew what the next question would be.

'Is she prettier than me?'

'No,' I said automatically. 'Anyway, she's different from you.'

'What color are her eyes?'

'Dark brown.'

'You know what color her eyes are and you didn't even think to tell me about her! I think you stink.'

'God! I'll tell you anything you want to know. What?'

Mr Howe came out of the house and sat quietly listening as Bridie asked every detail of my afternoon with Rebecca right down to a description of the dress she was wearing.

'Terrible for a little girl not to know if her mother and father are dead or alive,' said Mr Howe as he lit his pipe. 'Just terrible.'

'Did she pick up that cat's head with her bare hands?' asked Bridie after a moment.

'She didn't say. Maybe she used the handkerchief.' The cranking was getting harder and harder as the ice cream stiffened in the can.

'That's disgusting.'

'It was a caring thing for her to do, burying the poor cat's head. Things like that say a lot about a person.' Mr Howe was puffing thoughtfully, trying to keep his pipe lit. 'That ice cream should be about ready.'

'You can't marry her you know,' said Bridie out of the blue. 'You're a Catholic.'

'Marry her! Are you nuts or something?'

'She's Jewish. Jewish and Catholic shouldn't get married.'

'I think it's a mite soon for Finn to worry about getting married,' said Mr Howe. 'He's got a few years to think about it.'

'She's crazy.'

'Well, you can't. The Pope won't let you.'

'If I wanted to, I could. Pope or no Pope.'

'It's a mortal sin to talk nasty about the Pope like that.'

'Now, let's not start going on about sin,' said Mr Howe as he picked up the ice-cream bucket and started into the house. 'That's a subject we'd best leave alone.'

'You thought it was okay for Josie Cleary to divorce her husband and marry Laurie. And Josie Cleary's a Catholic and we can't get divorced.' I thought I had her with that argument but I should have known better.

'That's different.'

'How?' I asked.

'Well, if you don't know, I'm certainly not going to tell you.' She went into the house and I followed.

The subject of my mixed marriage to Rebecca was dropped as Mr Howe dished out the delicious ice cream. We never gave it time to mellow because as far as we were concerned time couldn't improve on perfection, and maple ice cream, Mr Howe's specialty, was about as perfect as anything could ever be.

'Maybe he shouldn't have gone back,' said Bridie, licking the back of her spoon.

'Who?'

'Rebecca's father. Maybe he shouldn't have left her and gone back to Germany.'

'I reckon he had to,' said Mr Howe. 'His wife is there and he wanted to get her out. A man can't desert his family when they need him, you know.'

'I guess not.' Bridie helped herself to some more ice cream.

A vision of Mom sitting alone and abandoned on that cold, bare sun porch flashed into my mind and although I had no idea it was happening the plan for her liberation was starting to gestate.

We heard about Simon being wounded from his cousin in Trenton. One night, when Bridie and I were doing the dishes, Pop answered the phone and we knew right away, from the tone of his voice, something was wrong. After he hung up he sat for a minute with his head in his hands and I thought something terrible had happened to Mom or Fritz.

'What's wrong?' Bridie leaned against Pop as she always did in her private moments with people.

'Goddamn it,' he stood up and started pacing. 'Simon's been hurt. He's coming home.'

'How bad?' I asked.

Pop put his hand on my shoulder. 'I don't know. His cousin said he'd call as soon as he knew any of the details. Goddamn it!'

'He's going to die, isn't he?' Bridie started crying.

'No, he's not going to die. He's wounded and that's all we know. Let's not borrow trouble.' He sat at the kitchen table and cradled Bridie in his arms. 'Finn, pour me a little Irish, please.' As I poured the whiskey he rocked Bridie, who was sobbing uncontrollably. 'Hey, Joe Louis, I thought you were tougher than this. Christ, Christ, Christ!' he said angrily. 'He's just a kid.' He drank the whiskey. 'I wonder if Fritz knows?'

It was weeks before we heard from the cousin again and discovered that Simon had been sent to a hospital in upstate

New York. Bridie and I were too young to visit but we talked with him on the phone and when we asked about his wounds he dismissed them by jokingly saying he had been hit by a bus. Bridie wrote almost every day and I sent him drawings of everybody and he graciously said he recognized the faces. Even though it was a long trip, Pop and Laurie went to see him a few times in the months before he was released. Pop described Simon's condition to us, but first he made it very clear that he was going to get well and be 'damn near as good as new'. Then he told us he lost his left eye and had a scar from his temple down to the corner of his mouth. He had other scars up and down the left side of his body and, after Bridie had gone home and Pop and I were alone, he told me Simon almost lost his left testicle but the doctors were able to save it. Pop's assurance that Simon would be all right did nothing to dispel a grotesque vision, like some Frankenstein monster in an army uniform, and when he told me Simon was going to come and live with us after he was discharged, I imagined a hunchback dragging his foot around our house, hiding in the shadows. Blind would have been one thing but the doctors had actually removed his eye and left a hole in his face. I couldn't confide my fears to anyone, especially Bridie, who had romanticized Simon's wounds and saw herself as the star of some wartime drama in which she was the heroic and stoic woman on the home front awaiting the return of her stalwart and battered man. From late August, when we heard about Simon, until December, when he came to live with us, I had horrible nightmares, born of guilt, in which I was running away from a monster who was asking me to help him, and everyone I knew, including Duke, was pointing a finger at me and telling me I should be ashamed of myself.

Even with Kitty in the picture, the question of Laurie's sex life, whether he actually 'did sex', as Bridie put it, was still un-answered as far as she was concerned. I had never told her that Tessie's Place was a whorehouse because, even though she

166

thought she was an expert on all things sexual, I didn't want to have to explain, in the vivid detail I knew she would demand, what a whorehouse was. I didn't really know that much about it anyway. Plus the fact that she knew Pop had been drinking at Tessie's with Josie Cleary and I didn't want to discuss that with anyone, not even Bridie. I assumed Laurie and Kitty were doing it and was shocked at Bridie's reaction when I said so.

'Why do you think that?'

'They're grown-ups and they're together all the time and –'

'She's a nurse, for cripes' sake. They're like nuns. They don't do it.' This was why Bridie wasn't threatened by Kitty Neal. She was absolutely blind to the relationship that had developed between Laurie and Kitty. As far as she was concerned Kitty was a caretaker, someone to look after Laurie and keep him sober but someone who could never, under any circumstances, become an intimate part of his life or replace her in any way.

'Nurses do so do it. Everybody does it. God!'

'How do you know so much?'

'Laurie and Kitty are together all the time. They're like Mina and Fritz. Anybody can see that. It's been almost a year.'

'They never talk about getting married like Mina and Fritz did.' That was true. There was never any discussion of marriage that we knew of.

'Maybe they do. Maybe they talk about it in private.'

'He'd tell me. Laurie and me don't keep secrets. Ever.'

'This is different. Kitty is a lady and ladies and men have their own secrets.'

'Shut up. You don't know anything. You can't even talk to Big Finn.' Bridie never minded resorting to cruelty to make a point. 'I don't want to talk about it anymore.'

'You started it.'

'Go to hell!'

'You, too.' I hoped that would be the end of it but I knew better.

Very early on a sweltering Sunday morning, when Pop was

still asleep and I was in the kitchen making his coffee, Bridie came running into the house in her faded old nightgown, all flushed and breathless.

'Come on. Hurry up, I want to show you something.'

'What?'

'Just come on, damn it.'

'Wait a minute, I have to put my brace on.'

'Forget the damn brace. It makes too much noise anyway.' She grabbed me by the hand and we ran across the empty street and started up her front steps. She motioned to me to be quiet as we crept up the stairs into the house and tiptoed our way to the second floor, along the hall, until we got to the front bedroom. All the time I had this frightening feeling she was going to show me something grisly, like a murdered body. The door was open a crack and Bridie peeked in. She turned to me and motioned once again to be quiet, then very slowly pushed the door open a bit more so we could both look into the room, and there were Kitty and Laurie, sound asleep, lying naked and uncovered on the stark white sheets. The room had a strange yellow glow from the morning sun coming through the window shades and, for some reason, the bed seemed to be floating a few inches off the floor. Kitty was on her back and Laurie was on his left side, facing away from us, and they both looked moist from the heat. He was snoring lightly and she was taking the long slow breaths of a deep sleep. Her right forearm was across her eyes and her kinky red hair was loose and covered the pillow. Naked, without anything to interfere with the lines of their bodies, they looked enormously elongated, as though some-one had stretched and re-molded them into lithe giants. Their skin, except where they had been covered by swimsuits, was the soft rosy beige the Irish call a tan. Kitty had a triangle of darker red hair between her legs, which seemed almost impertinent, like the wispy tuft in her exposed armpit. Her breasts were slightly flattened and her small, clearly defined nipples were the most tender, most private pink and I wanted to go to her and touch them. In contrast, Laurie's body had more visible bones and muscles and, with one foot shyly crossing the other, he reminded me of the long supple bodies, pale and vulnerable, of all the Christs I had seen on all the crosses. After the initial shock, there was nothing peculiar about seeing them lying there and I wanted to see them do something. I had no idea what Bridie was thinking but I wanted Laurie and Kitty to do everything I heard Fritz and Mina do in the dark. I wanted to see what caused all the moaning and sighing. Bridie stood there staring, her jaw set and her lips narrow and mean. Just then, Laurie exhaled loudly and rolled on to his back, exposing a huge erection, and for the first time I had the feeling we were watching something forbidden and personal and we should close our eyes and get out of there. I had seen Fritz with an erection and, having had nothing to compare it to, was very impressed. But this display of Laurie's was downright extraordinary.

'Well, for cripes' sake,' said Bridie in a whisper. 'Look at that thing.' Laurie's hand started moving toward Kitty and slowly slid across her belly until his fingers rested in her tangle of hair and I was scared to death I was going to get my wish and see them make love so I grabbed Bridie's hand and the two of us raced down the hall and steps and out the front door without making a sound. We ran down the alley and sat on her back porch, not looking at each other for a very long time. For a change, even Bridie was speechless. I didn't know what to say. I felt exhilarated but I couldn't tell if she was angry, amazed, embarrassed or all three.

'I guess you don't have to wonder anymore,' I said after I caught my breath.

'I hate them.'

'Well, what'd you expect?'

'They're disgusting. They make me sick.'

'You shouldn't have looked.'

'Well, you looked.'

'You made me look. You dragged me across the street like the house was on fire. I never would have known if you hadn't done that.'

'I hate them. She's a nurse, for cripes' sake. God will punish her.'

'I told you, a nurse isn't like a nun.' I knew I was wasting my time trying to reason with her.

'You don't know anything.' She started chipping at the peeling paint on the porch. 'And she's got ugly red hair down there.'

'Well of course she does. I thought you knew everything.'

'I do. But it's still ugly. I hate her and I hate him. I never want to see either one of them again.'

'Just pretend it didn't happen.'

'He doesn't care about me. I hate him.'

'I have to feed Duke. You going to eight o'clock mass?' She nodded. 'I'll see you later.' I started out of the yard and she stopped me.

'I just want to know one thing.'

'What?'

'What does Laurie do with that big old thing when he's got his clothes on? I mean, where does he put it?' So much for Bridie's sexual expertise. I didn't even try to answer her because I knew I would have been there all day.

For the next few weeks, Bridie spent most of her time at our house having as little to do with Laurie and Kitty as possible. Whenever we were alone she talked of nothing but seeing them lying naked in that bed even though she said she hated thinking about it. The whole idea of sex was downright disgusting to her, not to mention a sure-fire ticket to hell, especially in the case of two people who weren't married and didn't even talk about getting married. She calculated it as a double mortal sin, which was so grave nothing short of swimming to Italy and crawling to the Vatican on their hands and knees would earn them absolution. Sin was a big question mark to me. Of course, I believed in the important ones like murder, stealing, and cruelty to animals.

I knew there wasn't a commandment Thou Shalt Not Be Cruel To Animals but I thought it was such an obvious and serious sin, there didn't have to be. But sex was another matter. If beautiful little Mary Theresa Finnegan could be the result of Mina and Fritz committing a mortal sin then something was wrong somewhere. It just didn't seem that sex and sin were always one and the same. Once, when Fritz thought I was asleep and I caught him playing with himself, I accused him of committing a sin and he put me straight on that particular activity. He said he had always thought it was a sin, too, until he had his first wet dream and realized that if he didn't do it, it was going to happen anyway while he was asleep, so it was natural and there was nothing wrong with it and a person might just as well be awake to enjoy it. That made perfect sense to me and I was still waiting for my first wet dream and my license to endless nights of solitary pleasure.

The relationship between Bridie and Laurie, with all its enviable candor and honesty, was in serious trouble and Laurie had no idea why. Not only was Bridie not confiding in him, she was barely talking to him.

'Do you have any idea what's going on, Finn?' I was cleaning the pigeon coop and Laurie was leaning on the flyway. Out and out lying was also on my list of real sins so I didn't know what to say. I shrugged off the question with an unintelligible grunt, hoping that might satisfy him. 'I've never seen the likes of it. And it's not only something I've done. She's rude to Kitty, too. I thought she liked Kitty.' He waited for some comment but I busied myself raking up the floor. 'She does, doesn't she?'

'Well,' was all I could come up with.

'Finn, be a good lad and tell me what's going on. I know you know, so there's no point in pretending you don't.'

'I can't.'

'I thought we were friends.'

'I just can't.'

'Finn, I need your help. Please.'

'She'll kill me.'

'I won't tell her. I promise. I just have to know.'

'You're going to be mad.'

'I promise you on me mother's grave, I won't be mad. So, you can put that out of your mind. Now, what the hell is going on?'

'Well,' I was embarrassed and didn't quite know how to say it. 'She saw you and Kitty in bed naked,' I blurted out.

Laurie went pale and breathless and walked around in a complete circle. 'Jesus, Mary and Joseph, I was afraid of that. And us always being that careful. Shit.'

'I saw you, too.' I thought I'd better say it because he was bound to find out sooner or later.

'You saw us! How?'

'She came over and got me.'

'Christ, I'm lucky she didn't sell tickets.' He walked down past the vegetable garden to the chicken coop and turned around and came back, shaking his head and mumbling to himself. I was afraid he was going to start asking details of what we saw and I wouldn't know what to say. 'This is a wee bit embarrassing, I must say.'

'Oh that's okay,' I said, magnanimously giving him permission to forget the whole incident if he wanted to.

'So, Finn, what do you think?' What did I think about what? Was I supposed to say I was shocked or was I supposed to congratulate him?

'Well . . .'

'I ask you, is it such a terrible thing for a man to love a woman?'

'No,' I said. 'It's not terrible at all.' It was a question I could answer without thinking twice.

'I love Kitty Neal. She's a wonderful woman and I thank God every day that she came along. If it wasn't for her I'd be lying in me grave. And that's the God's truth and you know it as sure as you're standing there.'

'Yeah, she's nice.'

'I know it's not right, what with Kitty and me not being married and all, but sometimes things aren't easy. Someday, maybe, with the help of God.' He paced a bit then stood looking at the pigeons. 'You've beautiful birds here and you keep them nice, too. What do you do with all the shit when you've collected it?'

'We have a compost heap.'

'That's good.' He looked at the ground. 'A man can't always have things the way he wants them. Life don't work that way, now does it?'

'I guess not.' I didn't know what he was talking about.

'And a man has needs, too. You're a man, Finn, you understand these things better than Bridie.' I didn't really understand anything but he called me a man and suddenly I thought I did. 'We've been too close, her and me. Just too damn close. I never thought that could be a bad thing between a father and daughter but maybe I was wrong. God knows I've given her more than her share of troubles, and her being so young, and I'm sorry for that. Truly, if regrets were nickels I'd be a millionaire. But things were going good for us and now she won't even talk to me. Oh shit. What am I going to do? I'm at the end of me rope.' I didn't think he was actually asking my advice but he was. 'You know her better than anyone. What would you do if you were me?' All I could think of was Mr Howe. What would he have said if Laurie asked him that question?

'I think you should tell her what you just told me. I mean, how you love Kitty and how things aren't easy and that stuff.'

'You're right on the button.' His pale eyes brightened. 'We've never talked about Kitty, her and me, and I think maybe it's time. I won't say anything about knowing she saw us in our birthday suits like that.'

'Yeah, that's a good idea.' Bridie would have a fit if she found out I told Laurie.

'Thank you, Finn. I'll do just that. We'll keep this between us.'

'And don't tell Kitty, okay?' If I knew that she knew I saw her naked I'd never be able to look her in the eye again.

'Oh no. She'd die of shame if she knew. She's a sweet, shy thing, Kitty. Mum's the word as far as the women are concerned, you can bet on that. Thank you, Finn.' He started out of the yard and stopped at the gate. 'Kitty's a grand-looking woman, isn't she, boy?' He winked and smiled and left the yard, closing the gate behind him.

I don't know what Laurie told Bridie or if he ever even spoke to her because she never said a word about it. She did stop talking about seeing Kitty and Laurie naked so I assumed something had been said. But if Laurie took my advice and told Bridie the things he had told me at the pigeon coop, it didn't work. In December, when Simon came home, she and Laurie were still at odds.

Bridie and I went with Pop the day he picked up Simon at the veterans' hospital. The sky was gray and heavy with snow but all the way there and back we only ran into a few flurries. Billboards had Santa, with his arm around some well-scrubbed soldier, sailor or marine, selling us everything from Lucky Strikes cigarettes to Lifebuoy soap. It was a long trip and I got sick twice before we got there.

'You must be coming down with something.' Pop pulled over to the side of road for a second time and I threw up. 'You never get carsick.'

'I'll be all right.' My sickness had nothing to do with the car. I was afraid of what I might do when I saw Simon, afraid the very sight of his scarred, eyeless face would make me run away and make a fool of myself.

'It's cause you didn't eat any breakfast or lunch.' Bridie had a diagnosis for everything and most illnesses could be traced to food or the lack of food.

'I wasn't hungry and it's none of your damn business.' I hated her for approaching this whole scary incident as though she was going to the county fair.

'Now, don't you two start. Just get in the car.'

She sat in the back seat with me and after a few miles she reached over and held my hand. 'You still feel sick?'

'I'm okay.'

'I'm sorry,' she said after a moment, then put her head back and stared straight ahead and never said another word until we arrived at the hospital. Since she and Laurie had become estranged she was much nicer to me. All the warmth and concern, usually directed at Laurie, needed an outlet and I was the most convenient recipient. Also I was the next closest person in her life and she couldn't afford to lose me, too.

We sat in the waiting room while Pop went to help Simon with his things. There was a large Christmas tree decorated with strings of cranberries and popcorn and hundreds of greeting cards tied on with red ribbon. Crudely made wreaths hung in all the windows and garlands of pine boughs framed the doors. Bridie, frantic with anticipation, wandered around the room interrupting conversations to tell everyone we were there to take her one-eyed friend, Simon, home. I went to the bathroom several times just to get away from her. It seemed like Pop was gone for hours when the double doors opened and he walked through with Simon. Bridie ran to him without hesitation and he picked her up and they hugged and kissed but I couldn't take a step in his direction. When finally he stood still long enough for me to get a good look, I saw Simon, a little taller and thinner than I remembered, and maybe a little older, but it was just Simon, with a black patch over his eye and a thin red scar enlarging his already incredibly broad smile. He didn't look like a monster at all. There was nothing frightening or threatening about him. I was so relieved I almost wet my pants. Pop, who was carrying Simon's duffel bag, motioned for me to go to them. Simon put Bridie down and stood looking at me for a moment, as uncertain of my reaction as I had been. I went to him with my hand extended but he didn't take it. Instead, he knelt down and put his arms around me and held me very tight and said it was a hug from Fritz. I tried to hold back my tears but I couldn't. I was overwhelmingly happy to see Simon and I started crying so hard I don't remember anything but Pop carrying me out of the hospital to the car.

If Simon moved in with us because he needed a family, he chose a family that needed him even more. For Pop and I, it was almost like having Fritz back in the house and he did his best to be both older son and older brother. Without knowing it, he eased tensions between Pop and me and, all in all, things were much more pleasant. Never once did I forget that Mom and Fritz were gone but having Simon in the house helped fill the empty spaces. Bridie, who had always considered Simon her personal property because she was the one who had found him standing alone, waiting for the bus to Fort Dix, needed someone to replace Laurie who had, in her eyes, defected to the enemy. For her he was a combination of many things; father, friend and grown-up boyfriend, and if the burden was too much for any one man to carry, she didn't care. Even Mom was affected by his return. It may only have been coincidence but the first startling change happened right after Simon came home.

We had fixed up the little front room with new curtains and a new bedspread but Simon said he didn't like to be alone at night and asked if I would mind sharing my room. I was delighted. I had never gotten used to being alone. The first few nights we talked almost until dawn and I discovered that, like Fritz, Simon was a much better listener than talker. I told him everything that had happened to all of us since he and Fritz went overseas, in the most minute detail, and only stopped talking when I heard the faintest trace of a snore from across the room. Duke went from one bed to the other, tortured by his divided loyalties until finally, out of sheer habit, he settled down with me. Those first few nights, the mere presence of another body in my room was so comforting, so familiar and reassuring, I went to sleep feeling as safe and secure as I always had when Fritz was there.

Maybe Simon talked about the war and being wounded to Pop but he never did with me. He did joke about his scars and the patch and called them souvenirs from his trip abroad. As far as any information about Fritz was concerned, Simon didn't seem to know anything because he didn't remember any of the details of his being wounded. He was certain Fritz was fine, but that was all he'd say. He was interested in getting on with his life and his new job at the water company. Young men, even one-eyed young men, were at a premium and Big Tum, who had worked for the water company for so many years before his retirement, arranged for Simon to interview for a job and he was hired before the interview was over. He worked the same hours as Pop and made almost as much money, a portion of which he happily contributed to the running of the household. Dinner was waiting for Pop and Simon every night when they came home, and the three of us and Bridie, of course, fell easily into a comfortable routine. Mina and Maria visited several nights a week and we all took turns spoiling Maria, who was happy, darkly pretty and irresistible. Sometimes Pop and Simon would go to the Alley for a beer or maybe stop by and see Laurie at the Prussian Inn, but usually they listened to the war news on the radio and went to bed early. Except for the occasional Saturday or Sunday, when Pop took the car and went off by himself, he and Simon were almost inseparable. This was the first real family Simon ever had.

Crazy Mildred was very partial to Simon and if he had merely nodded in her direction I was sure she would have forgotten the toothless Teddy in a minute. Because of his eye patch and scar, she kept trying to get him to go to the men's ward, and only after weeks of insisting that he was a visitor did she decide to go along with his lie and not expose him for the patient he really was. It was Simon who actually got the first true response from Mom. One afternoon when we were visiting her, we were sitting on the sun porch in the women's building and Bridie was dominating the conversation with boring gossip about the kids in the sixth grade, especially her arch enemy, Frances Peart, who had little buds of breasts and was the envy of every girl in the class. Mom seemed to be listening and actually smiled when Bridie said something funny. Miss Webster was talking to Pop in her office, so it was just Simon, Mrs Ganis, Bridie and me. Simon casually asked Mom to take a walk with him and offered his arm and, as simply as if she had been doing it every day, she stood up and took it and they walked around the sun porch. Mrs Ganis slapped her hand over Bridie's mouth just as she was about to say something and break the spell and we all stood in stunned silence as Mom and Simon slowly circled the room. She didn't seem to be any more in touch than usual but she wasn't talking to her shadow people and she did follow Simon's lead.

'She heard you,' said Mrs Ganis. 'God in heaven, she heard you.'

'Mom?' She didn't pay any attention to me.

Pop and Miss Webster came into the room as Mom and Simon started around again. 'Jesus Christ!'

'The first time,' said Mrs Ganis. 'The first time in over a year she heard somebody.'

'Mae?' Pop went to her but she walked past as if he was invisible.

'We shouldn't get our hopes up.' Miss Webster was pleasantly cautious.

'Why not?' said Mrs Ganis. 'Simon asked her to take a walk and she did. That's a wonderful thing to happen, isn't it?'

'Mrs Finn? It's me, Bridie. How you doing?' Bridie took her hand and joined them for their walk around the sun porch.

'Who gave you permission to do that?' Mildred was standing in the doorway, hands on her hips and an officious scowl on her face. 'No one asked my permission.'

'That's enough, Mildred. You go back to minding your own business.'

'But it's my job to keep everything in order, Miss Webster. It's my job.' Mildred started to pout.

'I know,' said Miss Webster, 'but I'll handle this if you don't mind.'

'I love you. You're my favorite. All the other nurses are mean. Really mean. Goddamn sons of bitches.' She smiled sweetly. 'Everybody likes you, though.'

'Thank you, Mildred. Now, go about your business.' Miss Webster turned back to Mom and Mildred stuck out her tongue before slipping away down the hall.

'She stuck her tongue at you.' Bridie wouldn't let Mildred get away with anything.

'What does that mean, her getting up and walking like that?' asked Pop.

'I don't know. You'll have to talk to the doctor.'

'Can she come home?' I asked.

'No, Finn, I'm sorry. We'll have to wait and see about that. But you shouldn't get your hopes up. This is only one response.'

'It's a beginning, darling,' said Mrs Ganis. 'And we'll all keep our hopes up.'

'We have to be realistic about these things.' It was Miss Webster's quiet, smiling admonition of Mrs Ganis.

'Like hell we do,' Mrs Ganis smiled back.

'I'll talk to Dr Lorman.' Pop went to Mom and put his arms around her. She didn't push him away but she didn't seem to react at all. She just stood there, letting him hold her. Mrs Ganis and Simon took Bridie and me into the hall and Miss Webster went back to her office.

Riding home, Bridie and I made plans for the party we'd have for Mom when she was released from the hospital. Pop reminded us to be sensible and 'keep our feet on the damn ground' but there was something in his voice, a kind of energy, which I hadn't heard for a long time, and I knew he was almost as hopeful as us.

'I don't know how you did it, Simon, but you did it.' Pop was smiling almost as broadly as Simon.

When we turned into Livery Street, we knew right away that

something was wrong. Mr Ganis and Laurie were sitting on our front porch and Mr Pascali and Big Tum were leaning on the banister, talking to them.

'Something's up,' said Pop as we pulled in front of the house. Simon jumped out of the car and went to the men.

'Maybe you should wait a minute.' Mrs Ganis tried to restrain Bridie and me but we opened the door and ran to the porch.

'I think we should go inside, Tom.' Laurie opened the front door and they all started in.

'Oh Christ, what is it?' Pop's jaw was tight and he was pale as ash. Bridie and I pushed past everyone and went inside. The house smelled of fresh coffee and the shades were down in the living room and there was a pervasive sense of foreboding. Mina was sitting on the sofa with Little Tum and Mrs Shultz was pacing up and down rocking the baby. When Mina saw Pop she screamed and went to him, burying her face in his chest.

'What's happened to Fritz? Jesus Christ, what's happened to my boy?'

'They delivered the telegram to Mina this afternoon,' said Mr Pascali quietly. 'He's missing in action.'

As far as I was concerned, missing in action only meant Fritz was temporarily misplaced. He would be found and he would be in one piece and there was no other possibility. Masses were said for him and candles were lit and I thought it was all a waste of time because he was merely not where he should have been whenever the army was looking for him. Everyone was reassuring; Simon, Pop, the Ganises and Laurie. Even Mrs Cavanaugh. But I knew in their hearts they didn't really believe there was nothing to worry about. Pop started going to mass with Mina and the Pascalis during the week and his secret weekend trips, which I knew were to visit Josie Cleary, were fewer and further apart. Simon must have felt he had to shoulder more responsibility because he worked even harder at being the perfect son and brother. Several nights, soon after the telegram arrived, I heard him crying when he thought I was asleep. Bridie spent many an afternoon kneeling before her personal good friend, the Blessed Virgin, asking for yet another miracle, even though I told her a miracle wasn't necessary. I was the only one who was absolutely certain that somewhere in Europe the missing Fritz was alive and well, just waiting to be found.

It was almost the last day of school when Charles, the huge black man who had carried Laurie out of Tessie's Place, was standing, obviously ill at ease, with all the mothers collecting their children at three o'clock.

'It's that giant.' Bridie grabbed my arm and stopped me as we started down the front steps. There were only two black kids in all of Our Lady of Perpetual Help grammar school and I knew their parents so I didn't think he was there to meet them.

'I wonder what he wants?'

'Let's go back in school and wait until he's gone.' She started up the stairs.

'Come on. We didn't do anything.' I grabbed her hand and as we went through the heavy iron gate, Charles came to us.

'Tessie wants to see you.' He was nearly as gruff as he had been the last time we saw him.

'We didn't do anything,' said Bridie defensively.

'I didn't say you did, did I? Tessie wants you to come and see her. Now.' He turned away and started up the street.

'Well, for cripes' sake,' said Bridie, 'what's that all about?'

'Let's go see her.'

'No. I don't like that place.'

'Come on. We can see Honey again.' I walked away knowing Bridie would follow. We had only seen him once but we had never lost our fascination with the strange and beguiling Honey and I was sure Bridie would risk everything if there was a chance of seeing him again.

'You think he'll remember us?'

'Why not? We remember him.'

'We're not supposed to go there again. Big Finn will kill us if he finds out.'

'He won't find out.' I hurried to catch up with Charles as Bridie tagged along.

'How come you're so brave all of a sudden?'

'I'm always brave.'

'Like hell,' she said.

'Come on.' The truth was, I had been anxious to go back to Tessie's ever since Fritz told me it was a whorehouse.

Tessie was sitting in one of the big fan-shaped chairs, smoking a cigarette. The window shades were down and the lights were dim and the perfume smell was stronger and sweeter than I remembered. She was dressed in a tight, light brown lace dress, almost the color of her skin, and her hair was piled on top of her head and studded with small white flowers. Her beautiful milk-chocolate face was perfectly made-up and her lips were a moist, glistening, dark red. Another woman, white and younger and not as pretty, with platinum hair and pale, translucent skin, got up and left the room when Charles brought us in. She wore a thin nightgown and wrapper and as she passed us she touched my cheek and smiled and I could see her nipples through the flimsy material.

'That's Iris,' said Tessie. I knew Iris had to be one of the whores, and her touch was positively electric.

'Hi, kids,' she said as she went into the hall.

'That's bad news about your brother,' said Tessie and she took a deep drag on the cigarette.

'He'll be all right, thank you.'

'He is one fine-looking boy. Looks like your daddy.'

'You know Fritz?' He never told me he met Tessie.

'He came in with some friends a few nights before he went in the service.'

'For a drink or what?' I couldn't imagine why Fritz would want to be with another woman when he had Mina to love.

'That's none of your business,' she laughed and started

coughing. 'Sit down, I want to talk to you about something.'
Charles indicated the sofa and Bridie and I sat and I had the
feeling that meeting with Tessie was not unlike an audience with
the Pope. 'You want some ginger ale?'

'Yes, please,' said Bridie who was sitting so close to me she
was practically in my lap. Tessie motioned to Charles and he left
the room.

'How's your daddy?'

'Fine,' said Bridie. 'Sober as a judge.'

'That's what I heard.' Tessie took another drag on the cigarette. 'We lost a damn good customer when that man climbed
up on the wagon, I can tell you.' She laughed a deep throaty
chuckle. 'He still seeing the nurse?'

'You know everything,' said Bridie grudgingly.

'You're right about that, girl.' Tessie turned to me. 'Your
mama's still up at the Village? That's too bad. It must be cutting
your daddy up something terrible inside.' Charles came in with
the ginger ale, saving me from discussing Mom.

'My mother's fine. She'll be home soon,' I lied as I took the
cold glass. 'What do you want to talk to us for?'

'Darlin', you going to be a good businessman. A little small
talk and get right to the point. I like that.' She recrossed her legs
and smoothed her dress. 'It's about Honey. He has never stopped
talking about you two. He likes to drive me crazy. Still. Pestering
me all the time about Bridie and Finn. He gets something in his
mind and he sticks to it like a fly sticks to flypaper. He kept
hoping you'd come back and see him.'

'We wanted to but we couldn't. That's the truth, isn't it,
Finn?'

'We aren't supposed to be here.'

'How come?'

'My father said so.'

'Oh he did did he?'

'Where is Honey?' asked Bridie.

'At the eye doctor with one of the girls. His kind always has bad trouble with their eyes. He's getting new glasses.' She stubbed out her cigarette. 'I want you to play with Honey. Whenever you can. I'll pay you.' It was a flat-out business offer and she leaned forward, waiting for an answer.

'We couldn't take money for that,' I said.

'How much?' asked Bridie.

'Two bits. Every time you come here.'

'How much is two bits?'

'It doesn't matter,' I was trying to stop the transaction. 'We can't take money just to play with somebody.'

'I thought you were a businessman.'

'How much is two bits?' Bridie insisted.

'Twenty-five cents.'

'Twenty-five cents every time! Even if we come seven days a week?'

'That's my offer.'

'We'll do it.'

'No, we won't.' I was ready to leave but Bridie grabbed my arm.

'For cripes' sake, it's a job. Think of all the money we can save.'

'No. Pop will really kill us if he finds out.'

'You got to gamble a little if you're going to get someplace in this life. And that's the best piece of advice you're ever going to get.' She lit another cigarette. 'You holding out for more money?'

'Of course not.'

'Don't you like Honey?'

'Yeah, Finn. You said you liked him.'

'Sure I do but . . .'

'He's a real smart kid. He got brains like his daddy and me. We're all smart.'

'Okay then.' Bridie turned to Tessie. 'We'll do it. Don't worry if he doesn't want to do it now. He will.'

As we walked up Allen Street, I didn't even want to look at Bridie let alone talk to her.

'We could save a lot of money.' It was a weak argument coming from someone who was incapable of saving two cents longer than five minutes. 'We'll start saving our money and then someday we'll buy a house in New York City so you can be an artist and paint your pictures and I can be a Rockette or something.' She managed to find ammunition everywhere, even in our dreams, which, at that moment, I regretted ever having shared with her. We were walking along the high black bars enclosing the town cemetery and I was going so fast she had to run to keep up with me. 'Doesn't your damn leg hurt? Slow down for cripes' sake.' I had enough guilt without taking money to spend time with someone who didn't have anyone to play with. I was already certain I was somehow responsible for Mom being in the hospital, and Fritz being missing, and Pop sneaking off to see Josie Cleary. Even the loss of Simon's eye was on my list of things to feel guilty about. 'I don't know what the hell is wrong with you. Money is money.' She was puffing hard as she tried to keep up with me. 'Okay, okay, I won't take any of it. You keep it all.'

'I don't want the dumb money.'

'Okay, then, we'll do it for nothing.'

'Just shut up and leave me alone.' I started running to get away from her but she jumped on my back and wrestled me to the ground. 'Get off me, damn it, or I'll punch you in the mouth. I swear to God I'll do it!'

'You and whose army?' She was trying to pin my arms down but I managed to graze her chin with a wild punch and she fell back as I got to my feet and ran into the cemetery. 'I think you knocked my tooth out, you bastard!'

'Good.'

'I'll get you!' With the burden of a brace, at full speed, I was no match for her and in a minute she was on my back and we were rolling around among the tombstones. We both got in a few good slaps and she tried to bite my nose before I managed to get her down by lying across her body with my full weight and holding on until she was exhausted from the struggle. 'You son of a bitch,' she panted. If there were ghosts hovering around, watching us fight, they were subjected to language no good ghost should ever have to hear.

'You give up?'

'No, goddamn it!'

'Watch your mouth. You're in a cemetery.'

'So what!'

'It's a sacrilege.'

'No it isn't. This is a Protestant cemetery. Get off me.'

'No.'

'It's not fair. I'm a girl.' I knew she was really defeated when she stooped to that argument.

'Who cares! Just shut up and listen to me.' And right there, in the Wiggums family plot, gasping for breath, I told her we couldn't visit Honey for two reasons, one honorable and one practical. First, it wasn't fair to take money for something like that, and second, he lived in a whorehouse and if Pop and Laurie found out they'd probably send us to St Stephen's Orphanage for the rest of our lives. I felt the fight go out of her as she relaxed and curiosity took over.

'What's a whorehouse?' I rolled off and we sat up and leaned against the tombstone and I told her everything I knew, everything Fritz had told me, and everything I imagined a whorehouse to be. It was only moments before the pieces started to fall into place and she realized Laurie had been a regular at Tessie's for more than drinking. 'I hate him.' Her eyes started to fill with tears and I knew, from the set of her jaw, these were tears of rage. 'How long did you know?'

'Fritz told me that night. When we brought Laurie home.'

'And you didn't tell me? You're mean. You're just plain, damn mean. I'm never telling you anything again, you bastard.' I thought she was going to get up and leave but she sat quietly thinking, digging a hole in the sod over one of the Wiggums with the heel of her shoe. 'You think Laurie did it with that Tessie?' she said, angrily wiping her nose on the back of her hand.

'I don't know.'

'Can colored people and white people do it with each other?'

'I don't know. I guess.'

'Maybe he did it with that Iris. You could see right through that thing she was wearing.'

'I know.'

'How many more ladies work there?'

'How would I know!'

'Well, we're going to find out.' She got up and started for the gate. ''Cause we're going to start work tomorrow after school.'

'No we're not.'

'Oh yes we are. If we don't, I'll tell Laurie you told me he did sex with Tessie and Iris and all the other ladies who work there. And I'll tell Big Finn, too, and he'll give it to you good. Your skinny ass will be so sore you won't be able to sit down for ten years.' She walked away with all the arrogance and swagger I had come to detest every time she won.

'Damn you.' I tagged along in abject and humiliating defeat because there was no defense against the threat of telling Pop something I didn't want him to know.

'We're going to be rich and we're going to get away from Livery Street and everybody can go to hell.' She started skipping and I had to run to keep up with her.

On June 6, 1944, D-Day, the British and Americans staged the most spectacularly organized invasion in the history of warfare. A thousand aircraft, four thousand vessels and some forty-five thousand men landed at Normandy, attacking the most impregnable defenses ever erected. The spirit of the nation skyrocketed as everyone celebrated what they thought was the beginning of the end of the war in Europe. I celebrated for a slightly different reason. I was convinced that each and every one of those forty-five thousand men were jeopardizing their lives for the sole purpose of finding my brother.

*

By midsummer, Mom was taking regular walks, not only around the sun porch but also on the grounds of Franklin Village. With the trees in bloom and the flower beds and lawns well tended, it wasn't nearly as foreboding as it had been in winter. Italian and German prisoners of war, assigned by the government to work wherever they were needed to replace the shortage of manpower, did most of the grounds work. Two of the prisoners, Ugo and Francesco, who looked like a couple of high-school kids, became friends because Mina spoke Italian. There were always a few army guards looking after the prisoners but Franklin Village was fenced and posted and if they weren't on an actual work detail they were free to move about. Ugo and Francesco watched for us on the weekends when we usually visited and when they'd see us strolling along the paths with Mom they'd follow close behind, repeating over and over, 'Hello, how are you?', the only English they knew. If Mina was with us they'd speak Italian and she'd translate. Ugo was from Palermo and Francesco was from Rome and they had no idea what the war was about and couldn't wait for it to end so they could go home. They missed their families and every time they talked about them they cried openly. Ugo wanted to be a stonemason with his father, and Francesco wanted to be a movie star married to another movie star so, naturally, he was Bridie's favorite and she flirted with him shamelessly and asked Mina if she would teach her how to speak Italian so she could talk to him. They were both so young, so eager and open, it was impossible to think of them as the enemy and when I thought about Fritz fighting soldiers like them, war made no sense at all. Pop said they were more like two boys Fritz might have played basketball with and brought home to sit around the kitchen table rehashing the game.

In spite of my insisting we not take the money, Tessie forced it on us and, true to her word, gave us each twenty-five cents every time we went to see Honey, which was almost every day once school let out. I saved most of mine but Bridie had usually spent hers before we got home. I told her not to let on to Honey that we were being paid, that it would hurt his feelings if he knew we weren't spending time with him just because we wanted to. But Honey was aware of every heartbeat in his small world and after only a few weeks he told us we could have held out for fifty cents and Tessie probably would have paid. Aside from Iris, there were two other girls working for Tessie. Elizabeth, who was tall, thin and very dark, was moody and aloof most of the time but she liked to knit and once she relaxed and accepted us she taught Bridie. The other girl, Cat, was white and slightly overweight and childlike. She agreed with any point of view and she was very accommodating and laughed too much and Bridie swore she was feebleminded. But on many a rainy summer afternoon, the two of them played dress up and Bridie put on enough rouge and lipstick and eye shadow to look absolutely ridiculous.

Most of the time, Honey and I stayed in his room poring over all the maps and planning trips to places with impossible names to pronounce, or we worked at the kitchen table making model airplanes while Charles cooked delicious meals and all kinds of luscious cakes and pies. For whatever reason, rationing was not an issue at Tessie's, butter, meat, coffee, sugar, even chocolate, were always available and apparently in unlimited supply.

As Honey and I got to know each other I discovered there was something about him that reminded me of Rebecca Steinman, some elusive quality of not quite participating, of always standing outside and watching. They both seemed old and wise and I felt they knew things I'd never know. Like Rebecca's photo of her parents in their backyard in Munich, Honey had a picture he liked to look at, too. It was a tattered picture of a large black family posing on the porch of a well-kept Victorian house. It had to have been taken many years before because the women were in long dresses and some of the men were wearing straw hats and arm garters. There must have been twenty people of all ages, grandparents and tiny babies, pretty young women and strong young men, fat, complacent aunts and uncles and unruly children. It was a photo Honey found in one of his books and Tessie had no idea who the people were but he liked to pretend it was a picture of his family in Georgia at a picnic in the summertime. He said if he stared long enough he could see himself sitting on the front step between an enormous woman holding a baby and a skinny young man with his arms wrapped around his bony knees. Sometimes we'd both stare at the picture and pretend we were there and after a while I could see myself sitting right next to Honey and everyone made us feel so at home we didn't look white at all.

At first, Tessie wanted us to stay in the house all the time but after coaxing and pleading and wearing her down we started to go on little excursions and, in no time at all, as long as Honey was protected from the sun, we were free to do whatever we wanted. We introduced him to the wonders of Stony Brook and the fine art of catching salamanders and crawfish, and we took him to the old quarry behind Devil's Cave where there were always blacksnakes or garter snakes or copperheads. We went to the riding stables and watched the rich kids take lessons and sometimes the buxom German teacher, Miss Haas, in her jodhpurs and scuffed boots, would let the three of us straddle a tired old trail horse and ride bareback around the training ring. We fished off the towpath between the lake and the canal and caught calico bass and sunfish and eels and Bridie and I swam in our underwear off the Mule Bridge while Honey watched from the shade of a big silver maple. We stood under the trestle and screamed as loud as we could when the train crossed the canal but we couldn't hear anything over the squeal and clatter of the wheels on the tracks. At the university, we sat by an open window, under a wisteria vine coiling around the music building, and listened to free concerts as students practiced, and on rainy days we went to the museum and wondered at the enormity of the dinosaur skeleton and the birds'-egg collection and the mummy with the lipless, brown-toothed grimace, wrapped in dusty russet rags. Showing Honey all the things that over the years we had come to take for granted gave me a wonderful sense of rediscovery and appreciation and I remember thinking that whenever the day came for Bridie and me to make our big move to New York, leaving home would be a very difficult thing to do.

One afternoon after school, as we started up the back steps to see Honey, we ran into Mr Rose, the pharmacist from Winter's Drug Store where Bridie and I spent a good chunk of our money at the soda fountain. He was very thin and balding, with big spaces between his teeth, and he always seemed to be preoccupied. The hallway was dark and it took a moment for him to realize who we were but when he did he froze and his lips went white and he looked as though he was going to faint.

'Hey, Mr Rose,' said Bridie. 'What are you doing here?' I poked her hard with my elbow.

'Well, I . . . ah. . .' the veins in his skinny neck started pumping.

'You a friend of Tessie's?' she asked.

'No, no. Well, ah . . . yes.'

'That's nice.'

'I . . . ah. . . was just delivering a prescription.'

He started down the stairs but Bridie couldn't let it go at that. 'Who's sick?'

Tessie appeared at the top of the stairs.

'I don't know.' He took two steps at a time as he passed us. 'Christ,' he muttered and ran out the door.

'See you at the drug store!' she yelled. Tessie started laughing so hard she had to lean against the wall. 'Who's sick?' asked Bridie.

'I can't stand it,' she said, trying to catch her breath.

'What's so funny?' Bridie was completely bewildered. 'Somebody's sick, aren't they?'

'No, you dumb cluck.' I was starting to feel as embarrassed as Mr Rose. 'He was probably here to see one of the girls. Use your damn head once in a while.'

'Iris,' said Tessie, trying to stifle a scream. 'Oh my God, I think I'm going to wet myself.' She ran back into the apartment, laughing uncontrollably.

'Mr Rose and Iris!' Bridie was truly shocked. 'But he's married.'

From then on a signal was devised and we had to pay strict attention whenever we went to visit Honey. Charles painted a small square of wood, green on one side and red on the other, and hung it on a nail by the backdoor and whenever it showed red, we hid in the bushes and waited until the client left and Charles came down and flipped it over. Mr Rose wasn't the only married man in town who visited Tessie's.

When we were with Honey, we always stayed away from the railroad station so Pop wouldn't see us but one hot afternoon, when we were sure he was at work, we stopped by my house to wash up before we went to a movie, and he walked in. Honey was looking around the house the same way he looked at things in the museum.

'I always wondered what your house was like. Somehow, I thought white people live different.' He looked at the picture of Deirdre on the radio. 'That's your baby sister, huh?'

'Is anybody else as hot as me?' Bridie was fanning herself with a newspaper. 'I could sit right in the icebox.'

'You got a picture of your mother?'

'Yeah, up in my room. Come on.' As we started for the stairs, the front door opened and there stood Pop. I thought I was going to throw up.

'Hey, who's this? Honey, I guess.' He went to Honey and they shook hands but Honey didn't say a word. Pop looked at me for some reaction but I was so frozen I couldn't even blink. 'It was so goddamn hot at the baggage room they sent us home. I'm going up to take a shower.' Bridie and I just looked at each other. 'So, Finn,' said Pop as he passed me, 'cat got your tongue?' There was something mean in the way he said it. 'I don't miss a trick, sport. Not a trick,' and he went upstairs, leaving us speechless.

It was weeks before I found out that Tessie had told him.

'Darlin', your daddy and me go way back. Of course I told him. Didn't he tell you? I called and said nothing funny was going to go on. I gave him my word. You were coming here to see Honey and that was all. I wasn't about to sneak around without saying anything. No, darlin', I don't do that.'

'Does he know you pay us money?' I asked.

'Hell no, he does not. A man's finances is his own business and nobody else's.'

'I don't understand why Big Finn didn't say something,' said Bridie on our way home that day.

'Me neither.'

'We could have just relaxed and stopped all that worrying if we knew.'

'Yeah.' And I thought to myself, that's probably why he didn't tell us.

'I heard Miss Webster talking to the doctors and they're thinking about doing it.' Mildred was being more officious than usual as we sat on the steps of the main building watching Bridie and Pop and Mina walk Mom among the flower beds. It was the Saturday before Labor Day, and our last weekend before going back to school. The whole week had been sweltering and my leg was giving me trouble so I decided to sit in the shade by myself and enjoy the solitude and draw but I had just gotten settled when Mildred found me. 'In my professional opinion, they should go ahead and do it. But do they ask me? Oh, no. They think they know it all. Sons of bitches.' She was looking over my shoulder. 'Hey, you're a good artist.'

'Do what?' I was half paying attention to her as I drew the people milling about the common.

'Give Mae the shock treatments. She's not getting any better, you know.'

'What are you talking about?'

'Remember in *Frankenstein* when they hooked all those wires

193

up to the monster and sent him up into the storm and the lightning went into those things on his neck and he came to life? Remember that? Well, that's what we do to people here. We just shoot them full of electricity and it's supposed to make them better. What it does is give them convulsions and it doesn't always work but when we have patients as truly crazy as Mae, what else are we going to do?'

'Frankenstein!'

'Didn't you see that movie?'

'What do you mean they're going to do that to Mom? How do you know?'

'We had a conference about it. Miss Webster, the doctors and me. It's under consideration. My personal recommendation is that we do it. It worked wonders for Teddy. Of course, that's how he lost some of his teeth. But it's better to have your teeth knocked out than to be crazy. Don't you think I'm right?'

'You don't know what you're talking about.'

'I think I deserve an apology from you, young man. One more word and I'll put you on report.' She got up, brushed herself off, and walked away, mumbling about having me transferred to another hospital.

Before I said anything to Pop I went looking for Miss Webster to ask if it was true. She was in her office, standing in front of a noisy fan by the open window, trying to cool off.

'Lord, Finn, you should know by now not to pay any attention to Mildred. She hangs around corners listening to conversations that are none of her business and does nothing but cause trouble.'

'It's all a lie?'

'I think you should talk to your father.'

'Then Mildred was telling the truth. You are going to shock Mom!'

'It's something the doctors are considering. And it's nothing at all like Mildred said. Frankenstein!'

'Electricity kills people.'

'For heaven's sake, it's not the electric chair. Don't you worry about it. Just run along and visit with your mother and put all of this out of your mind.'

'She said it gives people convulsions.'

'Well, yes, but it's different than it sounds. Not nearly as bad as Mildred says. Lord, before we know it she'll be hanging up her shingle. I'm not going to stand here discussing this with you. You'll never understand it anyway. Now run along and stop worrying about it. I have work to do.'

I knew, whenever an adult dismissed me on the pretext of my not understanding what they were talking about, that it was something they didn't *want* to talk about. One thing was certain. They were going to put electricity in Mom and there was no doubt about it and it caused convulsions and that's what killed my baby sister, and I was sure, when Pop heard about it, he'd put a stop to it. As I went to look for him I thought of Rebecca's father going back to Germany to try and save her mother because of Hitler and the war, and I remembered Mr Howe saying it was the right thing to do because a man can't desert his family in time of trouble.

'Christ, Finn, you get yourself all worked up over nothing.' I had pulled Pop aside so Mom couldn't hear what I was saying because I was sure Mom heard everything everyone said.

'It causes convulsions. That's what Deirdre died from.'

'That was different. Your sister, God rest her soul, had the measles. Anyway, the doctors know what they're doing and they don't need any help from you or me.'

'Then they are going to do it?'

'Finn, listen to me.' He put his hand on my shoulder and his voice softened. 'Would I let them do anything to hurt your mother? Use your head, for Christ's sake. I love her and I want to see her get well so she can come home to us. Don't you want that, too?'

'Yes.' I was thinking about him loving Josie Cleary and maybe he didn't really want Mom to come home.

'And don't you think we have enough trouble with your brother being missing and all?'

'Yes.'

'Then do me a favor and don't make things any worse than they are. I'm trying my best, whether you know it or not. I could use a little help from you. We have to stick together, you know.'

'But they're going to put electricity in her.' He didn't seem to have any idea of the horror of what was going to happen to Mom.

'Christ!'

'You can't let them do that.'

'Now that's enough, you hear what I'm saying? I'm telling you the doctors know what they're doing.' His voice was edgy and I knew he was losing his patience.

'But she could die.'

'Goddamn it, I said that's enough! Not another word. And I mean it, mister.' He left me standing in the middle of the path and ran to catch up with Mom and Mina and Bridie. At that moment I knew exactly what I had to do and I went off to find Mildred.

That night, when Bridie and I were sitting on her bed counting the money we had saved since we started seeing Honey, I told her my plans. Reluctantly, Mildred the escape artist had shown me where there was a break in the fence behind the coal piles next to the utility plant. I tricked her into telling me by promising her a date with Simon. There were loose bricks in a pillar and a section of the black iron bars could be pulled open wide enough for a person to slip through. She said it was her job to know about things like that but she never told anyone at the Village because she and Teddy sometimes went outside and walked along the creek. She was talking about Greigg's Creek, which meandered through miles of rural and wooded countryside, ending up in the brackish, back-bay area of the Jersey pine barrens.

'For cripes' sake, you'll never get away with it. They'll catch you and put you in jail.'

'No they won't. Not if we get a head start. I'm going to do it Monday during the Labor Day picnic. There'll be so many people they won't notice we're gone for a while.'

'I think you're nuts.'

'Would you let them put electricity in Laurie?'

'How much money have we got?' Somehow, despite Bridie's penchant for spending, we'd managed to save twenty-six dollars and fifty cents.

'And I have my war bond and my Hanuka and Christmas money.'

'Well, that should keep us going for a while,' she said, putting the quarters back in the coffee can.

'Us! You're not going with me.'

'Oh yes I am.'

'No, you're not.' I had thought of Bridie coming with me but I decided I'd have a better chance of getting Mom out of Franklin Village by myself.

'When are you coming back?'

'Maybe never. I'll get a job someplace. I can make enough money for me and Mom.'

'You're never coming back and you want to go without me! Are you going to leave Duke, too?' I had forgotten all about Duke.

'I guess I'll have to.' I felt a stab in my heart. 'Maybe someday I'll sneak back and get him.'

'You would really leave me and Duke? I'd never do that to you. Not in a million years. And what about Big Finn? You just going to leave him?'

'He's got Simon.'

'And Laurie has Kitty Neal. So, I'm going with you.' And the decision was made, Bridie was coming with us, so we started mapping our strategy.

*

'Where's your brace?' Pop was checking the water in the radiator of the car.

'It's bothering me. Can't I leave it off just for today?' I had decided not to take my brace because it slowed me down. Bridie came over and leaned on the fender.

'What the hell's the matter with you two, wearing sweaters! It's a hundred and ten in the shade!' We were taking two cars because there were so many of us going to the Village. Mrs Ganis and Simon, Laurie and Kitty, Mina and the baby and Pop and Bridie and I were all helping load the picnic things into the car.

'I'm sweating just looking at you,' said Mrs Ganis, dabbing at her upper lip with her handkerchief. 'You look like refugees, for God's sake.' Bridie and I couldn't take a suitcase so we had to wear all the clothes we were taking with us. Aside from the sweaters, we each had on three pairs of underwear and three pairs of socks and she had a pair of shorts on under her favorite dress.

'This is only a picnic,' said Laurie, 'not a ball for the King of Rumania. You think you might be a bit dressed up?' He was referring to Bridie's jewelry. She was wearing most of the gaudy, castaway, clunky bracelets, necklaces and rings she had collected since her days in Boston with Aunt Theresa. Mom and Mrs Ganis, Little Tum, Kitty, and even Iris and Tessie, were all represented.

'You look like a Gypsy kid. Like you're going to tell fortunes,' said Mrs Ganis.

'I want to look nice for Mrs Finn.' Bridie climbed into the back seat trying to dismiss the subject. 'Besides, I look pretty, don't I, Finn?' I thought she looked stupid but I nodded yes.

'And you,' said Pop, 'you never wear your brother's watch. Aren't you afraid you might lose it?'

'The strap is real tight.'

'You better not let anything happen to that watch, mister.'

'I think it looks great on you, Finn.' Simon was always coming to my rescue. The one thing they didn't notice was that I was having a terrible time keeping my pants up because I had a penknife, some string, two corks with fish hooks stuck in them, and twenty-six-dollars-and-fifty-cents-worth of quarters in my pockets.

The night before, I said goodbye to Duke. Pop and Simon were listening to the war news on the radio and I went upstairs early so I could write goodbye notes to them and Mr and Mrs Ganis, Mr Howe, Honey and Rebecca Steinman. Bridie was leaving a note for Laurie. I told everyone we loved them and hoped to see them again someday and not to try to find us. Fritz's letter was special. No matter how hard I tried I couldn't say what I really felt so I told him I would bring his watch back someday and we'd all live together in the house in New York when I was a rich and famous artist and he wouldn't have to work because I'd have enough money for everybody. I folded them neatly and put them in my underwear drawer where I was sure they'd be found the day Pop finally accepted the fact that I was never coming home again and gave my clothes to the war relief. When I finished, Duke and I got in bed and had a long talk in private. I didn't tell him we might never see each other again, I just said I was going away with Mom and Bridie for a while and as soon as we could we'd come back and get him. As always, he understood, and I knew if he could have told me he would have wished me luck and said he'd be waiting for me. I had promised myself I wouldn't cry and I didn't because he would have suspected something. But after he fell asleep I lay there in the dark listening to the muffled sound of the radio coming from downstairs, knowing that the next morning I'd have to say goodbye to the best friend I ever had, and I buried my face in my pillow.

When the cars were packed and everyone was settled and ready to go, I saw him sitting on the side porch, watching us through the railing. Bridie saw him, too, and reached over and took my hand just as Pop started the car.

'Wait a minute!' she yelled. 'Why don't we take Duke? It'll be a surprise for Mrs Finn.' It was the greatest idea Bridie ever had, or ever would have, and it never once occurred to me.

'We can't take Duke.' Pop was ready to go.

'Why not? It's a picnic. Dog's can't go to picnics?' said Mr Ganis.

'Yeah, Pop.'

'Please, Big Finn.' I hoped Bridie could work her usual magic on Pop.

'Mae loves that dog, Tom. It would maybe make her happy. So what do you have to lose?' Mrs Ganis winked at us.

'Why don't we?' said Mina, who was sitting in the front seat holding the baby.

'Well . . .' Pop was outnumbered and beginning to weaken.

'I'll keep him on the leash, I promise.'

'What's wrong?' called Laurie from his car.

'We're taking Duke,' said Pop.

There were so many blankets and folding chairs on the lawn, it looked more like the beach at Seaside Heights than Franklin Village. Doctors and nurses and orderlies were milling about visiting with the patients and their families, and Mildred, a few steps behind Miss Webster, was making notes on a beat-up clipboard for her report. Mom was wearing one of her own dresses and someone had made up her face with more lipstick and rouge than she had ever worn and she looked frighteningly garish.

'Darling, you're beautiful,' said Mrs Ganis, hugging Mom. 'Doesn't she look like some famous lady? Greta Garbo, maybe?'

Pop had managed to squeeze our blanket into a shady spot under a huge chestnut tree on the edge of the common, right next to a family of people so pale they looked like they were in the process of disappearing. They were a mother and father, two teenaged girls and a young man about twenty who was obviously the patient. He sat on the edge of the blanket rocking back and forth, repeating the States in proper alphabetical order and folding and unfolding a paper napkin.

'That guy really has a screw loose,' whispered Bridie. 'He gives me the creeps. When are we going to get out of here?'

'Shut up, somebody will hear you.'

'You two are so perfect you can whisper about sick people? You should be ashamed.' Mrs Ganis shook her head in disgust and turned back to unloading the picnic basket with Pop and Simon. Kitty, who had once worked at the Village, went off with Laurie to look for a nurse friend and Mina took the baby for a walk among the flower beds. Duke lay quietly next to Mom, who, with the trace of a smile, sat contentedly petting him. Dance music was playing over the loudspeaker and every once in a while there'd be an announcement about a lost kid or an upcoming activity. I pulled Bridie aside.

'We'll go after we eat, when they start the games.'

'Can we wait till after the three-legged race?'

'With my leg!'

'Not you. I was going to ask Simon.'

'Why don't you just stay and run your damn race. Mom and I will go without you.'

'All right! Don't be so touchy. God! I only asked.'

'The games will begin in five minutes in the field near parking lot C.' The voice boomed over the loudspeaker.

'Let's go,' said Pop. 'We want to be able to see.'

'Duke hasn't gone to the bathroom since we got here.' My heart was beating hard and I felt I couldn't catch my breath.

'Oh Christ, all we need is for him to mess on the lawn.'

'I'll take him over to the field,' said Simon.

'No!' Bridie jumped in. 'Finn and me will take him.' She touched Mom on the shoulder. 'You want to come, Mrs Finn?' It was all so natural no one could ever suspect a thing. Bridie was perfectly cool but I felt my hands shaking and the sweat coming out of every pore.

'You want to go, Mae?' asked Pop, and she just sat there with her enigmatic smile.

'Sure she does,' I said as Bridie and I helped her to her feet. 'We'll meet you over at the field.' As we walked away, I looked back once and they were all busying themselves with packing things away and I thought they should be watching us go because it was probably the last time they'd ever see us.

'Don't walk so fast,' said Bridie, 'people will catch on.' I slowed my pace and tried to be as nonchalant as possible but I was having a terrible time keeping my pants up and holding on to the leash because Duke was pulling to greet everyone we passed. When we got around the corner of the main building we started walking as fast as we could.

'Come on, Mrs Finn, we're getting you out of here.' Bridie had Mom by the hand and it seemed as though she knew what we were saying because she started walking so fast we had trouble keeping up with her. Duke thought it was all a game and started barking.

'Shut up,' I said, but he only barked more and started dancing around in circles.

'For cripe's sake, he might as well be an air-raid alarm. Can't you stop him?' I shortened the leash and looked him square in the eye. 'If I let you off the leash will you stop?' He was panting hard and his hazel eyes were bright with excitement but he seemed to understand so I undid the clasp and, once free, he was too busy sniffing to bark, so we took off in the direction of the utility plant.

'Where do you think you're going?' It was Mildred, running to catch up with us. 'I've been keeping an eye on you. Not much gets past me, you know. That's my job.'

'Oh cripes! Get away from here you crazy lady.'

'I'll put you on report, little missy. Don't you get bold with me.'

'We're just taking the dog for a walk, Mildred. We'll be right back.'

'You have to stay with the group. That's one of my rules. And I don't like people to break the rules.' I thought we were finished before we even started when suddenly I had an idea as brilliant as Bridie's idea to bring Duke with us.

'Did that doctor find you?'

'What doctor?'

'You know, the head doctor.'

'Dr Blumenthal was looking for me? What did he want? What did I do?'

'He wanted to ask your advice about something.'

'He did!' Mildred was finally receiving the recognition she thought she deserved and she was beaming.

'What, is he nuts, too?' said Bridie.

'Shut up.'

'Oh, I love Dr Blumenthal. Where is he?'

'Out front someplace. You better go find him.'

'I will, I will. You have a nice walk with your dog.' She was being very gracious. 'How do I look?'

'Real pretty,' said Bridie, catching on and anxious to get rid of her.

'Thank you. Thank you so much. I really love you. You're my favorites.' She hurried away, talking as she went. 'I'd like to stay and chat but Dr Blumenthal and I have work to do. Have a nice walk, Mae.'

'Let's go,' I said, and we started running. We went through the parking lot and past the women's building and started across the field toward the utility plant. Bridie held tight to Mom and I held up my pants. Duke seemed to know where we were going and led the way but when he got to a little island of growth in the middle of the field, sumac trees and wild cherry and brambles, he stopped running and started wagging his tail and barking. I thought it was probably a rabbit or bird so I told Bridie to keep going but before we could pass Ugo and Francesco appeared.

'Hello. How are you?' They almost said it in unison. They offered us some food but we tried to tell them we were in a hurry and started running and they followed us, laughing and talking in Italian like it was some kind of game. Even Mom started laughing. With Duke joyfully running in circles and jumping all over everyone, me pulling up my pants and Bridie jingling along with her jewelry, we must have looked like some kind of saturnalia rather than a group of people trying to escape from a mental institution. We reached the utility plant and right behind the coal piles, just as Mildred had said, we found the loose section of bars. I pulled them open and Bridie squeezed through and for the first time Ugo and Francesco realized what was happening. They started shouting and slapping their foreheads and squeezing their eyes shut and they must have said no a hundred times.

'They don't want us to go.' Bridie's face was pressed between the bars.

'No kidding,' I said as I started to push Mom through the opening. Ugo grabbed her arm and held her back as they both pleaded with us in Italian. At any moment I expected to see Pop and soldiers and Mildred running across the field so I tried to explain how critical our escape was by pantomiming lightning coming down from the sky and going into Mom's neck, but it was apparent they hadn't seen *Frankenstein* so the performance was wasted.

'Damn it, let go of Mrs Finn!' Bridie reached through the bars and hit Ugo. 'I mean it. No, no, no!' They let go and Mom slipped through, followed by Duke and me. My pants were riding on my hips as we half ran and half slid down the embankment to the creek while Ugo and Francesco stood on the other side of the bars yelling at us. I'll never know what made them change their minds but by the time we reached the water they were sliding down the bank behind us.

About a quarter of a mile downstream, where the woods eased into a pasture, we found a rowboat. We could see the roof of a barn over the crest of a hill but, except for some uninterested cows, the place was deserted.

'Let's take the boat, I'm getting tired of walking.' Bridie sat down and took off two pairs of her socks.

'We can't steal a boat, things are bad enough already.' The truth was, I never liked to be on the water. Being in it was one thing but being on it, looking down into that distorted unknown, was another. Pop had told me a story he once read about a man who was fishing and his hook got caught on something and he thought it was a submerged branch but when he pulled it up it wasn't a branch, it was a dead man and the hook had snagged him under the chin. He had been in the water for a long time and he was waxy and colorless and his eyes were open and when his face broke the surface, he was staring right at the fisherman and the fisherman went crazy and fell backwards and drowned. I was always expecting that dead man's face to float up at me.

'What difference does it make? Besides, it'll be faster.' She was right. The creek was swollen from a particularly rainy summer and the water was deep and, dead men or not, we could make much better time.

'Okay. But there aren't any oars. We'll have to use branches for poles.' I turned to Ugo and Francesco. 'We need some long straight branches.' They just stood there smiling. 'Forget it.' Bridie and I found the poles while they looked after Mom.

Before we got into the boat I pointed to the big POWs printed on their shirts and told them to take them off. I figured we had enough red flags with a cripple, a Dalmatian and a Gypsy fortuneteller.

'Bridie, you sit in the center with Mom. Ugo up front and Francesco in the back with me.' I was either improving in my pantomiming skills or they were starting to understand English. When we were loaded the boat was riding dangerously low in the water and, with Duke excitedly moving from side to side, I thought we'd be swamped and sink. But we pushed off and once we hit the current, with Ugo and Francesco's adept poling, we were on our way. We moved quickly and quietly through woods and fields of wild aster and Queen Anne's lace, through pasture land, under bridges and past a deserted mill. Where it was too deep for the poles we drifted, while Ugo and Francesco, shirtless, bathed in the hot sun. Bridie held tight to Mom who in turn held tight to Duke. She seemed to be smiling at a world she had never seen before. Occasionally we'd pass a few fishermen on the shore and we'd wave and I'd ask, as casually as I could, if they were catching anything. It all seemed very wrong to me. I had expected a chase with bloodhounds and some kind of posse in hot pursuit and instead we were having an idyllic cruise on the creek.

'Do you think they know we're gone yet?' I was leaning over the side, looking at a school of minnows dancing in the shallows.

'Well, for cripes' sake, it's been hours. If they don't, they're pretty stupid.'

'Stupido!' said Francesco, recognizing the word.

'That's right,' Bridie smiled. 'I have to pee and I'm getting hungry. Can't we stop?' I motioned to Francesco and he told Ugo and they poled to shore. Bridie and Mom went into the woods and I unloaded my quarters and gave them to Ugo and Francesco to carry. We were at a wide point in the creek, where the water was fairly still, and I thought it would be a good place to fish. There were plenty of worms in the damp leaves and under the rocks along the shore so, while Mom dozed in the shade, the four of us took turns fishing. Bridie was as good at it as me. She had always baited her own hook, artfully slipping the sharp point through the worm so it wouldn't fall off, and she never complained about gutting and cleaning her catch. Pop said she had a fisherman's hands, that she could feel through the line if there was a fish within whistling distance. In no time at all we caught several catfish, a few suckers and some bluegill. Ugo and Francesco were too excitable to be good fishermen. Every time they got a bite they shouted and scared the fish away so I sent them to get firewood. While Francesco started a fire with the crystal from Fritz's watch, Bridie and I cleaned the fish and stuffed the cavities with wild onions for flavor, the way Fritz and I had done on our camping trips. There was plenty for everyone, including Duke, and when we were finished eating, we put out the fire and covered the ashes and were back on the creek.

All afternoon we drifted and poled, passing through cool, deep shade and hot, late-summer sun, listening to the birds and the rhythmic lapping of the water on the side of the boat plus the occasional uncontrollable outburst of Italian song. I was running away, breaking every rule, defying all kinds of intimidating authority from Pop to the United States army, and yet I never remember a time in my life when I felt more content. If there were dead men waiting to float to the surface, they were friendly dead men. For those few hours, the creek had all the power and responsibility, taking us down a course it had followed for thousands and thousands of years, and I didn't have to think about a thing.

At dusk, when we were all starting to feel hungry again, Bridie announced she wanted something besides fish. 'Can't we just go to some little country store and get some bread and stuff?'

'By now, everybody in New Jersey will be looking for us.'

'Well, I'll be damned if I'm going to eat fish for the rest of my life.'

'It's brain food.'

'I got enough brains. I want something good to eat.' I wanted something besides fish, too, but I was in charge and I felt I had to resist any change in my original plan to live off the land. 'If you didn't want to eat fish you shouldn't have come with me.'

She turned to Ugo and Francesco. 'You don't want to eat fish tonight, do you?' They smiled and nodded. 'See. Nobody wants fish.'

'They don't even know what the hell you're talking about.'

'What's that got to do with anything?'

We decided that between the two of us Bridie should be the one to look for a store because our escape might have been on the radio and they might be looking for a crippled kid.

'Take off that jewelry. You look like you robbed the five-and-dime.'

We saw a family camping on the bank and two kids swam out to us and we asked if they knew of a store near by and they told us there was a bait shop just around the next bend. It was sort of a bait shop and general store combined. We drifted past, checking to see if there were police or soldiers but, except for an old woman fishing off a rickety dock, the place seemed deserted. We went around the next bend and poled the boat to shore where nobody could see us.

'Don't talk to people and try not to spend too much money,' I said, giving her a handful of quarters.

'It's my money, too.' She started along the bank.

'That money has to last us.'

'I know, I know.' She disappeared around the bend and Ugo and Francesco started talking to each other, probably trying to figure out what was going on.

She was back in half an hour with bread, a can of Spam, peanut butter, a jar of jelly, tomatoes, chocolate milk and a bag of penny candy.

'Did you see anybody?'

'Two men were in the store just sitting and drinking coffee and that old lady who was fishing was the owner.'

'Did they ask any questions?'

'Nope. I told them I was camping with my mother and my brother and two friends from a foreign land.'

'Oh my God! And how did these friends from a foreign land get here? There's a war on, you know. People aren't doing a lot of traveling. You didn't have to say anything. I told you not to talk to strangers.' Francesco and Ugo were listening as if they understood what we were saying.

'You're so damn perfect, aren't you!'

'No, I'm not perfect. Get in the boat. We have to keep moving.' We helped Mom in and pushed off. 'Did you say anything else?'

'No. And if I did I wouldn't tell you.'

We drifted along in silence, passing the milk bottle from one to the other as we ate tomato-and-Spam and peanut-butter-and-jelly sandwiches. The penny candy was dessert.

Just as it was getting dark we pulled into shore and settled down for the night. Everyone was exhausted and fell asleep almost immediately. Bridie snuggled up next to Mom and I settled down with Duke between Ugo and Francesco. The air was hot and thick with moisture and the stars seemed to be within reach as I lay there in the dark listening to the tree frogs. I thought about Pop and how worried he must be and I thought about never seeing the Ganises or Simon or Mr Howe and Laurie again and for the first time I wondered if I was doing the right thing.

It was first light when Duke's growling awakened me. I heard a twig snap and before I even opened my eyes I knew someone was there.

'Duke, ssh.' Looking around, I saw that everyone else was still asleep. There was movement in the brush but I couldn't really see anyone until a State trooper and a soldier came toward me, motioning for me to keep quiet. The trooper extended his hand and made a large circle, indicating that we were surrounded. I didn't understand what was happening. I took Mom away from Franklin Village so why weren't they grabbing me and taking me off to jail? The soldier motioned for me to go to him just as two other soldiers came out of the woods and went toward Mom and Bridie. Suddenly, there were police and soldiers everywhere. The two soldiers put their hands over Bridie's and Mom's mouths and had them up and into the woods before I realized what was happening. They started to struggle and Duke started barking and all hell broke loose. Before Ugo and Francesco could sit up there were police and soldiers all over them. I couldn't really tell but it looked like they were hurting them.

'Stop that!' I screamed. 'What are you doing?'

'Get their weapons,' said one of the soldiers.

'They don't have any weapons.' I tried to pull away from the policeman holding me.

'Take it easy kid. Everything's going to be okay, now.'

'Hey!' yelled Bridie, 'Don't hurt them! Finn, stop them!' But before I could say anything else, Ugo and Francesco were taken away and we never saw them again.

At the police station there were reporters and radio people and a man who said he was from *Movietone News*. Mom was taken back to Franklin Village and when she left the police station she didn't even look back at us. They locked Duke in a cell to keep him out of the way while the police questioned us. They wanted to know if they hurt us.

'No. They were friends.'

One of the policemen leaned down to Bridie. 'Did they touch you or the Mrs in private places?'

'They certainly did not. What the hell's the matter with you?' Bridie was indignant. We tried to tell everybody that Ugo and Francesco didn't do anything wrong but they wouldn't listen to us. They kept saying there was nothing to be afraid of, to relax and tell the truth, that the POWs couldn't do anything to us anymore. But the harder we tried the more they believed whatever they wanted to believe.

Pop and Simon and Laurie came to get us and when Pop saw me he was so overcome he had to sit down and they brought him a glass of water. He kept thanking God over and over. Laurie picked up Bridie and hugged her and Bridie started crying and it just made everything worse. The police asked the reporters to leave and, after a while, Laurie and Pop went into an office with some of the police and Simon took Duke outside and, for the first time since we were caught, Bridie and I were alone.

'Everybody thinks we were kidnapped. They think Ugo and Francesco kidnapped us so they could get away.'

'I know.' She was taking off her extra underwear.

'They think they kidnapped us and those guys didn't even want to go. They tried to stop us for God's sake.'

'Well, we tried to tell them, didn't we? Can we help it if they don't believe us?'

'I think they only went with us so they could take care of us in case something bad happened.'

'You think?'

'Yes, I do. We can't let them take the blame.'

Bridie came to me and sat very close. 'Well, we should think about this.' She leaned her head on my shoulder. 'They're already prisoners. It's not like anything new is going to happen to them now that they're caught.'

'What the hell's the matter with you?' I got up and moved away from her.

'If we tell them the truth, we'll get in trouble.' She followed me, talking in a whisper so no one would hear. 'We stole a damn rowboat and took your mom out of the hospital and stuff. Laurie and Big Finn are real happy to see us now but if they find out, they will kill us.'

'You knew that before we went away.'

'Yeah, but I didn't think we were going to get caught. I thought we'd be living in New York City or something.'

'We can't let them take the blame. God will strike us dead.'

'No. He won't. We'll just go to confession and everything will be all right.'

'I can't do that.'

'Then do good works for the poor or something like that. For cripes' sake, you're going to grow a halo and wings if you don't watch out.' She took a deep breath. 'I don't want to get in trouble and the way it is now, nobody knows. Duke can't tell them and neither can Mrs Finn. And those two guys only talk in Italian and even if they did tell nobody will believe them.' I hated to admit it but she was making sense.

'But what will happen to them?' I was weakening.

'Well, let's see.' She hesitated a moment because she knew she had to come up with a very good scenario. 'Okay, the war will end and they'll go back home and everybody in Italy will think

211

they're brave cause they tried to get away. And there'll be a parade in their honor and they'll all eat a lot of spaghetti and drink a lot of dago red and we'll be seeing Francesco in the movies.' She had an answer for everything.

The newspapers had a field day with the story. Some were more sensational than others but they all accused Ugo and Francesco of taking us hostage. The local papers, stagnant from years of battle statistics for headlines, reported the incident as though it was the most exciting news since the kidnapping of the Lindbergh baby. One short column in *The New York Times* cautiously reported POWs escaping by abducting two children and an inmate from a mental institution somewhere in New Jersey. The *New York News* gave us the whole second page and reported a cripple and a mental patient being held at gunpoint by ruthless Italian POWs. Even the *Saturday Evening Post* did a story, with illustrations of two snarling men holding a woman in a torn dress, her eyes wide and filled with terror, while two innocent children clung fearfully to her legs and held on to their dog. No matter who did the reporting, they all agreed on one thing. Ugo and Francesco were villains.

And so we started the seventh grade as heroes, having lived an adventure even Bridie's nemesis, Frances Peart, couldn't match. Whatever residual ridicule we suffered from our encounter with the Blessed Virgin, it was completely forgotten. Public affirmation was strong stuff. Sister Mary Assumpta, coolly elegant and worldly, treated us with deference and, if for no other reason, Bridie enjoyed her celebrity because, as she put it, 'I got a nun eating right out of the palm of my hand.' Because we agreed not to lie about anything, we figured the only sin we were committing was a sin of omission, which we didn't take too seriously. We talked about our trip down the creek in the rowboat, about fishing, even about Ugo and Francesco, but we never said they kidnapped us. Of course, there were enough newspaper accounts and articles, absolutely fabricated, to substantiate anyone's fantasies. Bridie dramatized the hardships of life on the run, making it all sound twice as exciting as it actually had been, and I must admit there were moments when I had an irrepressible urge to tell everyone about the dead man with staring eyes, floating down in the seaweed, that I'd hooked under the chin and pulled to the surface.

The one very positive result of our misadventure was Bridie and Laurie's reconciliation. Bridie even made peace with Kitty. But only, as Bridie told me, after Kitty offered to get out of Laurie's life for ever. She wanted what was best for Laurie and Bridie, even if it meant giving up her own happiness. I didn't believe it for one minute but Bridie swore it was true. So, as long as Kitty put Bridie before herself, Bridie could magnanimously allow that Kitty was probably the right woman for Laurie. And, having convinced herself that she was coming out the winner, they could all relax into some semblance of a family. Laurie and Kitty bought two acres out at the Junction where they planned to build a house when the war was over and things got back to normal. But there was still no mention of marriage.

Pop and Simon never once questioned me about Ugo and Francesco and I couldn't figure out why. For a while, after he brought me home from the police station, Pop was different toward me. He was no more demonstrative than he had ever been but he was different. He seemed to listen to what I had to say and he even asked my opinion about things. I'd expected, when Pop and Laurie came to get us, that I'd be blamed for everything. It *was* all my fault and I knew it and I was sure he knew it, too.

'Why is Pop so different to me?' I asked Simon one night after we turned out the light.

'What do you mean different?'

'I don't know. Just different. He talks to me different.'

'I didn't notice anything.' He sounded too casual, like he was hiding something and wanted to dismiss the subject. I waited, hoping he'd say more but he didn't.

'If I had a secret I thought you should know, I'd tell you.'

'I don't have a secret.'

'Did something happen to Fritz? Are you guys hiding something bad?'

'No. Jesus, don't you think we'd tell you? We haven't heard anything, good or bad.'

'Fritz and I didn't keep secrets. You know what I'm saying?'

'It's not exactly a secret. Shit! I shouldn't be telling you this.'

'What is it?' I sat up so quickly I scared Duke.

'He read the letter you wrote to him and me when you ran away with your mother. Shit, I said I wouldn't say anything.'

'But the letters were still in my drawer when I came home. I tore them up.'

'When the police called and said they found you he told me to get some clean clothes in case you needed them, and when I went to get your underwear I found the letters.'

'And you read them?'

'Only the one addressed to him and me. After he read it he sat on the bed not saying anything for a long time. Then he took the clothes and went downstairs and the only thing he said was that you have guts.'

'You knew all along that those guys didn't kidnap us?'

'He told me not to say anything. And you can't say anything, either. I shouldn't have told you.'

I promised I wouldn't but I wanted to ask Pop why he didn't tell me he knew? And why didn't he get mad? And most of all I wanted to ask what was different?

'I have something I have to talk about.' It was almost Christmas and Duke and I were visiting Mr Howe and the guilt of living with what Bridie and I allowed to happen to Ugo and Francesco was unbearable. It had occurred to me to confess to Father Boyle but somewhere in the back of my mind I didn't quite trust the Seal of the Confessional. I also thought about telling Mr and Mrs Ganis but I knew what their response would be. 'You didn't hurt anybody, we love you, you were doing it for your mother, what people don't know won't hurt them and next time don't do such a stupid thing and give everybody a heart attack.' Honey knew. I told him right away and he thought I did the right thing trying to get Mom out of there but he was glad I didn't get away with it because if I had we'd probably never see each other again. And Rebecca knew. I was sure she'd read about it in the paper so I wrote and told her what really happened. I was embarrassed to have her think of me as some kind of hero. She responded right away, saying she respected me for trying to save my mother and, as far as the rest, what happened to Ugo and Francesco, it was fate and I had no control over it, therefore I was innocent. Everyone, including Pop, was forgiving me and I was desperately looking for the kind of absolution that only came with punishment. So there I was, telling Mr Howe.

'I don't know what you're asking me, Finn,' he said when I finished my story. 'You can't do much for those Italian boys. After all, they were prisoners and they did escape.'

'Why didn't Pop say anything?'

'Well, I'm not sure about that,' he said, pouring our tea. 'A lot of possibilities come to mind and I'll just throw them on the table and if you don't like them you can just throw them on the floor. First off, maybe your father isn't the bogeyman you always made him out to be. You see what I'm saying? Maybe you should give him the benefit of the doubt, so to speak.' I nodded agreement but even though I was baffled by Pop's behavior I didn't feel any differently toward him. 'Then, and this is pure speculating, could be he admired you for what you tried to do. Even though it was wrong and I'm not saying it wasn't. You see what I'm saying? You tried to save your mother from something you thought was bad and that's a thing to admire in a fella.'

'Yeah, but I was wrong about that, too.' The doctors started the shock treatments a few weeks after Mom was returned to Franklin Village and the results were remarkable. She knew who

Pop was. I wasn't allowed to see her yet because she was dealing with so much, trying to fill in all the details of the last two years. They did tell her about Fritz, and Pop said she understood and took it as well as could be expected. I had no idea what that meant.

'Finn, I think maybe you're being too hard on yourself.' He gave Duke a piece of a cookie. 'Anyway, one other thing comes to mind. In fact, I was thinking about it even before you brought up the matter at hand.' He leaned across the table and looked me square in the eye. 'You're not the little fella I picked up in the barn all scratched and torn by that owl anymore. You're growing up.' His eyes softened and he patted my hand. 'If I had anything to do about it, I'd hold that off for a few more years. But there's no stopping time, boy, no matter how hard you try. You're growing up and your father knows it just as sure as he knows time's going by for him, too.' He leaned back in his chair. 'Now, that's why I think your father is acting different toward you. Cause he knows that in the blink of an eye he'll have a man to reckon with, not a boy.'

Pedalling home I thought about what Mr Howe said, and he was right. I was growing up. Next year the eighth grade and after that high school and, then, the rest of my life. I wasn't at all sure I wanted to do it.

The news of President Roosevelt's death in mid-April was shocking and sorrowful. As Father Boyle had done at Mario Pascali's funeral, the press likened him to Moses leading the Israelites out of darkness to the Promised Land, and, like Moses, who died before he got there, Franklin Delano Roosevelt died when the world was on the brink of peace but he never lived to see it. A few weeks later Adolph Hitler shot himself and was burned with his mistress, by his officers, in a ceremonial Viking hero's funeral, and a few days later the fighting in Europe stopped. We sat in dark movie theatres watching the newsreels, one moment elated by our liberating troops and the next, horrified and sickened by what they found in the concentration camps. We watched as the Allied prisoners were released and we waited at home for the phone call or telegram telling us the army had found Fritz and he was alive and well. But we heard nothing from the war department. And then, in August, a single bomb was dropped on Hiroshima, killing almost 70,000 Japanese, and people all over the globe were dancing in the streets. World War II was over.

And so we tumbled toward the long-awaited peace. Rationing stopped and the boys started coming home. Air-raid drills and blackout curtains were a thing of the past. Women left the work force and returned to the home, and war brides became a permanent part of the landscape. Pop stopped disappearing on Saturdays and I didn't know why until one afternoon, when Bridie and I were browsing in Ferris's Department Store, we saw Josie Cleary, still looking like a movie star, shopping with Mr Cleary. The war wasn't the only thing that ended.

'I'm about froze,' said Honey. 'You two must be ready to die.' Simon was driving and Bridie was in the passenger seat and they were both soaking wet. Honey and I were hunched together in the back waiting for the heat to kick in. The rain was coming down so hard the windshield wipers were useless.

'Look at how pretty this is.' Bridie was looking at a shell she'd picked up on the beach. 'The inside is all creamy and pink. Not a bad house for something as disgusting as a clam.'

'I'm hungry,' Simon was wiping the steam off the inside of the window. 'Let's stop.'

'I'm going to get killed when I get home. My daddy's going to be worried sick.' Honey untied the scarf holding his straw hat and took it off. 'But let's stop anyway. What difference does another half-hour make?' We were on the rickety plank bridge crossing to the mainland and every time the lightning flashed the bay lit up and we could see the fishing boats in their moorings riding the choppy water. Simon pulled into a place just off the bridge, a small restaurant connected to a boat rental, and, except for a few scattered, off-season customers, it was all ours. A tiny old lady with dyed black sausage curls and dark blue eye shadow took our order.

'You know, it's good luck to touch an albino,' she said, rubbing Honey's shoulder. 'I bet I win at bingo tonight.'

'It's even better luck to kiss one.' Bridie leaned over and kissed Honey softly on the lips. When the waitress left the table she said, 'That skinny old witch must dye that hair with shoe polish. Cripes!' While we were waiting for our food, she and Simon went off to the restrooms to dry off.

'You think Bridie loves Simon?' Honey was playing with the oyster crackers, putting them in the squares on the checkered tablecloth.

'Yeah, sure. Bridie loves everybody.'

'I mean special like. She loves Simon special.' He popped a few crackers in his mouth. 'She told Elizabeth and Cat. She say she love Simon a whole lot. They told me she say that.' He stared at me through his thick glasses for a moment. 'You love her?'

'Not like you mean.' Simon had always been a favorite of Bridie's. He was her discovery, her private property. I knew that. But when Honey talked about her loving him in a special way, I got a peculiar kind of sick feeling. 'Simon's too old for her.'

'She don't think so.' He turned his attention to the rain on the window. 'Sometimes I think maybe I love her.' He ate a few more crackers. 'Cat let me play with her tits once.' He looked at me but before I could comment Simon and Bridie came back to the table. She had combed her hair back and it was slick and flat against her head and her cheeks were flushed and her eyes as green as grass. I don't think she ever in her life looked as beautiful as she did that day.

While we ate we talked about Thanksgiving. It was the first big holiday since the war and everyone was planning to make it special. Mr Stebbins, Honey's father, was taking him to Georgia to meet all the aunts and uncles and cousins he had never met. It was the first family reunion since before the war and Tessie wasn't going to be able to go because she always did exceptional business on holidays. She said she got every man in town who didn't have someplace else to go so Charles always made a nice big buffet. Honey was going to have a picture taken with all his relatives so he wouldn't have to look at the tattered photo of the people he didn't know and pretend they were his family anymore. Laurie and Kitty and Bridie were having dinner at their house and Bridie, who always loved a party, was doing all the planning. The guest list included Pop and Simon and me, the Ganises, Mr Howe, Mrs Shultz and Big Tum and Little Tum. Pop was cooking the turkey because he did the best turkey in the neighborhood. His secret was basting it every fifteen minutes with white wine while it slow roasted. Little Tum was making the desserts and Mrs Ganis was making her famous noodle pudding. Kitty and Bridie were going to shop for new dresses and all in all, as Bridie put it, 'It's going to be the best damn dinner since the Pilgrims had their wingding with the Indians.' Mina and the baby were having dinner with the Pascalis but they planned to come up to Bridie's in the late afternoon.

It was still raining when we dropped Honey off and as he got out of the car he saw his father standing in the doorway with Charles.

'He's going to kill me.'

'Boy, you got a lot of explaining to do!' yelled Mr Stebbins.

'Hi, Mr Stebbins,' Bridie was trying to sound casual. 'We were just having so much fun we forgot the time.'

'I'll show him some fun. You get on upstairs. Where is your head? You had us worried sick. What is wrong with you, boy?' Honey waved and went in the house, followed by his father and Charles.

By the time we got to our house the rain had stopped but the gutter was full and when Bridie got out of the car she purposely stepped in the water.

'The damn shoes were ruined anyway,' she said as she crossed the street. Simon and I had barely gotten in the house and taken off our coats when we heard her scream. We ran out the front door and she was on her porch, just standing there screaming. Mr and Mrs Ganis came out and we all started across the street just as Mrs Cavanaugh appeared in her ratty fur coat.

'What's the matter?' Simon had her by the shoulders trying to calm her down but she kept screaming. Mr Ganis ran into the house and Mrs Ganis and I followed and there was Laurie, in his bathrobe, lying on the kitchen floor. His face was contorted and his skin was blue and I knew right away that he was dead. Mrs Ganis started crying and Mr Ganis knelt down to see if he was breathing.

'Oh my God. Oh my God. Call a doctor . . . an ambulance. Oh my God.' Simon brought Bridie into the house and Mrs Ganis went to her. He came into the kitchen and felt Laurie's neck for a pulse.

'Jesus Christ.' He made the sign of the cross as he went to the phone.

Bridie pulled away from Mrs Ganis and went to Laurie. 'He's all right, isn't he?'

'Darling . . .' Mr Ganis tried to soothe her.

'Laurie, wake up.' She started shaking the body. 'Damn it, wake up, you hear! You fell off the wagon, didn't you? Goddamn you, anyway.' She slapped him and Mr Ganis grabbed her hands. There was an open jar of peanut butter on the table and on the floor, next to Laurie, was a tablespoon with some dried peanut butter on it.

I called Pop at the railway station and he came right home. He got there before they took the body away, while the house was still filled with people. Someone had called Kitty at the hospital and she was in the kitchen, holding Laurie's hand, telling him she loved him. When Bridie saw Pop she ran to him and he held her and she said over and over, 'Make it better, Big Finn, make it better.'

'Oh Christ, I wish I could.' Mrs Ganis, whose face was all swollen and smeared with make-up, started crying again. When Pop and I went to the kitchen they were putting the body on a stretcher. Kitty was sitting at the table, looking down at her folded hands. Pop stopped the men carrying Laurie out, pulled back the sheet and looked at the twisted blue face. 'You poor son of a bitch.'

From what the police could piece together, Laurie had taken his bath and was getting ready to go to work. The soapy bath water was still in the tub and his shaving brush was caked with lather and there was a wet towel on the toilet seat. He must have gotten hungry and gone downstairs and taken a big tablespoon of peanut butter, which lodged in his throat and he choked to death. They said he had been dead for over an hour when Bridie found him.

That night, Bridie slept with me in my bed. She hadn't talked much to anyone all day and when it came time to go to bed she wouldn't sleep alone. Kitty offered to stay with her but she wanted to be with me. Pop gave her hot milk with honey and whiskey and once we were in bed she started to doze right away. She didn't want to talk and she didn't want to be held, she merely wanted to lie next to me. Simon slept on the sofa that night. I was awake until the early hours of the morning listening to Bridie whimper in her sleep and thinking about Laurie. I remembered him lying next to Kitty, alive and rosy from the sun, and I thought it all had to be a mistake. Death was for old people and soldiers, not for someone like Laurie. I could hear Pop walking around in his room mumbling and I stopped breathing so I could hear what he was saying. He wasn't mumbling, he was crying.

Bridie's Aunt Theresa came from Boston and she and Pop made all the arrangements. When Deirdre died Pop bought a plot in the corner of the cemetery big enough for the whole family. When our time came, he, Mom, Fritz and I were to be buried right next to her. Pop didn't want Laurie to be off by himself, surrounded by a lot of strangers, so he asked Father Boyle to bury him in our plot. Maybe he thought there was room for Laurie because in his heart he didn't expect Fritz to ever come home. He asked Aunt Theresa if she thought Laurie might have wanted to be buried near his wife but she said it was impossible because Bridie's mother was buried in Ireland. As far as she was concerned, Our Lady of Perpetual Help was the perfect place for him.

The wake was at McConnell's Funeral Home where he was laid out for two nights. He was dressed in his good gray suit and after Bridie combed his hair the way he always wore it, even with the make-up, he looked just like himself. He had a handsome profile and silhouetted against the ivory satin of the coffin lining he looked like a matinee idol. The parade of people coming to pay their respects was never-ending. There were the regular customers from the Prussian Inn, Kitty's friends from the hospital, the neighbors, all the kids in the eighth grade, the Rosary Society and several people no one ever saw before. Two women, one slightly plump with a black half veil and the other with short auburn hair and horn-rimmed glasses, stood in the back the second night and stayed until everyone left. Mr Howe couldn't attend any of the services because he was suffering from pleurisy. The plate next to the coffin was piled high with mass cards and there were so many flowers they spilled out into the hall. The second afternoon, before people started coming for the viewing, Bridie and I read all the cards on the flowers. There was a large bouquet of orchids and white roses and the card read *With condolences, Tess Stebbins and friends*. Someone had placed a small bunch of flowers in the coffin and that card just said *Remember*. And there was another little bouquet, a few yellow roses with white carnations, from Iris, and Bridie and I finally knew who Laurie visited back in the days when he went to Tessie's Place.

The family and close friends gathered at McConnell's the morning of the funeral to say a final farewell before the coffin was closed. While we took turns filing past Laurie, Mr McConnell waited in the shadows, anxious to get on with his job. Pop and Simon went to the coffin together. Pop had asked me to go with him but Bridie held my hand tight so I waited to go with her. They knelt and said a silent prayer, blessed themselves and kissed Laurie on the cheek before going into the hall. Aunt Theresa was next. She rearranged the rosary entwined in his fingers, then leaned over, very close to his face.

'Don't you look grand lying there in all your glory. You were a sweet lad and a sweet man as well. There's not a soul can say a bad word about you and that's the truth. You did your best little brother. And now you're with the angels and Mam and Da. God love you.' She kissed him, touched his cheek and went outside. Bridie and Kitty looked at each other, wondering who should go next. Kitty smiled and held Bridie for a moment then went and knelt. She whispered whatever she had to say but we couldn't hear her, then she held his face in her hands and kissed a long kiss before she left. I was feeling sick because everyone was kissing him and I didn't want to kiss a dead man. Bridie and I were the last. We walked to the coffin and I started to kneel down but she held my hand so tight I couldn't. She just stood there looking at Laurie and I thought I should pray or something because I knew Mr McConnell was watching from the shadows.

'He shouldn't have done it,' she said. I could feel her whole body trembling.

'Aren't you going to pray or say something to him?'

'Why? He's dead. He can't hear me.'

'Well, damn it, you have to do something. Kiss him goodbye.'

'Why should I?' Her voice was shaking. 'He didn't kiss me goodbye.' She dropped my hand and left me standing there. In a way she was right. He was dead and he probably couldn't hear anything but there was always the outside chance.

Mr McConnell came toward me. 'Please join the others outside and we'll proceed to the church.' I knew he was going to close the coffin and Laurie would be gone for ever.

'Wait.' I leaned down. 'This is from Bridie and me,' and I kissed the cold, unyielding lips.

We stood at the graveside and Father Boyle reminded us that, like Laurie, we would all soon return to dust. One of the altar boys, standing just behind Father, was dancing from side to side as if he had to go to the bathroom. Most of the people who had been at mass had gone home but, apart from us, there were small groups standing off to the side. Tessie and Iris were there with Honey who winked at me every time he caught my eye. And Mattie Horn was there wearing the same coat Laurie had thrown up on when she'd helped Kitty get him home in his drunken stupor. And there was a group of men, I assumed they were cronies from the Prussian Inn, standing huddled together, their collars turned up against the cold. The two women, the one with the veil and the one with the horn-rimmed glasses, were holding on to each other. Father blessed the coffin with holy water, said his amen and headed down the path with the altar boys close behind. The Ganises left and Aunt Theresa, flanked by Simon and Pop, was next. Bridie let go of my hand and slipped her arm in mine.

'That's that.' There were tears coming down her cheeks. 'Let's go.' As we walked away the woman in the veil approached us. I could just see the tip of her nose and her mouth and chin and she looked familiar.

'I'm sorry about your father,' she said.

'Thanks.'

'He was a good man.' Bridie started to walk away. 'You're very pretty. A very pretty girl.'

'Let's go,' said the other woman. She smiled at Bridie. 'We have to be going.' She took the woman with the veil by the arm but she pulled away.

'You're very tall for your age.' She reached out her hand as if she was going to touch Bridie's face but she stopped herself. I kept trying to remember where I had seen her before.

'How did you know Laurie?' Bridie asked.

'It was a long time ago.'

The other woman was getting very nervous. 'We have to go. Now. You promised.' She tried to take the arm of the woman with the veil but again she pulled away.

'Just a minute more.'

'Who are you?' said Bridie. Just then I realized where I had seen that mouth and chin. It was Bridie's face. The woman was her mother.

'Bridie, come along right now.' Aunt Theresa was suddenly there between Bridie and her mother. 'Simon, get her out of here.' The other woman was dragging Bridie's mother across the cemetery toward a car parked on the street.

'You couldn't leave well enough alone, could you!' Aunt Theresa said viciously.

'I have a right!' screamed Bridie's mother.

'You have a right to nothing. And don't you ever forget it,' said Aunt Theresa.

'Wait,' said Bridie, pulling away from Simon. 'Who is she?'

'Bridie. I love you!' her mother yelled as the other woman forced her into the car. And then Bridie knew.

'Mother!' she cried. 'Mother, wait!' She fought to get away but Simon and Aunt Theresa held her back. 'Mother!' And the car drove away and disappeared around the corner. Bridie fell to the ground crying and calling Laurie and her mother, over and over again, like some lost child. Pop came back when he heard the shouting and picked Bridie up and started toward home.

We were sitting at the kitchen table, Pop, Aunt Theresa, me and Bridie. Bridie wouldn't talk to anyone. She was rigid, her mouth set and her eyes furious.

'You were never supposed to know,' said Aunt Theresa, trying to explain. 'What was the point? It would only hurt and we loved you that much we didn't want anything in the world to hurt you.' Bridie wouldn't even look at her. 'All right. I guess it was wrong but for the love of God at least let me tell you what I know.'

Bridie's mother left Laurie and Bridie when Bridie was a baby, without any explanation. She left a note in Bridie's crib and it had one word written on it. *Remember*. Off and on, Laurie received letters saying she was well but he never knew where she was. He tried to find her, even hiring detectives, but she seemed to have disappeared. The first few years she sent Christmas and birthday gifts to Bridie but that stopped after a while and from then to the moment Aunt Theresa saw her standing in the back of McConnell's Funeral Parlor, there had been no word at all from Kathleen Brennan O'Connor. And that was why there had never been any mention of marriage so far as Kitty and Laurie were concerned. Laurie, in the eyes of both Church and State, was still married. 'Now, that's the truth. I swear. We only did what we thought was right.'

Without saying a word, Bridie got up, put on her coat and went out the front door.

'Let her be,' said Pop. 'She needs time to herself to think things over. Christ knows she's been through enough.' But by nine o'clock, when she hadn't returned, Aunt Theresa was ready to call the police.

'I think I know where she might be,' I said. 'I'll go look for her.'

'Where?' asked Aunt Theresa. 'Where would she be going at this hour?'

She was squeezed into the big fan chair with Tessie, and Mr Stebbins and Honey were on the sofa.

'You want something to eat?' Mr Stebbins patted the sofa next to him and I sat down and he put his arm around my shoulder.

'No thanks.' Bridie didn't say anything. I wasn't even sure she knew I was there.

'My mama left me, too,' said Honey. 'I was just telling Bridie.'

'She was just a kid herself,' said Tessie. 'She didn't know what the hell she was doing.' It was strangely quiet and I wondered where the ladies were.

'Can I call home and tell them she's okay? They're worried.'

'Help yourself,' said Tessie. 'And let me talk to your daddy.' Simon answered and I told him Bridie was all right and asked him to put Pop on the line.

'Pop, hold on, Tessie wants to talk to you.' I handed her the phone.

'Tom? Everybody's safe and sound here so don't worry. Listen, it's starting to rain so, if it's okay with you, we'll just keep the kids here tonight ... No, no, no, nobody's working. They went to the movies ... Okay, they'll be home in the morning. Bye.' She hung up the phone. 'Okay, girl, we're going to put you to bed cause you are one exhausted child.' They put Bridie in Tessie's room, in the big bed with the satin sheets, and Charles brought her a tray with milk and cookies and put it next to the bed. Bridie still hadn't said anything. I stood in the hall and listened to Tessie talking to her.

'Don't you be too hard on your mama. Life is meaner than cat shit and most everybody's trying to do the best they can to get through it. Someday you're going to understand that it takes all kinds to make up this world and you don't want to look back and remember bad things you felt or said. It just ain't worth it, girl.' She started to hum. 'I'm going to stay here until you doze off, then I'll be right out on the couch. Now, close your pretty eyes and try to sleep. Things are always better in the morning.' She started humming again and closed the door.

After Mr Stebbins had turned off the light and told Honey and me not to talk all night we lay in bed listening to the rain on the roof.

'If there's a God,' said Honey, 'why does he kill people? That don't make no sense at all to me.'

'Me neither. Sister says it's cause He loves the person so much He wants them in heaven with Him.'

'Bullshit. If He loves them, how come He don't let them stay here and have a good time?'

'And how come He takes little babies?' I said, thinking about Deirdre.

'Yeah, how come?' We listened to thunder rumbling off in the distance. 'I don't even think there's a heaven.' I wanted to, but I didn't really know what I thought because it changed every day. I didn't want to talk about it anymore.

'What did Cat's tits feel like?' I asked.

'Nice. They was real nice. Big as cantaloupes.'

'Is that all you did?'

'So far. But when I'm ready she said I can do everything. That she'd teach me good.'

'You think she'd teach me, too? I mean when I'm ready?'

'Oh sure. Cat's real nice.' And so, the subject of death was replaced by sex, which was life and immortality and ultimately a hell of a lot more fun to talk about in the middle of the night in a storm.

The next morning, the storm had passed and Bridie and I walked home through the crisp, cool, rain-washed day and she said that, except for me and a very few other people, she didn't trust anybody in the whole goddamn world.

'They were only trying to protect you –' was all I got out.

'I'm warning you right now, if you take their side I'll never speak to you again. The Japanese could put splinters under my nails and I still wouldn't speak to you. You're my friend and don't you ever forget it as long as you live.'

'Okay, okay. Damn. I was only going to say –'

'I know what you were going to say so just forget it.' We walked along in silence for a while. 'You think she was pretty?'

'Yeah. She looked just like you.'

'I'll probably never see her again.'

'Maybe you will.'

'I don't even know where she lives. If I did, I'd write her a letter. I want to ask her why she left us.' We turned into Livery Street. 'I always knew she was alive somewhere.'

As soon as we walked in the door, Pop pulled me aside. 'For Christ's sake, don't say the two of you spent the night in a whorehouse. Theresa will have a shit fit. I said you were with friends.' There was something very reassuring and comforting about having my own father conspire with me.

'I won't say anything.'

'Aunt Theresa,' said Bridie, 'I did a lot of thinking last night and I'm not going back to Boston with you.'

'And who ever said you were? You're in school here and you should stay until you graduate. I've arranged for you to stay with Kitty Neal until June. Then we'll talk about what happens next.'

'I'm not staying with Kitty Neal. I want to stay right here.'

'Here! There's no room for you here.'

'Yes, there is,' I said. 'The little room in the front. We fixed it up for Simon when he came home.' I turned to Pop. 'Is it okay?'

'Please, Big Finn? I want to stay here with you and Finn and Simon. Please?'

'Well, it's fine with me, darling. If that's what you want.' He turned to Aunt Theresa. 'What do you say?'

'I'll pay her share.'

'Now, there'll be no talk of that.'

She smiled and nodded her head. 'I'll get my things. You can take me to the train station.'

And Bridie moved in with us.

PART THREE

Bridie parked under one of the few old maples left standing. The sun was blazing.

'Let's sit outside.' I picked up the lunch bag and started out of the car.

'No, there are ants all over the place. Anyway, it's no cooler out there.' We opened all the doors and Bridie pulled her skirt up to cool her legs. She poured ice tea from the thermos and I dug out the sandwiches. A slight breeze moved through the car.

'God that feels good,' she said. Workmen, on their lunch break, sat in the shade of the heavy equipment and we could hear them laughing and swearing. 'How much do you think a house will cost here?' she asked.

'A hell of a lot. Look how big those foundations are. These houses are going to be like the houses uptown.'

'I bet Mr Howe is turning over in his grave.' She took a bite of her sandwich. 'It looks so different with everything gone. Where was the barn?'

'Right over there,' I pointed to a patch of bare earth. 'And the house was there.'

'It seems like just yesterday that I saw that old house and barn for the first time.'

'It's eight years.'

'Oh God. Eight years since I saved your skinny little ass from dying of owl fever?'

'Eight years.'

'How depressing. Why did they have to cut all the trees? And the orchard?'

'Those old apple trees were all dead, anyway.'

'I guess. I hate this. I could cry.'

'We shouldn't have come here.'

'I just get so sick and tired of eating lunch the same place every day. Don't you?'

'I like to listen to the music.'

'Students practicing is not always music. You want a concert, go to Carnegie Hall.' We sat quietly eating for a while. 'It's only a week till Big Finn's birthday. What are we going to get him?'

'I can't think of anything.'

'I still say a TV.'

'He doesn't want a TV.'

'Cripes, we're the only family on Livery Street without a TV. We might as well be in the Dark Ages.' She turned on the motor.

'Are we leaving? I haven't finished yet.'

'I want to listen to the radio.' She tuned in a station and Nat King Cole was singing 'Mona Lisa'. 'I hate work. You think it's too late to become a Rockette?' She laughed, pulling her hair up to cool the back of her neck and I could see damp little curls sticking to her skin.

'You just started your job. Jesus, you got the rest of your life.'

'Thanks for reminding me.' She mopped her forehead with the hem of her skirt. 'How come you don't sweat?'

'Cripples don't sweat. It's our trade-off with God. Didn't you know that?' I sipped my ice tea. 'This is depressing. It's so bleak.'

'Where was that little spring? You know, where we used to pick watercress?'

'It was right on the edge of the cornfield.'

'Where was the damn cornfield?'

'Come on, let's look for it.' I got out of the car and started across the field.

'We'll get all sweaty,' she turned off the motor and followed.

'You will, not me.'

As we passed the workmen one of them whistled and Bridie turned to see who it was. She half smiled her arrogant, uninterested, flirty smile and turned to me. 'That guy is cute.'

Without even looking, I knew her behind would be swinging ever so slightly more than it had before the whistle. She was all legs and dark hair and lustrous skin and her walk was easy and confident. She rarely wore make-up and little or no scent but there was always a sexy, soapy clean fragrance about her and when she did sweat the fragrance intensified. Bridie had grown into a naturally graceful young woman with an innate, unselfconscious elegance. Her style was no style, yet she always looked fashionable, even with the chunky, cheap jewelry she refused to give up.

'Which one is cute?' I said.

'The one with the undershirt.'

'He's not the one who whistled. It was the big fat guy sitting next to him.'

'You rat,' she said, taking a swipe at me. We looked for the spring but we couldn't even find a damp spot. All those years that little spring bubbled up from some underground stream and now, like everything else of Mr Howe's, it was gone. The machines had chewed up and carried away every brick and piece of wood, every nail and hinge and window frame. All tangible evidence of Mr Howe and his Miriam were erased and it was time for new people to build new memories where the new houses were being built. We were standing in what had been the orchard and I could feel the cool shade of the old trees as I used to when Duke and I lulled away our afternoons deciding what to do with our future. Ghost pigeons flew around in a phantom barn and shadows of kids on bicycles circled in the dust. I could almost hear the clatter of teacups on saucers and smell Mr Howe's pipe tobacco.

'Let's get out of here.' We headed for the car.

'You want to go to a dinner dance with me?' she said on the way back to work.

'No.'

'Aw, come on, Finn. I have to go and I don't know anybody in the office yet. You know how weird that is. Standing there, wondering if anybody is going to talk to you. Come on, I really do have to go. It's at the Prussian Inn.'

'No,' I repeated. 'You know I hate stuff like that. Ask somebody who can dance.'

'You're good at the rumba.' She started laughing. It was her contention that the rumba, with all its disjointed hip action, was the perfect dance for the handicapped.

'No.'

'Don't be such a shit. I'd do it for you.'

'I wouldn't ask you to.'

'Please, you know how much I hate to beg. Really. It means a lot to me.'

'Okay. But I will not, I repeat *not*, dance. Even the rumba. Get some other asshole up to dance.'

'I owe you one.'

'You owe me a lot.'

She dropped me off in front of Finegold's. 'That dress is cute,' she said, looking at the mannequin in the window, frozen in a breezy wave to passersby. 'Can you get me a discount?'

'Sure.'

'See how much it is, okay?'

'Okay.'

'Oh, by the way,' she put the car in gear, 'you have to rent a tux.'

'A tux! Do you know how much it costs to rent a tux!'

'Hey, I'm worth every penny.' I could hear her laughing as she drove off.

After Bridie moved into the house we spent the next several years trying to find her mother. Almost every day we called information in a different town in New Jersey and asked if they had a listing for Kathleen O'Connor. If not, we asked for Kathleen Brennan. And if information happened to have one, we nervously called the number but it was never her mother. We had a road map and we circled every town we tried so we wouldn't repeat ourselves. We were certain she was somewhere in New Jersey, and probably close by, because Aunt Theresa said she didn't know where she was so the only way Kathleen could have learned about Laurie's death was by reading it in the paper. We didn't know the name of the woman with the cropped hair and horn-rimmed glasses so there was no way to track her down. Bridie did hear from her mother a few times. Not long after Laurie's funeral, she received a letter with five one-hundred-dollar bills. She told Bridie to let her know if she ever needed her but she didn't give an address or phone number. The postmark was Cape May but there was no Kathleen Brennan or O'Connor in the Cape May phone book. I almost dropped down dead when Bridie gave me the five hundred dollars to keep for her so she wouldn't spend any of it. Without telling her, I opened a savings account in her name at the First National Bank and a week later, when she asked for some of the money and I told her what I did with it, she slapped me. Bridie also started receiving cards on her birthday and at Christmas, always with different postmarks and always with some money, which she stopped giving to me to hold for her.

The house across the street, without Laurie and Bridie, sat eerily empty for several months. What little furniture there was was sold because Bridie wanted none of it. She ignored the very existence of the place but the bare windows, staring blindly at passersby, made me lonely for Laurie. I kept expecting him to come through the front door with Kitty Neal but the front door never opened until the contractors started renovating. The owner was converting it into two apartments and they were both rented to students, returning GIs and their wives, before work even started. What had stood for almost a hundred years as a single family dwelling was the first house on Livery Street irreversibly altered to accommodate the changing times.

At first, life with Bridie wasn't that much different because ever since she moved to Livery Street she spent most of her evenings with us as Mom worried about her being home alone when Laurie worked. It did complicate things in the morning because there was only one bathroom and she was in there all the time. Also, at night, when everyone was trying to fall asleep, she'd leave her door open and talk to anyone who happened to be listening about anything that happened to cross her mind.

'Mrs Cavanaugh stopped me today. I can't stand that woman. And if you get downwind of her you could faint from the stink. God, doesn't she know somebody invented soap? I wonder who did invent soap? She should be reported to the board of health. You could catch something just breathing the same air as her.' A second or two would pass. 'I'm going to make some special cookies to take to Mrs Finn this weekend. With nuts. She loves nuts. I just hope that Mildred doesn't get her hands on them. She doesn't need nuts, she's already a nut.' Another second would pass. 'I heard women get brain tumors from bleaching their hair. Did you ever hear that? The bleach goes through their scalp and they get brain tumors and die. I mean, who the hell would bleach their hair knowing they're going to get brain tumors? Isn't that stupid? Finn, you want to go to the movies Friday? Bette Davis. I love her. Sometimes she bleaches her hair. I wonder if she knows about those brain tumors. Maybe I should write her.'

The actual running of the house had always been fairly efficient. Pop and Simon were both very tidy and I did my best even though it took a conscious effort. But Bridie put herself in charge and organized and ordered us around with the authority of a drill sergeant. She planned menus, always featuring the foods Simon was particularly fond of, and demanded everyone always be on time for meals even though she wasn't doing all the cooking. For the most part, Pop and Simon were amused while I was usually irritated. But Bridie was happy. She had control and that always made her happy. And she had the added advantage of keeping herself so busy she could avoid mourning Laurie.

Honey never returned from his Thanksgiving trip to Georgia. Mr Stebbins came back, picked up his things, all his books and maps and model airplanes, piled them in the car and took them to Honey in Valdosta, where he was staying with his great-aunt and uncle. Mr Stebbins told us it was a good-size town in the middle of cotton country and they grew tobacco and water-melons, too. It wasn't far from the Florida State line and about an hour's drive from the Okefenokee Swamp. Honey always wanted to go to places with exotic names and Valdosta and Okefenokee sounded wonderfully exotic to me.

'It was time for him to go live someplace else,' said Mr Stebbins. 'It's not right for a boy to grow up in a whorehouse.' Bridie was sitting with Cat and Elizabeth at the kitchen table and I was helping Mr Stebbins load the car. 'Honey didn't know anyplace else but this. He spent all his time here. It's just not right.'

Tessie was standing at the top of the stairs, crying. 'Well, it's not right to just take the boy away, either.'

'He wants to stay there. Son of a bitch, you make it sound like I forced him.'

'I mean from me. It's not right to take him away from me. I raised him and he's all I got. He's mine.'

'No, he's not. He's mine and I want what's good for him.'

'Don't you think I did good for him?' She lit a cigarette. 'Jesus, I gave the child everything he ever wanted. When you were in the army he had the best of everything. He always had the best of everything. I love that boy. If I knew you were going to do this I never would have let you take him to Georgia.'

'Tessie, he is my son. I can take him anywhere I want. I don't have to get your permission.'

'And just like that, all of a sudden, I don't have nothing to say about him!' She started crying again.

'Finn,' Mr Stebbins took a box out of my hands, 'you go in the kitchen and get yourself something to eat. Tessie and I got to talk.'

'You're damn right we got to talk,' she said as I went. Bridie and Cat were drinking coffee and Elizabeth was knitting.

'Tessie's mad, huh?' said Bridie.

'More sad I think.'

'It sure is going to be different with Honey gone.' Cat was stirring her coffee thoughtfully. 'Poor kid, growing up in a whorehouse and he didn't even get to lose his cherry.'

'Oh yes he did,' said Elizabeth quietly.

'He did!' Bridie's eyes lit up.

'When?' I said it without thinking. 'I mean, when did he have time?'

'Hell, baby, it only takes a few minutes.' Elizabeth poured herself some coffee. 'He wasn't a bit nervous. Well, maybe just a little. But he's a natural. He's going to make some gal very happy.' She laughed, which was unusual for Elizabeth. 'That's my professional opinion.' Honey never told me. It had to have happened between the night of Laurie's funeral and a few days later when he left for Georgia.

'He was kind of young, wasn't he?' said Bridie.

'Old enough, girl. Old enough.' Elizabeth laughed again.

'I was only eleven,' said Cat. 'I mean the first time.'

'Cripes!'

'You going to tell that rabbit story again?' Elizabeth went back to her knitting.

'They haven't heard it.'

'Well, do the short version.'

'God,' Cat pouted for a moment. 'Well, we had big old rabbits, my daddy used to raise them to eat, and one time I was watching a mother rabbit nurse her babies and I wanted to know what it felt like so I played a game with my little brothers. We went out behind the spring house and I was the mama and they were the bunnies. I don't know why I wanted to do that, I didn't even have breasts yet. Anyway, they were sucking away and my cousin Dwayne came and saw us. He was just a little older than me, not even a year, and I liked him a whole lot. Well, we did it. Right there with my little brothers watching. We used to do it all the time. I thought I'd marry him when I grew up but he got kicked in the chest by a mule and got his heart squashed and he died. I really liked him. Anyway, my uncle was madder than all hell at that old mule and he shot him in the middle of a field and just left him there in the sun to rot. He swelled up like a big old balloon and there were big black buzzards and crows and all kinds of nasty bugs hanging around for weeks.' She smiled. 'I think I loved Dwayne.'

As we were walking up Allen Street Bridie said, 'I told you that Cat was feebleminded. Who would want to play mother rabbit? And she did it with her own cousin. That would be like me doing it with you. God, that's sickening! And she was only eleven. I just don't get it.'

All I could think about was Honey. He was gone and I didn't know if I'd ever see him again. He should have told me he wasn't coming back. There were things we had to say to each other. But he was gone without saying anything. Just like Laurie. They were both gone. How could someone be there one minute and be gone for ever the next? It was as easy as taking a

Thanksgiving trip to Valdosta, Georgia, or eating a tablespoon full of peanut butter. I didn't know which was worse, death or separation. When someone was dead at least you knew where they were. But when they just went away they were having a whole life without you and that seemed impossible. I thought of Honey the first time Bridie and I saw him, pale and tentative, emerging from the shadows, asking if we went to school. He could have been asking if we went to the moon, he said it with so much wonder. And now he was gone. He'd stepped into that tattered old picture, to sit on that front porch with the family he always wanted, perhaps for ever.

The one change that seemed to occur right about the time Bridie moved in, was the change in Simon. Almost imperceptibly, he began to have a life of his own, separate and apart from us. It was only a missed dinner or a night out without Pop but there was never any explanation of where he had been. Bridie, exercising her territorial imperative so far as Simon was concerned, would fret and ask questions but he always dismissed her with vague references to doing something with one of the fellows at the water company. It wasn't that he was unpleasant. Simon was naturally considerate and warm. But now, he was also secretive and moody and much less communicative. Our talks at night when the lights were out, the comforting reminder of the days when Fritz and I shared the bedroom, were shorter and only about subjects I initiated. He confided nothing and when I asked if there was a problem he always said it was simply a matter of being tired and all conversation ended and he went to sleep. Whatever was happening, it wasn't something he wanted to share.

He did have one consuming passion and that was his search for Fritz. We all wanted to know what had happened to Fritz but with Simon it was manic. The war was over and he didn't understand why the government couldn't give us more specific information. There were organizations effectively helping displaced persons from all over Europe yet some of our own servicemen were still missing. He wrote letters to senators and congressmen, to the war department and even to President Truman, demanding a more extensive investigation. He wrote to editors of newspapers and veterans' organizations, the American Legion and the Veterans of Foreign Wars, and he contacted other people who had a loved one still listed as missing in action. He was determined to discover what had happened to Fritz and he was not about to give up. He had to know if he was dead or alive.

We thought Mom might be home in time for our graduation from Our Lady of Perpetual Help but the doctors felt she needed more time in the hospital. Her progress was steady and promising and Pop was told he could expect her to come home in the near future. Thanks, Miss Webster said, to the new psychiatric breakthroughs resulting from all the work done with returning servicemen.

The first time Bridie and I saw her after her return to the world she looked thin and tired. It was in the spring and when we arrived at the Village we found her sitting alone in a small gazebo on the edge of a flower garden, reading. It seemed wrong seeing her sitting there without supervision. And she was *reading*, something she hadn't done in years. When she saw us coming across the lawn she got up and started toward us and Bridie and I ran to her.

'Hey, Mrs Finn, how you doing?' Bridie hugged her.

'Oh Bridie, look at you! As pretty as a picture.'

'Hi, Mom.' I suddenly didn't know what to say.

'Well, Finn, you're getting so tall.' She hugged me and held me close for a minute and tears came to her eyes. She put her arms around both of us and held tight. 'Thank God and Saint Jude,' she whispered.

'I'm not as tall as Bridie.' It was the only thing I could think to say. Pop kissed her and we sat in the gazebo and for the first few moments even Bridie was at a loss for words. Miss Webster said Mom was like someone who had been on a long journey and we should try to think of her that way. Sitting there, wondering what to talk about, I tried but it didn't work. If she *had* been on a journey we could have questioned her about the places she saw, food she ate or the people she met. But none of us knew what questions to ask someone who'd recently returned from hell.

'Now,' she said, putting us at ease, 'I know about Fritz and Laurie,' she took Bridie's hand. 'He's with the angels, sweetheart. I know it as true as I'm sitting here. And Fritz is in the palm of the Lord's hand. So, we don't have to be afraid to talk about them. God's will be done, yes?' She smiled and slipped her hand into the pocket of her dress and I could hear the tinkle of her rosary beads. 'We have so much catching up to do. I want to know everything that's happened. Please, don't be afraid to talk about anything.' And for the rest of the afternoon we talked. But it was measured talk. There was nothing spontaneous about Mom. Each new subject was considered for a split second and then approached with a controlled rationality. This was not the Mom I remembered. I had expected her to be just as she was before she started getting sick. I wanted the bursts of laughter and the little rages, the scolding looks and the compassionate smiles, but instead there was a quiet, automatic acceptance.

She did have plans and she was enthusiastic about the future. Now that the war was over and she was no longer needed at the depot, when she was able to come home she wanted to go back to teaching. Whether or not that was even a possibility, I didn't know, but Pop sat nodding encouragement so Bridie and I agreed with everything she said. She was looking forward to seeing Mina and the baby. She had yet to meet her only grandchild, who was already walking and talking. Pop didn't say anything but he was annoyed with Mina because she rarely came to the house with Maria. She worked at the telephone company, which was right around the corner from our house, but she never dropped in to say hello or called to see how we were. We had presents for the baby that sat for weeks on the sideboard in the dining room, presents she never would have received if we hadn't finally delivered them. Pop didn't say much but he was hurt. Yet if Bridie and I said anything he'd make excuses for Mina and defend her, saying her life was wrapped up with the Pascalis and we had to understand that. Pop had given Mom some pictures of Maria which she carried in her pocket and showed to anyone who would take the time to look at them. She laughed and said the nurses started running when they saw her coming, afraid she'd have yet another batch of pictures.

Before we left that afternoon, Mom asked to speak privately with Pop. There was the matter of gifts for certain people who were graduating from grammar school, as Mom put it. Bridie and I went looking for Miss Webster. We were still famous at Franklin Village as the kids who were kidnapped by the Italian prisoners so everyone knew us and they all greeted us. One of the nurses in the women's building told us Miss Webster was in the reception hall, in the records room.

'What do you want to see her for?' asked Bridie as we walked around the side of the building.

'I want to ask her something.'

'What?'

'Something about Mom.'

'What about her?'

'You'll see.'

'She won't tell you anything. She'll just say Big Finn should ask the doctor.'

'She'll tell me.'

'You always have to be right, don't you?'

'Why don't you just go back and wait with Pop. I'll be there after I see Miss Webster.'

'No. I want to hear what she says.'

We found her sitting at a desk with another nurse, going over some records. I was surprised to see her smoking.

'Well, Bridie and Finn. What did you think of the change in Mrs Finnegan?'

'It's wonderful. She's just like her old self,' said Bridie.

'She is not.' I wanted Bridie to leave me alone to ask my questions.

'She is, too.'

'No, she's not.' I turned to Miss Webster. 'There's something different about her. She's like . . . slow or something.'

'Finn, you should be a doctor when you grow up.' She smiled at the other nurse. 'Your mother takes medicine to keep her calm. That's all it is. After electroconvulsive therapy patients take certain medications. When she's a little further along she probably won't have to take anything but right now it's necessary. She'll be fine. Finn, you're going to be old before your time, you worry so much.'

'He does,' said Bridie. 'He worries about everything. God, he worries cause he doesn't have anything to worry about. No kidding. If you lived with him he'd drive you nuts.'

'Look who's talking about somebody driving a person nuts!'

'And he flies off the handle at nothing. Just listen to him.'

'Why don't you shut up for a change?'

'All right, you two, that's enough.' Miss Webster went back to her work.

'Thanks, Miss Webster,' I said as I left with Bridie trailing behind.

'Now you're mad, aren't you? You know what you are? You're moody, that's what. I'm sorry but you *do* worry all the time. It's a pain. Your mother is fine. For cripes' sake, relax.'

We were starting down the steps when I turned to her. 'Why don't you go to Boston and live with your Aunt Theresa and stop sticking your nose in my business. Go away and leave us alone. I don't want you in my house. This is my family, not yours.' Without even thinking I said the meanest thing I could ever say to her. That she wasn't wanted. She was so hurt she was paralysed. I should have apologized but I didn't because I really meant to hurt her. I was sick of her constant questioning and I was tired of her candor, which everyone else seemed to find so charming. She could say any hurtful thing she wanted to me and I was expected to accept it good-naturedly but if I said anything to criticize her she was stricken. Bridie was always good at dishing it out but she couldn't take it.

She usually sat in the front seat with Pop when there were only the three of us in the car, but riding home that day she sat alone in the back, brooding.

'Did you kids fight again?' It was obvious to Pop because neither of us was talking. 'Christ!' We didn't say anything. 'What did you do?' he said, looking at me. In this particular case I was at fault, but even if I hadn't been he would have blamed me.

'He didn't do anything,' said Bridie, grudgingly, and we rode the rest of the way home in silence.

Bridie went about proving she belonged with a vengeance. In fact, she did everything she could to make me feel like the outsider. She arranged to go to a movie with Simon at a time when I wasn't available because I promised to help Mrs Ganis beat her rugs. They spent all of a Saturday afternoon together, lunch at Winter's soda fountain, the movie, and a stroll through the university to look at the spring flowers in bloom. All she talked about during dinner that night was the dogwood and the magnolias and the daffodils and I knew that she didn't give a damn about what was blooming. She made little jokes and giggled and acted like a fool until Pop asked if she was sitting on a feather. Then she carried on like Pop said the funniest thing she ever heard. And no matter what Pop did or said she flattered him and hugged him and just couldn't keep her hands off him. Of course, he fell for it because as far as he was concerned Bridie could do no wrong. She was a girl and she was an orphan and, Joe Louis or no, she needed him and he was going to do everything he had to to make her happy.

Things were still very strained by graduation day. I bought Bridie a diary, which she was always talking about keeping, and when I gave it to her she thanked me and said she didn't get anything for me because she didn't like me. However, when I received a gift from Rebecca Steinman, a copy of a book I wanted, *Snakes Of The World*, Bridie was upset.

'What a stupid present to give someone for graduation,' she said when I showed it to her.

'I wanted this book.'

'How'd she know what you wanted?'

'I told her in a letter.'

'Is that what you write about in those letters? Stupid crap like books on snakes?'

'At least she gave me something.'

'Yeah, well, she doesn't have to live with you.'

Rebecca and I had only seen each other once, the day she told me about the cat's head, and we talked on the phone very occasionally and wrote letters, and yet Bridie hated her. She always wanted to know what I wrote to Rebecca, assuming I was saying bad things about her.

The night of graduation, with Bridie dressed in her long white gown with a wreath of flowers in her hair and me in my new blue suit, Pop gave us our presents. She received a gold charm bracelet with two charms, an Irish harp and a tiny graduation hat, and my present was a gold pocketknife with my initials engraved on it. Pop said he and Mom had talked it over and these were the gifts they decided on. Most everyone else gave us money. The Ganises, Simon, the Pascalis, Big Tum and Little Tum and Aunt Theresa, who came down from Boston, all gave us the telltale, long thin envelopes designed to exactly fit a bill. Mr Howe gave Bridie a garnet necklace of Miriam's which she had always admired and he gave me a gold chain for my pocketknife. It was a chain his father had given him along with his pocket watch which Mr Howe said would be mine when the Lord called him and he had no more use for time. But Kitty

Neal gave Bridie the most impressive gift. The two acres at the Junction had been in both Laurie and Kitty's names and when Laurie died the land went to her. But now it was all Bridie's. Kitty had tried to stay close to Bridie after Laurie's death but Bridie was little more than polite to her. The night of our graduation, Kitty, who had no family, told us she was leaving town. She was going to California to take a job in a veterans' hospital. Mrs Ganis said distance and time both helped ease the pain and thought it was a good thing for Kitty to try to start her life all over again. Mr Ganis told her to mind her own business. Everyone but Bridie hugged and kissed Kitty and wished her well. Bridie coolly shook her hand and politely thanked her for the land.

We filed through the sea of folding chairs in the school auditorium, with parents and families craning their necks to get a good look at the graduates. Bridie was my partner and she was slightly taller than me and had purposely bought shoes with a heel to make me look even shorter. All the nuns were there, sitting in a group in their stark black and white, like a pod of killer whales, wearing their best toilet water and dusting powder with looks of amazement on their faces, probably because they couldn't believe they'd managed to get yet another class through all eight grades. Father Boyle sat center stage, on what was essentially a throne, waiting for us as we parted and the boys went up the left stairs as the girls went up the right and we moved quickly to our assigned seats. Before Father gave the commencement address and handed out our diplomas, for some unknown reason, we sang 'Trees'. Either it was symbolic of something, perhaps growth, or it was simply a favorite of Sister Mary Alphonsus', who, year after year, organized and produced the graduation exercises with pride unbecoming to a nun. Father spoke about fledglings leaving the nest, soldiers going to battle, trains pulling out of stations, ships leaving port, mountain climbers starting up mountains and the Israelites marching out of Egypt and going to the Promised Land, which was clearly one of his favorite themes. But this time he failed to give Moses a mention. We had been drilled by Sister, to the point of perfection, once our names were called, to accept the diploma from Father, bow or curtsey, as the case may be, and return to our places, acknowledging applause with nothing more than a humble smile. I felt my face redden as Father called my name and I went to the podium.

'And may God bless you, Timothy Finnegan.' He said it while people were applauding. 'Your mother would be very proud if she was here.' I bowed and returned to my seat. When Bridie's name was called I knew by her smile and the bounce to her walk as she approached Father that she was not about to settle for a curtsey. I couldn't hear what he said to her but when he handed her the diploma she turned to the audience, bowed, and gave them Winston Churchill's victory sign. Everyone laughed, including Father Boyle, and there was a distinctly visible shudder in the pod of nuns. All I felt was anger. Once again, Bridie did things her way and there would be no repercussions and no reprimands. She was funny and charming and that seemed to be all that mattered.

We could have gone to the public high school in town but I had never been to a public school and the prospect was unsettling so I opted to travel eleven miles each way to Trenton every day and go to Immaculate Conception, the nearest Catholic boys' high. I also wanted to get away from Bridie. She hated the idea of spending four more years with the nuns at St Mary's, the Catholic girls' high, also in Trenton and across town from Immaculate Conception, but she thought she might be missing something if she stayed in town while I traveled every day so she put off deciding where to go until the last minute. Pop left it up to her completely. When Aunt Theresa came to our graduation, she talked it over with Bridie and Pop and they all came to the conclusion that Bridie should stay with us. Pop said the house on Livery Street was her home and we were her family. A part of me resented the decision but the truth was I couldn't imagine Bridie living anywhere else. She belonged with us and we belonged together but I was still happy we weren't going to the same high school. At the eleventh hour she decided to go to St Mary's, which meant we had to ride the bus together, she in her green plaid jumper and me in my blue blazer and gray pants, for the next four years. But at least, during the day, I was on my own.

There were times when having a handicap definitely worked to my advantage and my freshman year at Immaculate Conception was one of those times. My limp appealed to some core instinct for caring, supposedly present in all clergy, and the Franciscan priests who taught us, even if it wasn't part of their nature, faked compassion for a while. The older students, sophomores, juniors and the exalted seniors, were another matter. There were some mature, centered individuals in every class but most of them were tribal and the first few weeks, until everyone had pissed on their territory and boundaries were set, were hell for all the new boys. There were no girls present to distract or civilize so it was all challenges and threats and bullying, persecution, name calling and open warfare. I was the only kid in the freshman class with a limp so if I wasn't being ignored I was treated with a mixture of pity and disdain. The most and worst I had to endure was being called gimp or crip and even that lasted only a short time. But there were others in the class, misfits by the standards of the tribe, fat and skinny, too short and too tall, spastic and epileptic, introvert and loner, and slow kids and brains, who were forced to band together in order to survive. One of them was Alex Potts, and we became friends.

Alex was a misfit by choice. There was nothing noticeably different about him. He was a brain but otherwise he was average in every way with his medium height, medium weight and medium brown hair. His teeth were crooked and he had a small scar in his right eyebrow but those were distinctions he shared with half the boys in the school. He was a misfit because he disagreed with the tribe and had contempt for everyone and everything they held in esteem. I think he probably had contempt for most of the misfits, too, but for some reason he tolerated me. He attacked everything from the football team to the hierarchy of the Church. He even questioned democracy as a viable form of government, suggesting communism as an alternative. The priests were threatened by his perception because he dangerously encouraged students, if not to think for themselves, at least to question. He credited his parents, who were as old as everyone else's grandparents, with his radical approach. Them and his brothers and sisters, who were as old as Mom and Pop.

'I was *misconceived* when my mother was forty-six and my father was fifty-five,' he said one day when we were sitting in the lunchroom, at a table full of misfits, drinking chocolate milk. 'I am walking proof that the Church should not only permit, but encourage, birth control. My father certainly didn't want another child and I'm sure my mother is still in shock. The idea that they were even sexual at that age is downright ludicrous. When my mother told my father she was pregnant he stopped talking to her and he hasn't spoken to her yet. They write notes.'

'My mother and father stopped talking for a while before she got sick. It was terrible.'

'Actually, I like it. It makes for very peaceful meals.' He looked around at the sea of blue blazers bent over the tables. 'Look at them. Worse than pigs at a trough. Hitler was right. Certain people should be exterminated. He just had the wrong people.' I had never heard anyone say anything even remotely nice about Hitler. 'The world is like a hunk of rotting meat and we're just maggots crawling all over it.' Right then, I knew Bridie would like Alex.

I had written Honey two letters since he went to Valdosta, Georgia, but he never answered and I promised myself I wouldn't write again until I heard from him, but high school was something I had to share, so I wrote.

Dear Honey,

Did you forget how to write? I got your phone number from Tessie but Pop said it was too much money to call long distance so once again I am writing to you.

Finally, I'm in high school. I'm going to Immaculate Conception and Bridie is going to St Mary's. The priests are a lot harder than the nuns. Bridie doesn't believe me when I say that. My homeroom teacher is Father Patrick. Is he Irish? No, he's Polish. Ha ha. I like changing classes. It makes the day go faster and you get to move around so your ass doesn't go to sleep. (Don't let anybody see this.) I'm not taking French I'm taking Spanish which everybody says is much easier. And Latin which is really hard.

Duke is all confused. He still goes to Our Lady of Perpetual Help every day to meet us after school but we're not there. Sometimes he waits for hours before he goes home. I told him we're taking the bus but he just won't listen.

I haven't had time to do any drawing lately. If I do I'll send you a picture.

Mom will be coming home soon. That's what the doctors tell Pop. I can't wait.

Bridie and I haven't been to Tessie's for a while because school keeps us busy. The last time, Tessie was feeling sick. She misses you. Charles and I started to make a model airplane together. He's good at it. I hope you are happy there. I miss you a lot.

Your friend,
Finn

PS They still can't find Fritz.

I sent almost the same letter to Rebecca but I left out the information concerning Tessie. About two weeks later I received an answer from Honey.

Dear Finn,

Hello from Georgia. It's me, Honey. No I didn't forget how to write. Guess what. I'm in school. I took a test and they said I should be in the seventh grade. I like it a whole lot. My teacher is real nice. I'm the only one in the whole school like me. Everybody else is really colored. White kids and colored kids go to different schools here.

A whole lot of things is different here. There's a man in our church that's albino, too. His eyes are so pink he looks like a Easter bunny.

My Aunt Mussie and Uncle Moon are real good to me. His name is Moon cause he was born when it was a full one. I don't know why her name is Mussie. It's funny cause my name is Honey and Uncle Moon's is Moon. That makes us Honeymoon. We laughed a lot about that.

I miss you a lot, too. I hope Aunt Tessie is better and nobody else is sick. Send me a picture of you and Bridie. I'd like that a lot.

> Your friend, too,
> Honey

PS I still love Bridie special. Tell Duke I miss him and I got chickens and ducks and a goat named Bathsheba.

I didn't show the letter to Bridie because I didn't think she needed to know Honey loved her special.

'All they talk about is hair and nails and make-up and boys. Cripes, it's enough to drive a person nuts.' Everyone was in bed and Bridie was continuing a conversation she had started at dinner. Simon had said good night but I knew he was lying awake in the dark. 'And all those fat rear ends with green plaid stretched over them! It makes me sick to my stomach. Between them and the nuns, believe me, I will never last four years in that hell hole.' I heard Pop clear his throat. 'The Japanese wouldn't have to put bamboo splinters under my fingernails to get me to tell secrets. All they'd have to do is threaten to send me to an all-girls school. Hell, I'd tell them anything they wanted to know.'

'The war is over!' I yelled.

'So what?'

'Don't start.' Pop coughed again.

'You getting a cold, Big Finn?'

'No, I'm fine. Now go to sleep.'

'You think the nuns at Our Lady of Perpetual Motion were bad, well you ought to get a load of these tomatoes. They all look like they got the same false face on. And big! I bet two of them can't pass each other in the doorway. I don't know what they feed them but they all look like Big Tum in a nun's habit. And the girls! They are so stuck-up. Who do they think they are anyway?' I thought I heard Simon laugh. 'And they talk about the dumbest stuff. Who gives a damn about shampoo? None of them even knew China had a population of four hundred and fifty-five million people. Imagine all those Chinamen in one country.'

'How'd you know that?' I couldn't believe Bridie knew the population of Livery Street, let alone China.

'Everybody knows that. Besides, it's on the back of the Corn Flakes box.' Simon laughed out loud and a second later I could hear Pop laughing. 'What's so damn funny?' She sounded indignant. 'When I told those dumb girls about China they looked at me like I stepped in dog dirt. They just stared like I had two heads or something. Well, I showed them. I said, America is smaller. I wanted to tell them how many people America had but I couldn't remember. I got out the Corn Flakes box when I came home from school and America has one hundred and forty million in case you want to tell somebody.' I started laughing, too, because Pop and Simon were laughing so hard. 'What are you laughing at, Finn? This is all your fault. We could have gone to high school right here in town but that wasn't good enough for you. Thanks a lot.'

'You didn't have to go to St Mary's just because I'm going to Immaculate Conception.'

'You say that now, but you begged me to go.'

'I never said a damn word.'

'God, you are such a liar.'

'That's enough,' said Pop, trying to stop laughing.

'Well, I don't see what's so funny. I think you all have a screw loose. None of you knew how many Chinamen there are.' Pop and Simon only laughed louder and harder. It was the first time I had heard Simon laugh in a very long time.

One cold autumn Saturday afternoon I went to my favorite place for privacy, the music building at the university, to listen to the students practicing and do some thinking. I had decided I wasn't going to wear the brace anymore and I had to confront Pop so I needed to be by myself to plan my strategy. That summer I had grown so much I was finally taller than Bridie but everything hurt and it was time to get a new brace and I simply didn't want one. After all the money spent, I knew Pop would be mad as hell but I didn't see any improvement and I was tired of dragging the brace around and I was quite content to go through my life with the limp I had always had and considered as much a part of me as my blue eyes and brown hair. If other people had a problem with my leg they'd have to learn to live with it. I had made some of my weightiest decisions sitting there, under the wisteria vine, listening to the musicians in the making, and this, this decision to confront Pop, was a big one. There had been several frosts and all the leaves had fallen and the vine looked like a pencil sketch up the side of the building. The dried seed pods rattled in the wind, competing with the stop start of the music. I pulled the collar of my peacoat up as I hunkered against the building under a slightly opened window, wishing they'd play whatever it was they were playing, just once, from start to finish.

'Hey, what are you doing there?' A young blond man, who

looked to be about twenty, was smiling down at me from the window.

'Just listening.'

'Well, come on in. We need an audience.'

'Really?'

'Yeah. You must be freezing your ass off out there. Come on.'

The room was big and empty except for a small platform, which served as a stage, and a few folding chairs. It wasn't at all what I had imagined it to be. I expected a place where music was made would have red velvet curtains and gilt box seats but it was more like a gym. It even smelled like a gym.

'Sit down and make yourself comfortable. I'm Steve and those other guys don't matter,' he laughed, referring to the three young men seated with their instruments, discussing the music on the stands in front of them.

'My name's Finn.'

'You a music lover, Finn?'

'I don't know much about it. I liked what you were playing.'

'Tchaikovsky. *Andante cantabile*.'

'Boy, that's a mouthful.'

'They all are. I'll write it down for you.' He went to a stack of books and tore a piece of paper from a notebook and wrote the name for me. 'We'll play it through without stopping. Just don't be too critical.' He handed me the piece of paper and I folded it and put it in my wallet. 'Okay guys,' he said to the rest of the group, 'from the top and no stopping. We have an audience.' They settled down and after a few moments of absolute silence Steve nodded his head and they started to play.

I don't know if the piece of paper with Tchaikovsky's name made the difference but for the first time, sitting there listening to my own private concert, I realized music was the product of a person. It didn't just show up on the radio. Someone actually sat down and wrote it from something they heard in some mysterious chamber in their brain. The realization was so utterly astounding, for a moment I felt lightheaded. And the idea that someone else could look at the written music a hundred years later and play what the composer had heard, was overwhelming. There I was, listening to four students play something that had been written in another time in another country and it seemed like nothing less than magic. The music was mournful and anguished and all I could think about was how unhappy Mr Tchaikovsky must have been when he wrote it. Whatever his pain was, I thought I knew exactly how he felt. There were no boundaries and no limits and it was all mixed up with loss and inevitability, Mom, Laurie, Fritz and Honey, and urgency and expectations. My thoughts didn't make any sense and yet they seemed perfectly clear. I wasn't sitting in the rehearsal hall listening to the students any longer, I was in some transitory, otherworldly place Tchaikovsky was sharing with me. And then I saw Bridie's face in the window.

At first, I tried to ignore her but she did everything but stand on her head to get my attention. Her face was strained and it looked like she had been crying. She motioned for me to go to her but I thought it would be rude to get up and leave while they were still playing so I just sat there, staring straight ahead, trying not to look at her. When I did, she was gone from the window and a moment later I heard the door open and I turned and there she stood. I wanted to stay and listen to the music but I was certain she wouldn't leave me alone so I went to her.

'What do you want?' I whispered.

'Oh Finn,' big tears started to roll down her cheeks, 'I have to talk to you.'

'Now?'

'Please.' I knew it had to be urgent because she never said please to me. I turned to the musicians but they were so engrossed in the music they weren't even paying any attention to us so I took Bridie's hand and we slipped out, closing the door behind us.

'What's wrong?'

'Come on,' she said and led me to our spot under the wisteria vine. We sat down and she put her head on my chest and I held her while she cried. She was shivering, so I unbuttoned my coat and wrapped it around her and she slipped her arms around my chest and we held each other close. I could feel the warmth of her body and smell her hair as I sat there listening to the music, waiting for her to run out of tears. It was the closest I had been to her since the night Laurie died, when she slept in my bed with me. Only then she didn't want to be held and now she did.

'Are you going to tell me what's wrong?' I said after a few minutes when she seemed to settle down a bit.

'Oh God,' she took a deep breath which caught in her throat as she tried to calm herself. She didn't look at me but instead played absent-mindedly with one of the buttons on my shirt. 'I think Simon is in love with somebody.' She started to cry again. I felt a sudden rush of anger and I wanted to tell her to grow up and stop acting like a baby but I knew she was truly hurting so I said nothing. 'He doesn't love me.' Less than a month before, on the way to school, it had been a completely different story.

'He loves me, I know he does.' It was raining and the bus smelled of wet clothes. 'All I have to do is get through these next four years then Simon and I can get married and I can tell the nuns and school to go jump in the lake.' It was too early in the morning to listen to her fantasies. 'Mrs Simon Drubecki. Bridie Drubecki. God, I wonder if anybody will ever be able to say it?'

'What makes you think Simon wants to marry you?'

'He says so all the time.'

'When you were little, maybe. A lot of men say that to little girls. "I'm going to marry you when you grow up." They must think it's cute.'

'He means it. Besides, who else would he marry?'

'How the hell would I know? He could be seeing all kinds of girls when he stays out. And who says he wants to get married, anyway? A lot of people don't, you know.'

'Priests and nuns, maybe.'

'And regular people, too. Anyway, he's too old for you.'

'Cripes, he's only eight years older. In the olden days girls always married older men. Bette Davis always marries older men.'

'Yeah, and half the time she shoots them.'

'So? She still marries them.'

'Jesus! That's the *movies*.'

'Don't say anything nasty about Bette Davis. I love her.' She looked out the window at the rain for a moment. The stopping and starting of the bus, combined with the exhaust fumes, was making me feel sick. 'Don't you want to get married someday?'

'Yeah, when I'm seventy.'

'No, seriously, Finn. Don't you want to get married and have kids someday?'

'I guess ... someday. But I'm not wasting time thinking about it now.'

'Don't you think Simon loves me?'

'Sure. Doesn't everybody love you?' I meant it sarcastically but it went completely over her head.

'I want Simon and me to have a wedding just like Fritz and Mina's.'

'What happened to living in New York City and me being a painter and you doing whatever you wanted?'

'Finn, that was just kid's stuff. God, grow up.' She started rambling on about wedding dresses and houses and babies and it was so boring and ridiculous I couldn't pay any attention to her. The dream of living in New York may have been kid's stuff to her but it was very real to me and I knew that one day I'd do it. Bridie decided high school gave her license to be the one thing she wanted more than anything, an adult, and all of a sudden everything that happened before was childish. The very first day, going to school on the bus, she started planning the rest of her life. Pop and Mom and I would always be a part of it but Simon was to be the core. She didn't have all the details worked out but she knew they'd have a glorious life together. I was to be their best friend just like all the romantic couples in the movies always had a best friend. So what she was planning was a major change in her life but my life was to remain *status quo* to suit her purposes. I had other plans.

'How do you know he loves someone else?' The Tchaikovsky had stopped and I could feel a cold wet spot on my shirt from her tears.

'He practically said so.'

'What did he say?'

'Oh, I don't know. All kinds of things. It was just after you left the house and we were in the kitchen and he was polishing his shoes and I was fixing the spring in the window shade and I thought it would be just like that when we got married, the two of us doing little things like that, and I said so. He looked at me real funny and started to laugh, kind of embarrassed like. Then he said something about being flattered that I wanted to marry him but it being impossible. I was shocked and I told him I always thought we were going to get married and he said he was sorry and didn't know where I got that idea. Then I started crying and I don't know what the hell he was talking about. Stuff about me growing up and him not noticing it, and needing to know what happened to Fritz so he could get on with his life, and making a mistake coming to live with you and Big Finn. Stuff like that. I told him we had to get married because I loved him and he said he loved me, too, but not in that way. He thought about me like a sister and you like a brother and I said bullshit, that I didn't want to be his sister.' She stopped to take a breath and started crying again. 'Oh Finn, why can't you be Simon?' I had a peculiar, almost sick, feeling in the pit of my stomach. The music started again and she held me even tighter as we sat there listening. After a very long time she mumbled, 'The hell with him, he's only got one good eye, anyway.'

*

Simon didn't come home for dinner that night. Pop had been to see Mom and he was telling us about his visit and didn't notice how quiet Bridie was. Her face was still slightly swollen from crying off and on all afternoon.

'She's put on a bit of weight and looks good. Like her old self again. I talked to the doctors and they said any time now. Christ, they've been saying that for a month of Sundays but I guess they know what they're doing. Miss Webster was asking for you and so was your old friend, Mildred. She's nuttier every time I see her. She thinks she's the head of the hospital now. Sad to think she'll never get out of there. Jesus, when I see the likes of her, all I can say is, we have a hell of a lot to be thankful for.' We sat there eating in silence for a moment. 'You know, I was thinking maybe we should repaint the house. Inside and out. Before your mother comes home I mean. Maybe a different color . . .' He stopped and looked at Bridie and me. 'What's going on? How come I'm doing all the talking? Did you two have a fight?' Bridie started crying and left the table and went into the living room. He turned to me. 'What the hell did you do to her, now?'

'I didn't do anything.'

'Don't give me that, mister.'

'I didn't. I swear. Why do you blame me for everything?'

'Because I know you. You're always causing trouble.' He said it angrily and for a moment I thought my head would explode.

'You don't know me at all, goddamn it!' I shouted before I had time to think. His hand shot out and he slapped me hard across the face, knocking me and the chair over.

Bridie came running in. 'Stop it! Finn didn't do anything.' She tried to help me up but I pulled away from her.

'Leave me alone.' I got to my feet and went to the hall and grabbed my coat.

'Where are you going?' said Pop. He had never hit me like that before. Maybe a smack on the behind but never anything like a slap in the face, and there was remorse in his voice even though he was still mad.

'What do you care?' I said and started out the door.

'Don't you give me any lip, you hear me?'

'Finn, come back.' Bridie came to the door.

'Just leave me alone. Everybody, just leave me alone.' I slammed the door hard behind me and ran down the steps.

It had started raining and the street lights were just coming on, reflecting on the wet sidewalks. I went to the corner and stood in the entrance to the telephone company, out of the blowing rain, trying to decide where to go. I hated Pop and I hated Bridie and Simon, too. The last thing I wanted was to be around people who would ask me what was troubling me. I wanted to be left completely alone and the only place I could think of was church. The rain was coming down even harder as I crossed the street and entered the Gothic doors. The choir was practicing and two nuns were putting vases of purple chrysanthemums on the altar in preparation for the next day's masses. Several people were lined up waiting to go to confession so I sat in the back pew, pretending I was praying, knowing no one would bother me. When I thought about it, church was the last place I should have been, feeling so much rage. Why Pop hated me, I didn't know. I kept trying to figure out what terrible thing I had done. What was it he couldn't forgive? He never treated Fritz the way he treated me. Of course, Fritz was perfect and never did anything wrong. Fritz was perfect and I wasn't. Could it have been that simple? Because of my leg? In retrospect, I suppose I always knew that was the reason. His enormous disappointment because of the imperfection confronting him every time he looked at me. Even Mom withheld affection in an attempt to make me strong and independent. She knew, having grown up an orphan, how necessary strength was for survival. The sad thing was, her own strength never lived up to her expectations. Fritz was the only one who had loved me just as I was, expecting nothing more or less than the person I could be and, although I didn't want to admit it, there was one other person. Bridie. My leg meant so little to her she could even make jokes about it. But Bridie loved Simon and Pop loved Bridie and Mom was dealing with her own problems and Fritz was almost a memory. I was alone in my family. The organ was blasting out and the choir was singing about God's great glory when I got up and left.

There was hardly anyone on the street as I walked uptown. The rain was hard and steady and it was getting colder and in no time I was drenched through to the skin. I hadn't eaten much and I was hungry so I stopped in the diner. The greasy smell of the grill, mixed with cigarette smoke, hit me as soon as I walked in the door but it was warm and dry so I took off my coat and hung it up and sat at the almost empty counter. One man was sitting on a stool at the other end, talking to Esther, the owner's wife who worked behind the counter, and Carrie, the waitress, was taking an order at a booth in the back. The rain, streaming down the windows, was colored magenta from the neon sign flashing out front.

'Hey, Finn, aren't they serving at your house tonight?' said Esther as she came toward me.

'I'm going to a movie and I thought I'd eat out.'

'Simon, too?'

'What do you mean?'

'He's back in the corner there with a friend.' I turned to look and just as I did Simon looked over his shoulder and saw me. He was sitting with a fellow about his age, someone I had never seen before. He said something to him and got up and came and sat on the stool next to me.

'Boy, you're drenched. What are you doing here?'

'Well . . .' I didn't feel like telling him what had happened, 'I just wanted to get out of the house.'

He looked away. 'Trouble?'

'I don't want to talk about it.'

'Sounds bad.'

'Forget it.'

'Did Bridie say anything to you?'

'Yeah.'

'Shit. I feel lousy about it.'

'She'll live,' I said.

'Yeah, I know. I still feel lousy.' We sat there for a minute not saying anything. 'You want to come back and sit with me and my friend? Come on, I want you to meet him. I told him all about you.'

'No, I don't feel like it. Not tonight.'

'You sure?'

'Yeah.'

'Okay.' He got up and started away but stopped and turned to me. 'This thing with Bridie. We'll talk about it later?'

'Sure.'

He went back to his booth and Esther came to me. 'You two have a fight or something? How come you're not sitting with Simon?'

'I just want to be alone.'

'You and Garbo. So, what'll you have?' I ordered a piece of apple pie and a cup of tea and finished it as fast as I could because I felt uncomfortable with Simon sitting in the back.

The rain hadn't let up at all when I came out of the diner so I headed back to Livery Street but instead of going home I went to the Ganises'. Mrs Ganis answered the door.

'Finn, darling, look at you. Come in. You look terrible. So, what's wrong?'

'Who is it?' said Mr Ganis, coming down the hall. 'Finn. A nice surprise. You're all wet.'

'Can I stay here tonight?'

'Oh my God, he ran away. Finn, darling, did you run away?'

'What run away?' said Mr Ganis. 'When a person runs away he runs *away*. He doesn't go two houses down the street. Anyway, it's none of your business. Of course you can stay here, Finn. As long as you want.'

'Of course, darling, as long as you want. I'm going to run a hot tub for you so you shouldn't get sick and die. Come on, take off those wet clothes.'

When I was settled in the steaming tub for a few minutes there was a light knock on the door.

'Finn, are you all right?' It was Mr Ganis.

'Yeah. I'm okay.'

'Can I come in?'

'Sure.' I covered myself with the washcloth. He came in and closed the lid on the toilet and sat down.

'You feeling better?'

'I had a fight with Pop,' I said, staring at the ceiling.

'I thought maybe it was something like that. You want to talk about it? Maybe get some hair off your chest.' I looked down at my perfectly smooth chest and laughed.

'I don't think so.'

'Listen, I understand these things. A man doesn't want to talk, he doesn't want to talk. But do you mind if maybe I talk?'

'No.'

'I had a father once, too, you know. It was a long time ago but the funny thing is the older I get it doesn't seem so long. Anyway, we lived in a small village. It was so small we used the next village over as a landmark to let people know where we were but nobody ever heard of that village either. So, my father was a rabbi, but you already know that. And my brothers and sisters, we were all afraid of him. If we needed anything or even wanted to talk about anything we always went to my mother. You would have loved her, believe me. And vice versa. She would have loved you. But my father! Oh boy, he was something. We weren't allowed to bother him when he was studying. The trouble was he was always studying. He didn't have time for us but because he was a rabbi he had time for everybody else in the whole village. Anybody could come to him and he'd smile and be nice. Anybody but us. God could strike me down for saying this but I didn't like my father very much.'

'What are you talking about in here?' Mrs Ganis came in with a cup of tea.

'Hey, hey! This is for men only. He's naked in the tub.'

'So, who can see? He's underwater, for God's sake. This will make you feel better.' She handed me the tea. 'Sam, get your wool robe for him. And pajamas.' She turned to me, 'Maybe you should take a couple of aspirin.'

'No, thanks, I'm fine.'

'I'll turn down the bed for you. Drink your tea.' She closed the door behind her.

'So, I'll get your pajamas and the robe. What I'm saying is, all boys have trouble with their fathers. It's not the same trouble but they all got trouble. Who knows, maybe God meant it to be like that. If I could do it all over again and be young, I'd try to *like* my father as much as I loved him.'

Later, lying in the warmth and comfort of the bed, listening to the rain coming down harder than ever, I thought it would be easier to have a rabbi who didn't have time for his children for a father than Pop. I wished Mr Ganis was my father and wondered why he and Mrs Ganis never had any children.

The next morning, when I went home to change for mass, Bridie told me Simon spent the night out, too. She was in the kitchen fixing breakfast and Pop hadn't come down yet.

'Where's your coat?'

'Mr Ganis hung it up in their basement. It was soaked.'

'Where in hell did you go when you ran out of here?'

'Around.'

'God, I was worried sick.'

'Is he mad?' I asked.

'I don't think so. Mrs Ganis called and said you were there. But that's all she said.'

'I mean is he mad about me yelling at him last night?'

'Well, I told him it wasn't your fault. But I didn't say anything about Simon and me. I don't know why, I just didn't. You want something to eat?'

'Mrs Ganis gave me breakfast. You been to mass?'

'No, I waited for you. We can go to ten o'clock. It's always shorter.'

'What about Simon?'

'He's not back yet. You think he stayed with one of his girl-friends?'

'I saw him last night at the diner. He was with a buddy of his.'

'Did he say anything?' She didn't look at me as she turned the bacon in the frying pan.

'He said he felt bad but that was all. We didn't talk much.' I sat down at the table and Duke came over and licked my hand. 'Did you feed Duke?'

'Yeah. Don't you want some coffee or something?'

'No, I'm full.'

'I'm glad you're home.'

'So am I.' It was Pop, standing in the doorway. He went to the coffee pot and poured himself a cup. 'You all right?'

'Yes.' I tried not to sound angry. 'I'm fine.'

'I'm sorry,' he said. 'I'm sorry I slapped you.' He didn't look at me. 'Bridie told me you didn't do anything. I'd still like to know what the hell is going on. But I'm sorry. I don't know, I've had a lot on my mind. I mean, your mother and –'

'I have to get ready for mass.' I got up from the table and headed for the door.

'Wait a minute.' He looked at me for the first time. 'I'm trying to apologize. Christ, I said I'm sorry.'

'I heard you,' I said as I left the kitchen with Duke trailing behind.

'Christ Almighty! I tried. You heard me, I tried,' I heard him say to Bridie as I started up the stairs.

Simon came home late that afternoon. He didn't say where he had been and nobody asked but Pop winked knowingly. Bridie was embarrassed and avoided talking to Simon and finally, on the verge of tears, made some excuse about having to do schoolwork and went to her room. Simon was obviously upset and after a quick cup of coffee went upstairs to take a shower, leaving Pop and me sitting in the kitchen.

'What the hell is going on?' He said it quietly, looking at the floor.

'I'm not going to wear the brace anymore.' I hadn't planned to say anything and without thinking it just came out.

Pop's head snapped up and he looked at me in shock. 'What are you talking about?'

'I don't want to.'

'Jesus Christ!'

'It's not doing any good anyway.'

'It takes time. Dr Whiteshield said it takes time.'

'I'm not going to wear it.' His eyes narrowed and he sat looking at me without saying anything. 'It's heavy and it hurts.'

'Do you know how much money we spent –'

'I'll pay you back.'

'That's not the point, goddamn it! Why are you doing this? To get even cause I hit you? Is that what this is all about? I apologized, for Christ's sake.' There were tears in his eyes and I almost felt sorry for him.

'That's not the reason. I just don't want to wear it.'

'You want to always be a cripple?'

'It doesn't bother me.'

'Well, it bothers me.'

'I know it does.' It was the first time either one of us was perfectly honest with the other and we both knew it.

He was visibly shaken and went pale. 'Okay,' he said, getting up, 'don't wear the goddamn thing.' He pushed his chair into the table and went to the back door and opened it. 'Don't set a place for me at supper.' And he left, quietly closing the door behind him. I had won the battle. Duke came to me and put his head in my lap. There was no victorious feeling and no triumphant satisfaction. It was more like a realization that something had fallen into its proper place. I don't know how long I had been sitting there when Simon came into the kitchen, dressed in a bathrobe, drying his hair.

'Where's your father?'

'He went out.'

'Bridie still in her room? I didn't hear anything up there.'

'She didn't come down.'

He sat across the table from me. 'I'm causing a lot of trouble, huh?'

'Pop and I had a fight. It didn't have anything to do with you.'

He looked at me for a moment then turned away. 'I'm thinking of moving out.'

'Why? I told you, this isn't about you. You can't move out. This is where you live. Pop doesn't even know about what happened with Bridie.'

'I think maybe I have to.' He got up quickly and went to the back door and stood looking into the yard.

'No you don't. Bridie's crazy. She makes all this stuff up in her head and thinks everybody feels the same way she does. It's not her fault, she's always been like that. But she'll forget all about this. You wait and see.'

'It's not because of Bridie.' There was a hopelessness in his voice. 'I do. I have to go.'

'Did I do something?'

'Oh no.' He came back and sat down again. 'I don't want you to think that.' He shook his head. 'Goddamn it.'

'Then why? I don't get it.'

'I can't explain.'

'You can tell me. I won't say anything. I swear to God I won't.'

'Finn, I can't, okay?' He almost sounded angry. 'I never should have come here. It was crazy.' He started out of the kitchen.

'Simon, I'm not a little kid anymore.' I grabbed his arm as he passed. 'I tell you things. Why can't you tell me?'

'I wish I could.' The words seemed to be stuck in his throat. 'But I don't want you to hate me.' He touched my shoulder and left. I couldn't imagine Simon ever doing anything to make me hate him.

It was the following summer before he left. Just after we

received news of Fritz from the war department, Pop threw him out.

Bridie didn't get over Simon as quickly as I had predicted and her reaction was something completely new to me. In place of the usual angry, pugnacious need to get revenge, there was withdrawal. Both she and Simon were uncomfortable and avoided each other as much as they could. At first, Simon tried to be casual and joked with her as he had always done, but Bridie wanted no part of it and he gave up and stayed away more and more. When he was home, he was even more preoccupied and distant than he had been, even to me, and I blamed it on Bridie. He was like a boarder in the house, coming and going as he pleased and no longer a part of the family. He even stopped going to Franklin Village with Pop, always with some excuse about work but I had the feeling, for some reason, he didn't want to see Mom.

I did quit wearing the brace and Pop never said a word about it. The day after I told him I wasn't going to wear it anymore, I put it in the corner of my closet and covered it with an old coat so I wouldn't have to look at it. Whatever truths Pop and I faced that day in the kitchen, whether we articulated them or not, resulted in a cold and edgy truce, and we tolerated one another. I think, more than ever, we both looked forward to Mom coming home, hoping her presence would somehow ameliorate a very uncomfortable situation. Bridie, estranged from Simon, divided her attention and affection between Pop and me, and our favorite meals started to show up while Simon's very noticeably disappeared.

Fortunately, high school kept Bridie and I busy enough to escape, at least some of the time, into our books. Neither St Mary's nor Immaculate Conception permitted freshmen to participate in extracurricular activities, in the hope that we would concentrate on our schoolwork. We were expected to 'develop the work habits and discipline' necessary to see us through the rest of our academic careers. However, we were allowed to take an elective course and both schools offered music and art. Bridie, who couldn't draw a stick figure, opted for music and I took art. Bridie hated every minute with the Teutonic monster, Sister Joseph of Cupertino, while I counted the minutes to get to my classes with Father Blaise Marat. The class was comparatively small, with fifteen students, and Father Blaise made each of us feel as though we were the only one in the room. He was in his late twenties, tall and angular with sandy hair and intense hazel eyes. His energy and enthusiasm were almost uncontrollable and he had a childlike quality which wasn't unusual in young priests who had, since puberty, always been in the protective, unreal world of Holy Mother Church. Whatever ability I had as an artist, he recognized and nurtured, and in no time at all I thought he was the most extraordinary teacher in the world. When the story circulated that I was the kid who had been held hostage by Italian prisoners of war, and the school paper did an article about me, I told him the truth. It was a guilt I still carried and I was afraid if I didn't tell him the truth, one day he'd find out and we'd no longer be friends. He said it was time to put the guilt aside. I had tried to tell the truth and he was certain that was enough for God, who didn't hold grudges. He asked me about Mom and Bridie and Pop and by the time I finished I had told him everything about my life, with the exception of spending a lot of my free time in a whorehouse. Somehow it didn't seem like the right thing to tell a priest. Even a priest as nice as Father Blaise. I was vague about my connection with Honey but I did tell him he lived in Valdosta, Georgia, and I wanted to do some drawings for him and Father suggested I do a book of sketches of places Honey and Bridie and I had enjoyed together. He gave me a bound book of drawing paper and some pencils and charcoal and said I could do it for my class project and send it to Honey when the school year was over. On the front page I wrote in big block letters, *HONEY'S*

BOOK and every weekend I went to all the places we had shared and drew the best pictures I could. Pictures of the Mule Bridge, the museum, Tessie's Place and the riding stables, the music building and the trestle and the footpath along Stony Brook. I did sketches of Tessie and Charles, Iris, Cat and Elizabeth and a full page of Mr Stebbins. In the middle of the book, when I knew I was halfway through, I drew a two-page sketch of a dinosaur skeleton with Bridie, Honey, Duke and me looking up at it. As I recall, the figures really didn't look very much like us but I knew Honey would appreciate it.

St Mary's was much closer to the bus station than Immaculate Conception so Bridie usually took an earlier bus than me. By the time I got home she had changed out of her uniform and had supper started. She was very protective of that hour or two when she had the house to herself to do whatever she wanted with no men around, so I knew something was wrong the day I saw her standing at the bus stop, waiting for me. It was spring but the air was cold and I could see her as the bus pulled up to the curb, still in her uniform, without even a sweater around her shoulders. She was wiping her eyes with one of Pop's big linen handkerchiefs. It seemed to take for ever for the driver to open the door and while I waited I imagined all kinds of terrible things. The house burned down or Pop or Simon were in an accident or dead. I even thought something might have happened to Mom.

'It's Duke,' said Bridie as I stepped off the bus, 'he was hit by a car.' She was fighting back tears.

'Oh God, no. Oh Jesus.' I started pacing, afraid to go anywhere because I didn't want to know how bad it was. 'Oh Jesus God.'

'He's home in the kitchen. The man that hit him took him to the vet. Big Tum went with him. He's hurt real bad.' She gently put her hand in mine and led me across the street, almost against my will.

'Oh God, oh God. Please don't let him die.'

'It happened right in front of school. Just before lunch.'

'That stupid dog!' Duke was still going to Our Lady of Perpetual Help to meet us and walk us home for lunch and at three o'clock. He had been there every day for eight years, waiting for us, and he hadn't figured out that we weren't there anymore. I started to run and when I turned into Livery Street, I dropped my books. Bridie helped me pick them up.

'The yelp was that loud, I could hear it in the basement.' Mrs Cavanaugh was sitting on the rocker, leaning on the porch rail. 'I knew it was your dog the minute I heard it. I thought it was dead already, what with it screaming as loud as it did. Jesus, Mary and Joseph, it was enough to make your blood run cold.'

'Shut up you old bitch!' I screamed it loud enough for everyone on the street to hear.

'Well, I didn't hit your dog, you dirty little cripple. You need your mouth washed out with soap, that's what you need.'

'You need everything washed with soap!' yelled Bridie, running behind me with my books. Mrs Cavanaugh sputtered something back but I couldn't hear what she said.

Duke was lying on the floor in the kitchen, near the back door, wrapped in a blanket. All I could see were his head and his tail. Big Tum and Mr Ganis were sitting at the table. Duke's eyes were closed and I thought he was dead.

'Duke?' I could hardly get his name out as I knelt down. He looked at me but the light that was always there when he hadn't seen me for a while was gone. He managed to wag his tail a few times.

'He just walked in front of the car. The fellow driving feels real bad. Real bad.' Big Tum's voice was quiet. 'He's got dogs of his own and he feels real bad.'

'Is he going to be okay?'

Mr Ganis sat next to me on the floor. 'We have to wait and see. The animal doctor did what he could, so now it's up to God.' He put his arm around my shoulder. 'But, Finn, we maybe shouldn't expect too much.'

'Aw, Duke . . .' I wanted to pet him but I was afraid I'd hurt him if I touched him.

'He's got internal injuries. George Glass is a damn good vet but, like Sam says, we shouldn't expect too much.' Big Tum was whispering as though he were in a hospital room and didn't want the patient to hear. Bridie sat next to me and held me and we stayed there until Pop and Simon came home from work.

'Oh Christ! Poor Duke,' said Pop. 'He crossed that street a million times. Christ Almighty, I never thought this would happen.' He and Simon fixed sandwiches but nobody ate. We tried to get Duke to drink some water but he couldn't, he just lay there with his eyes closed. When it came time to go to bed, Pop got out the sleeping bags so Bridie and I could spend the night in the kitchen.

'If he's no better in the morning, you know what we have to do,' said Pop just before he went upstairs. 'We all love him and we don't want to see him suffer. You know that, don't you, Finn? It's what Duke would want, too. He's depending on you for that.' I nodded my head. 'If you want me during the night, you call. I won't be sleeping.'

'I'll stay here if you want?' said Simon.

'No, we'll be okay.'

'I'll be right in the living room on the sofa if you need me.' In the face of the tragedy, we were a family again.

'You watch and see,' said Bridie. 'Tomorrow, Duke's going to be better. I've been praying to the Blessed Mother.'

'We'll all do a bit of that, I think,' said Pop, and he went upstairs.

Several times during the night I checked to see if he was all right and when I whispered his name, so as not to waken Bridie, he always managed a feeble wag of his tail. I must have dozed off just before sunup and when I awoke Bridie was sitting with Duke's head in her lap and he was gone. As always, he didn't cause any trouble, he just slipped away while we were sleeping.

'Laurie, Laurie . . .' Bridie was rocking back and forth, calling her father's name over and over. I took Duke and carried him out to the yard and went into the pigeon coop and sat on the floor, holding him. The birds fussed and strutted and finally settled down and I don't know how long I was there before Pop opened the door.

'You all right?'

'He's dead.'

'I know.' His eyes were red. 'You stay here as long as you want. You don't have to go to school today. I'm not going to work, either. When you're ready, we'll find the right place to bury him.' He closed the door and went back into the house and I could hear Bridie calling for Laurie. After a while, I carried Duke out and laid him on the side porch. I carefully covered his face with the blanket and, without even thinking about it, went to the toolshed and got the sledgehammer. Then, I went back to the pigeon coop, opened the door and chased out all the birds. When I was sure they were all out and flying, I started to knock down the coop. The pigeons circled in confusion, watching their home being destroyed. Simon, hearing the noise, came out of the house and grabbed the sledgehammer, trying to take it away from me.

'Finn, what's the matter with you? Stop it.'

'Simon, leave him alone!' Pop shouted from the porch. He was holding Bridie, who was still calling for Laurie.

'He doesn't know what he's doing,' said Simon.

'Yes, he does. Just leave him alone.' It was a tone of voice no one would quarrel with and Simon let go of the sledgehammer and stepped back. 'Call Dr Lorman. For Bridie.' Pop took Bridie back in the house and Simon followed them. I started smashing the coop, time and again, lifting the heavy sledgehammer, and when I finished there was nothing left but splintered wood and tangled chicken wire and broken eggs. Somehow, I'd cut my leg and my cheek but I didn't feel anything and didn't notice until I saw the blood. The bewildered pigeons watched the whole thing from Mrs Shultz's roof.

'Get out of here!' I shouted. 'Go away! You don't live here anymore. Goddamn it, get out of here!' Simon came and took me back into the house and as we went up the steps I saw the Ganises and Mrs Shultz standing by the gate. He sat me down on a kitchen chair and washed the blood off my face and leg and bandaged the cuts. I could hear Pop and Bridie in the living room. She was crying and calling for Laurie and Pop was trying to quiet her.

She didn't go with us when we buried Duke. Dr Lorman gave her a shot and she was asleep, being looked after by Mrs Ganis, when Pop, Simon and I drove out to the country to find a place. Pop wanted a secluded spot where we could be sure he wouldn't be dug up so we went way past the edge of town. We drove down dirt roads I didn't even know existed until we found a quiet place and we buried him. It was a small clearing about fifty feet from a cornfield where the pheasants scavenged and the deer came out at twilight to feed. Pop said it was a place where nothing would bother him but also a place where he wouldn't be alone.

That night, I filled the rest of Honey's book with drawings of Duke.

Bridie didn't go to school the rest of that week. She spent most of the time in her room with the shades drawn, going through boxes of things she had taken from the house after Laurie died, and covering her walls with photos of just the two of them. She polished a pair of his brown-and-white spectator shoes and kept them on the dresser next to Laurie's birth certificate, his wallet and a white plaster statue of the Blessed Virgin, whose nose had been chipped off. I took most of her meals to her on a tray and as I went up the stairs I always had the eerie feeling I'd find Mom in her room. When she did come down to eat, she wore one of Laurie's sweaters or shirts and, on occasion, even a necktie. Pop told Simon and me not to comment on the way she was dressed and to talk about whatever she wanted. It was always about Laurie.

'Once, we stayed in a big gray house, all weathered from the salt and sea, on Cape Cod. Laurie was working in a hotel for the summer.' Supper was over and Simon and I were clearing the table. 'Anyway, the house was haunted. Honest to God, it was haunted. But the landlady, a real skinny little lady with a gold tooth, said only children could see the ghost. Well, I was scared spitless to stay in the room alone when Laurie was at work but he said it was just a tale to attract tourists. Haunted rooming houses always rented more rooms than unhaunted ones. So, the ghost was supposed to be the widow of a man who was lost at sea. He was a captain of a ship or something like that. And when she heard his ship went down and he drowned, she set herself on fire and jumped off the widow's walk, right into the ocean. It was something about there not being a lighthouse so she made herself a human torch for all eternity so sailors could find their way in a storm. Well, one night, the wind was blowing real hard and it was just about midnight and I woke up and there was this lady standing at the foot of my bed and she was all in flames. Then she jumped out the window and I started screaming. It scared the bejesus out of me. The lady with the gold tooth came running in and tried to shut me up but I kept right on screaming until Laurie came home. He said it was all in my imagination and gave the landlady hell for telling me the story. But I swear, I saw that lady in flames as plain as day and she was a ghost. Laurie held me that night and sang to me.' Her eyes started to well up. 'He sang, "I've been Working on the Railroad".' She excused herself and went back to her room.

Duke's absence was felt in every corner of the house, every moment of the day, but I missed him most at night when I went to bed. Sometimes I'd wake up in the middle of the night and for a moment forget he was gone and reach over to pet him. It seemed Simon was always awake and if he knew I was upset he came and sat on the edge of my bed and we talked, just the way we had when he first came out of the army.

'When I was a kid, we lived in an old milk truck. Five of us. My parents and my brother, Ethan and my sister, Lydia and me. I always thought that was a pretty name. Lydia.' Simon had never talked about his family, except for the cousin in Trenton, and I thought he was doing it to help get my mind off Duke. 'It was the Depression and a lot of people were out of work and lived anyplace they could keep dry. We didn't know any better so it seemed okay to us kids. It was kind of fun.'

'When did you have the Dalmatian?'

'I never had a Dalmatian.'

'You said you did that first day we met you. You told Bridie and me that you had a Dalmatian.'

'I did?' He thought about it a moment. 'Well, if I did I was just saying stuff to keep you talking to me. I never had a Dalmatian. I never had a dog at all.'

'Where's your brother and sister, now?'

'Oh hell, I don't know. When my father died my mother took up with another man and he didn't want all us kids so my father's cousin took me and that was the last I saw of any of them. They could be dead for all I know. That was a long time ago.' He didn't say anything for a while. 'You okay, now? You think you can sleep?'

In those first few months after Duke died, the chocolates flew from roof to roof, wondering what had happened to their coop, before returning to the wild. Some probably went back to Mr Howe's barn. There was a similar unrest in the house, a strange mixture of grief and calm. Pop did his best to be considerate and caring and Bridie and Simon got along as though they had never had words. We all talked more, unconsciously trying to counteract the resounding silence left in the wake of Duke. Simon was still secretive but we all accepted it and respected his privacy. Bridie, wanting to know everything about Laurie, especially about his life before she was even born, started writing long letters to Aunt Theresa in Boston, with page after page of questions. She also intensified her search for her mother and started a correspondence with Kitty Neal, who was settled in California, working at a veterans' hospital. She was as assiduous in her search for the facts of Laurie's life as Simon was about discovering the fate of Fritz.

We put off telling Mom about Duke for almost a month but one Saturday, on our way to Franklin Village, Pop said it was time and, like it or not, she had to be told. It was a warm, misty day and the sky threatened rain.

'I'll tell her alone,' said Pop, 'but I think it might be easier if the three of us are with her. You know how much she loved Duke.'

'We'll stay with you.'

'Thanks.' Our eyes connected in the rear-view mirror.

'I hope crazy Mildred isn't around. She drives me nuts.' Bridie was rubbing steam off the inside of the window.

'You know something, Mildred always reminded me of someone but I could never put my finger on who it was. Then one day it hit me.' Pop turned to Bridie sitting next to him. 'She reminds me of you.'

'Me!' Bridie's eyes widened indignantly. 'Are you crazy, too?' Pop started laughing and Bridie knew he was kidding her. 'Oh you big liar.' The mist turned to light rain as we pulled up to building H.

We found Mom folding linen with Mrs Lessing, a very tall and very dour nurse.

'Thank you, Mae. Take your family out on the sun porch.' She locked the linen closet and turned and walked away without saying anything to us.

Mom's physical recovery was obvious and remarkable. Except for her hair, which was now almost completely white, she looked like she did before her illness. Her weight was back to normal and her beautiful skin was as fresh as a young girl's. She still seemed isolated, though, with a slightly detached look in her eyes and a constant half smile that was more sad than happy.

Two old women were on the sun porch, sitting motionless like weathered statues, staring intently into nothingness. They didn't even look at us as we pulled chairs up to the window and sat watching the rain coming over the hill.

'I love rainy days,' said Mom, brushing Bridie's hair back from her face. 'I think rain is in our Celtic blood, don't you? I like the roiling of the heavens and the thunder and lightning but my favorite is a soft, misty rain like today. It suits spring, doesn't it?' She looked at us for a moment. 'You've something bad to tell me, haven't you? I can see it on your faces. What is it?'

'Well,' Pop pulled his chair closer to Mom and took her hand. 'It's Duke . . .'

'He's dead?' asked Mom.

'Yes. He was hit by a car.' Mom's hand went into her pocket and I could hear the tinkle of her rosary beads. She squeezed her eyes shut tight and threw back her head and Pop put his forehead on her shoulder, sharing her pain. I was aware of the easy, familiar touch that was routine even after the long separation. I automatically thought of Josie Cleary and Pop together and I wondered if, whenever I saw any intimacy between Mom and Pop, I would always think of Josie Cleary.

'We all loved Duke,' said Bridie.

'Well,' said Mom, opening her eyes, 'Duke's in heaven with Laurie and Deirdre. They'll take good care of him. Animals go to heaven, too, you know.' And the peculiar sad smile broadened into acceptance. 'We had him a long time. I guess it's God's turn. He wanted him.' It was the same stupid excuse for death the nuns always used and I hated it but I didn't say anything.

Later that afternoon, I said I had to go to the bathroom but I went looking for Miss Webster. Mrs Lessing was in the office, drinking coffee.

'Where's Miss Webster?'

'Off this weekend. What do you want?'

'I was wondering when my Mom was coming home?'

'Any time she wants to,' she said curtly.

'What do you mean?'

'Just what I said. Your mother can leave any time she wants. Your father knows that.'

I didn't believe her. 'Why's she still here?'

'Ask her. I don't discuss patients with their kids. Now, if you don't mind . . .'

On my way out of the office, I ran into Mildred coming along the hall with her clipboard.

'You shouldn't be here. I must insist children stay in the children's building. We must abide by the rules.'

'I'm just visiting.'

'Well, see that you return to your building as soon as possible. You heard, I suppose?'

'Heard what?'

'I've been appointed director of the hospital.'

'Congratulations.'

'It's an important job but it's also a shitty job. I have to be here twenty-four hours a day. And you know what bitches these nurses are. Just between you and me, I think one of them is screwing Teddy. If I find out who it is I'm going to transfer the bitch.'

Mrs Lessing came out of her office. 'Mildred!'

'Oh hello, Mrs Lessing. Don't you look pretty today.'

I didn't say anything to Pop until we got in the car and started down the driveway from the main building.

'Why isn't Mom coming home?' He must have been able to tell by the tone of my voice that I had heard something.

'She's afraid to,' he said after a moment. 'The doctors say she feels safe here.'

'She's afraid of us?' said Bridie incredulously.

'Christ, no. Not us. Things. The world. I don't know for sure.'

'Isn't she ever coming home?' I asked.

'Well, at first, maybe just for a few days. A weekend maybe. To see how things go.'

'How can she rather be there than home?' said Bridie.

282

'It's not what she'd *rather* do . . . Jesus, it's hard to explain. But I think I understand.' He looked at me in the rear-view mirror. 'It doesn't mean she doesn't love us. Or that she doesn't want to come home. You know what I'm trying to say, Finn?'

'Yeah. I do. It's probably real scary for her.'

'Real scary. Christ Almighty, just think what she's been through.' We didn't discuss it anymore. I wanted to go back and tell Mom it was a good time to leave and come home but as I looked at the fields sliding by in the mist I wondered if she'd ever come back to Livery Street.

Father Blaise gave me an A+ on Honey's book. He said the work was consistent and showed great promise. If I truly wanted it, and if I worked hard, he said I might have a future as an artist. I didn't much like the 'might' but I liked Father Blaise and even conditional praise was appreciated. Before I sent the book off to Honey, I went through almost every photo taken of Bridie and me until I found the one I felt was most appropriate and I pasted it on the inside cover. It was a picture of us with Duke. I was kneeling with him and Bridie was standing behind us and we were both squinting at the sun, our lips curling and our eyes disappearing. We were dressed in our Sunday best and we looked downright foolish. I knew Honey would get a kick out of it.

Just after school let out, Alex Potts came to spend the day with me. He lived in the country, way on the other side of Trenton, so his sister, Pompeii, drove him to our house and Simon offered to take him back after dinner.

'Pompeii Potts!' said Bridie when Alex introduced her to us. 'You're kidding.'

'Isn't it awful,' she laughed. 'My married name is Tharp. Not much better but you don't spit as much when you say it.' She was at least twenty years older than Alex.

'Our father is an amateur antiquarian,' he said by way of

explanation. 'We have a sister named Athena and a brother, Daedalus.'

'Cripes, and I thought Bridget was bad.'

We took Alex on a tour of our regular haunts and since Bridie had heard a lot about him but never met him she was all questions.

'Who are you named after?' she asked as we wandered through the museum.

'According to my father, Alexander the Great. But I looked up the name Alexander and decided my patron is Alexander the Fifth who was an anti-Pope. I like the idea of that. He was also not wanted by his parents and was raised by the Franciscans. There's something satisfyingly cyclical in that.'

'You're a show-off,' said Bridie. 'Finn said you were and you really are.' I could feel my face redden.

'Did you say I was a show-off?'

'I guess I did.'

'So what. I am a show-off.' By the time we got to the dinosaur skeleton, Bridie had just about had her fill of Alex.

'Someday,' he said, looking up at the skull, 'the human race will be extinct and creatures from other planets will come to earth and dig up our bones and they'll reconstruct us and we'll be in museums on Mars or Venus or some star we haven't even dreamed of, and aliens with two heads or four nostrils or seventeen ears will file by our skeletons, awestruck by the primitive beings who once destroyed their own planet.'

'We're not going to destroy our planet.' Bridie hated the idea of any kind of apocalypse.

'Einstein said when we split the atom it was the beginning of the end.'

'God,' said Bridie, whispering to me, 'he never quits.' She turned to Alex. 'I bet you don't know how many Chinamen there are in China.'

'How many?'

'Four hundred and fifty-five million. Give or take a few. Jeez,

I thought everybody knew that. And do you know how many Americans there are?'

'No.'

'Well,' she paused and I knew from the look on her face she had forgotten the number, 'a lot less.' She said it as though it was an exact statistic and smugly walked away.

'I really like her,' said Alex as we followed her in the direction of the Egyptian mummy.

'We'll never be extinct.' We were sitting at the soda fountain in Winter's and the idea of extinction was bothering me.

'That's what the dinosaurs thought.'

'Those big dumb things didn't think,' said Bridie, eating her cheeseburger.

'How do you know they didn't?'

'How do you know they did?' Bridie was ready to challenge Alex no matter what he said.

'I like to think all things are possible.'

'So do I,' I said. 'Father Blaise says we shouldn't put any limitations on ourselves.'

'Even if we don't,' Bridie leaned into Alex to make her point, 'there are some things we simply cannot do. For instance, I couldn't turn Chinese if I wanted to, or fly without a plane or some other man-made gadget, or hold my breath for an hour and twenty minutes. Am I right?'

'Well, technically –'

'Okay, I made my point.' She took a huge bite of her cheeseburger and chewed contentedly. Bridie loved to win. Especially when it was a victory over someone like Alex. I could see he was charmed and amused by her and now that she had won a few rounds it was obvious she didn't think he was nearly as bad as she had. And by the time we dropped him off at home, after we had stopped in the Italian section of Trenton and Simon bought us a tomato pie, I knew that the next day Bridie would be referring to Alex as *her* friend.

*

Mina brought the letter from the war department. I could tell by the expression on her face that she had heard something. We hadn't seen her or the baby for months and at first, when I saw her standing there, I didn't know what to say.

'Is Pop here?' She kissed me on the cheek.

'Yeah, everybody's in the kitchen. How's the baby?'

'Fine.' She took an official-looking letter out of her pocket as we walked through the dining room to the kitchen.

'Mina!' Simon looked startled to see her. Pop got up from the table and went to her and hugged her.

'I heard.' She handed the letter to Pop and he opened it and read it.

'What's it say?' said Bridie.

'They think he's dead. But they're not sure.' Mina sat at the table and Bridie held her hand. 'He may have been buried in a common grave by Italian partisans. It's a strong possibility but they're not certain. He isn't officially pronounced dead.'

'So, nothing's changed,' said Simon. His voice was dry and flat.

'There's still hope.' Pop sat with his head in his hands.

'No, there isn't.' Simon went into the living room.

'I'll see if he's all right,' said Mina and she went to look after him. I picked up the letter and started reading it and I could hear Simon shouting but I couldn't understand what he was saying.

'What the hell's wrong with him?' Pop got up. 'Maybe I should go in there.' He went into the living room and Bridie and I followed. Both Simon and Mina were crying. He was pacing, his fists clenched, beating against his thighs. Mina was trying to calm him. When he saw Pop, he went to him.

'I can't stand it anymore —'

'No, Simon. Please.' Mina buried her head in Simon's back.

'What's going on?' demanded Pop.

'Don't.' Mina's voice was muffled. 'Please, God, don't.'

'What's wrong with you?' Pop took Simon by the shoulders

and I had a terrible feeling, like we were all going to explode all over the walls.

'I love Mina,' said Simon. 'I've always loved her and she loves me.' I don't know whether I was surprised or shocked, but for a moment I stopped breathing.

'Oh God.' It was a pitiful plea from Mina.

'I've loved her since the first time I saw her. The night before the wedding. But Fritz was my best friend –'

'Shut up,' said Pop.

'I couldn't help it. I tried not to. I swear to God I did.' He sounded like a little boy. 'When he got letters from her, sometimes he'd read parts to me and I pretended she was writing to me. I couldn't help it.'

'No more,' pleaded Mina.

'And when I knew she loved me, too ... that was about a year ago –'

'I said, shut up.' Pop's voice was harsh and pinched. Bridie and I were at the foot of the stairs and, sensing some danger, she slipped her hand in mine. I knew what was going to happen and I couldn't do anything to stop it. 'You son of a bitch.' And Pop punched Simon in the face and sent him sprawling, knocking Mina down, too. 'All this time, you two were whoring around! Jesus Christ!' Simon had difficulty getting to his feet and Bridie and I went to help him and Mina. 'Leave them alone!' Pop screamed so loud I could feel his voice reverberating through the floor but we ignored him and Bridie helped Mina and I tried to help Simon. He was dizzy from the blow and couldn't get his footing. 'I told you to leave them alone.'

'Go on,' said Simon. 'I'll be all right.'

'I want you out of this house tonight, you son of a bitch. You hear me? Tonight.' He turned to Mina. 'And I never want to see you again.' He started up the stairs.

'Tom, wait, please,' said Simon, but Pop kept going.

'Pop, listen to him.'

He turned to me. 'That man was screwing your brother's wife.'

287

He said the words slowly and distinctly and, as though I had no control over my mind or mouth, I said, 'Like you were screwing Josie Cleary?' I wanted to suck the words back as soon as they were in the air.

'You can leave, too, if you want.' He said it quietly, matter-of-factly, then he turned and went up the stairs.

I was in the middle of my second year in high school before Pop spoke to me again. And then it was only because he was drunk. That night, the night he hit Simon, he stayed in his room while Simon packed and left the house.

'I'll stay with my friend from work. His name is Kevin. We used to meet there, Mina and me.' He pinched his eyes shut. 'Oh shit. You don't want to hear this.'

'Yes, I do.' And I did want to. I wanted to understand what was happening.

'We both felt so guilty. That's why Mina stopped coming here. She felt so goddamn guilty she couldn't look anybody in the face. I was sure everybody could see what was going on. I couldn't even visit your mother. And all the sneaking around. I hated that.' Simon was rolling his clothes and putting them in his duffel bag. His upper lip was split and he had a bruise under his ear. 'I hope you're not pissed at me.' The truth was, I didn't know what I felt.

'No, I'm not pissed at you. I don't think.'

'I wanted to tell you but I promised Mina I wouldn't say anything to anyone. Neither one of us knew what we were going to do ... you know, if Fritz came home.' He stopped for a moment. 'He still could.'

'Maybe.'

'I guess I can't do anything about your father.' He sat on the side of the bed. 'Christ, I hurt him so bad. And I love him. All of you. Mina wasn't the only reason I wanted to move in here after I was discharged. Fritz never stopped talking about you guys. Not only you, but the whole neighborhood. I wanted all of it to be as much mine as it was his. I never had anything like that. I wanted you for my family.'

'Well, we are your family.'

'Not anymore. Jesus, I fucked up everything.' He started packing again.

'What are you and Mina going to do?'

'I don't know. What can we do? They won't pronounce him dead . . . she's still married. For at least another four years. He's already been missing three.' He must have realized he was talking about the advantages of my brother being dead. 'Oh shit, I'm sorry. God, I don't want Fritz dead. I don't, I don't . . . I don't know what I want.'

'You don't want Fritz dead. I know that.'

'But sometimes I think I do. Oh Jesus, help me.' It was a cry from his heart. 'I want everything to be the way it can never be. I want you and I want Bridie and Mae and Tom and Mina. And Fritz. I want Fritz back, too.' He was in such torment he didn't know the tears were spilling from his eyes. Bridie came into the room and sat next to me on the bed. The split on Simon's lip opened and blood started running down his chin and I gave him an undershirt to wipe it away. 'I don't want to be alone again.'

'We don't want you to be alone, either. Do we, Finn?' said Bridie.

'I know you don't. I know that.' He held her face in his hands for a moment. 'I'm sorry I hurt you. I never meant to hurt anybody. Honest to God, I didn't.'

'It's all right. Finn says I make things up and hope they come true. It's my fault.'

'I have to go.' He picked up his duffel and went downstairs. 'I'll call you in a few days. I love you both.' He looked at us for a moment. Really looked at us. 'Lydia and Ethan.' He went out the door and closed it quietly behind him.

'Who's Lydia and Ethan?' asked Bridie.

'His real brother and sister.'

That night was the first night I spent in my room completely alone. Fritz was gone, and Duke, and now Simon. Simon, who was as much my brother as Fritz. I didn't think his loving Mina, their loving each other, was such a terrible thing. If Fritz had been killed in action in the war, Pop would have been happy if Simon and Mina fell in love. It would have made perfect sense. But not knowing, not having the war department officially pronounce him dead, kept Fritz alive even though I was certain he *was* dead and I was sure Pop felt the same way. I would never admit to believing Fritz was dead. That would be much too disloyal. But secretly, down in the dark part of me I didn't even want to acknowledge, I wished we knew he was dead so we could put to rest that person who every day faded more and more from my memory.

'You awake?' Bridie whispered.

'Yeah.' She closed the door quietly and came to my bed and got under the covers with me.

'Big Finn is really mad, huh?'

'He's mad, all right.'

'You think we'll ever see Simon again?'

'He said he'd call. He's going to stay with his friend, Kevin.' She made me feel uncomfortable.

'What do you think?'

'I don't know what to think.'

'You think he'll go away?'

'I hope not.'

'Simon and Mina love each other.' I knew what was going through her mind. It was all right for Mina to have Simon if she couldn't. 'I'm glad it's Mina and not some girl we don't even know.'

'Me, too.' I could feel her warmth radiating under the covers.

'Is that true about Big Finn and Josie Cleary?'

'You were there. You saw them together at the farm.'

'Yes, but they weren't doing anything.'

'She came into the barn with the kerchief off her head and Pop was mad enough to kill us for disturbing him.'

'You think they were doing it?'

'Where do you think he was going when he disappeared all those weekend afternoons?'

'To see her?'

'And you heard what Tessie said. She thought Mom had long dark hair. Pop was there with Josie Cleary and Tessie thought she was Mom.'

'Oh, that's right. Yeah, I remember that.' She didn't say anything for a moment and I looked at her and she was staring at the ceiling, her face almost glowing in the dark. 'Josie Cleary's beautiful, isn't she?'

'Like a movie star.' And I was thinking how beautiful Bridie was. She rearranged herself and I got a whiff of the sweetness of her skin and hair and I wanted to hold her and to feel us touching. I wanted to be a part of her and I wanted her to be as much a part of me as my arms and legs. All of a sudden, I knew I loved her every way two people could love and I had to tell her. She rolled on her side, facing me, and when she spoke I could feel her breath on my face.

'Finn,' she said. I turned to her and started to reach out my hand. 'I really like Alex Potts. Do you think he likes me?'

'Goddamn it!' I pulled my hand back and threw off the covers. 'Get out!'

'Why? What did I do?'

'Nothing. Go on back to your room. I want to get some sleep.'

'What did I do, damn it?'

'Nothing. I don't feel like talking about Alex Potts, okay? Get out of here.'

'Well, he's your friend, for cripes' sake. I think you're crazy. I didn't do anything.' She got out of bed.

'Close the door.'

'Honest to God, you're just like Big Finn.' She left, slamming the door behind her.

I was sure I was going to suffocate. My breath came in short gasps and I felt like I had to burst out of my skin to get any air. The bed was still full of her warmth and her scent and I wanted her and hated her. I thought I was going to throw up and I swallowed hard to fight off the nausea. Bridie wanted Alex, just as she had wanted Simon. But she didn't want me. I seriously considered Pop's suggestion that I leave the house, too. It wasn't as if I didn't have anyplace to go. Mr Howe would let me stay with him, and the Ganises said I was always welcome. I thought I might even take my money and go to Valdosta, Georgia, to live with Honey and Aunt Mussie and Uncle Moon. Tessie would take me in, too. Bridie certainly didn't give a damn where I went and Pop wanted me out of the house. And poor Duke, I didn't have to worry about him anymore. I was free to go if I wanted and no one would care. There was only one thing stopping me. Someday, Mom would come home.

Pop didn't eat breakfast the next morning or any morning for the next few weeks. He was gone when I got up and he came home long after dinner, just in time to go to bed. When he talked, only to Bridie, he never mentioned Simon or Mina's name. He didn't mention me, either. It was as though we never existed. Even when Mina and Simon left town, he didn't say anything.

It was a parish scandal. Mina Finnegan taking her baby and running off with her husband's best friend. And after Pop was so generous about taking Simon in when he was wounded and discharged and had no place to go. And the fact that Fritz was still missing, and therefore some kind of war hero, made it so much worse. Somehow, things got so twisted Pop became the wronged party and the Pascalis would have to live in shame until they went to their graves for raising a daughter as wanton as Mina. There was no compassion for the lovers. He was a man and the mere fact of his maleness did somewhat absolve him from some of the blame because, naturally, he couldn't control himself. But Mina was another story. Mina, sweet, delicate, dark and lucent Mina, was a slut and a whore and deserved the wrath of God. And to compound matters the two of them just sneaked away in the middle of the night. The truth was they did anything but sneak away.

'We're leaving town,' said Simon, looking into his coffee cup. He and Mina had asked Bridie and I to meet them at the diner.

'No, you can't.' Bridie couldn't bear the thought of anyone else slipping away from her.

'There's no other way.' Mina took Bridie's hand. 'We've tried to think of everything.'

'We even talked to Father Boyle. Shit, that was a waste of time. His advice was to wait and see what happened and to stay away from each other. Four years from now, if there was no word of Fritz, we could start keeping company, as he put it, and then be married in the church. Can you believe that? Jesus.'

'My parents thought it was the only way,' said Mina. 'They just don't understand.'

'I went to the depot twice to talk to your father but he wouldn't see me. Give him this, will you?' Simon handed me a sealed envelope. 'Maybe someday he'll read it and he won't hate us.'

'Where will you go?' I took the envelope.

'We're not sure. Mina writes to Kitty Neal. Maybe we'll visit her. Maybe we'll try living in California.'

'She loves it out there,' said Bridie. 'She's got a lemon tree in her yard.'

California seemed like the end of the earth to me. 'Do you have to go so far?'

'There are a lot of opportunities there. It's really opened up since the war. A lot of people are moving there.' Simon sounded as though he was trying to sell me on the idea in hopes he'd sell himself.

'We didn't want to leave without saying goodbye.' Mina's black, antelope eyes misted. 'But most of all I wanted to tell you something.' While she talked, Simon's thin hands, like great spiders, moved nervously on the table. 'I loved Fritz. You must know how much I loved him. And I still do. Please, please believe me. But I know in my heart he's not coming back. We were one person and if he was alive I'd know it. He would have contacted us by now. I'm sure he would.' She looked at Simon. 'I don't know if you can understand this, but Simon and I love each other . . . and Maria loves him and we all need each other . . . and I know Fritz would want us to be together . . .' She broke off and Simon took her in his arms.

And that night, after saying goodbye at the curb in front of the diner, all of us reflecting the magenta of the neon, Mina and the baby and Simon climbed into his used Dodge and left town. On the way home, Bridie and I didn't say very much. She was still annoyed because I'd thrown her out of my room without explanation, and I was still jealous because she liked Alex Potts, but that was overshadowed by the departure of Mina and Simon and the baby. Walking along in silence, I thought about the day Mr Howe said I was growing up and there was no way to stop it happening. Only a few years earlier, Mina and Simon wouldn't have tried to explain their love to me. My role was that of a kid brother. But now I was a person to talk to and be reasoned with. A person to be counted as a friend and confidante. Where before, as a kid, I could have railed at Simon and Mina leaving me, I now had to accept it as a fact of the changing landscape of my life. Bridie was crying and, without thinking, took my hand. At first, I wanted to pull it away but her hand was warm and her touch was comforting. We walked the rest of the way home, each lost in the loneliness of our diminishing world.

With only the three of us in the house it seemed sadly empty. The dining-room table was larger without Simon and there was always leftover coffee in the pot. In the middle of the night, if I woke up, I'd look at his bed, expecting to see him, curled on his side, facing the window. Pop sat alone, listening to the radio programs, and without his and Simon's running commentary, the radio seemed too loud. I made a few feeble attempts at talking to Pop that summer but I might as well have been invisible. Luckily, most of the time, there was no one in the house but Bridie and me and after a while we settled into our old routine. She immersed herself in her correspondence, which now included Simon and Mina in California, and forgot about the incident in my bedroom. I couldn't do that. I still wanted her, and every night remembered her lying next to me in my bed, and I still resented her interest in Alex Potts.

'I love all these funny names,' she said, looking at the map spread out on the living-room floor as she was trying to choose a town in her continued search for her mother. 'Hopatcong, Allamuchy, Musconetcong . . .'

'They're Indian names.'

'I wish I could speak Indian.'

'You just did.'

'Oh yeah.' She went back to circling her map.

One of the consequences of Simon's leaving, a consequence which wasn't being discussed, was a sudden drop in the amount of money coming into the house every week. I knew it was a problem when I saw Pop sitting at the kitchen table, carefully meting out his weekly paycheck.

'I'm going to look for a job.'

She stopped reading the map. 'Why?'

'Pop needs the money.'

'Did he say something?'

'No. But I know he does. No money's coming in from Simon.'

'Why don't we sell the acres? That would get some money. And my savings account.'

'Pop wouldn't let you do that.'

'Well, I don't need that land. I don't even want it. Besides, Big Finn's the one who pays the taxes on it.'

'I'm telling you, he would never let you sell it. All he talks about is how valuable it's going to be for you someday.' I started upstairs. 'I'm going to change my shirt, then I think I'll take a walk uptown.'

'What kind of job could you get? You don't get home from school until almost five o'clock.'

'Maybe nights. Or on weekends.'

'Then I'll get a job, too. I'll go uptown with you.'

'Do you have to do everything I do?'

'Yes.'

The only business we could find that was looking for help was the bowling alley. There was a placard in the window advertising for pin boys. Bridie was out of luck because they wanted *boys*, literally, and they weren't about to take responsibility for a cripple getting hit by a pin or a ball so that left me out, too. We bought the *Town Times* and went to Winter's and had an ice-cream soda and read the want ads but there was nothing right for us.

'I wish I was a damned accountant,' said Bridie, digging into the bottom of her glass for the last bit of ice cream. 'Every other ad is for an accountant.'

'You know what we should do? We should ask Miss Haas if she needs anybody at the stables on weekends.'

'Cleaning out stalls! I don't want to do that.'

'Well, I don't think she'll ask you to be a riding instructor, for God's sake.'

'I would rather sell the damn land than shovel horseshit.'

'Well, you don't have to do it. Okay? But I wouldn't mind. Come on, walk me down so I can ask her.'

'I do not want to work at the stable.'

'Fine.' We paid the check and started up the street.

'I mean it. I really do.'

'Fine.'

'Okay,' she said, as the last word.

The following weekend, in spite of Bridie's fervid objections, we started working at Miss Haas's stable for fifty cents an hour. Since there was always work to be done, Miss Haas left our hours up to us and if we put in long days, between the two of us, we could make almost twenty dollars in a weekend. It was hard, but I loved being around the horses, not to mention all the dogs and cats which were part of the menagerie, and after a while even Bridie formed attachments to certain animals. She hated cleaning stalls but in time she could curry a horse better than anyone at the stable. And she could work as hard as any man. Miss Haas, with eyes as blue as ice and wispy blond curls framing her constantly tanned face, liked Bridie and me and always gave us an extra dollar or two when she paid us. She was embarrassed by affection or gratitude and when we tried to thank her she dismissed us by telling us we talked too much.

'What is this?' said Pop, looking at the eighteen dollars Bridie handed him after dinner one night.

'Money, you dummy,' she said. 'From Finn and me.'

'What's it for?'

'You. For whatever you need it for. We got a job.'

He still wasn't talking to me but he looked directly at me for the first time since the night of the fight with Simon. The eye contact made me uncomfortable. He turned to Bridie. 'What job?'

'At the stables. Finn and I work there. Weekends. Didn't you smell us? Cripes, we smelled like Mrs Cavanaugh.'

Pop closed his eyes for a moment. 'I can sure use it.'

'That's what Finn said.' Bridie touched Pop on the shoulder as though inviting him to say something to me. He shook his head slightly in acknowledgment but he didn't look at me.

'Thanks.'

'And if you need more money,' said Bridie, 'we have some saved. And we can sell the acres.'

'No, you won't sell the acres. That's yours for the future. Christ, they'll be worth a lot of money someday. You mark my words.' Pop was happy with what we had done and his face smoothed out to the face of a boy. He folded the money and put it in the drawer of the hutch. 'This will help a hell of a lot and I'm proud of you.' Even though he didn't look at me, I knew the *you* was meant for me, too. I felt something that I could only describe as feeling bigger than I actually was and I wondered if my skin could contain me. It was a combination of how I felt after a good meal and a hot shower and a good sleep.

'We won't be able to visit Mrs Finn as much,' said Bridie.

'Well,' Pop sat back at the table, 'maybe you won't have to worry about that as much.' He echoed Bridie's tone. 'She's coming home for Christmas. Just for a visit, mind, but at least she'll be home.' Bridie hugged Pop and turned and hugged me, and while her arms were around me I felt his hand pat me on the back. But he still didn't say anything to me.

I'm sure Alex wondered why I was cool to him when we first went back to school that fall. But, because he expected everyone to accept his peculiarities, he didn't question the peculiarities of other people. He asked about Bridie and I offered little more than the assurance of her well-being. Our tenth-grade homeroom teacher, Father Gabriel, short almost to the point of dwarfism, had the embarrassing task of teaching us hygiene, which included sex education. Now that we were past the first year and accustomed to the rigors of high school, we were apparently considered sophisticated enough to hear the whole truth about the most taboo subject carefully kept under wraps in the Catholic school curriculum. There was little any of us didn't already know about so we were anxious to see Father Gabriel squirm as he went into the graphic details. He saved sex to the last, after talking about clean hair and nails, showers and proper brushing of the teeth.

'So far as sex is concerned,' he said, his cheeks darkening, 'well, you all know it's a sin unless you're married. All sex, except married sex, is a sin and then you only do it when you absolutely have to. To have children. So, in the meantime, don't think about it. Impure thoughts only get you in trouble and it's unhealthy, not to mention sinful. My suggestion is not to touch that thing except when you urinate. Class dismissed.' And he quickly left the room and we were supposedly sexually educated. Like everyone else in the room I was preoccupied with sex, and I thought Father Gabriel might at least offer some suggestions as to how to deal with the chronic preoccupation. But he had been in the seminary since he was practically a child and I realized I had more experience than him. However unsatisfactory it was, I had at least been in bed with a girl.

We didn't get the outside of the house painted in time for Mom's visit. All we managed to do was the kitchen and the bathroom. But Bridie and Mrs Ganis made new curtains for all the rooms downstairs and matching bedspread and curtains for Mom and Pop's room. Since we were busy every weekend at the stables, we had to work on the house at night and do our homework on the bus and during study halls. It would have been unbearably uncomfortable, with Pop and I not talking, if Mr Ganis hadn't helped with the painting, all the while filling us in on everything he read in the paper or heard on the radio.

'So, I read where one million veterans enrolled in college under the GI bill. It's the least the government could do. Finn, you missed a spot. Right up there to the left.' We were in the kitchen and Mr Ganis was taking a break. I never figured out how he could focus on a particular place with his crossed eyes.

'If they're smart, they'll get all the education they can,' said Pop. 'They're going to need it. Things won't be like they were in my day. Christ, if you don't have an education you'll be out in the cold.'

'It's a whole new world. A new world.' Mr Ganis shook his head in wonder. 'And now what have we got? We got flying saucers, yet. Who needs them? We got enough troubles without little men from someplace else. Tell them to go home.'

'I'd like to see somebody from another planet.' I thought of Alex and his aliens taking our skeletons to some unknown star.

'Who needs them? Who we already got here can't get along.' Mr Ganis started painting the woodwork around the windows. 'So, Finn, what do we hear from Simon?' It was deliberate. He knew what Pop's reaction would be but he couldn't abide the shattering of the family.

'I'm going down to the basement to soak these brushes. I'm finished for the night.' Pop took some brushes and a bucket and hurriedly left the kitchen.

'It was a try, what can I say?' He lowered his voice. 'How can a man not talk to his son for so long? Stubborn mick!' I never told the Ganises that I had confronted Pop with Josie Cleary and they were gracious enough not to ask when they realized it was a private matter.

'We haven't heard from Simon and Mina in a while. I guess they're okay.'

'Finn,' Mr Ganis pulled me aside and whispered. 'I can't say this to your father. He wouldn't listen. And he's too goddamn proud.' He hardly ever swore. 'You and Bridie working so hard at the stables, that might not be so good. You got school to worry about. Mrs Ganis and me, we have some money aside for a rainy day –'

'No, thanks. We're doing fine. And we like working at the stables. It's fun.'

'Cleaning up after horses is fun? I guess you got to be young. Anyway, we got the money if you need it. You'll come to me? Promise?'

'I promise.' We went back to our painting and Mr Ganis continued his running commentary.

'I read about a musical show in New York you might like to see. Maybe Sophie will take you and Bridie. *Finian's Rainbow*. It's about a leprechaun.'

Pop didn't come back to the kitchen that night.

Mom's visit was only an overnight. Pop picked her up Christmas Eve day and she went back to Franklin Village Christmas afternoon after dinner. Bridie and I stayed home and took care of the last-minute decorations and Mrs Ganis rode along with Pop because he was nervous. Bridie wanted a party but Dr Lorman said it would be hard enough for Mom to deal with being home and he thought a lot of people would only upset her. Our tree was the best we ever had. It filled the bay window, and the lights, all green, blue, red and white, could be seen up and down Livery Street. We carefully put each strand of tinsel on the branches and the finished tree looked as though it had been brushed with silver. Mom particularly liked the crèche under the tree, with Mary and Joseph and the Baby Jesus surrounded by the Wise Men and the animals and shepherds. I painted a new sky full of silver glittery stars for a backdrop and we made forests of little trees with the tips of the pine branches. Bridie thought the Baby Jesus' face looked faded so she touched him up so much he looked like a Kewpie doll, grinning grotesquely at the Magi. She was in and out the front door so much, watching for the car, that the house was cold when they finally arrived. Mom looked beautiful. Under a dull cloth coat she was wearing a flowered print dress, and her hair was up and held in place with barrettes with small poinsettias.

'Does she look a fashion plate or what?' Mrs Ganis was holding her hand as they came into the house. 'When you come home for good, Mae, we'll go shopping for the New Look. Hotsie totsie.' Mom hugged Bridie and me and stood in the doorway of the living room like a stranger looking at a place she had perhaps read about but never visited.

'The tree is beautiful. We have a very nice tree on the sun porch. We made all the decorations. What time is it?'

'Almost three,' said Pop, looking at his watch. 'Why?'

'I just like to know the time. We have a big clock on the wall in Miss Webster's office.'

'How do you like the curtains?' asked Bridie. 'Mrs Ganis helped me make them.'

'I already told her,' said Mrs Ganis. 'I can't keep a secret.'

'They're very pretty. Very pretty.' After Mrs Ganis went home Bridie and I showed Mom around the house while Pop stayed in the kitchen fixing tea. She looked at each room curiously, either trying to remember or trying to forget.

'Laurie was very handsome,' she said, looking at Bridie's wall of pictures. 'This is a sweet little room. You keep it nice, Bridie.'

'Laurie was born in Limerick. That's in Ireland. He weighed eight pounds nine ounces. He was twelve when they came to Boston. Aunt Theresa told me.'

'That's nice, dear,' said Mom with gracious uninterest.

'My grandfather had a tobacco shop. Do you know what your grandfather did, Mrs Finn?'

'He worked on the railroad. All the men in our family worked on the railroad.'

'Just like Pop,' I said.

'Oh, that's right.' It seemed she had forgotten what Pop did for a living. 'I thought it was a much bigger house,' she said to no one in particular as we went downstairs.

She had been away so long she behaved more like a visitor than a member of the family. If she wanted anything, she politely asked for it rather than presuming to get it herself. She chatted politely, never interrupting, and avoiding any mention of Simon or Mina or Fritz. Pop had told her about Simon and Mina right after they left town and he told Bridie that Mom accepted it as the will of God. I wasn't sure if it was her acceptance of the will of God or the pills she was still taking. All afternoon, whenever there was a lull in the conversation, she would ask the time.

'It's just after five,' said Pop.

'They'll be lining up for supper now. They're having creamed dried beef tonight and tomorrow they're having chicken. Roast chicken. Miss Webster told me the holiday menu.'

'We're having turkey tomorrow.' I wanted her to stop talking about the hospital. 'Mr Howe is coming. And the Ganises.'

'That's nice.' She sipped her tea. 'I'd like to go to church some-time.'

'Well,' said Pop, 'midnight mass is so crowded I thought we'd go tomorrow morning. Maybe ten o'clock.'

'That's fine. May I use the bathroom, please?' When she left the room, Pop got up and went out into the yard.

'She's just nervous,' said Bridie. 'Dr Lorman told us she'd be nervous.'

'I wish she'd talk about something besides Franklin Village.'

'Well, that's all she knows. You can't blame her for that.'

'Yeah, but it's scary.'

'Big Finn's upset, huh?'

'He's scared, too, I think.'

We opened our gifts that night but by then we were all so uncomfortable no one could work up much enthusiasm except Bridie, who did an extraordinary job of playing Santa. Mom's gifts were little and inexpensive because Miss Webster told Pop there was a lot of stealing at the Village and it was foolish to take a chance with anything of value. We gave her handkerchiefs and underwear and a bottle of Tweed toilet water, her favorite. Pop made egg-nog and we sat in the living room with the lights out, in the multicolored glow of the tree, and Bridie and I told Mom all about our jobs at the stables and school and any bits of gossip we thought might interest her. Pop sat next to Mom but I noticed they didn't touch. When it came time to go to bed, Mom asked where she was supposed to sleep.

'In your room,' said Pop as patiently as he might talk to a little child. 'I'll sleep down here.'

'What time is it?'

'Ten-twenty.'

'We don't stay up this late at the Village.'

'Then I think you'd better go to bed.' Pop sounded weary. 'Bridie, take her upstairs. If she needs anything, call me.'

'We go to bed at nine. That's when the lights go out.' Bridie and Mom went up to the bedroom and I cleared the egg-nog mugs and took them to the kitchen. When I came back, the lights were out on the tree and Pop was stretched out on the sofa. I wanted to say something but I knew he wouldn't answer me so I mumbled a good night and went to my room.

In the middle of the night I heard talking and I thought Pop had come up to their room. But as I listened I realized it was only Mom talking and I went to her door to try and hear what she was saying. Bridie came out of her room and we stood in the dark listening. I wanted to believe she was praying but she laughed a few times and I knew she was talking to her phantoms. Bridie followed me back to my room and when we got to the door we could hear Pop trying to stifle his crying.

'He must have heard her, too,' whispered Bridie.

'Poor Pop.' I wanted to go to him but I couldn't. 'You better see if he's all right.'

'Okay. I'll get him a whiskey.' She went down the stairs and disappeared into the darkness and I went back to my room and sat on the edge of the bed listening to Mom, wishing Duke was there. Or Simon. Or Fritz. Someone.

There wasn't an empty pew in the church. Half the people there were once-a-year churchgoers showing off their new Christmas duds and glowing with the spirit of the season as they sang about silent nights and first Noels. Pop and Bridie and I didn't sing. I'm sure they were as preoccupied with Mom and her voices as I was. But she joined in with her strong soprano, singing as loudly as she had sung 'The Star Spangled Banner' in the movie theatres during the war. Father Christopher, weary from being up late the night before for midnight mass, preached the capsule version of the standard birth of Christ and fulfillment of the prophecies sermon, and the whole mass, even with the long line of communicants, only lasted about forty-five minutes. When we left the church, Mrs Cavanaugh was huddled together with Mrs del Fiore and ancient Mrs Farrell and as we passed them, Pop on one side of Mom and Bridie on the other with me trailing behind, they stopped talking and stared at us as though we were lepers. I gave Mrs Cavanaugh the most withering look I could muster and she stuck her tongue out at me.

Dinner was less painful than the rest of the day because Mr Howe and the Ganises kept the conversation going even though it was mostly about how delicious the food was and how wonderful Mom looked. Pop was clearly devastated and Bridie had been withdrawn and ornery all day and I couldn't think of anything to say. Mr Howe, smelling of Bay Rum and dressed in his Sunday best, and Mrs Ganis, as colorful as the Christmas tree, did their best to keep up the holiday spirit but Mr Ganis seemed to sense something was wrong and kept looking at Mom. Every so often, she would ask the time.

'I can't be late,' she said anxiously when we were only halfway through the meal. 'They're expecting me and I don't want them to worry.'

'You won't be late.' Pop was embarrassed. 'I'll see that you're not late. Now, eat your dinner and relax.'

'This is so delicious,' said Mrs Ganis. 'So, who's the cook? You, Mae?'

'Bridie,' I said. 'And Pop.'

'Delicious,' echoed Mr Howe. 'You could open a restaurant.'

At five minutes before three, Mom was dressed in her coat and sitting in the chair nearest the front door, nervously holding the small collection of gifts on her lap. By then, Pop had given up any pretence and was as impatient as Mom to get the visit over with.

'We'll go, Mae. Let me get the car keys. Mr Howe, are you ready?' Pop was going to drop him off on the way to Franklin Village.

'Finn and I will go with you,' said Bridie.

'No, I want to talk to Mae alone.'

'Well,' said Mr Howe, 'I hope I don't have to wait to next Christmas to see you.' He had his big gnarled hand on my shoulder. 'I miss our talks.' With school and work at the stable, I had only seen Mr Howe once since Duke died.

'We miss you, too,' said Bridie.

'I'll be out to see you soon,' I said. 'I promise.'

'I'll hold you to it,' he smiled and patted me on the head.

Mom was so eager to leave she started out the door without saying anything to anyone.

'Hey, Mrs Finn! Don't I get a hug?'

'Oh, of course, I'm sorry.' And she stood there, allowing people to put their arms around her but tense with the overwhelming desire to leave. 'Thank you all very much,' she said formally, 'I had a lovely time. Really I did.' And she hurried out the door.

'It's going to take time, darling,' said Mrs Ganis, holding me close after they were gone.

'A lot of time.' Mr Ganis put his arm around Bridie. He smiled optimistically. 'Look how much she improved!'

'She's hearing her voices again.' After listening to her the night before, I had no illusions.

'Oh God, no.' Mrs Ganis finally let the tears, which she had been holding back all day, run down her fat cheeks. 'No, no, no.'

'Sophie, stop with the crying.'

'Don't tell me when I can cry. This is America, for God's sake.'

'What's that got to do with it?'

'You don't know anything.' And we all started to clear the table.

Pop came home long after Bridie and I went to bed. It was past midnight when I heard a noise and went downstairs. He was sitting at the kitchen table with the bottle of rock and rye in front of him and he was playing with a button that had come off his shirt. His tie and the jacket of his good suit were on the floor.

'Merry Christmas, sport,' he said when he saw me standing in the doorway. I picked up the jacket and tie and hung them on the back of the chair. 'My button came off.' He looked at it a moment as if he expected it to do something. 'Your friends at Tessie's said to wish you a merry Christmas. They miss you.' He had obviously had a few drinks but he wasn't falling down drunk.

'You want a cup of tea?'

'I've got my tea, thank you.' He poured himself a shot. 'You want a drink? How about that? A father-and-son drink. Jesus Christ, it's about time don't you think?'

'Okay. I'll have some whiskey.'

'No shit?' He was startled. 'You'll have a drink with the old man. Christ!' He chuckled. I got the whiskey and poured myself a little in the bottom of a coffee cup and sat across the table from him. He stared at me for the longest time and finally said, 'You're a nice-looking kid. You take after your mother.' The truth was, the older I got the more I looked like him. 'The whores like you.'

'I like them, too.'

'You like everybody, don't you?' He smiled broadly, flashing his strong, perfect teeth. 'Everybody but me.' He looked into his glass. 'Everybody but me.' I wanted to contradict him, to reassure him and say it wasn't true, but I couldn't.

'How was Mom when you got her back to the Village?'

'Delighted. She was delighted. Why shouldn't she be delighted? She was back home, wasn't she?' He looked away and smiled at the wall. 'She was back home.'

'Did you tell the doctors what happened?'

'It's Christmas. It's the Yule. No one was there.' He leaned across the table. 'You blame me, don't you? You blame me for everything that's happened to your mother. Well, let me tell you something, mister. I blamed me, too. For a long time, I blamed myself. Christ, I couldn't breathe with the weight of the guilt. But you want to know something? It's not my fault. I asked the doctors and they said it's a sickness . . . like any other disease. Your mother is sick and it's not my fault. Goddamn it, it's not my fault.'

'I don't blame you.' I didn't know what else to do so I lied.

'Bullshit, you don't blame me! You probably blame me for the fucking war, too.' There was more resignation in his voice than anger. 'Well, that wasn't my fault either. Your mother is sick. Whatever it is, she was born with it. Her father shot himself, for Christ's sake. You understand that?' He took a deep breath. 'I don't understand anything anymore.'

'Pop, why don't you go to bed.'

'I'm not drunk. Not that drunk, anyway. Don't try and get me to bed. We haven't finished talking. Drink your whiskey.' I took a sip and he lifted the glass to his lips but put it down again without drinking. 'Fritz isn't coming home. You know that don't you? You know it as true as you're sitting there. He's dead. Simon and Mina killed him off once and for all.'

'They didn't kill Fritz!'

'They drove the last nail in his coffin, for Christ's sake! He never even met his own baby and they took the baby away. Now he's laying in some lost grave with nobody to visit him or bring him flowers. Why bring flowers to the dead? Doesn't make much sense, does it? Oh Christ!' He stopped talking and stared at the floor between his feet. I was beginning to feel the few sips of whiskey warming me. 'And we lost your mother, too. It's all over with her. We're just people she knew once. Not nearly as real as those ghosts she talks to. Sometimes I wish I was one of them.' He was saying everything I had been thinking.

'Maybe the doctors will do something –'

'No. We have to stop pretending. The doctors don't know shit. It's just you and me and Bridie. And that's the way it's going to stay. Nothing's the way we thought it would be. Not one goddamn thing.' He was talking more to himself than me. 'Nothing worked out and nothing ever will. I'll never live on a farm. What a dumb shit I was to think I might live on a farm someday. Dreams don't come true, sport. Never. I wonder why we dream if they can't come true? God's getting even with us for something.' He suddenly looked at me. 'And it's not for the likes of Josie Cleary if that's what you're thinking. Who the hell are you to accuse me, that's what I'd like to know. You're a kid, for Christ's sake. You wouldn't understand even if I tried to explain. You're just a kid. Fritz would understand. If he was here, Fritz would understand.'

'I'm going to bed.'

'Drink your whiskey.'

'I don't want it.' I poured it down the drain.

'We haven't finished our talk yet.'

'It's a waste of time because I'm just a kid and I don't understand. If Fritz was here you could talk to him.'

'You're a cold little bastard, aren't you?'

'I guess I am. Good night.'

'Close the kitchen door.' I closed it behind me. 'It's not my fault.' His voice was muffled.

Instead of going back upstairs, I went out on the front porch and sat on the steps. It was bitter cold and I huddled close to the house with my bathrobe pulled tight under my chin. Most of the houses on the street were dark but a few had night lights dimly shining like the soft light of fish tanks. I imagined everyone tucked in their beds, secure and warm, looking forward to the next day with all the promise each sunrise is supposed to bring. They didn't know Fritz was dead and Mom might just as well have been. Pop had decided and I had to admit I agreed with him. But I envied Mom and Fritz. Short of the end of the world death or madness seemed like the only way to escape, and since I didn't think I was going to die or go mad I sat there, shivering and turning blue with cold, praying for the end of the world.

Nothing as cataclysmic as the end of the world happened and life went on as usual until the following March when I had the flu so bad I missed two weeks of school. Miraculously, Pop and Bridie didn't get it. The first week I had a temperature most of the time and in my delirium visited with Fritz and Simon and Betty Grable and President Roosevelt. Dr Lorman considered putting me in the hospital but I raised hell so Mrs Ganis and Little Tum nursed me during the day and Bridie and Pop took care of me at night. Midweek the second week, when I was feeling better, I received an air-mail letter from Simon.

*

Dear Finn,

Bridie tells us you are sick. I hope by the time you get this you will be feeling better. Maybe you should come out to California for a visit and let the sunshine make you better? Mina and I would like that a lot. We miss you and talk about all of you all the time.

I'm thinking about getting my real-estate license. I don't want to be stocking shelves in a market when I'm fifty years old. Everybody seems to be moving West. There seems to be a great future in selling houses. Mina and I want a house of our own. Especially now. One of the reasons I wanted to write was to tell you we are going to have a baby. In September. You're the first person to know. I wanted it that way. We haven't even told Kitty Neal. We are very happy about it and I hope you'll be happy, too. You can tell Bridie. If you don't, she'll punch you out. If you want, you can tell your father, too. I hope someday he'll be able to forgive us. Did he read the letter, yet?

Kitty has been seeing an army major. He's a doctor and a very nice guy. He looks a lot like Laurie. She is happy and Mina says she thinks it's serious. You would like it a lot out here. We have coyotes and rattlesnakes and tarantula spiders as big as your fist. And we have mockingbirds and they sing at night. I really like them. There's all kinds of things for you to draw. Even movie stars, although I've never seen one.

Well, I hope you're all better soon. We love you and miss you more than I can tell you. I hope you think about us as much as we think about you.

Your 'brother',
Simon

I showed the letter to Bridie and her immediate reaction was anger because she had heard from Mina and Mina didn't say anything about the baby.

'Why didn't she tell me? I'm the one who writes to her all the time.' She was serving me a lunch of tomato soup and a cheese sandwich.

'Simon wanted me to be the first to know.'

'Cripes, you'd think you were the King of Egypt or something.'

'Maybe I am.'

'How can they have a baby? They're not married.'

'Don't be stupid.'

'I don't mean that! I mean the baby will be illegitimate. That's not fair to the baby.'

'Everybody thinks they're married. And someday they will be. The baby will never know.'

'I guess. And how come Kitty didn't tell me about that army guy? Nobody ever tells me anything.'

'Maybe she wanted to wait until she really had something to tell. Like she's getting married or something.'

'You think? I'm glad she met somebody. But I bet he's not as handsome as Laurie.'

'Probably not,' I agreed, knowing her image of Laurie was a mixture of saint, hero and matinee idol.

Pop fixed the sofa like a bed so I could stay downstairs and listen to the radio and I spent my days with *Mary Noble Backstage Wife*, *Pepper Young's Family*, and *Young Dr Malone*. Little Tum had an excuse, although she never needed one, to bake me the most delicious pastries I had ever eaten, and Mrs Ganis made anything I wanted. By the time I was feeling better, I was spoiled rotten.

Toward the end of the second week, when my strength returned and I was suffering from cabin fever, I decided to take a walk uptown just to get some fresh air. It was a cool day but the sun was strong and warm and it felt so good stretching my legs I decided to walk to Tessie's Place because I hadn't been there in a long time.

'Well,' said Charles when I surprised him in the kitchen, 'we were beginning to think you died or something. You are getting tall, boy. How the hell are you?'

'I'm okay –'

'Wait a minute,' his brows came together and he glared at me, 'what the hell are you doing here on a school day? You drop out?'

'No, I had the flu. I've been home sick.'

'Well, sit your skinny ass down and I'll give you some pea soup. Good for you.' He ladled the soup from a pot steaming on the back of the stove and slathered a thick slice of homemade bread with butter. 'How's my girlfriend?'

'Fine. We've both been working on weekends at the stables.'

'For that German lady?'

'Yeah, she's real nice.' The soup was delicious and warming. 'Where's everybody?'

'Iris ain't here no more. She went to work in a whorehouse in Cuba. Cuba for God's sake! Hell, she don't even speak the language. But they like blond white women down there and she thinks she's going to do real good and save lots of money. She wants to put some money away before she gets too old to sell her pussy. She's smart. You want some tea?'

'Please.'

'Elizabeth took Tessie to the doctor. She got a bad cough she can't get rid of. I been trying to get her to go to the doctor for two years. It's so bad now, she had to go. I think it's the TB but don't you say a word, you hear?' I nodded my head. 'My daddy had the TB and he coughed just like her. And I know she been spitting blood but she won't admit to it. I seen the blood in her handkerchief. And she don't weigh as much as a new pig. All skin and bones, her clothes just hanging off her. If you see her, you notice she got a kind of ashy color to her skin. Some black folks get that color when they're sick. And them beautiful eyes are all sunk and got no light in them.' His own eyes sparkled with tears and I realized that Charles was in love with Tessie. 'I think what made her real bad sick was cause Honey stayed in Georgia. That's the truth and don't you tell nobody I said it.' We traded information about Honey and I told him about Mom hearing her voices again and he said he thought the good Lord expected too much of some people. 'They say He never gives you a burden you can't carry but I think that's bullshit. Most folks just die from the weight of the burden. And that's the truth.'

'I thought I heard you talking to somebody,' said Cat as she came into the kitchen. 'Well, look who's here.' She kissed me on the cheek and I got a strong whiff of her perfume. Her robe was open and I could see the shadow of her nipples and the hair between her legs through the flimsy nightgown and I felt an electric shock ripple through my body.

'How are you, Cat?'

'Getting fat. Fat Cat, that's me. But look at you! You're growing up. Where's Bridie?'

'School. I've been home cause I had the flu.'

'I guess it's going around.'

'You want anything?' asked Charles.

'No thanks.' She sat at the table. 'Iris is gone.'

'Charles told me.'

'To another country. I never knew anybody who went to another country. She said she was going to send me a postcard. I hope she remembers. Imagine something coming from another country with your name on it. That's like magic, isn't it?' She leaned into me. 'Tessie's sick.'

'I know.'

'Real sick, I think.'

'Let the doctor be the one who says how sick she is,' said Charles defensively, as if he hadn't already diagnosed her tuberculosis.

'I got a new doll,' said Cat, changing the subject. 'Her eyes open and close and they're glass. A real pretty blue. Come on, I'll show her to you.' She got up and started out of the kitchen.

'Let the boy finish his soup.'

'Okay,' she said. 'When you finish your soup.' She smiled her child's smile and left.

Charles sat across from me. 'You ain't been broken in yet, have you?'

313

'No.'

'Well, now's your chance. Cat's real good. And she keeps herself clean, too. She's good at breaking boys in.'

'I don't think so.'

'Hell, don't think about it. Just do it. She's always been partial to you. You and Honey. She's still mad cause Elizabeth broke Honey in. Shit, you be doing her a favor.'

'Well . . .'

'You know you want to. When she bent over and kissed you I could hear your pecker twitching clear across the kitchen.'

'I'm too nervous.'

'Everybody is the first time. But you get over that fast enough when you see how good it feels. Now go on. Get out of my kitchen.'

'What if she doesn't want to?'

'If she don't want to, she'll tell you and you go home.'

Cat must have had thirty dolls. Dolls with real hair and porcelain faces, rag dolls and dolls with eyes that followed you around the room. They all had little dresses and aprons and socks and Cat kept them as clean as any good mother kept her kids. The light in the room was pink from the red scarf draped over the lamp on the night stand and the wallpaper was patterned with big rust-colored roses and there were ruffles everywhere. The curtains were ruffled and the bedspread and the skirt around the dressing table. Cat was sitting on the bed with her new doll.

'Look, when you bend her back her eyes close. Come here.' I went to the bed. 'Look at her eyelashes. They're real hair. Isn't she beautiful?'

'She's real pretty.'

'I call her Iris. You think Iris would like that?'

'Sure she would.' I sat on the edge of the bed and I was shaking so much my leg was jumping uncontrollably.

'Don't be nervous. I know what you're here for.'

'I just came to see your doll,' I lied.

'You big fibber. It's okay. It is, honest.'

'I don't have any money with me. I could pay you later.'

'A million dollars couldn't pay for what I'm going to do for you.' She rubbed my lips with her fingertip. 'You have pretty lips. Soft and shaped real nice. Real pretty lips.' I expected her to kiss me but she didn't. 'You want to play baby bunny? I'll be the mama rabbit and you be the bunny.'

'Okay.' I was beginning to shake all over. She stood up and slipped her robe off and I could see her round body through the nightgown. Her breasts were huge and her nipples were brown and the size of silver dollars.

'The baby bunny sucks the mama's titties. You think you'll like that?'

'Yeah.' My mouth was so dry I could hardly talk.

'I'll be right back.' When she got to the door she turned. 'Take off your clothes.' And she left. I looked at all the dolls staring at me accusingly and I wanted to run. But more than that, I wanted to stay. Very slowly, I unbuttoned my shirt and took it off. Then I sat on the edge of the bed and took off my shoes and socks. I stood up and started to undo my pants but the dolls scowled at me and I had the feeling they were closing in. So I just stood there, shirtless and shoeless, for what seemed like hours before Cat returned. She carried a basin of water and a towel and a washcloth and put it on the night stand.

'You still have your pants on! You afraid to let me see your bad leg?'

I hadn't even thought about my leg. 'It's not that.'

'Well, don't be shy with me.' She took a dish with a small piece of soap out of the night stand. 'You haven't got anything I haven't seen.' Before I knew it, she had pulled her nightgown over her head and sat on the bed, stark naked. She reached out and put her hands on my hips and pulled me closer and unbuttoned my pants and pulled them down along with my underwear. I had no idea my own pants, sliding slowly down my legs, could be so tortuous and exciting.

'Step out of your pants. A man looks stupid with his pants

down around his ankles.' I did exactly as I was told, kicking my pants across the room. 'Well, look at you. You're all ready to go, aren't you.' I was too embarrassed to look down but I had the feeling that every atom of my body had gone to one place and was sticking straight up from between my legs. 'This is what we do.' She wet the washcloth in the basin and rubbed some soap on it, making a lather, and started washing me. It was ecstasy. A naked woman was stroking me with a warm, wet, soapy cloth, a woman with a scent and breasts and a mysterious promise between her legs.

'I don't think you better do much more of that.'

'Tessie makes us do this every time.'

'Yeah,' I was frantic to have her stop before it was too late, 'I took a shower just before I came here.'

'I'll just rinse off the soap.' As she dipped the cloth in the warm water, I tried to think of anything but what was happening to me. I thought of dead people and accidents and operations where people were cut open and bleeding but in the back of my mind I knew she would come back and rub me again with the warm washcloth and I didn't know how long I could last.

'Can you wait just a minute? Please?'

'Sure. You are anxious, aren't you.' She didn't touch me for a few moments but she started touching herself and that was just as bad. She made big circles, flattening her breasts, and I could see her nipples start to harden and I wanted to tell her to stop because I felt like she was touching me. I looked at the dolls, hoping their disapproval would do something but I was on the edge and nothing seemed to help. 'You have a nice smooth body, Finn.'

'Thank you very much.' I didn't want her to say anything because her words were as exciting to me as her touch.

'Just like Dwayne. That was my cousin. He had a smooth body, too. He got killed by a mule. Did I tell you about Dwayne?'

'Yeah. The mule kicked him in the heart.'

'That's right. I loved him.' She leaned forward and kissed my right nipple, flicking her tongue back and forth. It was like a hot coal on my chest and I pulled away.

'I'm sorry. I'm ticklish, I guess.'

'We have to get all that soap off before it dries. Dried soap can burn a person.'

'Yeah.' I took a deep breath and bit the inside of my cheek and thought of people going up in flames in the pit of hell but when she started rubbing me with the wet cloth, it was all over. I was mortified. 'Oh God, I'm sorry,' I said. 'I didn't mean to do that.'

'Don't you fret about it,' she said, cleaning up.

'I mean it. I'm sorry.'

'It happens all the time. In fact, it happens to the chief of police every time he comes here. He has a problem. But I just think you were at the starting gate too long. That's your only problem. We'll wait a while and try again.'

'I have to go home.' I was too embarrassed to stay there. I grabbed my clothes and started getting dressed and Cat put on her robe.

'It'll be okay in no time at all. You'll see. You guys got your pistol loaded all the time. I know what I'm talking about. Five minutes and you'll be raring to go again.'

'Maybe some other time.' I pulled on my pants and stuck my underwear in my pocket. Then I put my shirt on and left her bedroom, carrying my shoes and socks.

'Come back later,' she said as I was leaving. 'Any time. I mean that. Any time.'

'Thank you very much. Goodbye.'

When I passed the kitchen Charles was leaning in the doorway. 'Well, that was fast.'

'Yeah.' I hurried toward the back stairs.

'Hey! Where you going in such a hurry? Don't you want to talk about it?'

'About what! I didn't do it. It was over before it started.'

'Well, that happens. You just want it so bad you can't wait.

Hell, that happens to every man sometime. Now don't be hard on yourself, boy. It happens to every man.'

I ran down the stairs and didn't stop until I got to the garbage cans on the side of the building. My heart felt like it was coming out of my throat and I sat on a can, catching my breath and putting on my shoes. I was completely humiliated and all I could think of was Elizabeth saying Honey was a natural when he did it. And I was a failure. Cat had done her best but I failed. I couldn't even get through the preliminaries. It was all that damn washing. Charles said it happened to every man but I didn't believe him. I was sure I was the only person on the face of the earth who ever experienced such abject degradation.

On the way home I wondered if I was still a virgin. I wasn't quite sure if sex with a woman, no matter what kind of sex it was, constituted the loss of virginity or not. By the time I got home I was certain of one thing. Cat knew what she was talking about. I was raring to go again.

Charles was right about Tessie. She did have TB and in less than two months there was no more Tessie's Place. Bridie and I went down to say goodbye the day Charles carried Tessie to the waiting car. Mr Stebbins, who was in television sales in Harlem, came over to drive Tessie to her people in Georgia. Charles was going with them and after a short visit was going to take Tessie to a place in Arizona that was supposed to be good for people with tuberculosis. She was, as Charles had said, ashen, and she tried to cover it up with too much make-up and she looked like one of Cat's overly painted porcelain dolls.

'I'll give Honey a kiss for you,' she said when she was settled in the back of the car. She had a slight fit of coughing and turned her face away. Bridie crawled in beside her and hugged her. 'Not so tight, girl,' said Tessie kindly, 'you'll squeeze what little life I got left out of me.'

'Don't you kids pay any attention to her,' said Mr Stebbins. 'She's too damn mean to die.'

'And that's the truth,' said Charles, loading the last of the bags in the trunk of the car.

Cat and Elizabeth were there and a cab was waiting to take them to the train station. Cat was going home to visit her parents in West Virginia and then she was going to join Iris in Cuba. Tessie was paying her way. Elizabeth was going to Philadelphia to stay with a married sister and she planned to open a knitting shop with the money she had saved.

While Bridie was saying her goodbyes, Cat pulled me aside. 'Imagine me going to a place where they speak another language.'

'That's great. You'll learn Spanish.'

'Hell, I can hardly speak English. That's one good thing about being in this business. Language got nothing to do with it.' She laughed.

'Say hi to Iris for us.'

'I will. And I'll send you a postcard.'

'Okay. I'd like that.'

'We didn't even get to play mama rabbit.' She touched my lips with her fingertip and I could feel my face redden. 'You're a sweet man.' She didn't even say young man.

'Thanks,' I said. 'I wish it had been different.'

'Maybe you and Bridie? Huh? It's real nice when you love somebody. You take care. I'll be thinking about you.' And she kissed me on the cheek. Even Elizabeth, as cold as she usually was, kissed us goodbye.

When I went to the car, Tessie waved me away. 'Get out of here, boy. I'm tired of saying goodbye.' She held out her hand and I took it. It was as cold and frail as a dead baby bird. 'Besides, you'll make my mascara run and there's nothing worse than an old whore with runny mascara. You grow up nice, you hear me?' She turned to Mr Stebbins. 'Let's go. Jesus, we'll never get to Georgia.'

'Tell Honey to come back for a visit!' yelled Bridie as they pulled away.

When they were all gone and Bridie and I came around the side of the building, past the For Sale sign, and started up Allen Street, we saw some of the regular customers, sitting in their cars and leaning against trees, hiding in the shadows trying not to be seen, ashamed to say goodbye but there, nonetheless, to bid silent farewells.

Pop never missed a weekend visiting Mom but he was right when he said she was never coming home. She didn't completely retreat again but her reality was the hospital and the people inside her head, while we were part of a past life which she remembered less and less as time went on. Over the next few years doctors tried electroshock several more times and, although she improved for a while, eventually she withdrew into the security of her other world. We were never told it was hopeless but we knew that Mom, like Mildred and hundreds of other patients at Franklin Village, was a permanent resident. In time, she stopped talking about Fritz or Simon, or anyone from her past. If she didn't see people with some frequency they simply ceased to exist. When we visited her she reacted with a formal deference, as she reacted to the doctors and nurses and anyone else she saw with some regularity. And it wasn't long until our primary purpose was to supply her with everything and anything she wanted. Most of the time she asked what we brought her before she said hello. But we never, among the three of us, ever discussed her not leaving the hospital. That Christmas night in the kitchen, when Pop sat across the table from me, half drunk and accusatory, was the only time he actually said she was never coming home. And too many people had already slipped away from Bridie so she was content to live with the illusion that, somehow, we would all live happily ever after.

Because of work at the stables and taking care of the house, Bridie and I never joined any clubs or participated in any extracurricular activities. School was merely that, nothing more and nothing less. We both did only as much homework as we had to to maintain slightly above-average grades and that was usually done on the bus going to and from. I did do a little artwork for the *Campanile*, the school paper, because Father Blaise was the faculty advisor and he asked me to help on certain projects. But it was always something I could do during study hall or in my lunch hour. And so Bridie and I made no friends, with the exception of Alex Potts, and, somehow, in spite of Bridie's affinity for him, Alex and I managed to get along. I suppose we were his only friends, too. He was a year older than me and by the end of the summer before our junior year, he got his driver's license and whenever his father gave him the car he came to Livery Street. Most of the time he sat around the stables waiting for us to finish work but on the odd day we did take off, we hit the road. A car gave us the kind of freedom we had only dreamed of and when we had the time we went to the shore or the Poconos or to visit Mom. We even drove into New York. And it was because of Alex and his car that Bridie found her mother.

It happened when we were looking for a gift for Mina and Simon's baby. He was born the end of September and they named him Thomas, after Pop and Fritz. Simon called, all excited, with the good news that both mother and baby were healthy. Pop wasn't at home. Simon and I had hardly spoken when Bridie took the phone and laughed and cried as she asked all kinds of questions about weight and hair and time of birth. When Pop came home from work and we told him, without saying a word, he went upstairs and locked himself in the bathroom for over an hour. Bridie and I were fixing pork chops for supper when we heard him come into the kitchen. He had showered and changed his clothes.

'I'm going out. I don't want anything to eat.'

'Big Finn, it's almost ready. It's pork chops. You love pork chops.'

'Not tonight.' He stood there for a moment before he said, 'Send a gift. From the two of you. Something nice.' Bridie went to him and hugged him before he left.

'Where do you think he's going?'

'I don't know,' I said. 'Maybe the Alley.'

'He'll get drunk.'

'Jesus, I hope not. He'll want to have a father-and-son talk and I'm not up to that.'

'He said to buy a gift.'

'I know. I heard him.'

'He cares about Simon and Mina. I knew he did.'

'Maybe.'

'Cripes, we have to tell somebody about the baby. I'm going to call the Ganises.'

'What about the pork chops?'

'The hell with the pork chops.' She called and shrieked and squealed and by the time she was finished I was so caught up in the moment I called Honey in Valdosta.

'Yes?' it was a woman's voice, soft and rich as syrup.

'Is this Aunt Mussie?'

'Yes. Who is this?' she said warily.

'I'm Honey's friend in New Jersey.'

'Is this Finn? Calling all the way from New Jersey? You don't mean it!' Her voice went away from the phone but I could still hear her. 'Moon, go find Honey. He got a long-distance phone call from Finn in New Jersey. Hurry up. It costs a lot of money.' She spoke into the phone again. 'It's not something bad, is it?'

'No, it's good. A friend of ours had a baby.'

'Jesus love the sweet little thing.' There was a slight pause. 'Well, Finn, you sound all growed up. I guess I always think of you as little because the picture Honey has is when you was kids. You should see how big Honey is. He's near a man already.' She chuckled. 'Now I got a voice to put with the face.' I could hear mumbling in the background. 'Here he is now. It was very nice talking to you, Finn. Come see us sometime, you hear?'

322

'Hello?' the voice was breathless. It was a voice I didn't recognize. A man's voice. 'Finn?'

'Honey, how are you?'

'Man, I can't hardly believe it. All this time and you finally calling.'

'God, you sound different.'

'Well, you do, too.'

'Simon and Mina had a little boy.'

'Oh, that's good. Man that is real good. Way out there in California, huh? What your daddy say?'

'We should buy the baby something. That's all.'

'Where's Bridie?'

'Right here, trying to yank the phone out of my hand. How's Tessie? You hear from her?'

'Yeah. Charles calls every week. She's in a hospital in Arizona somewhere. He said she's doing pretty good.' There was a pause and I realized we were having trouble talking to each other. For a moment I thought about asking Bridie to leave the room so I could tell him what happened with Cat but something stopped me. I had the terribly lonely feeling that I didn't know him well enough. 'Yeah, she is doing good,' he said, breaking the silence. 'It's dry there and healthy for people with the TB.'

'I'm glad. You wait and see, she's going to get better.'

'Yeah.'

'Well, I better put Bridie on. She'll have a shit fit if I don't. You take care, you hear?'

'Write me a letter. I like getting letters.'

'I will. You write, too. See you.'

'Not if I see you first.' He laughed and I handed the phone to Bridie who carried on as though she had only seen him the day before, easy and unselfconscious and relaxed as an old friend should be. But I couldn't think of anything to say to the stranger on the other end of the line and I knew he felt as awkward as me. It was easy to write a letter to the boy I had known but I had no idea how to talk to this new person. Too much time separated us. Enough time to make us cautious and unavailable and exclusive from one another. Maybe if we were together again for a while and had an opportunity to get to know the people we had become, maybe we could relax with one another. But, meanwhile, I knew I'd never be able to tell him about Cat.

Bridie couldn't decide on a gift for the baby. It had to be something special, something no one else would ever think of and something the baby would cherish until he was an old man. She was sure she'd know the right thing when she saw it and she finally did see it in the window of an antique shop in New Hope, Pennsylvania. Alex picked us up early on a Sunday in mid-October and we went up to Washington's Crossing and along the Delaware to Lambertville. The leaves had turned and were at their brilliant best as we drove along the canal, which looked so inviting we stopped and sat on the bank, watching two painted turtles basking on a log, absorbing as much warmth as they could before their long winter sleep started. A water snake lazed its way along in the shallows, apparently in no rush to go anywhere, and a dragonfly zoomed past, impressing us with his sensational aerodynamics. The sun shimmered on the water and the air was warm and thick with autumn and it was so pleasant I couldn't pay any attention to Alex and his usual tirade against the human race.

'If everything is so rotten, why don't you just shoot yourself and get it over with?' said Bridie, her eyes closed and her face turned to the sun.

'Because I want to be around to see my predictions come true.'

'You're full of shit,' I said.

'Ah, but you have a way with words, Finn.'

'Come on,' said Bridie. 'Let's get something to eat. I'm starved.' We drove on to Lambertville and had lunch in a small restaurant on the river, then we crossed the narrow bridge to

New Hope, parked the car and went browsing through the galleries and shops.

'Look at that,' said Bridie, stopping to look in the window of an antique shop. 'That's perfect for the baby.' She pointed to a set of very old, hand-carved alphabet blocks. The letters were crude but there were beautiful flowers and birds intricately woven around them and the wood had mellowed to a soft, rich patina. 'Aren't they great?'

'They'll probably cost an arm and a leg.'

'Maybe not. Come on, let's see.' We went into the cluttered shop and the dusty, musty smell of old things, mixed with the sweetish smell of potpourri, made me feel slightly nauseous. A plump, dark-haired woman came from the back of the shop and as she approached us I immediately recognized Bridie's mother. Bridie's back was to her and before I could say anything her mother asked if we wanted help with anything.

'How much are the –' Bridie stopped mid-sentence as she turned and realized who she was talking to. 'Jesus!' She sounded as if the wind had been knocked out of her.

'Bridie?' Her mother backed up a step. 'My God!' I thought she was going to faint. 'I knew that someday you'd walk through that door. I knew it as true as I'm standing here. I said it a hundred times. Someday Bridie is going to walk right through that door. Oh my God, you're beautiful.'

The woman who had been with Kathleen at the cemetery came from the back room. 'Is something wrong?' she asked.

'It's Bridie. Can you believe that? I told you she'd come walking in one day. Didn't I, Leah? Didn't I say she'd come walking in some day?'

'I'm Leah Harris,' she said, extending her hand to Bridie.

'This is Finn and Alex. Cripes, I can't believe this.'

'I saw you at the cemetery.' Leah shook my hand. 'We don't have to stand here.' She was completely in control of the situation. 'Please come in the back and I'll make some coffee.'

'I'm Kathleen.' She took Alex's hand. 'I'm Bridie's mother.'

'Your mother!' he said to Bridie. 'I didn't know you had a mother.'

'Do you want to stay?' I was afraid it was all too much for Bridie.

'I guess.' She turned to Kathleen. 'I've been calling all over New Jersey trying to find you. Why didn't you tell me you were here?'

'Well,' her mother looked at Leah, 'we thought it was best this way.'

'Why? God, I knew you were alive. Why shouldn't I know where you lived? I have so many questions. Stuff I want to know about you and Laurie.' Kathleen moved slightly toward Leah.

'Let's go in the back and talk about this,' said Leah.

'You go,' I said to Bridie. 'Alex and I will take a walk and come back in about an hour.'

'Why?' asked Alex.

'Because it's none of your damn business.'

'You be back. One hour, you hear?' said Bridie.

Alex and I walked along the narrow streets of the town and finally went to the river and watched people feeding several ducks and two Canada geese. He asked me questions about Bridie and her mother but I told him, in all honesty, I didn't know very much. I did tell him about Laurie's funeral and Kathleen's sudden appearance but when I said that was all I knew he thought I was lying. When the hour was up and we got back to the shop, Bridie and Kathleen were standing out front and Bridie was holding a neatly wrapped package. As we approached, Kathleen waved and went back into the shop and Bridie came to us.

'Let's go home,' she said, and started off in the direction of the car. Her face was drawn and I knew it wasn't a good time to ask her what was said.

'How much were the blocks?' I asked.

'They gave them to me. They're over a hundred years old.

The Q is missing. There's a piece of paper with the name of the man who carved them. He worked on a ferryboat someplace. He made them for his kids.' She walked ahead and I knew the conversation was over. Alex started to say something but I grabbed his arm and he shut up. When we got to the car she sat alone in the back, as she had done as long as I had known her when she didn't want to talk. The afternoon sun cast long shadows and the leaves looked more dramatically beautiful than they had on the trip up the river. We rode along in silence until we left the river and started toward home.

'She didn't walk out on me,' said Bridie, finally. 'She took me with her but Laurie came and got me and took me back to Boston. He had a job and she didn't and he threatened to go to the authorities.' I looked over my shoulder and she was crying so I reached back and she held my hand. 'She didn't walk out on me. Aunt Theresa's a damn liar. Kathleen said she always wanted me with her.'

'Why did she leave Laurie?'

'I don't know. She just said she had to. That she wasn't meant to be married. I don't get it. But he was never mean to her or anything. I asked her that. She said he didn't have a mean bone in his body. And she said she always loved him.'

'She was ahead of her time,' said Alex. 'It won't be long before marriage is obsolete. A wedding license is nothing more than a permit to breed.'

'Why don't you shut up, Alex,' I said.

'All that time we were looking for her in New Jersey and there she was right across the river in Pennsylvania. Why didn't we think of that?'

'Too easy, I guess.'

'God, I can't believe it.' She asked for my handkerchief and we rode the rest of the way with Alex asking questions that neither Bridie nor I answered.

'I think Alex is a jerk,' she said after he dropped us off at home.

'Really?' I felt enormous relief. She had outgrown the only existing competition.

'Yeah, really. A big jerk.'

'I kind of like him.'

For the next few weeks, Bridie kept to herself in her room. I told Pop we met Kathleen and he tried to talk to Bridie about it but she wanted to be left alone. Then, one night, she took down the shrine to Laurie. The walls of her room were stripped of his pictures and everything was carelessly thrown into boxes and hidden under her bed. She did keep one picture of him on the dresser next to the statue of the Virgin with the chipped nose. I was never told any of the other details of her conversation with her mother and I never asked. Apparently, Bridie was satisfied with what they talked about and although she and Kathleen kept in touch and occasionally saw one another, it was too late for them to be any more than casual friends. At first, Kathleen wanted more but friendship was the most Bridie could give. Just knowing where her mother lived seemed to put things into some kind of perspective for her. Laurie lost his position as a deity but she didn't cherish the memory of the mortal man any less.

'What if,' said Pop, driving slowly through the light snow of a late winter storm as we were heading home from a visit with Mom, 'what if we sold the house?'

'Sold the house!' I leaned forward so I could get a look at his face to see if he was serious.

'Why would we sell the house?' asked Bridie. 'Are we broke?'

'No, no. It's not that. Just listen to me. The town has grown so much since the war, and all these professional people, your doctors and lawyers, are buying people's houses to turn into offices. We're only half a block from the main drag, for Christ's sake. We could probably make a fortune. I've been thinking about it.'

'Where would we go?' I had never lived anyplace but the house on Livery Street.

'Well, now, I've been thinking about that, too. Say we get a good price for our house. Okay? I buy the two acres from Bridie and we build a house in the country.' So, I thought, his dream wasn't dead.

'I told you before, you can have the acres. I don't want them.'

'No, I'd never do that. I'd pay you whatever acreage is going for. And we could put up a nice little place. What do you think?'

'But, we've always lived in our house –'

'Then it's time for a change. We could have a bigger garden and chickens and maybe goats. I always liked goats. And a couple of dogs. What do you say?' He was so enthusiastic, I didn't know how to respond. He sounded like a kid, like he did when he and Mom used to talk into the night planning their future and Fritz and I lay in the dark listening to them. 'Come on you two! For Christ's sake you must think something.'

'Well, I don't know,' said Bridie. 'I guess it's okay. I never lived in the country. And I never lived in a new house.'

'It's your house,' I said, not meaning to sound argumentative.

'It's yours, too. So, tell me what you think.'

'What about . . . I don't know . . . Mom and Fritz and Simon and Duke . . . all the memories?'

'To hell with memories. I'm sick of memories. If you want memories you take them with you. Jesus, you don't have to be in a house to remember people. I remember my mother and father and I'm not living in the house I grew up in. That's bullshit.'

'Okay. You asked me.'

'Is that your only objection?'

'What does it matter? Sell the lousy house if you want. I don't give a damn.'

'Now, don't start fighting,' said Bridie.

'I'm not fighting. He asked me what I thought and I told him. Sell the house and build a new one. You're the one who has to live in it.'

'Oh?' he looked over his shoulder. 'And where the hell will you be?'

'New York.'

'Oh, that's right. You're going to New York next year.'

'I want to.'

'To study art, isn't that it?' he said sarcastically.

'That's right. I've been saying I was going to New York half my life. It can't come as a big surprise.'

'And where are you going to study?'

'Cooper Union if I can get in.'

'You've got the money for all this?'

'I'll work and go to classes at night.'

'You've got it all worked out, haven't you? And where you going to live? In Greenwich Village with the other freaks and the Communists?'

'Maybe.'

'Well,' he said mockingly, 'don't you think you're something else. Who the hell is going to pay good money for your *art*. Christ, there's a million people every year who think they can go to New York and become rich and famous. You know where most of them end up? In the street. That's where. What the hell makes you think you're so special?'

'Not you. That's for damn sure.'

'Don't you get smart with me. I just want you to keep your feet on the ground and not go off half-cocked.'

'Finn is good. Really he is.' Bridie was tentative because she didn't want to get into a fight.

'So are a lot of people. That doesn't mean shit. I'm only saying this for your own good. Wait till you see how tough it is out there in the real world.'

'I don't have to wait. You told me a thousand times.'

'And I'll tell you another thousand times if I feel like it. You've got a real smart mouth on you. You always know better than everybody else, don't you? Well, let me tell you, mister, you don't know anything. I want to see how smart your mouth is after life has kicked you around a bit.'

'Yeah, so far it's been a real picnic!' He slammed on the brakes and the car skidded to the side of the road and stopped.

'Please,' Bridie pleaded. 'Don't start fighting.'

'I'm not fighting,' said Pop angrily. He turned to me. 'Maybe you should walk the rest of the way home so you can cool off a bit.'

'Maybe I should.'

'Big Finn, it's miles. And it's snowing! Just calm down, the both of you.'

'Come on, Bridie. You like to walk in the snow.' I opened the door.

'Bridie's staying right where she is.' She didn't move.

'You don't have to stay if you don't want to.'

'I know,' she said in a small voice. She didn't look at me. Pop knew he had won so I got out of the car and he drove off before I had time to close the door.

The snow was coming down in big, fat flakes as I walked the three miles to town and the berm of the road was already deep with slush and my feet were soaked. I couldn't imagine never being able to go back to the house on Livery Street. I knew every inch of it as well as I knew my own face and the idea that other people might someday live in it had never occurred to me. When I thought about the future, about living in New York, Livery Street was always a part of it. I'd come home on weekends and holidays and nothing would change. It was the only absolute in my dream, the only anchor. But Pop's dream was to live in the country and he didn't care about or believe in mine. As I trudged along in the snow, I thought maybe he had good reason to want to run away from the memories. Maybe he wanted to run away as much as I wanted to hold on, and a part of me wished I could sympathize with him. But of all the sentiments I felt for my father, sympathy wasn't one of them.

As usual, he thought he was punishing me by not talking but I actually looked forward to those silences. As I got older they lasted longer and longer and they weren't merely silences, they were standoffs. But I came to regard them as periods of peace, when I didn't have to listen to his sarcasm and negativity. Bridie tried to defend him by placing some of the blame for the fights on me.

'You know how he is. Why do you provoke him?'

'I don't provoke him. I defend myself. Can't you see the difference?'

'He doesn't mean half the stuff he says.'

'Then he shouldn't say it. How come you always take his side?'

'I don't.'

'Yes, you do. Always. He kicks me out of the damn car and you ride home with him.'

'He didn't kick you out of the car. You didn't have to get out if you didn't want to. Besides, I wasn't wearing boots.'

'That's a load of crap and you know it.'

'Why are you picking on me all of a sudden?' She was trying to change the focus of the argument. 'You're the one who had the fight with him.'

'And you're sticking up for him.'

'Yes, I am. Cripes, Finn, you know he always wanted a place in the country. Why'd you have to shoot him down like that?'

'What about what he did to me? Jesus, he shoots me down every time I turn around. Don't you hear that? Are you deaf or something?'

'No, I am not deaf. I told you, he doesn't mean that stuff and you know it.'

'No, I don't know it. All I know is he's a son of a bitch.'

'God is going to strike you dead for saying that about your own father.'

'Don't start that crap.'

'When he's dead you'll be sorry you said mean things about him. I know what I'm talking about.'

'You really think you're going to make me feel guilty? The one thing I don't have to worry about is him dying. He's too damn mean to die.'

'Well, at least he's not going to sell the house. Not yet, anyway.'

'What do you mean?'

'He said if it meant that much to you he wouldn't sell it.'

'Yeah, sure. I'm his biggest concern, right?'

'Whether you know it or not, you are.'

'Bullshit. He can't stand to be in the same room with me. And I'll tell you something, the feeling is mutual. Anyway, it doesn't concern you. So why don't you just butt out.' I hated the idea that Bridie and Pop talked about me when they were alone. No matter what they said, as far as I was concerned, it was collusion.

Silence wasn't my only punishment. Pop knew that like every other kid my age I wanted to learn to drive more than anything else. So he taught Bridie but not me. They went down to the lake early in the day on weekends, before Bridie and I went to the stables, and practiced on the deserted dirt road. I was never invited. Bridie was embarrassed and I was angry and there were times when days would go by without either of us speaking. Alex tried to teach me but it was hopeless. He was so worried about something happening to his father's car that all we did was scream at each other. It was Miss Haas, finally, who taught me how to drive and Bridie was jealous but she couldn't say anything because Pop was teaching her and excluding me. Miss Haas and I would go out to the country in the Chevy pickup, and with her patient and expert teaching, dodging hayricks and tractors, I learned to drive on the narrow little macadam roads.

'I'm thinking of closing the stables,' she said one day as we crossed a rickety wooden bridge. 'I want to go back to Germany.' She lit a cigarette, cupping the match in her hand against the wind.

'Why?'

'Well, my family is there and I haven't been back since the war. My mother's getting old ... there are a lot of reasons.' I realized I knew nothing at all about Miss Haas. I didn't even know her first name.

'Won't you miss the horses?'

'Well, sure. Some of them. Especially Raven.' Raven was a gelding both Bridie and I were partial to. 'But we have horses at home. My family raised Württembergers. It's an old breed dating back to the sixteenth century.'

'I never heard of them.'

'They're gentle. A good riding horse. About sixteen hands. A pretty horse. I miss working with them.' We rode along in silence for a few moments. 'I didn't realize how homesick I've been all these years. Besides,' her mood changed, 'the town is getting too big. It's time to get out.' A rabbit darted in front of us and I swerved to miss hitting it. 'Hey, you're a good driver.'

'Hey, you're a good teacher.' She laughed and tossed her cigarette out the window. We drove past neat farms and pastures with freshly whitewashed fences and she told me about her family and about Germany and we talked about what Bridie and I were going to do after we graduated. We were on back roads I had never seen before but just as dusk was settling everything started to look familiar.

'I think I've been down this road before.'

'They all look alike to me. Watch what you're doing and forget the scenery.'

'There's something about this one . . .' and I realized it was the road that led to Duke's burial place. 'We buried my dog back here.' I turned into the rutted lane that ran alongside the cornfield and parked the truck. 'You mind?'

'No, no, go on. I'll wait here and have a cigarette.'

The earth was soft from recent rains and the mud sucked at my shoes as I searched for the grave. It wasn't hard to find because someone had put up a marker of field stones in the shape of a pyramid. There was something oddly pagan about it, as though Vikings or Druids had built a monument to Duke. Sticks and leaves had collected between the stones along with the dry, papery skin a snake had slipped out of. Velvet-textured mosses were growing in the shadow on the north side and toadstools were pushing their way through the leaf mold. As I knelt down to get a closer look at the pyramid I noticed some letters scratched on one of the stones and when I picked it up and turned it over I saw *Fritz* crudely etched on the side. Right next to it was another stone with *Duke* scratched into it. Only Pop or Simon could have done it because, aside from me, they were the only people who knew where Duke was buried. Neither one had ever said anything about visiting Duke's grave and it suddenly seemed sad and eerie and I felt like crying but I had no idea who I wanted to cry for. The pickup horn blasted and I put back everything, including the snakeskin, the way I had found it, and started down the path to Miss Haas.

'Was it the right place?'

'Yes.' I didn't want to talk about it and she sensed that and respected my privacy. Driving back to the stables, I knew I'd never be able to ask who made the pyramid. If it was Simon, it was his way of burying Fritz once and for all so he could love and live with Mina without any guilt. And if it was Pop, the pyramid gave him a place to mourn, and it buried Fritz with Duke, instead of in some unmarked grave with strangers, in a country none of us had ever even been to. I never did find out who scratched the names into the stones. And I never forgot where Duke was buried. I would always think of it as a lonely place, ancient and timeless and protected by the spirits of the stones. And I would remember it as my brother's grave.

The silence ended as abruptly as it had begun. One day, when I came home from school, Bridie, all excited, was waiting for me on the front porch.

'God, I thought you'd never get home. Have we got a surprise for you. Actually, it's Big Finn's surprise. Well, come on in and he'll tell you.' She went into the house and I could hear her telling Pop I was coming up the stairs. He suddenly appeared in the doorway, grinning from ear to ear and dancing back and forth with excitement.

'Christ, I thought you took the wrong bus and were off to Timbuktu or someplace.'

'You sold the house.' It was the only thing I could think of.

'No, I did not sell the house. Would I sell the house without telling you?' He looked over his shoulder at Bridie. 'He thought I sold the house.'

'I told you he wasn't going to sell the house, didn't I.'

'Did somebody die and leave you money?'

'Don't I just wish,' he said, laughing. 'No, no, it's not that. Here, let me hold your books.' He took my books and I thought I was going crazy. When I left for school that morning he wasn't even talking to me and now he was laughing and holding my books.

'What the hell is going on?' I tried to get past him to go in the house but he blocked my way.

'You stay right where you are. Okay, now, close your eyes.' My mind raced and the only thing I could think of was Fritz was home. 'Now, turn around and don't open your eyes till I tell you.'

'God, the neighbors will think I'm nuts.'

'Who cares about the neighbors,' said Bridie. 'Just turn around.' I did as I was told, wondering what the hell I was going to see.

'Okay, open your eyes.'

Very slowly, fearful of what might be standing in front of me, I opened my eyes. 'What? What am I looking for?'

'You see that red Pontiac across the street?'

'Yeah.'

'It's ours!' shouted Bridie. 'Yours and mine. Big Finn bought it for us.'

'For the both of you,' said Pop. 'I bought it for the both of you. It's only two years old. I got a real good deal.'

I was so confused I didn't know what to say. He wouldn't even teach me to drive and now he was buying me a car. 'I don't understand.'

'Well, it can't be that difficult, can it? I bought you a car.'

'How could you afford a car?'

'Don't worry about it. I'm paying the guy off. So, how do you like it?'

'It's nice. Really nice.'

'I knew you'd like it.' He put his arm around my shoulder and pulled me close. It was something he had always done with Fritz but he never ever did it with me.

'Come on,' said Bridie, running across the street. 'The interior is perfect. Red leather seats. They're beautiful.' She opened the car door and slipped in behind the wheel. I crossed the street and Pop was right behind me.

'So,' he said happily, 'don't expect a big graduation gift.' He laughed again. 'This is kind of a graduation present seven months in advance. Throw in Christmas and your birthday, too. Christ, she's a beauty, huh?'

'Come on,' said Bridie, 'let's go for a ride.' I automatically started to get in the back seat but Pop stopped me.

'We can all sit up front.' He handed me the keys. 'Here, you drive. We'll take a spin around the lake.' It would be the first time I was driving with him in the car since I got my license. Bridie moved to the center and Pop got in the passenger side. I was so stunned I could hardly get into the car. 'Come on, sport, let's get going.' I turned the key in the ignition and the car started right away. 'Watch out, world, here we come,' he said as he reached behind Bridie and rested his hand on my shoulder. I pulled away from the curb, uncomfortable and thoroughly confused.

Everything changed. Pop was someone I didn't even know. He laughed and joked and played foolish little tricks on us and he even invited me to listen to the radio with him. There was an assumed camaraderie that had never existed and I found it embarrassing. We talked about Simon and Mina and the kids as if there had never been any trouble and he reminisced about the good times with Mom and Fritz and Laurie. He even talked about getting another dog and when I told him I didn't want one he seemed genuinely compassionate and said he understood, that perhaps it was still too soon after Duke died. He was warm and interested and giving and everything was perfect. But as much as I wanted to trust him and believe he really had changed I had the feeling it was all a mirage, illusory, temporary and deceptive.

'I don't understand it,' I said to Bridie one night when we were doing the dishes after Pop had gone into the living room to listen to the news.

'Why do you always have to question everything? Relax, for cripes' sake.'

'I just don't trust him.'

'Did you ever think that maybe he changed? That maybe he's trying to make things up to you?'

'Yeah. I still don't understand why.'

'Just be happy about it. God, Finn, when are you ever going to stop worrying about things? You'll be gray by the time you're twenty. Sometimes you really make me sick.'

'What are you getting mad at me for?'

'Never mind. Just dry the damn dishes.'

And it wasn't only Pop and life at home that changed. The whole world seemed to change. The neighborhood had the first block party since the war when the Republic of Eire was proclaimed in Dublin and Britain recognized its independence. Even the newcomers to the street, people who had no ties to Ireland at all, joined in the celebration. And when Israel was admitted to the United Nations we all got a little drunk with the Ganises. Both Mr and Mrs Ganis cried and laughed and yelled at each other and Pop and Mrs Ganis danced and we had a wonderful time. Rebecca Steinman, the friend I had only seen once, emigrated with her grandparents to Israel but we continued to write to one another. She was convinced her parents were still alive and she thought she'd find them among the refugees in Israel but, through the help of an agency in Jerusalem, she discovered they had both died in concentration camps. It was in a kibbutz near Tel Aviv that she found the spirit of her new family and her letters were happy and full of hope for the future. She sent me a picture of herself and I was amazed at how little her face had changed. It was the same pretty, dark, brooding face of the girl who'd buried the cat's head. Whenever I received a letter from her with the Israeli postmark, I thought of Cat and how she marveled at the idea of something coming all the way from another country with her name on it. I had the same sense of wonder. And Miss Haas did sell the stables and went back to Germany to try and pick up the pieces of her family business and start breeding Württembergers again. Before she left, she told Bridie and I she had a buyer for Raven, the black gelding, but if there was any way we could care for him, we could have him. The only place I could think of was Josie Cleary's farm but I knew that was out of the question. So, when we said goodbye to Miss Haas, we said goodbye to Raven and our life at the stables. I got a job on weekends in men's furnishings in Finegold's, the big department store in the new shopping center just north of town, and Bridie went to work at the ribbon counter in Woolworths.

Even Honey had a major change in his life. He was enrolled in a private school for blacks, Boggs Academy, which was somewhere outside of Valdosta. Tessie was paying for it and Pop just loved the idea that Honey was going to an up-scale, religious school on the money his aunt had once made in a whorehouse.

Mr Howe was cremated and his ashes scattered before we even knew he'd died. Mrs Fricker, the woman who called the police when I was scratched by the owl and fell in the barn, noticed we weren't at the small memorial service and took a cab to our house so she could tell us in person that Mr Howe had had a massive stroke and had died in his kitchen. Her habit was to check on him every few days and when she went to his house she found his body slumped over the kitchen table. Mr Howe had given her the phone number of his son in New York in case anything happened and she called him right away. She apologized for not phoning us but since she wasn't family she didn't feel it was her place and she thought that somehow Mr Howe Jr would have informed us of Mr Howe's death. Pop and Bridie and I drove her home and went on to the house to pay our respects to Mr Howe Jr. There were trucks in the yard and workmen were loading Mr Howe's furniture. Several of Mrs Howe's dresses, which Mr Howe had meticulously kept clean, were thrown in a pile in the dust next to her humpbacked trunk. Bridie picked them up and brushed them off and started yelling at the workmen. Pop pulled her away and Mr Howe Jr appeared in the doorway to see what the rumpus was about. He looked almost as old as his father but there was absolutely no resemblance between the two men. Mr Howe, with his long legs and thin, elegant body, had been naturally graceful but Mr Howe Jr was short and big-bellied and his movements were awkward and jerky.

'What's going on?' he said in a sharp, high voice.

'We were friends of Mr Howe,' said Pop. 'My name is Tom Finnegan. This is Bridie O'Connor and this is my son, Finn.'

'I'm Mr Howe's son. I was wondering how to get in touch with you people. There are packages in here for you. Come in.' He started into the house but stopped and turned to Bridie. 'If you want those old dresses, you can have them. There are some more out there, too.'

'Yes, please.'

'Take them when you leave.' He went in the house and we followed. The walls were stripped and the rugs were rolled up and almost all the furniture was gone. 'Wait here,' he said, and disappeared down the hall.

'Mr Howe would have a fit if he saw this.' Bridie was too angry to cry.

'Christ,' Pop shook his head in disgust.

'They even ripped some of the wallpaper. Why?' I said, trying to push the wallpaper back in place.

'Damn it!' Bridie handed me the dresses and went to the kitchen sink and carefully picked up the pieces of one of Mr Howe's teacups. 'Look what they did!'

'Now, don't get yourself all upset.' Pop put his arm around her shoulder. 'People don't respect the property of the dead unless they think it's worth a lot of money. It's a hard fact of life.'

'I can glue it together for you,' I said. 'Keep the pieces.'

'I have no idea what's in here,' Mr Howe Jr came down the hall carrying two neatly wrapped packages, one with *Bridie* printed in bold black letters, and one with *Finn*. 'You know how eccentric my father was, so it could be junk.'

'He was not eccentric,' said Bridie. 'He was a wonderful man.'

'I'm sorry.' He handed us the packages and went to the back door and opened it. 'As you can see, there's a lot to be done before I go back to New York.'

'You might have let us know there was a memorial service,' said Pop as he passed Mr Howe Jr. 'We were his friends.'

'I had no idea who my father's friends were.'

'You didn't know anything else about him, either,' I said.

'That's enough, now.' Pop pushed me ahead of him down the back path and Mr Howe Jr went in the house and closed the door. Bridie retrieved the rest of the dresses and we got in the car and left without looking back. The three of us rode home in silence, unable to talk because we were choking back a mixture of rage and tears.

Bridie's box contained Mrs Howe's jewelry. There were delicate gold filigree earrings and a long lapis lazuli necklace, a gold ring with black enamel and tiny pearls and an oval cloisonné locket with pictures, faded to sepia, of a very young Mr and Mrs Howe. It was all old-fashioned and out of style but Bridie thought each piece was as precious as the crown jewels. After I had glued the pieces of the teacup together, Bridie added it to her dresser-top collection of treasures and sometimes she put fresh flowers in it. She said the flowers were for Laurie, the Blessed Virgin and Mr Howe.

It was several days before I opened my box. There was a finality about being left things that I didn't want to deal with. Mr Howe had promised that when he ran out of time, his watch would be mine. And now it was. It was carefully wrapped in old, wrinkled tissue and as I unwrapped it I could feel him near by. The intricate etching on the back had almost worn away from sliding in and out of his pocket all those years and there was a chip in the scratched crystal. It was a watch that, lined up in a shop window with dozens of other old watches, would have no special appeal. But I had seen him look at it hundreds of times and when I held it in my hand, I could almost feel Mr Howe's dry, calloused hand close over mine. There was also the copy of *Great Expectations* and when I opened it to see if Mr Howe had written in the flyleaf, I found three hundred and forty-two dollars in assorted bills. The odd amount broke my heart. In a very studied hand he had written, *Dear Finn, a cup of tea, a warm fire and Mr Dickens. We shared the best life has to offer. Your friend, E. Howe.* It was dated January 15, 1947, three years before he died. He had expected the call from the Lord for a very long time and, as he'd wished, he was at home to receive it when it finally came. I couldn't fall asleep that night and whatever tears I shed were tears of enormous sorrow and undeniable remorse. For years before he died I had paid little or no attention to him. I suppose he didn't want me to grow up because he knew as I got older he would be excluded from my life. To this day, the one person I feel most guilty about is Mr Howe and when I think of him I wince and lower my head in shame.

We didn't tell Mom about Mr Howe because she would have smiled and said he was in heaven and then forgotten he ever existed. The truth was she really had no interest in anything that happened outside the fences of Franklin Village. Bridie and I went to visit her on a Sunday, not long after Mr Howe died, without Pop, who had a special meeting of the carnival committee with the Knights of Columbus. Bridie did the driving. My leg sometimes went numb if I kept it in one position too long.

'I'd hate to be cremated,' I said as we drove along the familiar road to the Village, my mind still full of Mr Howe and the image of his body being burned to ashes.

'Well, you can't be. You're Catholic. If your body gets burned up you won't be able to rise up from the dead at the Last Judgment.'

'You really believe that's going to happen?'

'It's kind of creepy, isn't it? Think of all the graves all over the world opening up and dead people climbing out of them. It's enough to scare the bejesus out of you.'

'What happens to people who get burned up in airplane crashes or other kinds of accidents?' I was thinking of a whole family that was burned to death when a Christmas tree caught on fire. 'What happens to them at the Last Judgment? There aren't any bodies.'

'God probably makes exceptions. He'd have to or it would be like the invisible man in heaven.' She chuckled. 'How do I know? What do I look like, a nun or something?'

'It's all so hard to buy.'

'I know what you mean,' she said, checking her hair in the rear-view mirror.

'When you come back, you're supposed to get all your missing parts, right? Okay, so somebody has his leg cut off and it gets burned up. And when he dies, the rest of him is buried. So, after the Last Judgment, where does he get a new leg?'

'From the spare-parts department.' She laughed. 'This is so morbid.'

'No, I'm serious.' But I could feel the laughter building up inside. 'Really, I am. Where do those parts come from?'

'Sears & Roebuck!' She screamed with laughter.

'It's not funny. We're talking about death and resurrection.' I knew what was going to happen and I tried to fight it. Whenever either one of us got hysterical with laughter the other one simply fell apart. 'This is an important philosophical discussion.'

'I know,' she said, but she could hardly get the words out.

'But don't you ever think of death and things like this?' I was trying desperately to be serious but I couldn't fight the laughter any longer.

'Stop! I can't take any more,' she laughed.

'I'm serious,' I said, howling uncontrollably.

'I think of death all the time.' She squealed and we both started laughing so hard she had to pull over to the side of the road.

'Stop it, stop it,' she said after we settled down a bit. 'Don't say anything else or I'll suffocate.'

'People can choke to death laughing.' I was trying to get my breath.

'Choke to death!' she wailed, and it suddenly sounded like the funniest thing either one of us had ever heard and we both started again. It must have been fifteen minutes before we were able to get back on the road. Every muscle in my chest and stomach and face hurt and the pain was absolutely delicious.

We sat with Mom on the sun porch with the usual group of ladies, staring or mumbling to themselves or asleep in their chairs, and talked about anything that came into our heads. She just smiled and nodded when we told her Pop wouldn't be there and waited for the next piece of information so she could agree with whatever it was. We told her about our plans to go to New York to see *South Pacific*. It was the biggest hit on Broadway and Mrs Ganis gave us tickets for a graduation gift. 'Some Enchanted Evening' was everyone's favorite song and you couldn't turn on the radio without hearing it. Even Mom knew the words and sang a few bars. Bridie and I couldn't wait because we were going to have a night on the town, all by ourselves. Mom got bored smiling after a while as she patiently listened to us talk about our trip, and finally told us visiting hours were over and it was time to leave. She was always so relieved to see us go. She had survived the trial of yet another visit and had a whole week before she had to suffer through it again.

Our night in New York was one of the best nights of my life. Bridie bought a new blue dress with my discount at Finegold's and I wore my gray suit, and Pop and the Ganises said we looked like fashion plates. I tried to talk Bridie out of some of her chunky jewelry but she told me to mind my own business and everyone agreed with her. Even though it was a warm spring night, Mrs Ganis, over vehement protestations, insisted Bridie carry a sweater. For special occasions, I had taken to wearing Fritz's wristwatch and carrying Mr Howe's pocket watch at the same time. I could never choose one over the other so I decided to carry both and it gave me a peculiar sense of security and I felt I was sharing my good times with both of them. We didn't drive because there was a new transit line with a stop on the corner of Livery Street and the bus went right to the Port Authority Terminal in New York. I planned to surprise Bridie and take her someplace special for dinner and Mrs Ganis suggested Sardi's because we might get to see some celebrities. She gave me the address from a copy of the *New Yorker* but when we got there we couldn't get a table so we walked around and finally ate at Downey's. Bridie was sure everyone in the place was someone famous but I didn't recognize a single face.

We decided to have a cocktail before dinner to celebrate our upcoming graduation but all we knew about cocktails was what we'd seen in the movies.

'I'll have a Sazerac,' said Bridie, with great aplomb, when the waiter took our order.

'A Sazerac for the lady. And for the gentleman?'

'And I'll have a Martini, please.'

'Up?' said the waiter.

'Up what?' I asked.

'With or without ice.' He smiled patronizingly.

'Without.' He started to walk away. 'Very dry.' I remembered William Powell saying that in *The Thin Man*.

'Yes, sir.'

'What's a Sazerac?' I asked Bridie when the waiter was gone.

'I don't know. Bette Davis ordered one in a picture and I never forgot the name of it. Maybe it was Joan Crawford. Anyway, it sounds so sophisticated.'

When the waiter brought our drinks we toasted each other with the frosty glasses and I took a mouthful of my Martini and thought I had poisoned myself.

'This is horrible. Like gasoline.' I drank some water to get the taste out of my mouth.

'Mine is delicious. Just like licorice.'

'My God, how do people drink these things?'

'Taste mine.' She handed me the drink and I took a sip.

'That's good. Taste mine.'

'That tastes just like cologne. Cripes, it's awful. Send it back.'

'I can't send it back! That waiter's so stuck-up. He'll know I never had a Martini before.'

'He'll know when you don't drink it, too.'

'No, he won't.' I drank some of my water and emptied the rest of the Martini into the water glass. 'I guess I have to eat the olive.' It was gin-soaked and I could hardly get it down. I looked around the restaurant to make sure no one had seen me dump the Martini and an older lady, sitting alone, was watching me, smiling, until I caught her eye when she busied herself with her menu.

The waiter suddenly appeared from nowhere. 'Another?' he asked as he took my empty glass.

'No, thanks. That just hit the spot.'

'Not too watery?'

'No. It was perfect.'

'Good,' he said, smiling knowingly. 'May I take your order?'

After dinner Bridie and I walked to the theatre. The streets were crowded with people hurrying to the different shows, and taxis and limousines were fighting for curb space. Liveried chauffeurs held open doors as people emerged, elegantly dressed in formal wear.

'You think those people are somebody?' asked Bridie as we filed past the ticket taker.

'Yeah. Somebody very rich.'

The middle-aged usherette showed us to our seats and we sat, strangers in a strange land, watching people settle in, wondering if, like us, this was their first time in a Broadway theatre.

'I expected it to be bigger,' said Bridie.

'Me, too.'

'Like Radio City Music Hall.'

Members of the orchestra straggled into the pit and took their seats and started tuning up their instruments, competing with the din of the people in the auditorium, and when the lights dimmed slightly Bridie took my hand and held tight. The conductor mysteriously appeared and made his way to the podium, and when the audience started applauding I wanted to applaud but Bridie wouldn't let go of my hand. He bowed to the audience, turned to the orchestra, tapped on the music stand and stood poised with his baton. The noise in the auditorium stopped and there was a moment of absolute silence, an expectant and breathless moment when I knew that some magical, marvelous thing could and would happen. The conductor's hand dropped and we heard the first haunting notes of 'Bali Ha'i' and I was bewitched, transported to a singular place that, in time I would discover, was only available in the theatre. And that was during the overture. The curtain hadn't even gone up.

When the show was over we were so full of the fantasy and Mary Martin and Ezio Pinza and Rodgers and Hammerstein we couldn't possibly jump on a bus and go back to reality so we joined what seemed to be a million other people and walked the streets of New York. We went up Broadway to Columbus Circle, along Central Park South to the Plaza Hotel and down Fifth Avenue to Rockefeller Center. A few of the people we passed looked as though they had some place to go but most everyone was like us, strolling along, talking and sharing the night and the city. Bridie held my arm and I was certain passersby thought we were the most handsome couple they had ever seen. It was a night neither one of us wanted to end but we had an hour-and-a-half bus ride ahead of us so we caught the one-thirty. I was so charged and excited my mind was racing but we were hardly through the tunnel and into New Jersey when Bridie put her head on my shoulder and fell asleep.

It was almost three o'clock in the morning when we got home and Pop was waiting up for us. He was sitting in the living room in his pajamas and I could tell he was angry but he was doing his best to control himself.

'Jesus, I was about to call the police.'

'Sorry, Pop.'

'Oh, Big Finn, you shouldn't have waited up.'

'I was worried. Who the hell knows what could happen to you over there in New York. There's all kinds of crazy people, for Christ's sake.' He got up and started for the stairs.

'We took a walk after the show, that's all,' I said.

'Oh, is that all!' He looked at me, barely able to contain his anger.

Bridie went to him and hugged him. 'You had nothing to worry about. Don't be so silly.'

He half hugged her back and it seemed to calm him. 'Well, you're all right. In one piece. Let's get to bed.' He started up the steps and turned and looked at Bridie. 'How'd you like the show?'

'It was wonderful. Mary Martin is the best,' said Bridie.

'And you, sport?'

'It was great.'

'Good,' and he smiled and touched Bridie's face. Without looking at me he went upstairs.

'He was just worried. He's not really mad.' She kissed me on the cheek. 'It was the best night ever, wasn't it?' She turned as she got to the top of the stairs. 'Really, he's not mad.'

*

Our graduations came and went in the blink of an eye and to the strains of 'Pomp and Circumstance', with diplomas in our hands, we marched away from the self-defining security of school into the frightening and precarious rest of our lives. There were important decisions to be made but we managed to put them off for at least a week by going down the shore every day. We had endured years of endless bus rides and the tyranny of the priests and nuns and we deserved a week off. Lying on the sand in the hot June sun we talked about going to New York, making the long-dreamed-of big move, until there was nothing left to say and we finally came to the conclusion that it might be best to postpone it for a while. The reason being any excuse we could conjure without admitting we were afraid. Bridie said we had to consider Pop, that we couldn't just walk out on him, and I agreed it would take some time for him to get used to the idea of our being gone in spite of the fact that we had talked about it for years. And I said we should save more money, even though my savings account was fairly healthy, and, of course, she agreed because she had practically nothing. Walking along the boardwalk, eating pork-roll sandwiches and salt-water taffy, we decided to work for a year at better-paying jobs, and then, with the wisdom and experience of a year in the business world, we'd take on New York. I couldn't find anything so I went on full time in the men's department at Finegold's but Bridie managed to escape the ribbon counter at Woolworths when she started working at AAP, American Attitude Polls, a public-opinion research company. The money wasn't great, but the benefits were good and public-opinion research was supposedly a career with a future.

She had only been working at AAP for about a month when, uncomfortable in my rented tuxedo, I escorted her to the company summer dinner dance at the Prussian Inn. We had only been in there once, when Laurie worked there as a bartender, and all I could remember were the old swords and flintlocks on the walls. The Arms Room, which was the bar, was the pre-Revolutionary center of the inn and the walls were field stone and the floors, wide chestnut planks.

'Did you know Laurie O'Connor?' Bridie asked the barman. 'He used to work here.'

'No, I guess he was before my time.' He put two coasters on the bar. 'What can I get you?'

'Two Sazeracs,' I said. Bridie straightened my bow tie. It was the first time I had ever worn a tuxedo and I felt a little foolish and very conspicuous.

'You know who you look like all dressed up in your tux?'

'Who?'

'That waiter at Downey's.' She laughed. 'I'm kidding. You look gorgeous. Like a movie star.'

'And you look prettier than any movie star I've ever seen.' She was wearing a white dress and her shoulders were bare and her hair was up and, instead of her usual gaudy jewelry, she wore Mrs Howe's long lapis lazuli necklace. She was beautiful in her simplicity.

'I feel naked without all my jewels,' she said, wiggling her bare fingers. People wandered into the bar and nodded and Bridie smiled politely and turned to me. 'Who the hell are these people? I've never seen any of them.'

'Don't ask me.'

'Well, think of tonight as an adventure. We're going to have a good time no matter what.'

'You bet your ass we are. This tux is costing me thirty-two bucks.'

'Shall we take our drinks and mingle?' she said grandly.

'After you, Mrs Astor.'

'Thank you, Mr Vanderbilt.'

We went out on the terrace, which overlooked the golf course, and a tall girl with a pointed nose and wispy brown hair came toward us.

'Her name is Camilla,' whispered Bridie. 'One of the few people I know. Don't get too close to her, her breath would kill a moose.'

'Hi, Bridie. You look fabulous.'

'Thanks, Camilla. So do you. This is my friend, Finn.'

'Hi, Finn, nice to meet you.'

'A pleasure,' I said. Camilla stayed a few minutes and she and Bridie tried to make conversation but they had very little to say to one another and Camilla excused herself and moved through the crowd in the direction of the bar.

'I do not fit in here. I think I'd rather be at the ribbon counter. Or back at the stables shoveling horse manure.'

The couples at our table at dinner were all friends and, after we introduced ourselves, never said another word to us. But the food was delicious and the dessert was baked Alaska and Bridie said that made up for being bored out of our minds. After dinner, when the tables had been cleared, a five-piece band, sweating in their shiny worn dinner jackets, played while couples fox-trotted around the floor.

'Don't even ask,' I said to Bridie. 'I do not dance.'

'Just one.'

'No. We had a deal. Not even a rumba.'

'Just one and I promise I'll never ask again.'

'No.'

'One dance and we can leave.'

'You promise?'

'I swear to God. Come on,' and she dragged me out on the floor. The band was playing 'C'est si bon' and I did my best but my feet simply didn't work and I felt horribly self-conscious and was sure everyone was looking at me.

'You're doing fine,' said Bridie.

'Do me a favor and don't say a word. Let's not talk until this is over with.' It seemed like hours before the band stopped but finally the number ended and I took her hand and led her off the dance floor.

'Can we go now?'

'You sure you don't want one more dance?' She was laughing.

'I would rather have bamboo splinters stuck under my finger-nails.' And we left.

'It's early,' I said in the car. 'Let's go for a ride.'

'The air feels so good.' She unpinned her hair and it tumbled down and she leaned back. 'Believe it or not, I had fun.'

'So did I.'

The moon was brilliant and once we got out of town, away from the lights, we could see the stars, as clear and bright as Christmas candles. The night air was cool and sweet with all the smells of midsummer and we drove until, without even realizing it, we were passing the stables. There was a Sold sign tacked on the gate.

'Stop,' said Bridie. I pulled in the driveway and turned off the motor. 'I wonder who bought it?'

'I don't know. They'll probably tear it down and put up a bunch of ugly houses.'

'Let's go in.'

'It's only going to make you feel bad. Remember what it was like when we went back to Mr Howe's?'

'I know, but I want to see it once more,' and she got out of the car. I took off my tux jacket and threw it over the seat. The gate was locked so we climbed over and walked up to the barn, past the flower beds that Miss Haas always took a special pride in but now were full of weeds. The big double doors were open and we entered, breathing in the rich, familiar smell. It was dark and lonely as we walked past the office and the tack room and the empty stalls, but the most disturbing thing was the silence. The stables had always been so overflowing with life, with horses neighing and dogs barking and kids yelling, and now it was as quiet as a church. I stopped at Raven's stall and I could almost see his black velvet muzzle back in the dark corner.

'I don't like this,' I said. 'Let's go.'

'Wait a minute.' She was halfway up the ladder to the hayloft. 'Come on, we can see the lights of town from up here.' I followed her and we pushed open the hay doors and the moon-light spilled over the floor like liquid, and past the trees, on the horizon, we could see the sky brighten. The breeze was cooler coming through the doors and we stood looking at the night as though we had never seen it before. I slipped my arms around her waist and she leaned her head back on my shoulder and I could smell the sweetness of her hair. She touched my hands and the touch electrified my whole body. It all seemed so perfect and so natural and I knew, for once, maybe the first time in our lives, we were feeling the same thing at the same time, and she turned to me and we kissed. It was a soft, tentative kiss at first but soon we were crushing our bodies together and the kiss was deep and probing and there was no turning back. We lay down in the hay and, between kisses, slipped out of our clothes and I held her close, skin to skin as I'd imagined a hundred times, and, as if we were two halves kept apart and aching to make a whole, in a violent, moist, sweaty tangle we became a part of one another.

We lay spent, our naked bodies milky in the moonlight, without saying a word. I wanted to know what she was thinking but I was afraid to ask. As far as I was concerned, everything made sense and nothing made sense. I was fearless and yet I was afraid. I was totally me, maybe for the first time ever, and at the same time I was a part of her.

'I love you,' I said after a long while.

'I know.' She kissed me and we got up and dressed.

'I don't want to go home yet.'

'Me neither. Let's go down the shore.' So we drove to the dunes and parked the car and watched the sun come up over the ocean. Bridie didn't want to talk but finally she said, 'I don't think we should have done that.'

'Please, if you have regrets, don't tell me about them. Not now.'

'I do have regrets but not for the reasons you might think.'

'I don't want to hear about them.'

'I'm sorry.'

'Tonight was the single most important thing that's ever happened to me and you have regrets! Jesus Christ, Bridie, give me a break.' I got out of the car and started walking along the deserted beach. The same beach where she and Simon had played in the surf.

'Wait a minute,' she said, following me. 'Tonight was wonderful. I'm not saying it wasn't. But it shouldn't have happened.'

'It was inevitable. Don't you know that? It had to happen. I could have told you it was going to happen when you walked into the fourth grade. I hated your guts but I knew then that tonight was going to happen.'

'It's complicated.'

'Not for me it isn't. I love you. I've always loved you. What's complicated about that?'

'I love you, too. But –'

'But what? I want to marry you. I want to be with you for the rest of my life. I want to go to New York and do all the things we said we were going to do. I want to have kids with you. What's so goddamn complicated about that?'

'Maybe we will someday.'

'But in the meantime, just forget it? God!'

'Don't, please . . .' she started crying. 'You don't understand.'

'No,' I said, walking away, 'I don't. I really don't.'

'Wait, damn it. It's not as simple as you think. Why the hell didn't we leave everything the way it was. Goddamn it! It's my fault. I knew better.'

'What am I missing? You knew better than what?'

'Oh, I can't stand this.'

'You knew better than what? What are you talking about?'

'Never mind. Let's go home.'

'No. Tell me what's going on.'

'No.'

'Is there somebody else?'

'Forget it.' She started back to the car.

'It's not Simon. He's in California. It's not Alex is it? You said he was a jerk.'

'Finn, stop, please.'

'Maybe it's Mr Ganis? Maybe it's the mailman?'

She turned to me angrily. 'Maybe it's Big Finn.'

'No!'

'Now, are you satisfied?' She fell to the sand, crying.

'I don't believe it.'

'Then it's not true. Does that make you feel better?'

'Oh my God.'

'Finn –'

'No!'

'Please, Finn –'

'He's a son of a bitch!'

'No, he's not. He's been very good to me and I love him.'

'That bastard. He made you sleep with –'

'He didn't make me do anything. I knew what I was doing. I'm almost nineteen, for cripes' sake. I did it because I love him.'

'You love everybody, don't you?'

'No, just you and Big Finn.'

I don't know what I did next but I remember Bridie trying to pull me out of the ocean. The water was up to my chin and she was dragging me back through the surf and we lay in the sand choking and trying to catch our breath. When I had the strength to move I went back to the car and got in and waited for her. We didn't talk all the way home. She tried a few times but I told her to shut up and I threatened to get out of the car if she said one more word.

Pop had gone to work by the time we got to the house. Bridie went to her room and closed the door and I went to the bathroom and threw up before I showered and shaved. I went into Pop's room and got his big suitcase and I took pictures of Mom and Duke and Fritz and Simon and packed as many clothes as I could along with my copy of *Great Expectations* and some of my sketches. I put Fritz's watch on and Mr Howe's in my pocket and went downstairs and out the front door.

Before catching the bus to New York, I closed my account at the First National Bank and started my new life with just under two thousand dollars in my pocket. I don't remember the bus ride at all but I clearly remember sitting in the Port Authority Terminal with my suitcase and no place to go. It was hours before I went to Travelers Aid and asked where I might find a room and they suggested the YMCA. I was there for almost a week before I found a cold-water flat on West Forty-third Street, just off Tenth Avenue. After registering at Cooper Union, I got a job as a clerk at the Doubleday Book Shop in Grand Central Station. Everything I had dreamed about I did but I was miserable because Bridie wasn't there to share it with me. Pop was right about dreams. They didn't turn out the way they were supposed to.

It was over a month before I called the Ganises and when Mrs Ganis heard my voice she started crying and I couldn't understand a word she said. When I asked about Bridie she told me she left home the same day I did but she told everyone she was going and said she'd let them know where she settled. She tried to tell me something about Pop but I wouldn't listen. The Ganises had a card from Bridie but there was no return address. The postmark was Chicago. I called her mother and Aunt Theresa and Simon and Mina and they all said they didn't know where she was but I didn't believe them. Even Honey and Kitty Neal said they didn't know anything. The police wouldn't let me file a missing-person claim because she had told people she was leaving and occasionally sent postcards. She was merely someone who didn't want anyone to know her whereabouts. I had to find her because I wanted to apologize for leaving her and I didn't care about what had happened and I could never love anyone as much as I loved her. Even after I stopped asking about her, I never really stopped looking for her. Someday, I thought, on a train or a plane, or in a bookstore or on the street, I'd find her. But Bridie vanished.

Alex moved in with me for a few months until he was drafted

into the army during the Korean War. I knew he received all kinds of honors but we never saw each other again. It was the inevitable natural attrition of moving on in life. The last letter I had from Honey, when he was a sophomore at Howard University, majoring in history, he told me Tessie had recovered from TB and had opened an interior-design business in Phoenix. Charles was still taking care of her. The Ganises, my last link to Livery Street, sold the house and moved to an apartment in Philadelpia. Not long after the move, Mrs Ganis died of a heart attack and Mr Ganis moved into a retirement home. When he died, many years later, he left me thirty thousand dollars. I've always been in touch with Mina and Simon. He became a very rich man selling real estate in California and they had four kids of their own.

Mom passed away in her sleep at Franklin Village in February of 1961 and was buried next to Deirdre and Laurie in Our Lady of Perpetual Help cemetery. I didn't go to the funeral. I visited her every month until she died, always going to the Village on a Sunday because I knew Pop went on Saturday. Only once did I run into him but I hid so he wouldn't see me. After Mom died, Pop finally realized his dream. He sold our home on Livery Street, which was converted into lawyers' offices, and built a nice house on the two acres and named it Bridie's Place. He died on the front porch when he was a very old man. All alone.

Now, I live there.

READ MORE IN PENGUIN

In every corner of the world, on every subject under the sun, Penguin represents quality and variety – the very best in publishing today.

For complete information about books available from Penguin – including Puffins, Penguin Classics and Arkana – and how to order them, write to us at the appropriate address below. Please note that for copyright reasons the selection of books varies from country to country.

In the United Kingdom: Please write to *Dept. JC, Penguin Books Ltd, FREEPOST, West Drayton, Middlesex UB7 OBR*

If you have any difficulty in obtaining a title, please send your order with the correct money, plus ten per cent for postage and packaging, to *PO Box No. 11, West Drayton, Middlesex UB7 OBR*

In the United States: Please write to *Penguin USA Inc., 375 Hudson Street, New York, NY 10014*

In Canada: Please write to *Penguin Books Canada Ltd, 10 Alcorn Avenue, Suite 300, Toronto, Ontario M4V 3B2*

In Australia: Please write to *Penguin Books Australia Ltd, 487 Maroondah Highway, Ringwood, Victoria 3134*

In New Zealand: Please write to *Penguin Books (NZ) Ltd, 182–190 Wairau Road, Private Bag, Takapuna, Auckland 9*

In India: Please write to *Penguin Books India Pvt Ltd, 706 Eros Apartments, 56 Nehru Place, New Delhi 110 019*

In the Netherlands: Please write to *Penguin Books Netherlands B.V., Keizersgracht 231 NL–1016 DV Amsterdam*

In Germany: Please write to *Penguin Books Deutschland GmbH, Friedrichstrasse 10–12, W–6000 Frankfurt/Main 1*

In Spain: Please write to *Penguin Books S. A., C. San Bernardo 117–6° E–28015 Madrid*

In Italy: Please write to *Penguin Italia s.r.l., Via Felice Casati 20, I–20124 Milano*

In France: Please write to *Penguin France S. A., 17 rue Lejeune, F–31000 Toulouse*

In Japan: Please write to *Penguin Books Japan, Ishikiribashi Building, 2–5–4, Suido, Tokyo 112*

In Greece: Please write to *Penguin Hellas Ltd, Dimocritou 3, GR–106 71 Athens*

In South Africa: Please write to *Longman Penguin Southern Africa (Pty) Ltd, Private Bag X08, Bertsham 2013*

READ MORE IN PENGUIN

A CHOICE OF FICTION

A Bend in the River V. S. Naipaul

'V. S. Naipaul uses Africa as a text to preach magnificently upon the sickness of a world losing touch with its past' – Claire Tomalin in the *Sunday Times*. 'Brilliant and terrifying' – *Observer*

The Human Factor Graham Greene

Greene brings his brilliance and perception to bear on the lonely, isolated, neurotic world of the Secret Service, laying bare a machine that sometimes overlooks the subtle and secret motivations that impel us all.

The Gift of Asher Lev Chaim Potok

'It will bring double joy to his many admirers, returning them to the world of the Hasidim but also to his artist hero ... It is very much a painter's story, enhanced by a painter's special perceptions ... an allegory of the artist's perilous journey from the stagnation of success to the renewal of creativity' – *Washington Post*

Humboldt's Gift Saul Bellow

'Memorable for its many comic moments, superb descriptive snapshots of Chicago and brilliant mimicry of lawyers, businessmen and crooks' – *The Times Literary Supplement*

The Vivisector Patrick White

In this prodigious novel about the life and death of a great painter, Patrick White, winner of the Nobel Prize for Literature, illuminates creative experience with unique truthfulness.

READ MORE IN PENGUIN

A CHOICE OF FICTION

London Fields Martin Amis

'*London Fields*, its pastoral title savagely inappropriate to its inner-city setting, vibrates, like all Amis's work, with the force fields of sinister, destructive energies. At the core of its surreal fable are four figures locked in lethal alignment' – Peter Kemp in the *Sunday Times*

A Bottle in the Smoke A. N. Wilson

'Stunningly funny ... Wilson's knowing mockery of the viler aspects of the London literary world and the "insane vanity" of authors is spot-on ... But there is a redeeming idea behind it all, about the fantasies people live by' – Victoria Glendinning in *The Times*

Brazzaville Beach William Boyd

'A most extraordinary parable about mankind ... quite unlike anything else I have ever read' – *Sunday Express*. 'Boyd is a brilliant storyteller ... a most serious book which stretches, tantalises and delights' – Mary Hope in the *Financial Times*

Paradise News David Lodge

'Lodge could never be solemn and the book crackles with good jokes ... leaves you with a mild and thoughtful glow of happiness' – *Sunday Telegraph*. 'Amusing, accessible, intelligent ... the story rolls, the sparks fly' – *Financial Times*

That Darcy, That Dancer, That Gentleman J. P. Donleavy

'Marvellously funny and poetic, as if James Joyce had sat down to write a Tom Sharpe novel ... he is able to mix a lovely lyricism with the broadest of bawdy farce' – Stanley Reynolds in the *Guardian*

READ MORE IN PENGUIN

A CHOICE OF FICTION

Father Melancholy's Daughter Gail Godwin

A young woman's poignant search for self-discovery, *Father Melancholy's Daughter* eloquently exemplifies the struggle within us all to attain grace, inspiration and wisdom in our daily lives. 'Skilfully written, accessible, funny, discriminating, readable and thoughtful' – *The Times Literary Supplement*

The Message to the Planet Iris Murdoch

'I suspect that when the intellectual map of our own times comes to be sketched out, Iris Murdoch will occupy a position analogous to Tolstoy and Dostoyevsky ... Her vision of the world is heart-rending, but ultimately celebratory' – A. N. Wilson in the *Guardian*

Hemlock and After Angus Wilson

'He was a very acute observer ... and it was this vigilance, allied to a profound curiosity about the world, that gave his fiction its zest and its social accuracy ... a great novelist' – Rose Tremain in the *Guardian*

July's People Nadine Gordimer

'So flawlessly written that every one of its events seems chillingly, ominously possible' – *The New York Times Book Review*. 'This is the best novel that Miss Gordimer has ever written' – Alan Paton

The Slave Isaac Bashevis Singer

The Slave is a powerful drama set against the exotic background of seventeenth-century Poland with all its superstitions, witchcraft and witchhunts, abundant life and appalling prejudices. 'The tale is tragic and warmhearted, full of mellow wisdom learned through suffering' – *Yorkshire Post*